NO TIME LIKE THE PRESENT

Daphne Berridge, who has never married, has retired to the small Yorkshire village of Heckcliff where she grew up, intending to write the biography of an eighteenth-century woman poet. Two younger women are interested in her project: Cressida, Daphne's niece, who lives in London, and is uncertain about the direction of her life; and Judith, who keeps a shop in Heckcliff, and is a divorcee. When an old friend of Daphne falls in love with Judith, the question — as for Cressida — is marriage or independence. Then Daphne also receives a surprise proposal.

Books by June Barraclough
Published by The House of Ulverscroft:

TIME WILL TELL
FAMILY SNAPSHOTS
THE VILLA VIOLETTA

After teaching and lecturing in a variety of institutions, June Barraclough began to write full-time in 1985. *No Time Like the Present* is her eleventh novel. She has also edited two anthologies and translated a philosophical work from the French.

Her interests include family history, the study of English Christian names and Yorkshire dialect, and nineteenth-century literature, both French and English. She is married to David Wedgwood Benn and they have a grown-up son and daughter.

JUNE BARRACLOUGH

◆

NO TIME
LIKE THE PRESENT

Complete and Unabridged

ULVERSCROFT
Leicester

First published in Great Britain in 1997 by
Robert Hale Limited
London

First Large Print Edition
published 1999
by arrangement with
Robert Hale Limited
London

British Library CIP Data

Barraclough, June
No time like the present.—Large print ed.—
Ulverscroft large print series: general fiction
1. Women authors, English—England
—Yorkshire—Fiction 2. Large type books
I. Title
823.9′14 [F]

ISBN 0-7089-4045-5

Published by
F. A. Thorpe (Publishing) Ltd.
Anstey, Leicestershire

Set by Words & Graphics Ltd.
Anstey, Leicestershire
Printed and bound in Great Britain by
T. J. International Ltd., Padstow, Cornwall

This book is printed on acid-free paper

To all my friends

'No Time Like the Present'
    The Lost Lover: Mrs Manley 1696

'What's Past is Prologue'
        The Tempest, Shakespeare

Prologue

January 1993

On New Year's Day 1993 at ten o'clock in the evening the telephone rang just as Lydia Robinson was running her bath. She had been looking forward to retiring to bed with a book. The Norwood Reading Circle would soon be meeting to discuss *Vanity Fair*, a novel that Lydia in her youth had never been able to finish. She still found parts of it hard going but was beginning to enjoy Becky Sharp.

She dribbled into her bath water a few drops of the scented oil that had been a Christmas present from her stepson's wife, wondering what Thackeray had really thought of his heroine. Lydia often felt too lazy to produce her own opinions at the meeting, felt she'd expended enough energy finishing a book. Some people — Sonia Greenwood for instance — loved to discuss their own reactions at length.

Lydia had joined the circle some time ago because she had not wished to sink into a state of mental lethargy at a time when she

1

was still a dutiful wife, before she had bought a flat in Manor Court in Heckcliff and a car of her own with the money her father had left her. All the members of the circle lived within five miles of each other; coffee and chat did not involve long journeys.

Sonia Greenwood, who was the moving, or rather driving, spirit, had been friends with the others since they were children in the village of Norwood whose fields spilled over to Heckcliff. They had welcomed Lydia, whose husband's job had brought her, his second wife, along with his son Tony by his deceased first wife, to live in the north. Maurice had upped and left when Tony was twenty-one but Lydia had stayed on. She realized now that she'd done too much for both Maurice and his son. At the time she married, nobody had expected a man to help at home, certainly not to child-sit so that his wife might go out alone in the evening with her own friends. In the early seventies men who liked cooking were often regarded with suspicion. There hadn't been any take-aways then either, apart from fish and chips, and she'd spent a lot of time cooking and shopping and cleaning and washing. Once she was divorced she'd had more time to attend the meetings regularly, and do other interesting things. She stood, half undressed, and picked up the telephone to hear Dorothy Grey's brisk warm voice in her ear.

'Lydia?'

What Dorothy had to say was shockingly straightforward. One of their circle had died.

Lydia said something incoherent. She felt cold, not able to take it in. Dorothy sounded excited, but might be holding back tears.

'I was just going to have a bath,' said Lydia. She felt foolish, not up to this.

'Now I have to ring Joy Wood,' said Dorothy — 'I'll ring you again tomorrow.'

Lydia put the telephone down with a shaky hand.

They had all met at Sonia Greenwood's before Christmas and all had been their usual selves: Sonia, Dorothy, Gwyneth Coultar, Evelyn Naylor, and herself — and the most recent member, Daphne Berridge. Joy Wood was never able to come now because she had an old and ailing mother-in-law to look after, but she had sent her usual note to apologize for her absence. In the last year or two many of the first members had fallen off in their attendance.

They'd arranged a meeting for early in the New Year, to discuss their holiday reading of *Vanity Fair*. One of them would not be there now . . . There'd be a funeral to attend . . .

3

Lydia drew her towelling robe protectively around her, no longer keen to step into the bath that awaited her, not wishing to confront mortal flesh.

Now she wanted only to get into bed, draw the blankets over her head and shut out the world.

1

1992

On a cold April morning in 1992 Daphne Berridge lay in bed trying to summon enough energy to get up. Her alarm had just sounded and she was thinking about the slogan she'd seen on her way back from Leeds. It had been in large black capitals, pasted over the whole of the remaining end wall of a half-demolished terrace. She supposed it was what they'd used to call a Wayside Pulpit. This one was clever in its use of the sacred and the profane when it said: THANK GOD FOR JESUS!

Daphne had retired the year before from her college lectureship in the same city — they were shedding a few of the older staff and she had been glad to go. She rarely thought about her old work, didn't miss it one jot, so happy was she now in Heckcliff, where she had lived as a child. Her new home was one of two houses created from part of the stable wing of a Georgian mansion; a horse drinking-trough and riding block still stood in the cobbled courtyard. Her house had been lived in before by a sculptor who had unfortunately been in arrears with his mortgage. He had gone abroad, had died on a Greek Island.

Daphne had no problems with her own mortgage. On retirement she had received a largish lump sum along with her pension, and her needs were not excessive. So long as she had books to read, could afford enough petrol to run her old car, pay her household bills with something over for an occasional holiday, she was content — luckier than the majority of the population. As she'd worked hard all her life she considered her present mild comfort was well-deserved. Sometimes though she found herself wishing that time would come to a stop and let her stay her present age for ever.

She had never married, partly because the right man had never appeared at the right time, but there had been several love affairs, all long past, probably forgotten, she thought, by those with whom she had been involved even if not by her. She had always enjoyed writing; as soon as she was retired she had begun 'reading round' for a study of an eighteenth century woman poet.

Reasonably sociable when it was required, Daphne also relished solitude and was in no way desperate for company. Most of the people she'd known as a child had long ago left Heckcliff. Those of her parents' generation were either dead or living at Sunny Lands, the retirement home. She had joined an arts organization in the nearby town but had not yet attended a meeting. It was her experience that if you went to any meeting more than once or twice you were rapidly co-opted on to a committee, and she had had enough of committees during her working life. Yesterday however she had received an invitation from a woman who lived in the next village of Norwood to join a reading circle. She thought about this as she dressed and fed her cat Widgery. How had S. Greenwood (Mrs) known about her? Perhaps Judith Kershaw had mentioned her name? A reading circle sounded a bit too much like her old job.

A few months ago she had struck up acquaintance in the library with Judith Kershaw, a woman some fifteen years younger than herself, who had been divorced for many years. Judith had once been an art student but now kept the village hardware shop, having brought up four sons. Over a cup of tea or coffee she talked about painting and Daphne about books. Daphne hoped very much that

Judith would take up her painting again seriously when she had a little more time to herself.

These chats, her regular walks, much reading and listening to music, and looking after Widgery, made for a quiet life. But she visited the city once a month to go to Opera North or a play or film with a friend from the old days. Most of her old friends now lived in the south.

The only other person in Heckcliff whom Daphne knew well was an erstwhile colleague, Alan Watson. For one whole winter twelve years before, she and Alan had enjoyed what she still did not think of as an affair, but a friendship that had included bed, that had arisen after the death of Alan's wife. Later, in the days when there was cash for new departments in outlying annexes, he had been away for some years setting up some new branch of the college.

Alan had chosen to forget, so she had complied with his obvious wish that she should too. Neither had known that the other had decided to settle in Heckcliff. If they chanced to meet at the row of village shops they greeted each other and had a short conversation. As far as she was concerned there was no need to feel embarrassed, certainly no notion in her mind of taking up their old intimacy.

This particular morning, after dressing and feeding her cat and herself she heard the sound of a letter plopping on to the mat. She recognized her sister's handwriting. Mary was married, lived in Berkshire, and had two grown up daughters.

Over the remains of her coffee, Daphne read the latest news of the younger of her nieces, Cressida, who had a propensity for falling in love with the wrong man. Her mother guessed that this had occurred once more and could not help feeling worried.

'Now you're organized up there, I wish you'd invite her to spend a few days with you sometime. I'm sure she doesn't eat enough — suffering from love sickness.'

Daphne finished the letter. Cressida was perhaps more like her aunt than her sensible mother, who, as far as Daphne knew, had only been in love once.

When the smallest bedroom had been repainted she would invite her niece to stay. She liked her, though she doubted that Cressy would want to waste her precious holiday — she worked for a publisher — on an old aunt who lived in the sticks.

★ ★ ★

In this last surmise Daphne was proved wrong. The invitation she despatched was to be taken up the following autumn. Before this, Daphne had agreed — with some reluctance — to attend Mrs Greenwood's monthly reading circle. It *had* been Judith who had inadvertently mentioned to one of her erstwhile teachers that her new friend Daphne Berridge had once been a lecturer in literature. Judith had been very apologetic — 'I didn't mean to involve you. It just came out as something to say to her, you know.'

The shop took up most of Judith's life; any energy she had over she was going to devote to her painting, even though she was full of self-doubt. Maybe after twenty years of bringing up boys and running a business single handed she'd find she had no talent left? When Colin, her youngest, departed in September for his round-the-world trip she had a little more time to herself.

★ ★ ★

The members of the reading circle reassembled at the end of September. Daphne was trying to keep a low profile. She might like to tell them about her own projected book one day. Not yet.

The women chatted as they sorted their

10

books and notebooks, until called to order by the chairwoman, at present Mrs Dorothy Grey. Lydia Robinson, whose flat was their present venue, came in from her clean bright kitchen saying — 'Coffee whenever you want it.' Lydia's flat in Heckcliff, on the ground floor of a converted mansion, was pleasant, the large sitting room light, airy and high-ceilinged. There was a pretty Chinese screen and a long sofa covered in a nubbly oatmeal fabric, and chairs with the same covering. All was very spick and span, several varieties of indoor plants and bowls of pot-pourri placed on window sills and small tables. In this flat there was no husband lurking elsewhere during the meetings as there had been in the summer at the house of a member called Evelyn Naylor. Daphne thought, if they ever visit me they'll think me very untidy. Sonia Greenwood polished her reading glasses, then put them on again. They soon slipped down her nose. That's the woman I've most in common with, thought Daphne.

Dorothy stood up, cleared her throat and read the minutes in a pleasant voice:

'Minutes of the last meeting held at Evelyn's. Present: Sonia Greenwood, Evelyn Naylor, Daphne Berridge, Lydia Robinson, Dorothy Grey. Apologies for absence: Joy

11

Wood' — there was a slight groan here from the assembled company — 'Pamela Reeve. Absent on holiday — Gwyneth Coultar.' *Adam Bede* was discussed, provoking much disagreement concerning Hetty's love affair. It was decided to devote the rest of the summer to a reading of *Middlemarch*. It was also agreed that the next meeting would be held on Monday, 21st of September 1992 at Lydia's.

'May the Secretary sign these minutes as correct?'

There was an affirmative noise. The secretary, Sonia Greenwood, took out her pen and signed them.

'How far have we all got with *Middlemarch*?' she asked, taking off her spectacles. Gwyneth looked vague. Dorothy opened her notebook. Lydia sighed but said, 'I finished it,' and Evelyn Naylor looked up, saying, 'It's very old-fashioned, isn't it?'

Daphne looked at Sonia with slightly raised eyebrows, but kept silent.

'I thought we might make a start by discussing the women characters?' suggested Dorothy. 'Do you think the author's hard on Rosamond?'

'How does she make us care more about Dorothea?' asked Sonia Greenwood. 'Does she tell us to despise Rosamond?'

12

'The authorial voice?' asked Dorothy.

'What does she actually say about the two of them apart from the words she gives them to speak, or the actions she makes them carry out?' pursued Sonia.

This galvanized the company to look at what Dorothy called the text. A useful discussion ensued.

Lydia said that Mary Garth was more important than you might think. Daphne held her peace. It seemed ages since she'd actually taught this novel, though she had never been sure how far novels could be 'taught'. How had mid-Victorian readers reacted to Dorothea? She'd bet that many — especially men — had preferred Rosamond.

Lydia got up to make more coffee, leaving the rest to quote bits of the novel to each other. Most of them had marked favourite passages. Daphne thought they were a darned sight more keen than most of her former eighteen-year-old students. Sonia was thinking that it was one of their most successful evenings, though weeks — months — would be needed if you were going to study this novel as it deserved.

The talk veered off Dorothea and Rosamond and Mary and Mrs Cadwallader and got on to provincial life in general. Lydia, from the Home Counties, listened to the others talking about their northern childhood, spent 'only a hundred years after the time of *Middlemarch*,' as Dorothy pointed out.

Suddenly Evelyn Naylor said, 'Nowhere is safe but the Past.' It was not the sort of thing they expected Evelyn to say and they looked up in surprise. Daphne thought, that woman is neurotic, though I rather agree with her. Sonia gave a semi-theatrical sigh. Dorothy said 'Oh, but — ' and Gwyneth Coultar who had so far said nothing, looked out of the window at the sycamore tree growing in the courtyard of the block of flats, and wondered how old it was.

I could have put it like that, Sonia thought — but perhaps it's *novels* from the last century that are the only safe things? Was Evelyn referring to the big world outside or to her own life? Was George Eliot's land really less safe than formerly?

'Even in Norwood,' continued Evelyn, 'vandals have smashed the paving stones down the Old Road — and they stole ornaments from the church. It was in the paper.'

Gwyneth woke up and said, 'It's the motorway bypassing the town — slicing across the countryside — that's where they come from, your vandals.'

14

The little towns they remembered were now just staging posts to somewhere else, not real places any more, thought Daphne. She said, 'George Eliot was writing about change', but the others seemed to want to talk about present day problems.

Lydia was listening from the kitchen door. As a child she had lived near London throughout the war so might be expected to know about danger. Evelyn went on, 'We never even thought of things like rape — or murder — or violent burglaries — we used to go out to play sometimes for the whole day — do you remember? Nobody worried about us.'

'Our parents were glad to get us out of the house,' said Sonia.

'But there *was* a murder in Heckcliff,' offered Daphne. 'Of Mrs Ironside — that young widow killed one Saturday morning by her lover. I went to school with Nancy Ironside. In the local paper they called it a *crime passionel*.'

'I remember it too,' said Sonia. 'Being in Norwood though, we didn't always hear about all that happened over in Heckcliff. Did it frighten you? It was shocking — but a very unusual thing to happen at that time, surely?'

'We didn't feel any fear walking home in

the dark,' pursued Evelyn. 'We weren't afraid of being mugged or attacked.'

'Murders are one-off crimes,' said Dorothy, who had once attended a course in sociology. 'Mrs Ironside's murder would be unusual even now. She was a nice woman — my mother knew her sister. I remember my parents talking about her. Perfectly ordinary looking she was.'

'It's not only the raving beauties who get themselves murdered,' muttered Lydia.

'I wonder if anyone knew before it happened that she had a lover?' asked Daphne.

'They kept quiet about such things in case young people might overhear,' said Sonia.

Lydia went out for more biscuits but speedily returned. When it was her turn the hostess did all the work, allowing the others to relax. It would be somebody else's job next time. Sometime next year she would have to offer hospitality, thought Daphne, drinking her coffee. What a bind.

Dorothy said, 'We had an exceptionally tranquil childhood, didn't we? I expect it was different for you, Lydia, with V1s and 2s?'

'It's how one feels about it that matters,' said Gwyneth.

'It wasn't particularly safe in London — but

16

I don't remember being frightened,' Lydia said.

'Once the past is over, it can't change,' said Sonia. 'I expect that's what you mean, Evelyn? Whatever happens in the future, at least that is safe — saved — for us?' There was a short silence. People put their books down, thinking it was nearly time to go. Sonia went on, 'There were lots of things *I* was frightened of as a child but they weren't terrifying enough to stop me wishing sometimes now that I could go back and live it all over again.'

'Whoever'd want to do that?' asked Lydia with an expression of horror.

'What kind of things?' asked Daphne.

'Oh, I did nasty things to other children. Telling tales — betraying people — fighting. Then I'd be frightened they'd take their revenge. I was very snobbish about the village boys, especially one of them who was sweet on me — quite a nice boy, I suppose, underneath — but his clothes smelled sour and his nose dripped. He once sent me a Valentine with 'From Arthur with love'.'

'Well at least he could write,' said Daphne, laughing.

'Yes. Agreed.'

'I never knew boys like that,' said Lydia.

'Well of course not at your convent,' said Sonia.

'More coffee anyone?' suggested Dorothy hurriedly. 'Then we'd better finish what we came for.'

'General Confession?' suggested Sonia.

She had told Daphne at her first meeting that others came to these discussions more for the sake of friendship than literature, a time when they could forget husbands and housekeeping and revert to their old selves. That had put Daphne off until Sonia had added that as far as she was concerned reading was a solitary pastime. Daphne had agreed. Sonia Greenwood interested her.

Daphne looked at them all now: Dorothy Grey with her faded prettiness, hair still fair, small hands and feet that assorted strangely with her strong fleshy calves and what people used to call dressing-table-stool legs. Now there were tiny wrinkles round her big blue eyes. Tonight she was wearing a paisley wool dress of greens and browns, looked respectable in a way Sonia, in a muddle of bright purples and fuchsias echoed in rings on her hands, did not. Like herself Sonia had once been a teacher and Daphne could imagine she had been in her youth a bit of what they used to call a 'bohemian'. She used her hands a lot, had better legs than

Dorothy, but when she stood up you were surprised to see she was not tall.

Daphne was glad she had put on her big garnet ring. It seemed to put her on the side of Sonia Greenwood. That was absurd — the women were all friends. Why should she be dividing them into camps?

Gwyneth Coultar must always have been a large woman and had now reached the age when her looks were fashionable. With her whitish silvery hair in a French pleat and her high cheek bones she could be an Amazon or an Aztec warrior, but was the most peaceable of women with a soft tentative voice when she did speak, which wasn't often. Unlike Sonia, Gwyneth obviously did not care what impression she made. She was wearing a pinafore dress tonight and Daphne had once seen her in a cloak; she too might be unconventional? Apparently she painted. Long earrings would suit her, thought Daphne, trying and failing to put her mind back on *Middlemarch*.

Lydia Robinson was the best dressed, probably because she had the cash to dress well and was also interested in clothes. She sat looking truly well preserved, her cleverly lightened hair dropping artfully from a side parting in lightly permed waves. Lydia favoured black, or fawn and beige, had good taste, or rather knew what suited her, which was probably the same thing. She wore ten-denier stockings and higher heels than the others and you could see she looked after her hands for they were well manicured, the nails polished and pearly. She must visit that salon on the way to the town where some women from the villages went for manicures and massage. Lydia would never let herself go. She had a slightly old-fashioned twang to her voice that Daphne had often noticed in middle-aged, middle class people born near London, rhymed golf with oaf and pronounced the 'y's at the ends of words. 'Lovelee,' Lydia would say and 'Practicallee.' I ought not to criticize people's clothes and accents, thought Daphne — I've no room to speak.

Evelyn Naylor was thinner than Gwyneth, tall, dark hair going grey but still springy and curly. Her pale blue eyes looked out with a faintly puzzled expression and her freckles were a parody of the ones she might have had in childhood. There was no doubt that Evelyn was dowdy and either did not care or had no idea how to improve herself. After that first meeting when Daphne had given her a lift in her car Sonia had told her that Evelyn's husband Ronald neglected her, so perhaps he would not even have noticed if his wife had sat down to breakfast dressed as Minnehaha. Evelyn gave the impression of being both older and younger than the rest, more like a girl who had in some ways never grown up but who looked like her own mother must have done thirty years ago. She wore greys and browns a good deal but quite different shades from Lydia's. Her hands, clutching her notebook, were rough and red though her wrists were slender. Her voice was harsh, strange for someone Daphne had been told was musical.

She said: 'Well, I still think life was better then.' She caught Daphne looking at her.

'Would you have preferred to have lived in the 1830s like Dorothea?' Daphne asked, trying to bring the meeting back to literature.

'I don't know — I suppose there were no aspirins then?' replied Evelyn. This lightened the proceedings and then Dorothy suggested they might read *Portrait of a Lady* for their next assignment.

Lydia might once have been a Rosamond, marrying the wrong man, thought Daphne. Had Rosamond ever realized that Lydgate had married the wrong woman? Lydia had not made a second marriage. Dorothy might have a bit of Mary Garth in her? Perhaps, though, she might once have been a Dorothea like her namesake? George Eliot would have recognized Dorothy's sterling qualities.

Sonia definitely did not belong to *Middlemarch*, was a grown up Maggie Tulliver, Dorothea with more passion and less smugness. She wondered what her husband was like. How would Gwyneth and Evelyn fit into the book? Or she herself for that matter?

It was getting dark outside now; the autumn nights were drawing in. The back end of the year they called it here. It was a chore going out in the evening but perhaps it did one good?

Sonia was not quite ready to end the discussion. She directed her next remark to Evelyn Naylor, saying: 'Parts of England do still exist where things haven't changed very much — you could even imagine you were back fifty years. On holiday in Norfolk last year I happened to be on a bus with lots of respectable looking matrons on the way to Norwich. Hair permed once a month, I'd imagine, and they carried old fashioned wicker baskets — the sort they used to sell in blind shops, you know? — and wore sensible brogues and pastel-coloured blouses. They looked so very calm. Happy, I think.'

Gwyneth sat regarding her hands. She often confessed she had not finished the long books her friend Sonia so delighted in and enthused over . . . well, Sonia *had* been to university. The meetings sometimes even allowed her a few minutes' meditation. The others did not mind since it gave them more time in which to express their opinions though they always politely asked her for hers.

The others were still listening to Sonia. 'The reason they were on the bus was probably because like me they couldn't — or didn't want to — drive, though they looked capable types who could turn their hand to anything. Perhaps their husbands had the family car to go to work in? Anyway, they looked like middle-aged women used to look, pillars of the Church or the WI. What I mean is, it didn't look as though the world had changed for *them*. They looked perfectly happy living in the present. I felt younger than they were even though I probably wasn't.'

'You mean because their present was like their past?' asked Evelyn.

'I suppose it was that — whereas we — '

'*I* live in the present,' said Gwyneth, looking up.

'So do I,' added Lydia. 'Where else can you live?'

Daphne was silent. Did she? Not all the time, not when she was writing about her poet, Anne Crystall. The present seemed so fluid, compared with the past. As you grew older, time just fled by. One day soon she must talk to Sonia about her plans for the book.

'Once middle-aged people start to live in the past or to think everything then was better than now,' said Dorothy severely, 'it shows they've given in to growing old.' Evelyn looked guilty for having introduced the subject.

Sonia was still thinking about the Norfolk women with their clean crisp shirt-waisters and pale stockings and leather handbags. They'd dressed in that way since they were thirty, hadn't changed, had been middle-aged all their lives. They were not yet 'old', not yet senior citizens.

'George Eliot usually set her novels about thirty or forty years before she wrote them,' Daphne was saying. 'Like *Middlemarch*.'

'Oh well — *writers*,' said Dorothy in a tone of dismissal.

I suppose this is what they — we — are here for, thought Daphne — to discuss what our reading makes us think about. Mary Ann Evans worried about the world too, tried to find what had gone wrong just before her own lifetime.

'Must go,' said Gwyneth, suddenly getting

up. With one accord they all began to sort their papers and books and close handbags. Why do I talk too much and then feel depressed? Sonia asked herself. Men who talk too much don't. Dorothy, as she wrapped a scarf round her neck in Lydia's hall said briskly, as she said every time: 'Somebody really must persuade Joy to come to the next meeting.'

'I doubt she will get away from her aged parent,' said Sonia.

'Parent-in-law,' Evelyn corrected her.

'But Mrs Reeve *has* promised to attend next time,' said Dorothy on the threshold.

Sonia was thinking it was always pleasant to see Gwyneth, who did not depress her. Although not so frequent a participant as the others here tonight she did make an effort to come more often than several other women who attended only sporadically, none of them here this evening.

As they said their good nights she wondered how Daphne Berridge saw them all. For that matter how would the ladies on the bus see them — see her? The talkative one? These women here were all comfortable with each other. It would not be the same if a man were present, though men had never been excluded. Something was obviously bothering Evelyn, apart from her worries over the present state of the country.

Daphne was to give Sonia a lift to her home on the outskirts of Norwood before returning to Heckcliff, only a mile away down the Old Lane, and Sonia was looking forward to exchanging a few words with her in the car. She had the feeling that Daphne Berridge also found parts of the modern world a trial, though she would do something about it, not get depressed like Evelyn Naylor. Gwyneth strode out to the bus stop, thinking how lucky they all were, all reasonably fit and healthy. She was not frightened of old age, not since she'd taken up Buddhism and yoga, and always had plenty of energy. She must telephone Joy Reeves who was worn out looking after her invalid mother-in-law, and try to cheer her up. Dorothy was the one who kept most frequently in touch with everyone: she was public spirited, had a social conscience. Gwyneth guessed that Sonia found Dorothy annoying, but then Sonia liked to pretend she was less charitable than was the case. Dorothy hadn't changed a bit — but none of them had really.

People don't change, she thought. I wonder what that Daphne was like at school. I expect she and Sonia would have been friends if they'd known each other then . . . they're both clever, so perhaps they'd have been rivals?

'My niece is coming to stay with me next week,' Daphne was saying to Sonia as she started up her car. It took only a few minutes to Norwood and back by road. Sonia had told her she used to walk over the fields and down the Old Lane but her husband didn't like her doing it now and he couldn't always drive her as he worked late at the university. Sonia would have liked to invite Daphne in, but it was late and she'd want to get to bed. Another time perhaps?

Lydia gave a sigh of relief when they had all departed, and began the washing up.

2

Cressida Miller came to stay in the frozen north at her aunt's at the beginning of October. Mary Miller had told her daughter that Heckcliff had changed a good deal since their childhood and that Daphne was mad to go back there. You could never dip your feet in the same river, and so on.

Cressida agreed that the past was past, but as she'd never known the old Heckcliff she wouldn't recognize the changes that had taken place there. She appreciated Daphne's house, and her books, and Widgery, and the peace of getting away from what her aunt, who had once worked in London, called the Smoke. There was relief too at being, if only for a few days, away from other complications.

She knew her aunt enjoyed being alone and was flattered that she was tolerated as a visitor. Fortunately they liked doing the same things: reading, tramping round a good deal, and digging the clayey soil in Daphne's share of the garden. This year her aunt was full of the book she was working on, the biography 'and critical study' she had added, of some long ago female poet. You were not allowed to call her a poetess. Cressida wondered whether anyone apart from her aunt had ever heard of her. She was slowly becoming enlightened.

'She lived in what is now your part of London. Of course it was a village then.'

'Wouldn't you like to live for a time yourself where *she* used to live — so you could get under her skin?' asked Cressida. Daphne suspected a slight plot. Her sister was always urging her to move south.

'I've only just discovered where she lived, from a reading of the poet Southey's letters.

It was just over the border of what is now your borough — the same parish though. People aren't sure where exactly the house stood in the 1780s and 90s — you might have a look round for me one day — they've probably enlarged or amalgamated some of those old cottages.'

'I'd love to — I like exploring with a purpose,' said Cressida, her hair a curtain before her face.

'To answer your question, I don't want to live in London. I don't need to live where she did — it's too far removed in time. I like to imagine it as it was then. I'll go and check up when I've done all my spade work and know what to look for.' They were sitting eating toast by the apparently old but actually new fireplace, its genuine-looking flames fed by gas. Outside, autumn rain was already darkening the tea-time skies. 'Anyway, Anne was born in Cornwall,' added Daphne.

So the poet was called Anne! thought Cressy. Daphne had never liked her own name; they had nicknamed her 'Dafty' at school, Cressy's mother had once told her, so she had preferred in her youth to call herself Anne. Cressy called her by her Christian name rather than 'Aunt' but sometimes tried to think of her as Anne. She wondered if

Daphne had chosen the poet because she liked the name.

Daphne went on 'I *dream* better in the north! That's another reason for staying put!' Perhaps, Cressida thought, her own dreams would improve in the presence of such an enthusiast.

The night after this conversation, Cressida did wake out of the depths of a most interesting dream. She had been in a walled garden, a summer garden, and there had been three crystal goblets with green stems standing on a white wooden table. There were at least three people in the garden. One was a man who had whipped out a large white handkerchief as though he was about to do a conjuring trick. Instead he had taken the goblets off the table, covered it with the handkerchief and then carefully arranged the goblets there, as if in preparation for painting a still life. That was all. Nothing else had happened, apart from the sense of a conversation going on which she could not quite catch. Yet it had been an extraordinarily vivid dream: the emerald green of the glass, the snowy whiteness of the cloth, all in the warmth of the sun. She tried to hold it all in her mind before falling asleep again.

Over breakfast she mentioned it, sure it

would be the kind of thing that interested Daphne. Most people were extremely bored by other people's dreams. Not Daphne, who enjoyed listening to them as much as she enjoyed recounting her own.

'Do you think the goblets were symbols?' she asked.

'No,' replied Cressida firmly. 'There were real people there so why should there be symbolic people as well? The crystal was very beautiful.'

Daphne said, 'You said crystal! That was *her* name — sometimes they spelled it differently.'

'I don't think you told me her surname?' Cressy was impressed by her own dream discovery. Daphne was looking thoughtful and was still a little abstracted when Cressida left to do some shopping for her in Heckcliff.

It was not a rural village though it had been once. Now it lay only three miles or so from the nearest sizeable town, twelve miles from the city, one of three original hamlets only a mile or so apart: Heckcliff, Sholey and Norwood. Heckcliff, the largest, had most of the shops people required for their everyday needs, as well as a branch library, a church, two chapels and a park. If these were provincial suburbs Cressida liked them.

The hardware shop had once housed a plumber too, but now sold paint and wallpaper as well as pots and pans and kettles and radios and cups and saucers and dusters.

J KERSHAW was written in curly capitals, navy blue on white, above the shop door, and there was the pleasant tinkling of a bell when you opened that door. Cressy had already met Judith Kershaw whilst on a walk with Daphne. She was a pretty woman in her early forties with short dark wavy hair and a cheerful voice. All Heckcliffians relished conversation and spoke slowly, clearly — and loudly. Cressy could not decide whether they thought that she as a southerner would not understand them if they did not, or because that was the natural way for them to speak.

This morning she needed only a torch. Daphne's was broken and they ought to have one when they went out looking for Widgery at night. Her aunt did not approve of leaving cats out all night in rain and cold and did not favour a cat flap either, since stranger cats were apt to follow her own into the warmth, or to share his meal.

'I expect you find it cold?' hazarded Judith, as if Cressida was over from Africa for a visit. It was only a signal that you were expected to say something about the weather. She complied with 'My aunt says the leaves have been 'mizzling down' early this year.' It had depressed Daphne to think that by the end of October all the deciduous trees would be bare. Judith looked puzzled. Daphne had said it was a dialect word, which gave an idea of mist and drizzle — but perhaps she had invented its application to leaves?

'More than five months of bare branches,' sighed Judith. 'Perhaps we'll have snow this year.'

'You could paint that, I suppose?' offered Cressida politely.

Judith looked suddenly shy. 'Do tell her I'm enjoying that book she lent me. Has the literary circle started up again yet after the summer holidays?'

That book was an eighteenth-century novel that Daphne had picked up in a second-hand bookshop in York, liking to try things out on others. Cressy remembered that Daphne had attended the circle just before her own arrival but had volunteered little about it.

'Yes, she went last week — I'll tell her you liked the book.' She had finally located the torches in a box under a shelf of tins for baking buns.

'Stephen promised to sort out those boxes

last Christmas — I never seem to have the time,' said the proprietor, wrapping up the torch.

Cressy knew from Daphne that Judith owned the shop. Mrs Kershaw's grandfather had been the village plumber and her grandmother had kept the shop in the old days. They had bequeathed it just before the last war to their son and he had in turn left it to his only child. This turned out to have been a good idea when Judith's husband left her the very same year for another woman and they were eventually divorced.

Cressida was just about to go and was studying her shopping list when the shop bell pinged again and an elderly man entered. He went up to the counter and immediately engaged Judith in quiet conversation, interrupted only by her 'Bye, then!' to Cressy. They were still talking quietly when she shut the door. Evidently a friend. But everyone in the village was friendly. It might become a nuisance if you lived here all the time, but it was nice to be noticed.

On her way home she stopped at the library where there was an exhibition of landscapes painted by local folk, several of them surprisingly good, one by a J. Kershaw.

'How was Judith then?' enquired Daphne on her niece's return. Cressida reported that she was enjoying the book.

'Written by a friend of Anne,' said Daphne briskly. 'Mary Hays.'

'She wanted to know if you'd been to your literary circle again yet. I said you had.'

'Yes, we've been discussing George Eliot. I should be able to do that! But I don't like to say too much — I don't know whether it's a good idea having an ex-English teacher attending their meetings. Mrs Greenwood was once a teacher too — of history, I think.'

Daphne returned to the subject of her critical study over the supper which Cressida had prepared — a mushroom omelette and a salad of frilly fresh lettuce and large sliced tomatoes bought that very morning and dressed with the balsamic vinegar she'd found in Daphne's cupboard. All was washed down with some of her aunt's favourite dry Italian white wine.

'Anne was unhappily in love,' said Daphne, pouring herself and Cressida a second glass. 'I don't think she ever married. No evidence that she did and I feel pretty sure she didn't.'

Like you — and probably me too — thought

her niece mournfully.

'Marriage is a lottery,' said Daphne. 'Especially at that time it was.'

'I know — 'When in doubt, don't' — but people don't marry so much now — not my friends anyway — or only some of them. Most just live together,' replied Cressida, savouring her wine.

'I expect that makes some of them feel insecure? Up here in Heckcliff the middle classes mostly marry, though there's some of what they used to call 'living in sin'.'

'Tell me more about Anne,' said Cressida. 'What exactly did she write? Ought I to have heard of her before?'

'Many poems, though only one collection of verse was published. She was quite well known at the time — that was in the 'revolutionary' decade — the 1790s. She knew Mary Wollstonecraft.'

'I must read her poems.'

'I've only got a photocopy of the collection,' confessed Daphne. 'There are only a few copies left of the book — the British Library and the Bodleian have them but I'm always hoping to find another in an antiquarian bookshop. Many of her poems were about unrequited love.'

'Nobody writes poems now about that!'

'Don't they?'

'Well, not to publish — '

'Anne wrote about other matters too. They all did. Lots of the women wrote about the ills of womanhood — they were mostly feminists, if not all revolutionaries.'

'Was Anne a revolutionary?'

'I shouldn't think so. Some of her friends were, quite apart from Wollstonecraft who was the most notorious.' She took another piece of crusty-bread and buttered it thoughtfully before adding: 'It's their day-to-day lives I find so hard to imagine. Anne had a brother who painted. He became much more famous than she did — but that's par for the course — he was a man!' Daphne was an old-fashioned sort of feminist.

Cressy and her sister Jessica had imagined that Daphne, if not their own mother, had had a few adventures in her youth. But when they saw their aunt she had always seemed too busy, too much wrapped up in her work, to be interested in 'love'. Of course she was too old for that now! thought her niece. Maybe her feminism had stopped her marrying?

'Had Anne a lover?' she asked, taking courage with her second glass.

'If you mean, did she go to bed with a man? No, I should think it unlikely. Most

37

of the extant verse was written before she was thirty when there was a man said to be 'Platonically' attached to her, with whom I believe she was in love.'

'Who did she live with in London?'

'With her mother and her sister — and the elder brother when he was at home. The father was by all accounts an unpleasant character. They were all glad when he was away on business. He was Scottish, so it was probably drink.'

'Did she work for her living?'

'There was only one thing that genteelly brought up young women could do,' replied Daphne, 'and that was the same as they did up till very recently — they became teachers. No merchant banks or law offices for *them*.'

'Was she a governess?'

'Apparently, though the records are sparse and say only that she — and her sister later — were 'engaged in tuition'. She went daily to a local family to teach their children. There weren't many schools with women teachers, except for dame schools, or the occasional boarding academy.'

'How did she get to know the people who published the book? Didn't you have to have some sort of a 'network'?'

'Oh, the brother had lots of friends who

came to the house, and they had friends, — it's usually like that, isn't it? They were mostly Dissenters who'd turned into Radicals. Joshua — her artist brother wanted to be a professional painter — he learned engraving to begin with. Her younger sister Elizabeth wanted to engrave too but she wasn't allowed to learn in a studio because she was female. Anyway, Joshua became a well-known water-colourist after a long period of penury. Eventually he got into the Academy and was one of the founders of the Water-Colour Society.'

'So your Anne met Mary what's-her-name through her brother?'

'Yes, Mary writes to Southey about Anne whom she had met through Joshua. Southey describes Anne in a letter saying she was a fine artless sensible girl — he meant she had 'sensibility'. I'll show you the quotation if you're interested. Mary was cross with Joshua — who didn't seem at the time to be bestirring himself to help keep the family. Before he learned engraving, and before his painting was at all known he was apprenticed in the porcelain and pottery retail trade and painted on china! Some friends of his left him a shop, and then he went to Shropshire to a Mr Turner's china manufactory near Broseley — he probably started his proper painting whilst he was there.'

'I'll take Anne's poems up to bed if I may,' Cressy said, thinking, like Judith Kershaw, another painter who sold pots!

She read:

> 'Unhappy maid,' she cried, 'thou art to blame,
> Thus to expose thy virtuous breast to shame:
> Poor heart! Thy love is laughed at for its truth:
> Yet, 'tis a holy treasure, though disdained,
> And wantonly by thoughtlessness profaned;
> Ah! why then waste the blessings of thy youth?
> No more fair reason's sacred light despise:
> Thy heart may blessings find
> That dwell not in the eyes,
> But in the virtues of the feeling mind.'

Poor Anne, she thought. Only twenty-six and already telling herself not to go by outward appearances. 'The virtues of the feeling mind' was a nice phrase. If only men looked for these virtues in women . . .

'Wasting the blessings of youth', also struck deep, and Cressida fell asleep wondering how

40

Anne had been rejected, and by whom. Or did the beloved never even know of her love?

Her sleep that night however was dreamless.

3

Sonia Greenwood's childhood had been lived, like Daphne Berridge's, under the shadow following that Great War to end all wars which, since it did no such thing, was later called the First World War. Both their fathers had been called up to fight in France in 1917 when they were no more than boys. The nineteen thirties' childhoods of both little girls had encompassed a slump in trade after the depression. More personally they had encompassed measles, visits to cemeteries, swings in the park, Saturday pennies, walks in nearby woods, Sunday school, the reading of many books, and the arrival of the Second World War only 21 years after the first had ended. This war had brought London and Channel Island evacuees to the villages. Soldiers too, on their way home from Dunkirk, had been billeted on local families. The children's pastimes had perforce included the making of scrapbooks of warships, the invention of secret codes, and the collecting of postcards of places occupied by Hitler. Both Daphne and Sonia had tracked imaginary spies; both had done without bananas and chocolate and filled themselves up with slices of bread and golden syrup and Victory V cough pastilles.

Born in 1949, Judith Jagger had known few if any of these things apart from the walks and the swings. By 1958 she was receiving the benison of television and, two years later, free secondary education. It was in the year 1968, when everything seemed to be in ferment, that she had been swept off her feet by Andrew Kershaw, seven years older than herself and crazy with love for her.

She'd had one year at art school and had mildly enjoyed it; at least it was better than secondary school. Andrew Kershaw was not however a revolting student or anything at all of that kind. That was why she'd found him so attractive. Older than her other friends, he was a commercial traveller of sorts and she'd met him not at a 'gig' but at the village Conservative Club, which her father frequented.

Usually she'd spurned her dad's invitations to 'meet some nice young people from Woolsford', but that night she'd been a bit bored and fed up, partly because her tutors at the college didn't seem to know how to teach — or she no longer seemed to understand what was expected. She'd begun to see her parents' point of view about painting: that it could be done perfectly well at home on her own terms and that even if she passed all the art school exams there would be nothing to do but teach. She didn't want to go 'commercial'.

Immediately she'd been introduced to Andrew — or rather, he'd pushed forward and demanded a dance — she'd thought he'd go far, had been amazed at his self-confidence, flattered by his remarks about her looks and general style, and perhaps a little frightened of him. After that first meeting things had progressed quickly and soon a sensual noose had been tightened around her and she couldn't have escaped even if she'd wanted to, which at that time she didn't. After all, many of her girlfriends were already married, and Andrew had more money to spend than their husbands had. Her parents were the ones who now murmured that it seemed a pity to give up her studies. Couldn't they wait? But Andrew could not wait. Not only did he want to be her lover, he also wanted to be her husband. She knew this was unusual, especially for a man whom she regarded as more sophisticated than most. It touched her that he wanted her 'forever', wanted her to be his wife. It was also very exciting, and continued to be so until after the birth of their second child when she was still not quite twenty-two. Their first son, Stephen, had arrived exactly nine and a half months after their wedding day and she'd been happy and thrilled — and also happy because Andrew was happy. For three years, from the moment they met up to the day their second son, Mark, was born, she hadn't been able to stop wanting Andrew to want her. It was exactly like a drug or an enchantment, had nothing to do with pleasure but was purely the proof that she was needed and that Andrew could not do without her body.

After Mark was born, it wasn't that she fell out of love with Andrew, or even stopped wanting to satisfy his need of her, but just that she was a bit tired and somehow the children had begun to be more important. *They* needed her too, more than a man could. Andrew's still imperious desires, which had so built up her own self-esteem, continued to fan the flames of sacrifice inside her but were powerless in the end to prevent her self-knowledge: she knew that what she wanted was a rest, an interval before another baby arrived. She took the pill, but it made her feel sick. Andrew said it was important for women to have children when they were young. She consoled herself with the thought that perhaps if she became pregnant again it would be a girl, and she'd always wanted three children. She'd only be twenty-four after all, so she resigned herself to another pregnancy, though it puzzled her that her husband did not worry about the future, or about finances.

It was another boy, and a demanding one at that. She was busy every minute of the day and half the night. Scarcely had she recovered from the birth and the chaotic six months that followed, with two small boys and a baby, than she realized that her husband had been saying for some time that four was a nice round figure and they'd both have plenty of time to enjoy themselves later: by the time their children were young adults she'd only be entering her forties. It wasn't that she didn't love her babies, she adored them, even though she made every effort according to the best women's magazine advice not to neglect her husband but to make him feel he still came first. She did love him, and they'd bought a house on a new private estate. Everything should have been perfect.

By the time she was twenty-five, with yet another baby on the way, she felt like a machine that washed and cooked and fed and cleaned and ironed and shopped and washed again. One day she suddenly realized that Andrew Kershaw loved sex more than he loved his wife or his children and that he needed to wield power over a — willing — woman. He was not a bad father and did his bit when Colin was born only fifteen months after Ben, but she could see that he was hurt that she no longer seemed able to put him first.

Perhaps he'd fall out of love with her? The prospect didn't even appal her, if only she could be left alone for a bit, principally to sleep. Not that with four small children she could ever now be really alone. She had hardly any time to think about her marriage but she was determined Colin would be the last, and told her husband so.

'We're not Catholics, Andy,' she remembered saying. 'We don't have to have a baby just because you want to make love to me a lot.'

This had the effect of making him sulk. She also discovered more about his own background, about which he'd always been vague, saying both his parents were dead. He'd been fostered after his own parents had split up and had never met his mother again until she was with another man and had had another five children. He told her all this in a rush one Saturday morning. Could anything so simple account for his desperate desire (she saw it now as desperate) to found his own family and have something he could call his own?

Another thing happened. All that randiness, her willingness to be subjugated to another person's wishes, by passion, had completely evaporated in her. She didn't know whether she'd ever want to feel it again. Neither did she want to go in for a mechanical sex life if it didn't mean anything any longer. All her energies went into her babies. She was sure she wasn't the only woman to whom this had happened, though there seemed to be a conspiracy of silence around what women after the first flush of youth really wanted. She was still grateful to him but she was in love with her babies now. It was natural, wasn't it? Life could just be managed with four, no more than that — she knew her own limitations. She often wondered what kind of sex life married people had had in the village in the previous century when they'd had nine or ten children over twenty or so years. Surely it had been just wifely submission, nothing exciting, no passion? Then she realized that she herself had been submissive and that the disappearance of submission had made her see herself and her husband, and indeed men and women in general, quite differently. Once she began to see that Andrew thought he had the right to her whenever he felt like it, she began to feel angry.

Then suddenly he stopped making love to her and she thought: he is thinking it over, and was for a time relaxed and tender towards him. She felt more herself, more light-hearted. Whatever had driven him to possess her had been the result of his own earlier insecurities, she was sure. Now they could walk on together through life, loving their children and making mutual decisions about their life together, be a happy family, love each other, be faithful, grow up at last! Love was what mattered, wasn't it? Their sex life had been like eating a big meal every time they felt a little peckish, until they found the larder empty. Or rather, though she tried not to believe this, like a woman baking for a man every time he was hungry for a sandwich, and partaking of the meal with him because he didn't like eating alone. She tried to intimate a little of this to him, tell him it was time now to take stock.

But apparently, men — Andrew Kershaw anyway — didn't see it like this. She'd never refused him, had always tried to show she loved him and had been grateful for his love for her even when she had not felt the old desire. Andrew reproached her when she at last got him to speak, reproached her with putting 'her' children first. 'But they are your children too!' she had cried.

Andrew's sports car was the pride of his life but he never took her out in it. A year or two earlier he'd gone into partnership with a friend, a Lancashire business man who manufactured cables, and they'd been doing well. Judith had brought her own little mini which was now too small for four children. They needed an estate car even if it took a bit of saving up for. They'd been married six years and the children took up every minute of her day. At night she was too weary to go out and enjoy herself.

People made jokes about the seven-year-itch in those days. One day an old school-friend told her that Andrew had been seen in his sports car on the moor with a young woman. She didn't believe her, said nothing at first to her husband. He might have fallen out of lust with her: lots of men did that, and their wives turned a blind eye, though she'd never have thought Andrew would be one of them. Then she began to wonder if it were true. Her pride was hurt but she still said nothing.

It was Andrew who spoke first about it. He was 'giving her a chance' to respond to him and if she didn't want him there might be those who did. Was this the young man with whom she'd been so besotted, the father of their children, this man who spoke of a woman as though she were a commodity? She was as shocked by his tone as much as by his possible goings on, could not speak. For six months he'd shown no interest in her, which had given her time to recuperate her strength, thinking him considerate. Now he was telling her she no longer matched up to him in desire!

But her husband had got her where he wanted her. Whether she cared or not, he could go and enjoy himself elsewhere as men always seemed able to do. That made her angry again. Perhaps he wanted her angry so that he could subdue her anger through his own angry love-making? The moment this thought came into her head, along with the thought that he may have wanted to see her jealous, her anger fell away. She saw only a man who wanted to have his cake and eat it. She would not sulk. No, she would tax him coldly with infidelity — though it was all such a cliché.

She did this one evening when he was for

once home early since he had a slight cold. She almost felt sorry for him as she spoke. But he did not attempt to deny the truth. There was no bluster. This surprised her. He couldn't care for her any longer then? Neither did he apologize, said only 'That's the way I'm made'. 'But your children — never mind me — your *children* need you!' As she said it she wondered if they did. He was a practical man who had helped around the house when he felt like it but he never spoke to his children in an intimate way, though he didn't mind clearing up after them.

It took a year of negotiation before he finally went off, for good, with an eighteen-year-old hairdresser. She did not beg him to stay. The new divorce laws soon came in and she petitioned for a divorce on the grounds of desertion. Right up to the last minute she wasn't sure whether she ought to want him to return. This was just at the time her father died, leaving her the shop. 'Don't you care at all about the boys?' she finally flung at him the last time they met. 'It was you who wanted me to have them, Andrew!' 'Oh I know you resent that you are tied up with them,' he replied. 'But Mandy's pregnant now!'

He did not try to get the boys away from her, her worst nightmare, and he had never been a drinker, never struck her. People could not understand the failure of her marriage. 'Too proud,' they said of her. Only Judith knew that sex was his drug. If at nineteen she'd had a bit of common sense, made him wait, got herself better fixed up with contraception as he would not use anything himself, had a childless affair and waited till it burned itself out — which they said usually took three years . . .

But *he'd* been the one who had insisted on marriage and she'd taken it as a compliment to herself. She'd been so naïve, had trusted her feelings.

Two of the boys were too young to miss their father, and Stephen and Mark were only six and four when he departed for good. The divorce came through and she sold the new house. She'd had the foresight to have herself put as joint owner, since half the money had been provided by her father. She moved in above the shop and got her mother to come over every day to baby-sit and collect Stephen from school, whilst she sorted out stock, and made plans to reopen it, though without offering the plumbing service. She debated whether to go back to her maiden name, keep the shop as Jaggers, but the boys were Kershaws, the product of a marriage she'd thought would last all her life, for better or worse, so she retained that name.

For seventeen years now she had built up the business, using the rest of the capital when her mother died. In all that time she heard only two or three times of her husband, who no longer even paid her maintenance. He had married his Mandy, divorced her after four years and two more children, gone over to Manchester, married for the third time: an older woman who ran a beauty salon in a small cotton town, moved to Mallorca and after several years there had been killed in a car crash, the result of his speeding.

In all those years she had never, curiously enough, missed a man in her bed, though she had often felt the need for a companion. Looking back she did not discount her ex-husband's initial attractions but could no longer understand how she had always done what he wanted. The boys seemed as the years passed to have nothing to do with Andrew Kershaw, since he had nothing to do with them. Ben looked a bit like him, but not one of them appeared to have inherited his character. She had dreaded that somehow they would be disturbed on account of their father's dereliction. The elder two had both gone to college, one on a business course, the other studying graphic design. Stephen was twenty-three now, Mark twenty-one, Ben twenty and Colin eighteen. Ben was the cleverest and was now reading law at university, and Colin had just left school to go on his tour round the world as so many young people of his generation seemed to want to do. Now she could at long last think about herself, even if her boys were never far from her thoughts. She'd come through by dint of hard work. But she often wondered what was left inside her. She'd done a few water-colours whilst she was thinking about her future, one of which appeared in the recent exhibition at the library.

It was three months before she saw Colin off at the airport that Alan Watson had appeared in her life. They'd chatted in a friendly way at the library one evening. Mr Watson had once taught her maths and had just retired. He was a widower without children, had taught in various grammar schools before going on to lecture at a college of education. He'd always greeted her if he'd seen her on a walk, or in the town, where she went once a week to do the shopping that could not be done in the village. After the talk in the library he took to coming into the shop on slack mornings for a chat.

Judith was quite aware that he found her attractive. You just sensed that sort of thing, though it hadn't happened to her very often in the past seventeen years, mainly because she'd never had any free time. She might even have stopped thinking of herself as a woman at all when she was so predominantly a mother. He made her think back to those early years with her children's father, which were now like scenes out of an old film in which she did not recognize herself. Her friends had not believed her when she'd confessed she'd never wanted to bother with men since Andrew left, but it was true nevertheless. Worse, it had not been a deprivation! How could you desire in a void? It had been one man she'd wanted 'like that' so long ago and even then it had had nothing to do with sexual satisfaction, only with the satisfaction of knowing for those few years that she was desired. She could have taken the upper hand, but out of inexperience she had not. Nowadays women's magazines went on and on about orgasms, but as far as she remembered it had been *his* pleasure she'd been drunk with! She realized she would have been a prime candidate for feminists, though it had been a bit too early for the new wave of them to influence her. Neither the babies nor the need to be needed had had any direct connection with passion, though on the surface they had everything to do with it. Passion might not be on offer from Alan Watson. She rather hoped it was not. But she liked talking to him. He treated her as an equal despite the difference in their ages.

They had been continuing one of their conversations the morning Cressida went into the hardware shop, had progressed from talking about the books they were reading and the television programmes they'd watched the night before to his telling her about new classes in Leeds being set up for painters who had never finished their training or had come to paint in middle-age. Somehow the old desire to make shapes and colours was still in her just as it had been when she was sixteen. Alan had been quite amazingly encouraging about her water-colour landscapes, and it was he who had persuaded her to send one to the exhibition.

★ ★ ★

There were only three days left of Cressida's holiday. For four whole days she had almost managed to forget Patrick Simmonds, with whom she had been in love for over a year. In love, but not happily, since Patrick was not in love with her. He liked her, was fond of her,

56

found her physically attractive, even perhaps loved her a little, but his feelings, unlike hers, could not be called all-consuming. Cressida would not have minded this; it was said that there was always one person who loved more than the other. Patrick however was one of that legion of young men who feared committing themselves. If his feelings were what he often said they were, then were not affection, regard, attraction and friendship enough to build a shared future? It appeared not. Cressida had got to the stage where she had begun to suspect that Patrick would never need or want to settle down: he was not a settling down kind of person. But it anguished her to think that she might be wrong and that even now there might be lurking some woman, or more likely some slip of a nineteen-year-old, with whom one day Patrick *would* settle down.

Settling down did not now have to mean marriage, as she had explained to Daphne. Nowadays there were many women who decided not to miss the opportunity of nest-building and they would stay with any man willing to share a mortgage without the sanction of law or church. But, perhaps sensibly, considering his temperament, Patrick Simmonds refused to contemplate this either.

Friendly affairs were what he was good at, he said.

Even if Patrick's feelings had matched hers, Cressida did sometimes wonder whether a shared romantic passion was the best basis for that commitment for which she yearned, which most women seemed to want eventually, but young men only rarely. If it was not, neither was a one-sided romantic infatuation. Wryly she wondered whether her unshared feelings made married happiness more likely or only half as likely — she was apt to torture herself with conundrums of this kind.

Some sort of accommodation seemed more likely to result when the passion was on the side of the man. In a world seemingly much improved for young women it was still true that a man could declare himself, and often be accepted, whilst a woman doing the same never could. Most women still expected to be courted; it would be so much easier if she were a man and Patrick the reluctant female!

'Are men and women really *so* different?' she asked Daphne.

'Absolutely,' replied her aunt. '*Young* ones at least.'

'I was always brought up to think they were equal.'

'Equal doesn't mean the same! My generation wasn't brought up to think they were the same in matters of love,' said Daphne. Cressida was silent, thinking she had never wanted to admit that. In matters of unrequited love, when one would think the sexes were at least equal in their suffering, it was far easier for a man to have his cake and eat it.

'Men have nice little cupboards in their minds where emotions, however devastating, can be stowed away,' said Daphne echoing her own thoughts. 'Also, many women are so grateful to be wanted they don't investigate the other cupboards.'

Since she had never married and could therefore be regarded as having lost in the romantic stakes, whatever had been her other experiences, Daphne was chary of saying more.

Cressida knew that her Patrick was not the kind of man who would ever be willing to live with a young woman on her terms. He knew himself too well, shrank from inflicting more pain than was necessary. Also he had the habit of looking ahead to disaster. There were men who never expected — or never perhaps wanted — a relationship to last; it was just her misfortune to be in love with one. In the past, she decided, women like

59

her might have got themselves pregnant and achieved shot-gun marriages. Marriage now being out of favour, guns were superfluous. She could become what was oddly called a 'single parent' — some new form of womanhood, achieving parthenogenesis? But that would only keep the situation running on into the future. Was it a baby she really wanted, more than a man? Her women friends who had shared a domicile for a time with boyfriends, grumbled later that they had had the worst of the bargain. One or two had moved out before it was too late. 'Too late' usually meant that the boyfriend had begun to fancy someone else. The woman might just as well have been a middle-aged wife, except that now she earned her own living!

Cressida was quite grateful that Patrick had not taken the easy way out and lived with her in a temporary sort of way. With Patrick it was all or nothing, and she had made the most of him whilst he was available. He had never said 'I love you', but they had had some good times together until she started wanting more. Her own feelings were so much stronger than his, which he must have known all along. It could be just that young men like Pat were more chary of using the 'L' word, the word young women liked to use? She herself had fallen in love so quickly, that was the problem, had been quite prepared to sacrifice everything for its sake. Had she been conditioned, and if so by whom or what? Would she now have to give up all thoughts of romantic love, of passion?

She'd realized that a strong desire for bliss in love often led to painful misery. She always missed Patrick when they were away from each other but he never seemed to have missed her. Was her love nothing but a desire to settle down monogamously with him? This notion shocked her for she did not relish the idea of being directed by the forces of nature, had always thought she would prefer a passionate love-affair to marriage. Had marriage all the time been lurking at the back of her mind? Was *that* why she had not so far cohabited with anybody? Why should she for heaven's sake wish to be married when so many marriages failed?

She discovered an answer to this that surprised her. It was the cheerful spectre of her parents' successful marriage that lurked at the back of her mind! Her parents were not especially conventional, certainly not religious, nor were they against divorce, and yet this idea of Happy Families seemed to be firmly rooted in her. Not that family life had always been ecstatic, but it had been a fixture in her life. And families had children. What was more, she saw these as yet imaginary offspring with a father who loved them and stayed with them. If he had wanted, Patrick would probably have been a very good father though he never seemed to have considered himself in this role. He'd said, a few weeks after his remark about short-lived happy affairs, that he 'might like to marry one day'. This had raised her hopes, only to have him continue — 'When I'm about forty.' This had brought a vision not only of the nineteen-year-old child-bride but pictures of children born *in the next century*. She wanted to have children before the next century!

It was hopeless. Yet if she loved him, why not go on making the most of him, continue to have a splendid fling, enjoy herself? No, it was too late. She had betrayed herself, told him she loved him. And she couldn't enjoy herself for long, knowing it wasn't going to last and that he was too sensible to hint at compromise. The bald truth was that she did not mean to him what he meant to her. She could continue to be his friend, his very special friend, but not his lover. It was an unusual situation; most young men would have encouraged her to go on enjoying the pleasures of sex. It wasn't that he had grown tired of that with her, for he had said it was perfect. He knew she loved him, knew that she wanted him 'for keeps' (how possessive that sounded even in her own ears), and was rational enough — or was it cold enough? — to discourage her in the midst of a mutually enjoyable affair.

There was, then, nothing to be done. She could give him up as a lover or wait till he ended it, which he was about to do. She'd miss the love-making which had taken place two or three times a week, and the intimacy. Might she just possibly come to terms with the situation and, one day, stop feeling miserable whenever she was not with him?

A complicating factor was the man whose letter she now held over her plate of toast and marmalade. So typical that Patrick never wrote to say he missed her, or even just to say he was still alive or looked forward to seeing her, whilst Jonathan Edwards kept in constant touch.

Jonathan liked her and she liked him. He did not however fill her with wild longing or excitement, with either misery or joy. In fact she had known him before she made the acquaintance of Patrick. Recently he had given her the impression of liking her more and more, might even be a little in love with her though she was wary of ascribing to any man the sort of longings that tormented her. He had never declared himself. He knew a bit about Patrick and her, probably guessed the rest.

Daphne was thinking, *someone* is fond of her, the handwriting on that envelope is the same as the one that came the other day. It must be the boyfriend?

Cressida opened the letter and read it as she ate her toast and drank the deliciously strong but creamy coffee her aunt provided for breakfast — after waking her an hour earlier with a cup of equally delicious tea.

Dear Cressy
I hope you are having a peaceful holiday, or change, or rest, whichever is most needed. Pity about the weather if it's anything like what we've had down here. Rain, rain and more rain. I've got tickets for a recital at the Wigmore — your favourite Liszt's Consolations *and* Pilgrimages, *for Thursday of the week after next. Would you like one of them? I shall be going . . .*

What a funny way of inviting her out! As though he might just catch sight of her in the audience when surely the tickets would be together? She read on — Jonathan's cooking triumphs, the novel he was reading, an exhibition at the Royal Academy . . . the news . . . Bosnia . . . Belfast, all terrible . . . his work (he was a solicitor). She looked up for more coffee when she'd finished it. Love from Jonathan. Two kisses.

She liked men who wrote letters. Did other men think they were sissies? She liked writing letters herself, come to that.

She refolded the letter and put it back in its envelope for reply.

'Lovely coffee,' she said. Daphne was deep in *The Times.* 'Can I do some shopping for you? I thought I might walk over to Sholey after the shopping, unless it begins to rain — '

'It won't rain this morning,' replied her aunt. 'Do you know, someone has called her baby 'Chrysalis' — do you think it's a misprint? But what for? Christabel?'

'No, it's just a New Age name, I expect, though you wouldn't think they'd read *The Times.*' Daphne put the paper down. 'The sun was lovely when I woke at seven — but it is a bit cooler. Get us some chops, will you — by Thursday my imagination fails. Or we could have some fish and chips — they do them well here.'

'What time does the library open?' asked Cressida, beginning to wash up.

'Ten. Shuts at lunchtime though. I'll give you a cheque for the paper bill too if you wouldn't mind . . . '

Everything was so peaceful, so ordered, such a relief from London. She could reply to Jonathan perfectly sincerely saying: 'I am having a very peaceful holiday, change, and rest.' She'd better look for some picture postcards in case she did not feel like writing a long letter. She'd accept the concert invitation.

When she had gone out Daphne went into the garden to cut some late, small, dark pink, button chrysanthemums. She did hope that Cressida would make a sensible decision about her life. Someone, probably that Patrick chap, had been wearing her down. It was such a waste. When *she* was twenty-eight she'd been about to recover from life with a man called Charles Armitage. Had Cressy's young man treated her as Charles had treated her long ago? She rarely dreamed of Charles now, but when she did they were happy dreams, which a few years ago they had not been. Something in her life must have changed for her subjective landscape to have changed. The mellowness of age? Memories of Charles flitted in and out of Daphne's head as she clipped the flowers. Several bold climbing nasturtiums were still splashing their colour around. If the weather turned colder they would soon look like drenched sea-weed.

She went in, tidied up, made her bed, glanced in at her niece's, which was neatly sheeted, slippers standing politely side by side under the bedside table, and then went into her workroom, with its window that looked out over the cobbled stable-yard. How lucky she was to live here. She sat down at her desk with her file of ideas for 'The Life and Works'. If only, like her niece, Anne could have had an occasional holiday out of London, and some leisure, to give her lyrical food. Daphne always thought of the poet's birthplace, Cornwall, as slightly similar to Yorkshire, and she was sure the woman had not liked London. Anne never seemed to go anywhere except now and again into the capital on the passenger coach, often accompanied by her artist brother Joshua. But she rhapsodized over flowers and storms, must have found in them the metaphors for her states of mind. Southey had written that she loved poetry and retirement and the country — and that 'her heart was alive'.

Yet her life was probably narrow, as far as experience of the world went. Except for her being unhappily in love. Daphne wrote: 'What did she really think of Mary W. — who was passionate and probably bossy?'

Had those turbulent 1790s that followed on their friendship changed her opinion of her friend? Many of the women writers were on the side of revolution — who could blame them? — though others were critical, frightened that the English 'mob' would follow suit. She amused herself for a few minutes wondering which side her new friends at the reading circle would have taken in their youth.

Sonia would have been a rebel but not a revolutionary . . .

Daphne was soon back to work filling in the blanks of Anne's life as she imagined they might be filled. Thoughts of Sonia — and of Charles Armitage — were banished.

★ ★ ★

The lamb chops bought, Cressida visited Heckcliff library again. On coming out, swinging an ancient string bag of Daphne's, she passed J Kershaw's.

Judith saw her from the window where she was balancing a new consignment of casseroles, and waved. Cressy waved back, walked on, turned right and went up the hill in the direction of Sholey.

The autumn sun was bright, but the wind

was cold and she walked as quickly as she could, for the exercise, and to feel warmer.

She found herself thinking neither of Jonathan nor of Patrick, rather of Judith Kershaw.

What on earth it must be like to be forty-three with four grown-up sons? She couldn't imagine that at all.

4

The week after the meeting at Lydia's Sonia was in the bus returning from a visit to the town dentist. She had *The Portrait of a Lady* on her lap but was more interested in the old Indian woman across the aisle who had knitted steadily all the way. If those Norfolk ladies had reminded her of her mother's generation at home, this lady reminded her of her grandmother's. Her turbaned husband — they must be Sikhs — was seated by her side but never addressed one word to her throughout the journey. How did she know they were man and wife? Somehow she did. They were living by the rules of the tribe, she thought, just like her Grandma Pollard had — her husband a man of few words, but orderly, thrifty. What were this couple's children and grandchildren like?

There had been an attractive man in the dentist's waiting-room and she had smiled at him to show solidarity in pain. He had turned his face away as if she'd committed some solecism! She ought to have realized by now that older women were either invisible or a positively unwelcome sight. He'd been forty or so, nearer in age to her children. A similar thing had happened at a party not long before when a man had been quite rude. He'd been at least forty-five, not young. Very young men were nice, talked to you as if you were a human being, but it was those in their forties who were the rudest, still bearing about them some waft of the Blessed Sixties when they had been adolescents. It was not a period she or her friends had made much of, being too busy with small children. The man at the party had looked so bored that she had finally stopped trying to talk to him. Did he think she was trying to get off with him? But when an attractive young woman about her daughter Anna's age had been introduced his face had lit up, hormones triggered by a reaction to surface beauty, she supposed. She ought to be glad that hers had stopped racing round, they drove your life relentlessly along sexual highways and byways when there were more interesting lanes to explore. Nothing was more interesting to young people than sex; she supposed she had once been the same herself.

She must stop thinking that she was beyond the pale; she was just *older*, that was all. Young people all came to that, though they didn't believe they ever would. It was amusing as well as chastening to realize your former attractions had been only surface ones.

The Indians got off at the stop before hers and she smiled at the woman who shyly smiled back. Women were so much nicer than men. She got off at the following stop herself, intending to walk across to Norwood and home, when a woman greeted her on the Old Lane. 'It's Sonia, isn't it?' Tall, greying, bowed . . . Goodness, it was Esther Rice who had once lived near her in those far off sixties she had been thinking about. Did she look as old as Mrs Rice? She ought not to mind if she did, having been thinking about some of the advantages of age! But people imagined everyone but themselves had changed. The two women stopped for a moment to catch up on their lives; it had been years since they'd even seen each other. Duty done, each turned in her own direction.

At the corner of her road, a beautiful

brown-skinned girl passed by, her hair in a little pony-tail. Lovely profile, thought Sonia. She was wearing a dark bluey-green overblouse — didn't they call that colour 'teal'? — and her long bare legs were in three-quarter denim shorts. How tall the young were! Didn't she feel the cold?

She put her key in the latch. The burglar alarm sounded as soon as she opened the inner door, and she turned it off, hating the noise. How many years separated tall Esther and the beautiful half-caste as they used to call people like her. One good thing nowadays was the Indian restaurant on the way to town that delivered you a decent meal of nice dry coriander-flavoured rice and pungent bits of chicken. She might order one tonight. Bob was still away, so she'd be making a solitary supper. No, she'd boil two eggs and read while eating them. She was used to the pleasures of grass-widowhood, had been used to them for years, her husband often having had to go abroad for his academic work.

Perhaps it was only because she now had more time to herself that she found her thoughts reverting to the past, the place Evelyn had said was 'safe'. Her own memories were mostly pleasant and even the unpleasant ones were somehow hallowed because they were hers. She was aware of her own egotism. It worried her though that people said it was in your second childhood that you wallowed in reminiscence. She remembered *so much*. Could one remember too much? Was it because her experience was undigested that the past kept on returning, and one went on chewing it like some comforting cud?

Her dreams were often of her paternal grandparents' house, its hall decked for Christmas, the large kitchen where they ate as a family, the home-made lemon curd on fresh white bread; the cold shelf in the cellar where you put your frozen pink Stop-Me-and-Buy-One if you wanted to save it for tea, large white bedrooms, and the dusty, uninhabited attics above them. She would like one day to exchange memories with Daphne Berridge, who was her own age. It was a pity they had never met before.

She went upstairs. From one window she had a view of magnificent skies high over the Pennines, where you could see sunsets of vermilion and green, turquoise and mauve. She was lucky to go on living in a place she found beautiful. Sunsets had not changed. Pollution had not yet tainted the colour of these skies.

How best though could you live in the

present when so much tugged you back to the past? She ought to count her blessings. So many people were alone at her age, had no children, or had never had a permanent partner — Daphne Berridge for example.

Now she really must concentrate on *The Portrait of a Lady*. Had it always been mainly women who read novels? She and Dorothy had been great readers when they were at school, sharing their favourite books, each having similar tastes when they were about thirteen, especially for historical adventures. Now for some time they'd no longer liked the same books. Time had made Dorothy forget old allegiances to introduce new ones, and Timothy her husband had changed her. He had not been awfully fond of his wife's friend; he used to say: 'Sonia needs something to believe in.'

Faith, either religious or political, still eluded Sonia. Yet it had been Dorothy not she who had had to face death: Tim's death. Dorothy had a married daughter, and now grandchildren, and trusted they would carry on where she and Tim had left off. For Dorothy, living one's remaining years on earth was not a theoretical problem so much as a practical test of energy and endurance. The past helped; you realized you'd survive worse tests. 'You are always saying things are getting worse,' Dorothy once said to her, 'but you've never been what you might call a contented person!' She'd made her sound like Evelyn.

Many people of their generation thought but did not like to say, for fear of being labelled reactionary, that their native land was going downhill. It was true that it had filled up with words for things and concepts that had not even existed not long ago. The newspapers talked of *privatizing, prioritising, deselecting, rate-capping* and *bonking*. There were *preppies* and *yuppies* and *pit bull puppies, stagflation* and *copy-cat crimes; sumo wrestling, animal righters, glitterati* . . . She often felt adrift in this new world of *virtual reality, CD Roms, motorways, karaoke, bytes, digital recordings and cable TV*; things that were *user-friendly*, jobs that were *hands on*, cars soon to be shuttled through the *Chunnel* . . .

Dorothy however, though she would listen patiently to Sonia's homilies, said she admired this changed world and suggested that Sonia felt so personally affronted by it because she had been such a rebel in her youth and had become a natural conservative. Tim had always said she was a romantic, and romantic rebels usually ended up as reactionaries.

'Sometimes I come to the conclusion a better world might be created if everyone were born *slightly* mentally subnormal — 'differently abled' as the Americans say,' Sonia had replied: 'They'd never invent anything beyond the wheel, probably not even that. It isn't nice to feel a stranger in the world. I know I'm not the only person to feel it.' Dorothy looked shocked.

They had known each other since they were eight, done everything together. One day in the war they had taken a tram to a beautiful eighteenth-century mansion open to the public. Its rose-gardens had overwhelmed Sonia who leaned down to smell the velvety-dark perfume. Never would roses be so blackly red or smell so wonderful as on that afternoon. Dorothy said she couldn't remember that afternoon. Their mothers, husbandless for a few days, had taken the two girls on holiday together. The mothers had been stiffly polite to each other, drawn together only because of their daughters. Trudging through the heather, almost beaten down by the icy winds, Sonia and Dorothy had discussed Life and Love and God and Nature — and School. Both had hated the same things then, above all the piercingly cold afternoons spent playing compulsory hockey, a winter sun always about to set. Dorothy was a chapelgoer and Sonia occasionally accompanied her friend there. The chapel had a pale blue smell, preached against sex and strong drink and swearing, which only made these indulgences appear the more exciting to Sonia. Occasionally, until Sonia gave it up, Dorothy went with her to the Victorian Anglican church with its square tower and its dark ruby-glassed windows, incense lingering from the strange practices of the Anglo-Catholic vicar.

Dorothy's mother's kitchen had had a special smell, a mixture of cinnamon and gingerbread and warm oven that permeated Dorothy's clothes. Smells had been Sonia's chief pleasure, not only roses, but the smell of yellow 'picric' lint in her old dolls' first-aid box, and the mysterious *Evening in Paris* smell of the box that contained the soap Easter eggs given to her years ago by her grandmother Pollard. In adolescence there had been new smells: cloying nail-varnish that was like pear-drops and the delightful scent of Dorothy's new bottle of Quink ink which they sniffled rapturously.

Sonia's desk looked like a tip and Dorothy tidied it for her and received a tube of fruit pastilles in return. Sweets were still rationed, so it was a real sacrifice on Sonia's part, but she bought the favourite Victory V tablets instead, which were not rationed and sucked on chlorodine that had the ether-like smell she remembered from the nursing home where she'd had her tonsils out.

Sonia did not always tell Dorothy everything in those days; she kept a few secrets. Now, when she would have been more willing to share her thoughts with her she was a little sad that they had drifted apart. She had hopes of Daphne Berridge though.

* * *

It was early closing day and Judith Kershaw and Alan Watson had gone out for an afternoon walk. Soon the clocks would be put back and light would have drained from the sky by mid-afternoon but today was sunny, not too cold, a sort of timeless time, a time when in the past nothing had happened of importance. Years ago on such an afternoon Judith would have been collecting the boys from primary school at half past three and Alan would have been teaching the last period of the day, waiting for the bell that signalled the end of boredom.

'I always looked forward to free afternoons,' he was saying. 'I can't quite believe they've arrived.'

'But when you were lecturing at the college

you had free afternoons sometimes, didn't you?' she asked. He seemed to have forgotten that there had been years of working in Leeds after leaving the old grammar school.

'Oh, Tuesdays and Wednesdays were usually spent on teaching practice — not mine — I mean going all over the place listening to students' lessons. It was very tiring and you never really knew what you could do to help the weaker ones.'

'I suppose teaching is really like being a poet? Poets are born not made.'

'Up to a point. Some people are born teachers — I'm not myself. Others can be given hints, but they're no good if the subject bores them — or children bore them too!'

They were getting on dangerous ground, she thought: children, her four grown-up ones, and his lack of any. She wanted to ask him why he didn't find a young woman still young enough to have children for him. Then there'd be a point to a second marriage. She said:

'We always thought you were a good teacher,' and then hoped that her reference to those days when he had been Mr Watson and she Judith Jagger of the Upper Fifth doing her maths O levels would not annoy him. He laughed. 'It was a doddle teaching you lot — you were all so polite.'

'Were you ever on the staff with Sonia Greenwood? She taught me for a year when I was about ten before she left to have a baby. She still lives in Norwood. Daphne seems to like her.'

'The one who was Miss Hartley before she was married? I didn't know she knew Daphne Berridge, thought she must be about the same age. She married Hugh Greenwood who teaches at the university. I think she left the school at the end of my first year's teaching.'

'Oh, they met at this literary circle Mrs Greenwood organizes. Daphne really has enough to do but felt she ought not to appear stand-offish. Shall we go up the lane?' she said, thinking how different their two perspectives must be on those long past days of thirty years ago. 'Right. We can turn down again towards the Hall once we're on top.'

They were walking so far much the same route as Cressida had walked; she however had not taken the lane across the fields that led to the Grange but continued down towards a small hamlet and rejoined the main road more quickly.

The Grange was a large old house hidden behind a long drive, a little older than the converted mansion where Lydia Robinson lived. It was rumoured that its owner had completely renovated its interior, put in bathrooms with gold taps. Outside, you could see conservatories with shining glass roofs.

All around them were the dry-stone walls of an earlier time and the lanes and farms which, Judith reflected, would certainly have been there should the writer of the book Daphne had lent her have visited the place. There were no other walkers; occasionally a car passed them on the way to the town. The sky was clear, but there was that smell of autumn, of decay from the drifts of sodden leaves beneath the trees which led from the bottom of the private path to the Grange. Judith sniffed the air.

'Autumn was always my favourite season,' she said. 'I don't know why — I suppose it's not very cheerful.'

'It was always the beginning of the year for me,' said Alan. 'My favourite term — with Christmas at the end of it. I didn't enjoy the spring term so much.'

'Well it's warmer now than it will be in March — we're very exposed to wind up here.' She wondered whether they would still be walking together next spring. They continued up the path and stopped when they came to the pillared gates that were shut against intruders. There didn't appear to be anybody around, though scents even more autumnal were drifting over the large gardens.

'Bonfires,' he said. 'Soon be Guy Fawkes.'

They turned now and went through an ancient stile and across fields that brought them back to the lane and led on to a few houses in a hollow: old houses, cottages mostly, and then, on the left, another narrower lane led to the Hall.

'A Grange and a Hall,' he said. 'There must have been money round here for years.'

'It was where all the rich from the cities came to live,' she said, picking up a conker now from a horse chestnut tree, one of many that followed the curving path. They passed another imposing gate and saw through to the large garden of yet another mansion. But then there was nothing but fields and ditches and the cawing of rooks. In the distance the church tower could be seen.

'Thank God they didn't put the motorway through here,' he said, and took her hand. He was such a nice man — but did she really want to exchange her new found independence and new freedom from a family of boys to embark on another sort of life?

It had to be confessed that she feared change. Yet, if she did not encourage any form of change, she would be stuck for ever with the shop, waiting only for grandmotherhood, alone in spite of her large family.

Alan knew that she had a good deal of wariness now in her nature that had not been in the fifteen-year-old Judith, the girl who had plunged a mere four years after that into what he could only regard as a disastrous marriage. The wariness would be, he guessed, for marriage itself, but it was up to him to show her how her life might improve.

'What used you to do on half day closing?' he asked her as they walked sedately down the little hill past the stream where once village children like Daphne and Mary Berridge had been wont to gather kingcups and marsh marigolds. Even cowslips had been there then, Daphne said.

'I was usually too busy to take a break,' she replied after due thought. 'I suppose when the boys were little I'd fill up the washing machine and then do the orders over tea.'

It seemed to Alan Watson a life denuded of anything but toil.

'Tea,' he said. 'I feel like a high tea, not 'afternoon tea' as they call it round here.'

'High tea is just *tea*,' said Judith. 'If you southerners had it later you'd call it supper.' Alan had worked in the north since he was twenty five so this was not very fair.

He dropped his arm from hers as they toiled up the hill and reached the main road. 'Can I give you tea then — high or low as you wish?'

'That would be nice.' He lived now on Braemar Road in a tidy bungalow, a survival from the twenties, with the park wall as one of the boundaries of his garden. A favoured position. It would be nice to be looked after, she could not help thinking. But it was supposed to be women who 'looked after' men of his age. He was spry, slim, did not look his years and coming up the hill had puffed no more than she had.

It was companionship she needed, that was it. But could you have companionship with a man without all the rest? She could not help knowing that others would see this as her last chance.

There had been progress, he was thinking. Even one walk accompanied by pleasant conversation added to their store of knowledge about each other. They were no longer strangers. However, unless he introduced the subject, she didn't talk about her paintings or about the books she was reading, though she was willing to do so if asked. He knew Daphne Berridge lent her books and considered her intelligent, which she certainly was. But he must not rush things. He knew very well her dilemma.

He had never been a lonely sort of man but he too yearned for companionship. He wanted to say 'We could travel together, and you could paint — France, Italy, Spain — whilst we — or rather I — am young enough to enjoy them.' But he would suggest that only when they knew each other even better.

At one time after his wife died he had wondered whether his colleague Daphne would have wanted to marry him. The affair with Daphne had helped him recover in the months after Celia's death, shown him he was still part of everything, not washed up into widowerhood. She had been kind to him, but they had both eventually realized that in more indefinable ways they were not suited. When she had seen that he was feeling better, Daphne had withdrawn into her own private world and appeared to find it satisfactory. Judith was a different sort of woman. Not just because she was younger but because she had never actually chosen to live alone; it had been forced on her by her husband's desertion. She should now by rights be the busy but contented wife of a reasonably successful businessman with a wide circle of friends and a pleasant social life, with time to attend classes in painting, to travel, to tend a garden, do all the wifely things. He knew he was old-fashioned, but Judith *was* a wifely sort of woman in spite of her long years alone with children and all the ups and downs of family life without a man to help. He wondered if she had ever had offers from other men but did not like to ask.

'How are you liking that novel Daphne lent you?' he asked.

'I'm enjoying it — but I don't know enough about the background to fit it all in. I suppose I do enjoy novels even more than biographies. For years I never had time to read any.' She knew that Alan was not such an addicted reader as herself; men usually weren't.

Once, he'd said that happy endings irritated him, but unhappy ones depressed him, so that in the end he wondered why he should concern himself with the stories of imaginary people. Wasn't there enough to get excited about or worried about in the real world? She rather cherished such remarks. He could be quite perceptive on the other hand about painting and certainly knew a lot more about music than she did.

Dusk would soon fall. His house, when they reached it, was welcoming. In no time at all he'd made toast, scrambled eggs and wheeled in a trolley with scones and jam. His wife must have trained him well and by now he'd had years of practice. They ate their tea at a table by the window where they could look out on the slope of the open park that had once been meadowland. But she had to get back to sort out some shop work for the morning.

'I'll run you back,' he said. 'Leave the washing up.'

After he had deposited her at her flat above the shop and said a cheerful goodbye she felt quite strange. Not exactly lonely — there was always so much to do. One of the boys would probably ring her that evening and there were some clothes of Stephen's to sort out and send on. She looked into the two rooms on the top floor that had been their bedrooms and still had the four divans and the chests of drawers. So quiet. So abandoned.

She pulled herself together. Once your children had gone they might come back from time to time but she had to get used to the fact that the flat was no longer home for two of them and would soon not be for the other two even if they came for holidays. She had to learn to stand alone, detach the support — or weight — of four pairs of hands and decide whether or not to encourage Alan

Watson, provider of conversation and meals and companionship. And perhaps more.

'She's kind,' Judith had once said to Alan about Daphne.

He had wondered whether Daphne ever regretted that episode with him after Celia had died and he'd gone round white-faced and lost. He and Celia had had a happy marriage, he'd told her, though they would both have liked children.

★ ★ ★

Cressida had been talking about children the evening before she left to go back to London.

'They are just like adults,' Daphne had said. 'The same proportion of nice and nasty ones, I mean.'

'I just can't see myself with a baby,' Cressida had confessed.

'That's what your mother always said,' Daphne answered, remembering her sister's amazement when she had produced her first child.

'I mean, what if I found I couldn't have children after I'd gone to all the bother of getting married?' Cressida continued gloomily.

'There are tests,' replied Daphne briskly.

'But *most* women seem to be able to.'

She was thinking, Celia Watson couldn't.

Later that night she thought before she fell asleep of babies and children. She wouldn't have minded having a daughter. She had done quite a lot for other people's children, her pupils as well as her nieces. Anne had had no babies either. But then Anne possibly went to her grave a virgin unspotted. Unspotted by what? Sin, she supposed.

When she finally slept and eventually dreamed it was of children, three children of about seven to ten in a small room with a fireplace and a white table. She knew it was somewhere in London because one of the children said 'We walked down Thames Street.' There was a woman sitting in an armchair and then suddenly there was an open door and a man standing there. He had a menacing air, was dishevelled, and she could smell whisky in the room. He picked up a bowl from the table and threw it against the wall. But the woman continued to sit in her chair and the two children stood silent. Then the mother said something in a cultured voice with just the faint overlay of a west country burr. 'Lie down, Alec, and the children will bring you some tea.'

The man began to shout but Daphne could not hear his words. The porridge on the wall continued to drip. Without anything being said she — the onlooker, the invisible figure at the window — knew that the man was insanely jealous of something, someone. Perhaps it was of his wife's culture or his children's not needing him. There was the feeling of his not being needed. But then she was outside again and there were lights in the distance and the mast of a ship and a salty wind. She must help those children. As she stood now on the opposite side of the street the man came out of the house, followed by the boy and they walked past her towards where she knew was the great river.

Daphne struggled as she woke, wanting to return to the room with the woman and the girl to tell them it was all right, he had gone. The dream stayed with her for several minutes as she lay in her own quiet room far away from the Thames or from sad children and drunken husbands, patient wives.

★ ★ ★

Sonia had also once upon a time considered herself unsuited to life with children but now looked back on those years through a haze of nostalgia. Busy they had certainly been, but never boring, and she had enjoyed bringing up Anna and Ralph for most of the time.

She had been immersed in the present, had a *raison d'être* approved of by everyone. Six years she had spent with them for company, before the part-time lure had taken her back for a time when Ralph, the younger, was not quite three, to teach in a small private school nearby.

Evelyn Naylor had lived at that time in a settlement of small modern houses not far away. The Naylor boys were a bit old for Ralph, but there were many other women she knew who had children of the same age. Ralph had not paid them much attention but Anna had been sociable. She had taken her children out regularly for walks in the fresh air or played in the garden or the house with them until they were of an age to play outside alone, still possible in the late sixties, early seventies.

The way we lived then, she thought, before the end of the 1960s the country changed. She remembered Ellen, the child of one of the many Americans who used to be their neighbours, over for a year or two's academic exchange. They always remarked upon the safety of the village. Sonia had thought, whatever can America be like? In those days she had been able to leave her bicycle unchained for hours outside Norwood shops, had never heard of a burglar visiting anyone she was acquainted with. But popular music had already changed by then; she remembered Anna singing, 'I love you, yeh, yeh, yeh', and a plastic yellow submarine of Ralph's.

It had been the sort of life some feminists despised. Colds and minor illnesses had been the only real bugbear, before 'people stopped behaving themselves' according to Sonia's mother.

Anna and Ralph had been at one particular children's party when Jim and Bob Naylor had spent the whole time fighting each other. Zoë Coultar had been rather boisterous too if she remembered rightly, a lanky girl of about ten who didn't often meet other children. Gwyneth must have been over on a visit. They all thought Zoë's mother was 'funny'. Dorothy's elder daughter had saved the day. Her Ruth was the oldest child there, must have been about twelve, and had helped Sonia with the little ones. Ruth's sister Elizabeth was rather sulky and Sam went out on the lawn by himself, cross because his mother had insisted he attend a 'babies' party. Odd to think it was Elizabeth who was the one now surrounded by children, whilst Ruth was living in Hampstead with a research scientist and working in a lab herself. Dorothy said Ruth didn't intend to have children, she was very 'green' and did not consider the world a fit place for new human beings, never mind the population problem . . .

'Do you remember how Tony Robinson fought Peter Wood the whole time?' Dorothy had asked her recently.

'Yes, the last time I invited boys older than Ralph to the house he came and behaved very badly! Thank goodness we don't have to give parties like that any more.'

She would not confess to Dorothy though that she wished she still had an excuse to enter a toyshop, or admit to keeping safe the prettiest baby clothes. It wasn't that she wanted to hold on tight to Anna and Ralph; life at present was certainly easier. Neither did she really wish she were thirty-five again — present-day women of her sort now felt guilty if they had no job in the world outside, tried to combine babies with briefcases. It was the inexorable nature of time passing that scared her, though she tried not to talk about that too much to Dorothy.

'The children won't remember all the things we used to do,' she said to her husband.

'Oh, they will remember a good deal,' Bob replied. 'Think how vividly you remember *your* childhood!'

Dorothy, all her life having seemingly led up to her status as matriarch, often confessed herself to have been a failure with Sam, her own changeling child. Lydia was childless — but did not seem to regret that, nor see herself at a disadvantage. Evelyn had her sons, and Gwyneth her daughter. Would they have been different women without them?

Those lost years were not lost at all but encapsulated in new adults. Those years when they had been too busy to think about themselves had been an exercise in partial self-abnegation. Women who put all their energies into bringing up their children were often disparaged, but nothing mattered more than bringing up children, and the years passed so quickly.

Nothing happened to me that did not happen to millions of other women, thought Sonia. Children took over my life, became my life; so it was hard to let them go; the more one puts into loving them the harder it is to see them alone, unsupported, even if the right true end of it all is their independence. The empty nest syndrome they called it. But there were compensations: seeing a baby that was not one's own responsibility when it yelled, for example. A relief to know they had survived, and their parents with them.

It was when the children were teenagers

that she'd gathered a few friends together to read and discuss novels. She consumed books avidly; there was a danger of becoming too solitary, spending all her free time reading.

A smart neighbour, Lydia Robinson, who was about the same age as herself had often stopped to talk as they walked back together from the village shops, Sonia not driving a car and Lydia walking for the sake of her figure. Sonia suggested she might like to join them one evening, come round for coffee and an exchange of ideas. She gathered Lydia was a reader, having often seen her in the library.

'Oh, I mostly read detective stories,' confessed Lydia. 'I've always been meaning to tackle what the nuns called double quotes 'great books' but they rather put me off them.'

'They thought reading for pleasure was sinful?' asked Sonia.

'I think they pretended they found a superior pleasure in the classics. I didn't believe they did! I caught one of them once with Agatha Christie in plain covers! I didn't think they were to be trusted — as in other matters!'

Lydia agreed to join Evelyn Naylor and Dorothy Grey one evening at Sonia's. Gwyneth Coultar was back from abroad and was roped in. 'Is it one of these graduate wife things?' she had asked. 'I don't think I'm really a suitable person.' She was always a bit behindhand in her notions. Being away had made her more so. By the time Gwyneth got round to reading year-old issues of newspapers, England had already forgotten the subject of their columns. But good novels were not like that.

Lydia had seemed a little uneasy.

'But she's just the kind of woman to put herself down,' Sonia said to Bob. 'I think she's a bit lonely and needs new friends. There were a few other women who used to go to the local authority evening classes and then they cut them. They might appreciate coming. It won't cost them anything but the price of coffee when it's their turn to be hostess.'

For a time their meetings had been attended by refugees from these classes but one by one they fell away. Those who had known each other as children — Sonia and Dorothy, Evelyn and Gwyneth, with the addition of Lydia, who had later moved over to Heckcliff, continued to attend each month. July and August were given a miss out of some atavistic memory of school holidays. Bob thought it was all rather sweet and idealistic, but was used to his wife's enthusiasms.

It was good to remind husbands that their wives did not need the presence of men to enjoy themselves. They had sucked nourishment from novel after novel, past glories feeding an ambivalent present, with enough novels to last them into the next century. Reading and talking about their reading they had begun increasingly to talk about themselves.

5

One of the troubles with Daphne's long-ago lover Charles had been that he was in love with a partial figment of his imagination. Only partial, because Daphne had liked to believe that some of the qualities he claimed to find in her were actually there. Another problem had been his determination, whilst he was re-inventing her, that she should become in other matters what he wanted her to be. This boiled down to a Daphne mysteriously more efficient in her twenties than anybody of that age could possibly be, a Daphne whose sheets were always ironed and fragrant, whose taste in wine was impeccable — Mouton Cadet, Puligny Montrachet — but only certain specified years — and who wore soft tweeds. This impossible ideal mixed badly with the waif-like qualities he found in her which also arose from his imagination.

Yet Charles had truly loved her, not only the parts he had invented, she had no doubts about that. There must have been something in her that had made his imagination take wings the way it did. She was beautiful (he said) and desirable (he said). His ideal woman. She had known even then that she would never find again with any other man the kind of sensual adoration which he proffered. Years later, Daphne wondered occasionally how long Charles's love for her — and hers for him — would have lasted if he had been free to marry her.

'A penny for them,' Cressida said, startling her. It was the last day of her holiday. That afternoon she was to return to London, a London changed utterly from the solid clean grey-monumented city Daphne had once lived in.

'Oh, I was just thinking how London had changed,' she said. 'More toast?'

'I had another interesting dream,' said Cressy. 'I'm sure it was in London, somewhere down near the docks, and there were four children, two boys and two girls, I think, and they had to walk to school across a bridge. I was walking with them but it was very muddy. It doesn't sound very interesting does it? I remember my boots were heavy and wet. I suppose it was the walk yesterday when I got over the wall into the field on the way back and found the grass all squelchy.'

'Down near the Syke?'

'Yes. I washed my socks when I came in in case you thought I might catch cold. I'm always telling Grandma that you can't catch cold from wet and cold, only from germs.'

'What did the children look like?'

'I don't recall their faces but I felt they were very close and I was an interloper — you know how in dreams there are feelings there aren't words for?'

'I always used to feel my dreams were trying to tell me something, but now I'm sure I must know already, though I can't remember what when I'm awake,' Daphne said.

Cressida had not told her aunt of the other dream she'd had after the first one. Quite a different dream: Patrick kissing her, so warm and blissful, the sort of bliss you just could not experience when you were awake. Why was that?

'I'm off to the post office,' Cressy said.

'I really enjoy walking everywhere — really healthy. Can I get you anything at the shops?'

'Some stamps, perhaps. What time are you leaving?'

'About three o'clock — the train goes at half past — I'll go into Woolsford on the bus.'

Cressy strode out to the village shops, hands in pockets, thinking that the bliss of the dream was akin to the effect of music she and Daphne had been listening to. The Liszt concert paraphrases of Verdi made her feel full of love for Patrick. Daphne too had looked dreamy as she listened. What had she been like when *she* was twenty-nine? She'd done without a husband and apparently thrived, so it seemed men were not always necessary for happiness, or at least sanity.

Whilst Cressida was out Daphne did her household tasks swiftly and went to her table. Her mind was seething with ideas she had had no time to write down. She was looking forward to solitude once Cressy had gone. She enjoyed her niece's company but there were some kinds of work for which you had to have long uninterrupted hours alone if you were to accomplish them satisfactorily. Her notes were in a large folder on her desk, neatly numbered according to the projected order of the book. The literary part of her research and her annotations of the poems had been thorough, but there was too much she did not know about Anne and her family, above all their childhood and adolescence. She'd read up the period in the biographies of anyone who might have known them. It was time to draw it all together, to recreate the woman. What had been Anne's thoughts as she went about her daily tasks, taught her small number of pupils, talked in the evenings to her brother, found a little fame when her slim volume appeared and was reviewed? Was love as often in Anne's thoughts as it was in the theme of so much of her poetry?

Daphne found the historical background the hardest to recreate. How much pain did people have to put up with? How much did they weigh? How many clothes did they possess? What possibility had there been for a 'respectable' woman of her day to have a love affair that was not anodyne or Platonic and did not lead to marriage? Mary Wollstonecraft had had such a relationship. Had Anne's being loved 'Platonically' by the man she was in love with been more of a comfort or a torture?

Outside today it was cool and bright. Widgery came in and rubbed against her legs. He would go to sleep all afternoon after his dinner, and when he woke up Cressy would be gone and she would have a long evening alone.

Cressy had told her last night that there was a young man called Jonathan with whom she had a 'Platonic' relationship that was very pleasant. Daphne had said nothing, sure that this Jonathan must harbour other desires which, Cressy being in love with the other chap, he knew better than to declare. Was life easier now for women of her niece's age, in spite of the modern lack of morals — or because of that?

'He is a safe sort of person,' Cressy had said.

They had talked about Judith Kershaw. 'She looks happy enough. She likes her own company?'

'She's hardly had much of it with those great lads around — a relief I expect, even if she misses them, to know she can now cook for one instead of five. You haven't met them, they are *enormous* . . . She's enjoying being alone though she didn't choose to be — it chose *her*. Bringing up four boys alone — I could never have done that!'

'What do children have to do with love? Is it just Nature's way of making sure of the next generation?'

'Being the result of sex, and love and sex seemingly connected?' Daphne asked dryly.

'I suppose children stand for continuity?'

'Continuity is in buildings and places too — old ghosts everywhere. You don't have to have children to feel fully alive,' said Daphne, obliged to defend her own way of life though heaven knew she wanted Cressy to settle down and have a baby. Why?

'I'm not sure how much I want what they call 'a family'. The *idea* seems different from just having a baby doesn't it?'

'Babies don't stay babies long. Soon they're big messy boys — or girls — with untidy bedrooms and football boots and pop records and homework, being tempted by God knows what — drugs? Drink? Sex again?' They laughed.

That conversation might possibly have led Cressida to be invaded at night by ghosts of children? Daphne felt sure the children in her own dreams were Anne and her brother. The feel, the atmosphere, had been right. Cressida could have dreamed of the same children.

She sorted out her papers in a rational rather than a ghostly frame of mind and was ready with some home-made soup when Cressida returned with the stamps and an invitation for her aunt to go round to Mrs Kershaw's next Sunday for tea and a chat.

'Come again soon and I'll be able to show you more of the book,' she said when her niece left for London.

'I'd love to. Thank you for everything.'

She hugged her aunt and was off, her last sight of Daphne was of her standing at the garden gate waving, the house solid behind her, drifts of rowan-tree leaves swirling round in a little wind. She didn't think she was going to be lonely.

Daphne went back into the house. It did seem quiet after Cressy had left. She settled down with *Portrait of a Lady*.

★ ★ ★

The next day she went for a walk to Sholey passing by the Hall and the Grange. She had met the Grange's owner at a garden party he had hosted the previous July for the benefit of the local arts council. Normally she would have wriggled out of attending such a beano and she had kept the invitation unanswered for some weeks. On the appointed day however the weather had been so heavenly that she had decided to go, though she'd been slightly put off by the curt female voice that had answered her telephone acceptance. The hour or two she had spent in the Grange gardens, which were extensive, had been pleasant. She gathered that their owner, one Roger Masterson, was a retired architect who often lent his grounds to good causes. She wasn't sure that the arts council was all that much of a good cause. Providing books for schools seemed to her more important than subsidising street art. But when she saw that the committee of the A.C. was agitating for the local council to grant more cash to the public libraries, a cause dear to her heart, she was all for it.

At the Grange she had spoken to only two or three people, of whom two were women, before wandering off alone to look at Mr Masterson's roses which in this northern clime were still out in profusion. As she sniffed some particularly fine Zephyrine Drouins she had been joined by a tall, silver-haired man who had engaged her in conversation. What she had said to him apart from expressing pleasure in the roses she could not now remember but he had been polite, guided her over to look at some shrubs which did not interest her so much, before apologizing that he must rejoin the 'committee'. When she described the tall man to Judith it turned out that it had indeed been her host, Mr Masterson.

Now she wondered who did his gardening; he had been fairly knowledgeable about his climbers, but somehow she had felt it was at a distance, that a gardener stood between him and them.

Today the high wall prevented her from seeing the garden — but there would be nothing to see in November. She walked along, and turned left. After a bend in the lane, Sholey Hall suddenly appeared on the right, set back only a little way behind a cast-iron gate, its handsome eighteenth-century front hiding the original building which you could glimpse at the back. It was said that someone was thinking of buying it, and there was talk of alterations and additions. So far they had not materialized. Daphne felt proprietorial — why should an owner be allowed to alter 'her' Hall? Ruefully, she recognized her own irrational belief that the place really belonged to her as it had in her childhood when she had built up an imaginary place from what she could see from the outside through the gates. The Grange on the other hand was solid, nineteenth-century, held no surprises, not even fake Gothic ones. The smaller more beautiful Hall would have already stood here when Anne was alive.

Pondering this now she walked on and was just about to reach the end of the lane which branched off to a wider modern highway when she heard a car engine purring behind her. Its driver slowed down a little as it passed and surprisingly lifted a hand in salute. She half lifted her own before she realized that it was Roger Masterson's BMW.

The car gathered speed and disappeared: he must have recognized her. That was surprising.

* * *

Unlike Sonia, Lydia Robinson no longer had occasion to visit her dentist, except to check that her dental plate was still a good fit. It was a secret between Lydia and her cat (a Persian of a more refined breed than Widgery) that her bottom teeth were false. She suspected that Dorothy might have guessed, having once glimpsed her furtively removing a grape-seed that had lodged behind the lower jaw plate so beautifully made by Mr Johnson's technician.

Lydia was very aware of all the unmistakable signs of ageing which, apart from teeth, plagued every generation as it approached old age and was now plaguing her own that had once been so young and healthy. Brown 'liver spots' appeared on hands — especially on Gwyneth's since she had seen more sun than the most of them; focusing became worse so that you were continually switching spectacles unless you could endure bi-focals or were lucky enough to have been born short-sighted and were now catching up; you woke up early in the morning or throughout the night on bad nights when no pillows could make your neck or back feel comfortable.

Even Gwyneth had complained that she could not always hear very clearly the dulcet sounds of her Swami — or Guru — or whatever he was called. Sonia had complained of a bunion, inherited, she said, from her grandmother. Dorothy had said it was more likely the delayed effect of the stiletto heels Sonia used to wear in her youth.

Evelyn had complained that her right knee often seemed about to give way coming downstairs but that she ought not to grumble, she didn't have arthritis like her great friend at church. Someone had chimed in with brittle nails, and Evelyn had then lamented her greying hair. They had all in the end admitted to aches and pains in muscles, and to forgetting people's surnames.

Sonia, who loathed growing older, said 'They never mention these things in nineteenth-century novels — only consumption or brain fevers were good enough for them!' The others had laughed, and Dorothy said,

'I don't suppose most people lived as long as we have, on the whole.'

'We're approaching sixty not ninety,' Lydia had muttered.

★ ★ ★

Whilst her husband had been alive Dorothy had organized her life around him, lived for him even more than for her children. She had been unselfish and placid, but in the years since Tim had dropped dead of a heart attack one cold morning on the way to work, she had changed. Sonia often wondered how Dorothy would react now if by some miracle Tim were suddenly restored to her. She knew that Dorothy needed to be near other people's busy lives, hated being alone. When her children, Ruth and Elizabeth and Sam, were in their early teens she had retrained as a social worker but after ten years had retired to fill her life helping the village children to learn to read, hospital visiting, having grandchildren to stay with her regularly to 'give Bess a rest'. She also gardened seriously, visited the theatre regularly and devoted some time to the baking of cakes, as once her mother had done, selling them at various charitable functions. She was also on the committee of a local art gallery and an active member of the Labour party. Her life was now just as full as during the years exclusively devoted to husband and family. Only her daughter Elizabeth took after her though even she did not bake very much. Ruth baked not at all. Dorothy's son Sam, who did not always see eye to eye with his mother, was unmarried, a property developer: a person very unlike his father.

Sonia admired her old friend's qualities but detected a certain priggishness, which she kept to herself, fearing it might reflect upon her own attitudes. Dorothy had substituted political involvement for religious enthusiasm — something Sonia could not join her in — and now confided less in her, seemed closer even to Evelyn, the accountant Ronald Naylor's wife.

Even Dorothy did not understand what Evelyn had ever seen in her husband, and was sorry for her. Evelyn still however gave piano lessons and, Dorothy's blind spot being music, she hoped, talking to her, that Evelyn's knowledge might rub off. She had also been a confidante when the Naylors' children had been 'difficult'. Christopher was now married and lived in Cornwall where he grew flowers and let flats to tourists; the other, Jim, was working in Australia.

Ron was only too pleased for his wife to be friendly with Dorothy.

Lydia thought Evelyn a bit of a drip. She went to church a lot, at St Boniface's, a High Church in town. Brought up a Catholic, Lydia had lapsed completely and got on better with the agnostic Sonia, though they had little in common except a certain scepticism.

'We are both rather self-contained,' Sonia had said once to Lydia, who had wondered what she meant. Of all people Sonia Greenwood did not appear self-contained — always bursting out with some enthusiasm or other. They had got to know each other better after Lydia's marriage had finally disintegrated. Sonia felt indignant when Lydia sketched in the story of her married life.

Gwyneth had for a time joined Evelyn at St Boniface's but had discreetly faded away and joined a Buddhist group. This had led her to Zen and to involvement with Eastern art, something for which Lydia had not much time.

Nobody had ever seen Gwyneth with a man since the fleeting lover who had fathered her daughter Zoë upon her had then departed. Twenty years before, she had found a job as housekeeper to an art collector in Italy, taken Zoë with her and stayed there for several years. Gwyneth had few wants; even before the Swami's time she had dressed at jumble sales and charity shops and was eating rice and beans before they became fashionable. On her eventual permanent return to England, so that Zoë might go to secondary school in her native country, Gwyneth had found a live-in post, a flat at the back of a minor stately home with a private art gallery, had kept the place clean and shown visitors round. There happened to be stables there and that was how Zoë had discovered her equestrian talents. When she was eighteen Zoë had got herself apprenticed to a wealthy racehorse owner as a stable-girl and then the stable-girl had turned into a champion horsewoman. Gwyneth's father had left his daughter enough to live on in retirement, and she now rented a small house in Woolsford, still travelling abroad when the urge took her.

Gwyneth would not disagree with anyone over anything and meant more to Sonia than Evelyn or Lydia did, or even Dorothy. She was a tolerant woman and sometimes drew on that tolerance to understand Sonia, who was so much sharper than she was. Sonia considered Gwyneth truly good — certainly an untaxing companion. Neither asked too much of the other. As they both enjoyed visiting galleries they often met to look at pictures.

One autumn Saturday they were together at an exhibition of some of the work of a nineteenth-century Yorkshire painter who appealed to Sonia because of his 'atmospheres'. Gwyneth didn't see his paintings in that way, looked carefully at his moons in scudding clouds, his wet pavements and mysterious serving girls, and the tracery of leaves on autumnal branches, and said, 'I wonder how he achieved his effects.' The pictures were well executed but didn't speak to her personally, as she knew they did to Sonia.

'They take you back, don't they?' Sonia said. 'Why did he paint the same lane and *almost* the same house over and over again? He was obsessed with them. Look! this title is *Sixty Years Ago*.'

'Nostalgia,' said Gwyneth.

His Golden Age then, thought Sonia, he's always trying to find it again. 'Like Daphne said about writers always setting their stories a while back?' Gwyneth offered. 'When things had the sheen of the just lost past.'

She often surprised Sonia with such remarks.

'Autumns however go on coming every year.'

Gwyneth peered at a date. 'This one's the year before he died — I do know he became a Catholic.'

'He was only fifty-six at his death,' said Sonia, looking at the catalogue. 'He must have been only in his early thirties when he was painting some of these. Nostalgic at such a young age!'

'Autumn is a Victorian subject,' said Gwyneth.

'Let's go and have coffee,' said Sonia. She thought, all these feelings have to be rooted in something — golden moments always happen *somewhere* at some particular time. Did Gwyneth with her recently discovered mysticism not really attach points of time any more to real time, real places?

'When you want to escape, to be taken out of yourself you go to older paintings — at least I do,' said Sonia when they had settled in the tea room. Older narratives too, she thought.

'Why do you want to escape?' asked Gwyneth with a smile.

'Why not? Does aesthetic response never link with other more common-place feelings?'

'You'd feel the same walking down that lane on a *real* evening looking at a *real* sky as you do when you look at his pictures? The feeling is the same?'

'Not quite, he's added something, but it corresponds to feelings I already have, links me to something — I don't know what. Did he make all his paintings from memories or create something new?'

Gwyneth was calmly eating a doughnut since even mystics had to eat and she didn't need to slim. Sonia went on: 'Do you think he was happy being sad? Or just sad?'

'Probably he felt happiness *ought* to make him sad?' suggested Gwyneth. 'I mean, knowing it wouldn't last.'

'There's something mysterious about the pictures — he's added something we couldn't describe in words, some sort of longing . . . Perhaps it was for past happiness.'

'Lots of the houses he painted were quite new then,' said Gwyneth, who had been reading the catalogue.

'But they're timeless too,' said Sonia. 'I find them attractive because they're like places I've known.'

'He lost eight of his children in infancy,' Gwyneth went on, looking up.

'His poor wife! They probably had something wrong we'd know how to put right. That particular reason for sadness wouldn't be there now for him. But nobody in the West

115

is really happy. We all know too much about what's going on elsewhere. Even if things are going well with us we feel guilty,' Sonia went on.

'I don't have television,' said Gwyneth. 'Most people in India get along with their lives — happiness doesn't count in the same way there.'

'I suppose we're spoiled for anything else,' said Sonia. 'We ought to feel less miserable about some things — at least *we* don't have eight children who die.'

'But the sun always goes in,' said Gwyneth teasingly.

Sonia looked up at her friend. 'That doesn't seem to worry *you* though — does all your Buddhist stuff help you escape from the present?'

'Buddhism isn't concerned with escape. The individual soul matters less, you see. It's about accepting everything — and purifying your inner nature.'

'I can't help feeling that individual souls matter,' said Sonia after a pause, 'individual imaginations, anyway.'

She envied her friend's calm. What did art mean to Gwyneth after all? She still painted. 'Painting is part of it all,' said Gwyneth as if in reply. 'Things sound so tawdry when we try to put them into words. There are

116

no words for certain states of mind — that's why I think this sort of painting is not the greatest.'

'Because we want to translate his paint into talk about 'feelings'?'

'Partly. You know, when I make pots — there's a sensation I can't put into words about the shapes and proportions. So few people nowadays bother with technique. If you can't *use* the pots you've failed. In the East, craft is all part of art.'

Would Indians appreciate these paintings? Sonia wondered. She couldn't do as Gwyneth did, and produce lemony water-colours or glazed mugs or get up early to practise meditation. Too lazy. Maybe that was what was wrong with her? Was it too late?

'Does Zoë practise yoga?' she asked, as Gwyneth sat quietly, a crumb of doughnut on her lip.

'No — but Zoë uses her physical body to express herself — '

'How's the riding coming along?'

'She may be in the next British Olympic team,' replied Gwyneth modestly.

Gwyn had always been one on her own. You would have thought she might never have bothered with men at all and all the messiness entailed by 'sex', except for the indubitable existence of her daughter Zoë.

She'd probably been celibate since the birth of her daughter over thirty years before! She had never wanted to keep hold of a man, and didn't need a husband's salary after her father's bequest. Unexpectedly, Gwyneth said, looking up shyly, 'Zoë's pregnant — but she'll have had the baby well before the next trials.'

'Oh, congratulations!' said Sonia in surprise. She could see Gwyneth as a grandmother more easily than she had ever seen her as a parent.

'The father's a married man.'

Thirty years ago it had been quite daring for an unmarried woman like Gwyneth to have a child. Had Gwyneth been in love with Zoë's father, or he with her? It wasn't the sort of thing you could ask about, and Gwyneth had probably forgotten.

How things had changed. What did Buddhists think about babies? Wasn't Buddhism one of those philosophies that played down physical urges? Gwyneth looked peaceful and healthy sitting drinking the herbal tea that the gallery now provided. 'You must be pleased,' said Sonia. 'Are you — is she, I mean, hoping for a boy or a girl?'

'Our family was always short of boys, but I don't think Zoë minds.'

Sonia changed the subject, began to talk of the novels she thought they might read after *Portrait of a Lady*.

'I think *Great Expectations* would be a good idea, don't you?' She thought, 'expectations' were what young professional men used to have, and middle-aged people had of their ancient relatives. Young women had usually just 'expected'. Like Zoë. So many friends were now grandparents. Was that why you had children, so that later you could see your genes circulating? Well, she would not be a reluctant grandmother but doubted *her* daughter was thinking of making her one yet. Gwyneth asked politely about Anna. Sonia told her the latest news of Anna's shop.

'See you at the next meeting,' she said when they parted.

★ ★ ★

Sonia's daughter Anna had some years ago converted a garage into a small warehouse for her 'Things You Used to Use' business. A stroke of genius, the kind of idea Sonia applauded. It might have been her own talking of all the things that had disappeared from people's homes in the last forty years or so that had given her daughter the idea.

Anna had started without much capital but had placed an ad in the county newspaper for people to bring or send her old-fashioned objects — things like wind-up gramophones and stone hot-water bottles, and hair ribbons and boys' knee-socks and garters and lace baby clothes and crocheted mats and table runners and antimacassars. Above all, things that were still usable, not just examples of forgotten fripperies. Children could still play with battledores and shuttlecocks and whips and tops and musical boxes and kaleidoscopes, and skipping ropes fitted with ball-bearings, but the things really needed not so long ago were the best: flat-irons and goffering irons and old box-cameras and bedroom ewers and shawls and pixie-hoods and patchwork quilts. Not modern copies but the genuine article. What had started off in a small way with a market-stall, almost an exchange between enthusiasts, was burgeoning into a very successful business. Anna had anticipated the vogue for imitation bakelite telephones and reframed cabinet portraits of 'ancestors'. Sonia, who was a bicycle and portable typewriter person herself, was amazed by her daughter's entrepreneurial talents and helped her with her first catalogues. It seemed the country was overflowing with the goods of yesteryear and there was also a ready sale for them. It also helped old people who were willing to part with things and who needed a bit of pocket money. Some of the objects were even sold on to various museums of social history. Anna preferred the decorative — the watches pinned on bosoms, the ivory pens with pictures of the Eiffel Tower in their insides that you saw through a small opening, and the pretty old pinafores, muslin jar-covers, curling-tongs — if not the liberty bodices, whalebone stays, and chamberpots. She drew the line at old ovens and washing-machines unless a museum expressed a need for them, but she sold velour hats, panamas with old school-bands, and the round spectacles of the 1940s, old cookery books with recipes for junket and 'shape', and bottles with the labels of Virol and Parrish's Chemical Food and Scott's Emulsion still stuck on the outside. She sold old books too and comics with Pip, Squeak and Wilfred, and children's books and annuals and the souvenir programmes and mugs of jubilees and coronations.

Anna's grandmother, Madge Hartley, had donated a golliwog. Where she had found it Sonia did not know, since her mother had always been a great thrower-out of junk. In her daughter's shop Sonia rediscovered the badges of long-gone clubs, Ovalteenies and Teddy Tails and the cigarette card albums of her childhood. She had not yet found the album of Kings and Queens with golden-haired Richard the Lionheart but was sure she would one day. Anna had sold her father an old stereoscope from the 1890s with the original cards of St Petersburg, and last year Sonia had purchased a kaleidoscope and a musical box for Christmas presents, then had not been able to part with them. She had given people butter-pats and ladies' garters instead.

What with pianolas, and props for outside washing, and 'possers' to stir the clothes in the dolly-tubs, and peg-bags and bead curtains, Anna was about to rent a second shop, had become more choosy and was now organizing an Exchange and Mart by mail order for the smaller things.

How long ago was it that most of these objects were still found in people's homes? Forty years? It was their own generation who had been the last to know these things. Why exactly did young Anna want to deal in them? It must be that she had guessed they would soon become fashionable, for she had a feel for the up and coming. Now they called it 'retro-chic'.

But the objects were often perfectly usable things superseded by the shoddy plastic of a later more spendthrift generation. Hating waste, every time Sonia went to the shop she found something she remembered from childhood or even from the fifties. One day she came upon an old wireless. It must have been made in about 1950, just before her own little Bush had been one of her most treasured possessions. It belonged to the time of Senior Service cigarettes and shut-up Sundays and sweets still rationed, a world of clean, reliable buses and dark stone buildings and coal fires and efficient steam-trains. Forty years was not all that long ago. Just before rock and roll, but long before freezers and word-processors and computers and seat-belt, and people saying 'fuck' out loud, and the Alternative Service Book, and pavement stones that tripped you up. She was the one who sometimes felt herself stuck in past grooves, who had to make an effort to belong to this new world, this new England, to live in the present. She must talk to Daphne Berridge about this too for she sensed in Daphne a similar slightly guilty hankering.

★ ★ ★

Evelyn was pursuing her own path to enlightenment. When she called in one morning to borrow a book from Sonia before the next meeting she said, as she lingered in the hall, 'You are a survivor, Sonia, aren't you?'

'We all are,' answered Sonia in some surprise. In her opinion anyone who could survive Ron Naylor ought to be given a medal.

You have your faith, she thought. Christianity must help people to get through life? 'How's Christopher?' she asked Evelyn.

'He's much more settled now, I think,' replied Evelyn. 'You know, I've had more time recently to think about things — '

She hesitated, then said, 'You feel as I do, I think — about the past — I don't like the way the world is going.'

Sonia was about to say, 'You fear it? Surely not if it's all in the hands of your God?' — but that sounded unkind.

Underneath are the everlasting arms . . . If only that were true! She tried to see the world through Evelyn's eyes, would like to be able to say that in her case it was not laziness or worldliness that stopped her attending church. Why though should faith be vouchsafed Evelyn Naylor and not Sonia Greenwood? Evelyn guessed the direction of her thoughts from her expression.

'Even if you have faith, life is always hard,'

she said. She seemed reluctant to leave.

Life was not hard so much as mysterious or meaningless, thought Sonia. How could you construct a meaning that would stand up to the rest of the years one was given, a rickety self-construction, not to be compared with a holy one?

Evelyn pulled the collar of her shapeless coat round her neck and said, 'I'm making a collection for Yugoslavia.'

Now why could she not have come out with that to begin with? She tucked a wisp of hair behind her ears and looked vulnerable and well-meaning and Sonia, who had been going to make a joke about the way news readers always called that country 'the former Yugoslavia', like a society commentator calling a married debutante 'The former Miss Fergusson', did not, but said instead, 'Oh, yes — we were meaning to send something but didn't quite know where to send it. Wait a moment.' She hunted down her handbag, found it under a mountain of books and newspapers, retrieved a five-pound note and handed it over. Evelyn said: 'That's *very* generous. Thank you, Sonia. Should I ask Daphne Berridge for a contribution, do you think?'

'Ask her at the next meeting — check up on us all!' answered Sonia.

She was relieved when Evelyn went. If only you could buy answers to questions about life as easily as buying off your conscience. Why should it be another woman of her age who had just lost her home and her possessions and was shivering in some Balkan cellar and not herself?

Did Evelyn ever have such thoughts?

6

Judith Kershaw telephoned Daphne to remind her she was invited to drop in for a cup of tea on her way back from her next Sunday walk. Daphne suspected she wanted to talk about her 'follower', Mr Watson, or Alan, as Judith now called him. She did not want to find him there when she arrived for her tea, so said 'Will you be alone?' before she put the 'phone down. Yes, Judith was to be quite alone.

Daphne did not mind Judith eventually discovering her own past involvement with him, but better from him in some intimate moment than from herself. It was not yet time for sisterly confessions. She knew Alan Watson well enough to know that he too might be a little embarrassed to have her witness the progress of what might be a new love in its beginnings.

Apart from the man himself, nobody in Heckcliff, including Judith, could possibly know of Alan's long-ago affair with her. But that Mr Watson was thick with Mrs Kershaw had been common gossip for the past few weeks and had arrived in Daphne's ears about the same time as Judith had mentioned him to her, saying that they 'got on well'. He must know that Daphne was a friend of hers. Daphne, who was naturally open, did not enjoy keeping her own past a secret but judged it wiser for the time being. Their relationship, whose mainspring had been Alan's grief over his wife's death, had been fourteen or fifteen years ago, long enough now for her to feel dispassionate about him. She wanted Judith too to see Alan as the quite separate person he was.

The afternoon which was to end with tea at Judith's was cold and bright. Daphne enjoyed her roundabout walk there, with fields and woods on every side and from 'the Top' a view of further hills. Here you could imagine yourself far away from any town. In her childhood she had taken for granted that beyond the hills to the west lay a pall of smoke over the town in its valley.

Now that had gone, along with the industry responsible for it, and the town had emerged as a new thing from its old chrysalis. It was almost unrecognizable and was on the way to becoming a tourist attraction.

Here, near where she was walking, were narrow 'cloughs', where gushed brown stony streams. They had not changed and she found them still beautiful. The skies here were usually grey, wrapped up in woolly clouds, changing into shot silk when light filtered through. Had Anne ever noticed such skies, she who had been alive at the same time as Wordsworth? There was little evidence in her own verse of any unconventional attitude towards the beauties of nature. 'The orient splendour of the morn' was about as far as she went, with the sun's 'wide glories blushing along the sky' — which Daphne supposed was not a bad description of dawn. She tried to remember any poems written by Anne about evening and recalled 'purple hills'. The main focus of her poems was the description of human beings — maidens and men, one unhappy maiden in particular. The cheerful fires of winter did however make their occasional appearance.

Daphne quickened her step and came out on the Top. All was quiet here except for the distant drone of a car or the cawing of a solitary rook. Up here was the church with the narrow tower that Anne could have seen if she had journeyed north after 1819, the date of its restoration. You came upon it unexpectedly when you followed the lane round. It had always looked lonely, often appeared on old engravings or newer picture postcards, but she had never found it an intimate building. It was too high up, enjoying its solitude, the elegant sentinel of her own country, the building she had always seen first in the distance when at the time Heckcliff still had a railway station she had come home on the train from Woolsford, the western skies lending a backdrop of colour to the church high on its rise.

She wondered when evensong would begin — if they still had evensong and were not rationed in their services. Hardly any churches used the old prayer book now, which made her reluctant to attend them. Like Cressy, Daphne was neither believer nor unbeliever, felt sorry for churches, hoped they would not disappear. If services came dressed in suitable language, she might have been prepared to rethink her religious attitudes, but knew this for hypocrisy. She often put money into the boxes of churches she entered, hoping it would go towards a building fund and not be used for the conversion of the Jews. Mary said nostalgia was in danger of becoming her religion, because religion was connected for her with a certain time in a certain place. The place of her imagination existed only in the old time; the present village with its present church and present skies, was not the same. Imagination working on a place in past time brought about her own creative energy. Mary was right in a way but Daphne also liked the village as it was now. It had changed less than many places. On such afternoons as this she made a bridge back over to that lost country of her childhood.

Dusk was not far off. The clocks had now been put back. She quickened her step and walked down the lane towards the crossroads a mile or so away where all roads met and led to towns, and where the green and orange double-decker buses going north or south used to meet the maroon single-deckers that made their way east and west. There were fewer buses now and thirty times as many cars as there had been in her childhood.

There was a light in the window above the hardware shop. Daphne rang the bell and waited for Judith to come down from her flat. She noticed that the shop window had a new consignment of casseroles: smart blue and grey ware, most likely French, France being the home of good cooking implements.

130

Many of the villagers were reasonably well off and Judith had told her she was still making a profit even in these times of recession, which did not so much affect those retired on good pensions from their firms. Frying-pans catered for the more unregenerate of the villagers.

Daphne made a mental note to invest in a new non-stick pan. At the back of the shop was a DIY section. She remembered Alan had been a confirmed do-it-your-selfer, neat and clever with his hands.

Here was Judith, also neat and tidy, hair newly washed, in a cloud round her head. 'Tea's ready. Crumpets,' she said. 'Will you be all right to walk back, though? You didn't bring the car or leave it anywhere?'

'It's only a mile,' replied Daphne following her up the narrow stairs, at the top of which a brown door opened on to a pleasantly furnished flat; sitting-room, bathrooms, kitchen (well-stocked with casseroles, she knew) and the three bed-rooms, two on the top floor, one here at the front, its window facing over the road, and into which Judith led her to divest herself of her jacket. The room had only a single divan — if Alan and Judith were conducting an affair it would be at the bungalow.

'Your niece got back all right then? She's a

nice girl, isn't she? She looks like your sister.' Judith had been a child when the two sisters used to visit their parents, still alive at that time. With her painter's eye she remembered the two young women.

'Yes — she rang. Has to get back to work — I think they'll all come to me at Christmas for a change. My brother-in-law's retired now and aims to go hill-walking up in Westmorland when Christmas is over.' She followed Judith downstairs.

'What a family for walks,' said Judith, setting a plate and a cup and saucer on a little tray and parking it on a small table at Daphne's side.

'You spoil me — how nice to have someone make your tea for you! Sunday is such a sad day, don't you think? I still can't work well on a Sunday — early training, I suppose. I read the papers and telephone my sister and then I feel restless and there's not much you can do in the garden at present apart from leaf-collecting and bulb-planting. How are the boys?'

Judith told her, said three of them would come home at Christmas but that she was thinking of a little holiday for herself after that, now that Christmas and the New Year merged in one long bank holiday.

'I was going to ask your advice,' she said

when they had each eaten one crumpet and the teacups had been refreshed. Daphne waited. No escape now.

'Alan Watson's asked me if I'd like to accompany him on a little jaunt abroad — one of those week-end breaks in capital cities, you know.'

'Good for your painting ideas,' said Daphne non-committally.

'Yes, but would it be burning my boats do you think? He says he wants a change and that it's more fun with a companion — you know for years I had no one to go with — apart from the boys — even if I'd been able to afford it. Anyway, what do you think?' Judith was looking expectant. For the second time recently Daphne felt she was being consulted as a sort of oracle about the lives of others. Who was she to judge? Alan hadn't yet got as far with Judith as she'd imagined.

'I suppose it depends on — well, on whether you want to encourage him?' she ventured.

'I just don't know! He's awfully nice — and very attentive — I think he wants some sort of — relationship — but I'm all at sea. I keep thinking it's not allowed!'

'I'm sure he's not the sort of man to take advantage of you,' Daphne said, 'I mean — you could go as friends — reserve your decision till later. It's a good idea for getting to know someone. Travelling with them makes clear their faults and virtues!'

Judith laughed, and Daphne knew she'd already made up her mind. 'Give him a chance,' she went on. 'You don't have much fun.'

'Well I'm not sure if fun is what he wants. Or perhaps it is!'

'I think a man of his sort — especially at his age — would be the marrying sort,' Daphne said after a pause, buttering another crumpet, which she would regret later but never mind.

'That's the trouble. I've never intended to marry again. Fun is perhaps what *I* need. But what if in fact marriage *is* what he has in mind, and I disappoint him or don't want to see him again when we get back?'

'Let that take care of itself,' said Daphne. 'People don't have to marry people nowadays just because they've — er, been on holiday together — '

'I know — but what will the boys think?'

'If you have a holiday I expect they'll be relieved. They know about him, don't they?'

'Yes, a bit, but if I decide to make things — permanent — there'd be problems wouldn't there? Colin's only eighteen and this *is* still his home — '

'He won't want to stay with you for ever, Judith — and there's nothing against mothers finding a life of their own again when children move away. And even if Colin didn't approve at first, he'd come round eventually. It's more your own problem — starting a new way of life. Beginning again. Changing. Young people will be as bad as people my age if you let them! They don't like changes made by *other* people. But it's just selfish of them — they soon get used to it. You do what you want. Your children will please themselves as far as their own lives are concerned.'

'Yes, I suppose so. Anyway, it's not come to that yet. But I can't stop thinking about the consequences of everything I do.'

'That was the legacy Andrew Kershaw left you.'

'I know. I've managed fairly well in the last seventeen years, haven't I? It's funny — as though I felt resentful in case anyone might want to muck up my life — !'

'Quite understandable,' soothed Daphne. 'But Alan would understand that. He's a sensitive man.'

'You knew him quite well, didn't you?'

'Oh, he was a colleague,' replied Daphne

vaguely. Not the time to go into things now. 'I really must be off — the cat will want to get in again. I left him over the garden wall looking for non-existent mice in the field.'

'You've been so kind listening to my silly problems,' said Judith. Daphne felt immediately guilty. Modern life certainly was complicated. Did situations like Judith's crop up two hundred years ago? There were plenty of widowed women then, and even separated ones, but divorce hardly existed. Second marriages were usually of widows and widowers, the latter after their first wives had died in childbirth.

On leaving Judith she walked briskly towards the park, deciding to return home through the Snicket. It was not a short cut, but the park was more pleasant than the road even though it was now dark. She was just crossing the road towards the war memorial that overlooked the expanse of grass sloping away towards the lower road when she heard a car stop behind her. Not usually a nervous person she was more wary now than she had once been — you read such terrible tales even in the broadsheet newspapers.

When she heard a voice — 'Miss Berridge — may I offer you a lift?' she turned in surprise. It was Roger Masterson poking his head through the car window.

She stopped. 'I really need the exercise' — she began. Then she decided to accept. It was dark and she wanted to be home now to feed Widgery and settle down with a book, perhaps a TV programme. Sunday was the only evening she watched.

'You must remind me where you live,' he said as she buckled her seat-belt. 'I know you like walking — since I see you now and again up near the Grange — you were walking there this afternoon, weren't you?'

'I live just behind the Snicket,' she replied. 'It's only a short walk.' She did not answer his question.

'Don't you mind then, walking alone in the dark?'

'Oh no!' she replied airily. It wasn't quite true but she resented his assumption that lone women might be foolish to do so.

'You must come and see my conservatories — I remember you admired my roses,' he said when she was fumbling with the seat-belt fastening. The journey had taken only a minute.

'Thank you — and for the lift.' What else could she say?

She was mildly irritated but also a little intrigued that she must have made some sort of impression on the handsome widower. He probably thought she was eccentric, needed saving from her own foolhardiness. Men of his generation, which was also hers, tended to the courtly in their dealings with women, whom they often called the ladies. Perhaps even Alan was like that now he was older? She certainly could not remember his ever having 'looked after' her fifteen years ago.

Roger Masterson dropped her at the gate to the old stables, saying: 'Do come and look round the Grange. I'm sure you would like my winter flowers.' She murmured something non-committal.

When she got inside her house she flopped down with relief, deciding to forbid for the moment any further consideration of Roger Masterson's interest in her. Over her supper she concentrated on trying to put herself in Judith's shoes, trying to deal with the problem with her intellect — which for as long as Judith had been speaking she hadn't been able to do. But she couldn't imagine herself as a divorced wife-cum-widow, mother of four sons, and with an elderly admirer. Had it ever been a tempting prospect to marry Alan Watson? Not that he'd ever asked her. She didn't think so. Even years ago she'd valued her own freedom too much to want to alter her life, fit it into the rhythms of someone else's. If it had been possible she would have married her earlier lover, Charles, to have a child.

She did not regret having led what some people might call a selfish life, she hadn't done any active harm to anyone as far as she knew. Charles's wife had survived.

She'd been good at her job even if teaching had not been her first choice of profession. She'd fashioned it into a reasonable career once she had left the schools and become a lecturer of future teachers. But even before she retired the job had changed, her own expertise had become less valued. She was better employed now writing about her poet. She might even dream of Anne again tonight . . .

At half past eleven Daphne settled herself for sleep, looking forward to Monday morning, when at least Sunday would be over. She did not dream of Anne at first — or even of Judith — but of Roger Masterson who — ludicrously enough — was offering her a pink rose.

★ ★ ★

Cressida was sitting next to Jonathan Edwards as he drove his little car (a reconditioned Morris Minor) back from his father's house in Wimbledon where they had been walking on the common. Usually, as he had explained to Cressida, he visited his father on Sunday afternoons before he returned to his own small flat in Bloomsbury.

Cressida found his company restful and had enjoyed the walk that had been almost as healthy as walking in Heckcliff, if warmer, and in tamer country. Yesterday she had been to the races with Patrick Simmonds. It was his kind of thing and served to distance him from whoever was accompanying him. She had known it would be impossible to talk to him properly there.

Now another man was driving her through South London's almost featureless landscape and she felt contentedly gloomy, if that were a possible state. They passed roads and roads of terrace houses that looked Edwardian, so they must have survived the war; then playing fields, small factories, more sports fields — like green lungs. If it were summer there would be cricket matches being played on every one of them. As it was November there had been football matches that morning; now there were only small knots of bystanders leaving. Some brave souls were even sitting outside a tavern, spinning out their Sunday before thinking of Monday. There was a common on the left further on, bordered by slightly larger houses, semi-detached, also pre-First World War, smarter and bigger than the twenties' ribbon development which wound round Outer London strangling the suburbs further east. Roads and roads she'd never heard of . . . London was just too big. Another common now, and blocks of flats built like liners — in the nineteen-thirties she guessed. All such a jumble. Further down now on the left, dingy council flats — the outposts of nastier places. South west changed imperceptibly to south east and it was not long before Jonathan gestured to his right and said, 'My old school.'

'Do you ever go back?'

'Once or twice — I liked my time there but most of my school friends went abroad — unless they'd already a niche in the City.'

She looked behind, craned her neck. In the distance the Crystal Palace transmitter pointed to the grey sky.

'My mother remembers hearing about that fire when she was a little girl,' she said. 'She didn't understand how glass could burn.'

'It was a pity it burned down,' Jonathan said. 'I always wondered how they transported it in the first place from Hyde Park. It only lasted eighty-five years, but the Eiffel Tower's still going strong after over a century.'

'No glass *there*,' she said. Jonathan's conversation was pleasantly soothing.

They passed several churches which looked as if nobody had prayed in them for at least a century though she knew that was wrong and they'd probably been full of worshippers that very morning.

'We've had Edwardian and the thirties, now it's the Victorians back,' she said as they drove through, past Forest Hill, the traffic building up now, people returning from their Sunday outings like lemmings towards Sunday evening. 'You can drop me in Lewisham, I can get a bus home.'

'Oh, I'll take you all the way if you don't mind crawling.'

'The traffic'll be awful back into central London — it'll take you at least another hour.' Then she thought, perhaps he thinks I can't be bothered to give him a cup of tea, and said, 'You can stay for supper if you don't mind boiled eggs.'

'No, really — I love boiled eggs but I must get back. No trouble honestly — I might go through the city — '

'Tea and toast then?' she said.

'That would be lovely.'

As they crawled through Catford she thought of Patrick, who by now would have been visibly impatient and probably swearing at other drivers. Not that he drove much, and certainly wouldn't spend an afternoon walking on Wimbledon Common. She would see him — probably for the last time — next week. On the Saturday he was off to the Far East for his firm of art dealers.

During the last proper conversation she had had with him he had obviously been holding himself at a distance, though she did not think he had intended to be intentionally off-putting when he had launched into a comparison between rock music and sex. 'The nearest thing to it,' he said. She supposed that a pounding beat, repetitious thuds and powerful rhythms must be connected with what men felt, whereas she felt it had no connection with any sort of pleasure, was more a pain. Not that Patrick had ever been anything but a most considerate lover; it just made one realize that what was going through a man's head at the most intimate moments was utterly removed from what a woman was actually feeling. And anyway rock music made her feel ill; it affected her brain, dehumanized her. Was that what he meant? Did one have to be dehumanized to experience sex? Yet his very elusiveness was attractive — until you stopped hoping you might understand him. She felt on the other hand that she understood Jonathan Edwards very well. Why should that make him less of a man in some people's opinion? She felt rebellious as they drove along, wished she could tell Jonathan about it, but that was not possible. Jonathan was the sort of man who was likely to commit himself, and that too had its dangers. And was the idea of 'security' a chimera? Her own needs and desires seemed so banal — settling down, having a baby . . .

Couldn't she feel secure without the hope of a shared future, however banal? If she gave Patrick up she might regret lost opportunities, freedoms. If she excluded the idea of a future, things would go on much the same — lust and agony in equal mixture, her life trickling away when she wanted to landscape it, make the water flow in a patterned way. One's life might trickle away like that — a thin rivulet, formless, meaning less and less as time went on. The beginnings with Patrick had been so auspicious, but the pattern seemed to have been laid down long ago by the man himself. He probably despised her, with her thoughts of a revelation at the end of it all, some sort of symmetry which she could find.

'The South Circular is a Platonic idea,' Jonathan said, breaking into her thoughts. 'It is said to exist but must lead on invisibly. I think we were on it just now.'

'Better than a motorway,' said Cressy who hated motorways, avoided taking a driving test because then you'd be expected to tackle one if you passed.

They arrived in front of her flat, the basement of a large house set on a private road, one of several built by nineteenth-century city merchants. She would tell him about her aunt's woman poet over tea, she thought, and one day soon they might explore the lane where Anne was said to have lived. Meanwhile there was work to do tomorrow, work which would enable her for the time being to afford this quiet road, her quiet flat. As Jonathan sat for a moment drinking the promised tea she thought he looked quite at home. He reminded her of the Thursday concert, and kissed her on the cheek when he left.

7

It was a blustery late autumn morning.

'Joy might as well be dead for all we see of her,' grumbled Evelyn. She and Dorothy were sitting in the latter's kitchen, Evelyn having been invited before Dorothy dispensed more general hospitality in the evening to the rest of the friends. She went on: 'It's very unfair.

Just when Peter seemed settled at last up in Cumbria she has to have her mother-in-law living with them — '

'What do you think Reggie thinks about it all?' asked Dorothy.

'At least he's not retired, so he can get out of the house to go to work. I expect he helps out at week-ends.'

'He never took much interest in his children though, did he? I expect he thinks even his own mother is his wife's province. Enough for him to have her living in his house, though I suppose he could have put his foot down and suggested a nursing home for her.'

'Oh, Joy wouldn't want to do that,' replied Dorothy in a shocked voice. 'It's not as if the old lady needs a nurse — not yet, anyway.'

'She might soon though,' said Evelyn. 'Then Joy will rejoice!'

Dorothy looked at her sharply. Evelyn was becoming quite hard these days. She replied: 'I do hope she gets a break soon — I rang her the other week and she said she was hoping to have Nick and Luke to stay for a few days at half-term since she can't get up north to see them.'

'Peter ought to suggest a swap. He and Paula could come down and look after his gran and let Joy go up to the boys for a change,' said Evelyn crossly.

'Men don't think of things like that, and I suppose as she isn't Paula's grandmother, Paula doesn't feel obliged to do anything.'

'Joy used so to enjoy our evenings, didn't she? She does need a break — surely Reggie could take over for one evening? She says he always gets back late from work after she's settled Mrs Wood for the night.'

'Well then, he could come back early for once — the old lady could go to bed earlier once in a while — or possibly one of us could offer.'

'You mean old-lady sit?'

'Mm — or we could go to Joy's with the coffee and some supper, do it all for her — she wouldn't have to lift a finger. Not much of a change for her, I suppose, but still . . . ' Dorothy tailed off with a sigh.

'She won't have much time for reading,' said Evelyn.

The conversation passed from the oldest generation to the youngest. Dorothy's younger daughter Elizabeth had just had a new baby boy, Tom, and his grandmother was delighted to talk about him. Dorothy had abandoned one of her committees and reduced her hospital-visiting to help Bess more with her eldest child Dorothea, named after her grandmother, and the middle one, Toby.

147

Evelyn could keep her end up here since her son Jim's wife in Perth was now pregnant.

'I don't know how you will bear it — not seeing the baby grow up and everything — won't you go out for a visit?' suggested Dorothy.

But Evelyn was less interested in her descendants than was Dorothy — or more fearful of interfering. And it was different, it being her son and not her daughter who had enrolled her in grandmotherhood. 'I may go out in a year or two — Ron won't though.'

Evelyn's husband was known to be 'funny' about lots of things. He had left the child-rearing to his wife, not being any different in this from most men of his generation, and he had since taken little interest in his progeny. Evelyn must have been thinking of herself when she was grumbling on behalf of their old friend Joy. 'He's been nicer about Chris though, recently,' Evelyn then added, accepting a second cup of Dorothy's decaffeinated coffee.

'How is he?'

'Fine — I don't think he'll ever come back to London permanently though, now the business is holding its own. Ron's finally accepted he isn't going to follow him in the firm. I think he's resigned to his partner buying him out eventually.'

Evelyn's Christopher had always flatly refused to join his father's firm of accountants. Now that he had changed tack completely he was enjoying life in Cornwall. 'Chris and Valerie seem quite settled — when I think how I used to worry about him . . . '

Evelyn asked, 'How is Ruth?' Dorothy's other daughter Ruth was the one who lived with the scientist, and had renounced the idea of marriage, she said for good. It was a sore point with Dorothy who thought it all a bit adolescent, though she pretended she didn't care.

'Oh, fine — she telephones me every week. I can't complain. They're all coming to me this Christmas — Ruth and her partner, and Bess and the whole family — I thought Bess needed a change, and it means I can help with Tom and keep an eye on Toby and see more of them all. She offered to do it all herself this year, but I felt it was too much, with a new baby and everything. Anyway, you know how I enjoy cooking and entertaining.'

'You really do!' said Evelyn wonderingly, who hated both.

'There's plenty of room here now my lodgers have gone.' Dorothy had had three students living with her till quite recently. She went on: 'There's room for quite a few

Christmases before I sell up and take a little flat for my old age.'

Evelyn wondered who would one day look after Dorothy. Since her husband's early death she had been so active — it made Evelyn tired to think of all that Dorothy did. But perhaps one day she'd slow down a bit.

Over lunch — home-made soup, cold chicken and tomato salad in a mustardy dressing and chocolate-chip cookies which her friend had baked for the evening — the talk passed on to Gwyneth and Sonia and the new member, Daphne. Whenever the friends were in twos or threes it seemed they could not avoid anatomizing the absent ones, though out of interest rather than malice.

'Who's coming this evening then?' asked Evelyn.

'Everyone except Joy and Mrs Reeves. Sonia, and Daphne Berridge and Gwyneth.'

'She never finishes the books, you know, Gwyneth!' said Evelyn critically.

'She rang to say she was to be busy at some meditation workshop today but hoped to come straight on afterwards. Now I come to think of it I'm not sure about Lydia — I had a card to say she'd finished the book but couldn't make up her mind what she thought about it. She says she doesn't

150

like Henry James's 'prissy morality'. Perhaps Daphne Berridge will say more this time.'

'Well, he does load the odds against the good characters, doesn't he? I wish he'd give them a break.'

'I suppose there wouldn't be any conflict then, would there? I think it's just like life — virtue is its own reward,' concluded Dorothy.

* * *

Upon entering Dorothy's sitting-room that evening Daphne thought it was too tidy, too bare, with its two or three abstract paintings, a big vase of bulrushes, a plain, pale-green carpet and cushions, and leather sofas. It was so unlike what she so far knew of Dorothy, though Sonia had hinted that Dorothy had been much influenced by her late husband, a clever, tidy-minded, rather dogmatic individual.

Sonia was at present thinking that Osmond in the novel they were to discuss reminded her a little of Evelyn's husband Ronald. He was no aesthete but always kept himself apart from his wife's friends and even from his wife and children, preferring his Bach organ fugue CDs, or office work which he was wont to bring home in great quantity. Could Evelyn remember why she'd married him? Why he had wanted to marry Evelyn was perhaps a more interesting question. Perhaps he was less self-sufficient than he appeared. If Evelyn ever left him he might realize what a big gaping hole his wife had filled. Evelyn, as Sonia well knew, had had no other suitors, had married Ronald Naylor because he had asked her. She must have assumed he loved her. He came from a respectable rather stingy family in the village, had been a friend of her brother Bill's and articled at about the same time. At least, thought Sonia, he was not physically repulsive. She had been repelled by Osmond, and wanted to talk about this aspect of the book with Daphne if she could draw her out. She must stop elaborating on her friends and friends' husbands and concentrate on the novel.

Evelyn was thinking about the cold supper she had left for Ron. She lived at stalemate with him. When the children were small she'd been free in the evenings to listen to concerts on the wireless, and now he didn't mind if she went to concerts with other people. I wasted my youth, she thought. Someone else might have wanted it. She had her children, and now there was the coming grandchild, so she supposed she was no unhappier than most people. The past *had* been safe as well as boring and predictable. She hadn't intended to burst out at the last gathering with that remark though. Sonia was now staring at her most strangely.

Daphne wondered whether she knew any of these women as well as she thought she knew Ralph Touchett and Isabel in the book. Was understanding real people different from understanding characters in novels? Almost all these women had known each other in childhood, and there was nothing like a shared childhood for allowing you to get to know another person. The difference between novels and life was that the novelist told you what was going on in the heads of his characters, whereas, unless you asked, you had no idea what was going on in some people's, and even then they might lie, or prevaricate.

She was recalled to the present by Lydia's saying 'A hundred years later than this book the couple would divorce, wouldn't they? There wouldn't have to be so many secrets either — illegitimate daughters, for example.'

How tactless, thought Dorothy. Gwyneth had an illegitimate daughter.

'Isabel would not divorce Osmond, even now,' said Sonia firmly. 'She'd abide by her mistake, I feel sure — unless he ditched her first.'

'She is noble,' said Daphne.

'Surely *now*, when relationships are so — fluid — she would leave him?' pursued Lydia. 'I mean, why ever not?'

'She's not a twentieth-century woman trying to 'find herself',' Gwyneth put in.

'She might not need a man for that,' said Daphne.

They'd all grown up before the new wave of transatlantic feminism had drowned some women younger than themselves. Until now Sonia had been regarded as the feminist of the circle. Was Daphne to outbid her? They all alerted themselves to another rebel in their midst.

Daphne was thinking that novels were also about misapprehensions as well as knowledge of others. Characters built castles in Spain upon their ignorance of others. These new friends were quaint and rather sweet in their earnestness. Most likely they thought she was just an old maid with no real worries.

As others see us, thought Dorothy. We know only bits of other people. I don't know if Evelyn ever loses her temper with that husband of hers, or if Joy ever complains, or what Daphne Berridge does with her time. Gwyneth and Lydia are just as mysterious . . . I think Gwyneth likes me, even if we haven't much in common. Lydia is

154

superficial. If you put her in a novel you wouldn't know what she was thinking about. She's all outward cut-and-driedness, but you could probably rely on her in an emergency. Would Sonia agree? It's years since we had a proper talk . . . Sonia didn't like Tim. Of course, she said nothing, but I could tell. She was lucky to find Bob Greenwood . . .

'How would you have behaved in poor Isabel's position?' Sonia was now asking. 'Would you have been taken in by Osmond? You wouldn't know as much about him as his author knows, would you? He wouldn't have been presented to you in an unfavourable light.'

'Can you talk about characters as though they were real people?' asked Lydia. 'We just don't know what he was *really* like — we only have him from the author's point of view.'

'But knowing at the end of the book what the heroine knew, would you have been so loyal to your husband?' Daphne asked.

Could *she* ever have been taken in by Osmond? Charles had not been any kind of Osmond; he'd been capable of passion for a person. She'd possibly been the object of more passion than some of the other women here. There was no way however of applying a thermometer to feelings. Dorothy or Gwyneth or Evelyn might once have been the objects of equal infatuation. Why was Isabel Archer so vulnerable? Too virtuous? Too moral? Too attractive?

As they took their coffee from Dorothy's pale grey cups Gwyneth was composedly sketching Evelyn as she sat frowning a little, rereading the last chapter of the book. Gwyneth sees a different Evelyn from the one I see, thought Sonia, so there are perhaps no misapprehensions, just different ways of seeing. She bent her head down to Miss Archer's problems.

It was peaceful and orderly in her home, thought Dorothy, Tim having imposed order once and for all upon her own untidiness. She had never looked back, had remained in his regard the woman he wanted her to be even after his death. Did wives have such influence over husbands? If Bob Greenwood were to die, would Sonia change? Women seemed to be more affected, more influenced, by the men in their lives. As well as men's characters often being stronger they were also more selfish. Women wanted to please. Isabel Archer had not been selfish enough, had been far too loyal.

Sonia had decided she preferred Henrietta Stacpole. She almost agreed with Lydia. Why did Isabel Archer have to marry *anybody*, she asked herself rebelliously. Were there no women a hundred years ago who didn't want to spend their lives with a man? And Isabel was rich, so could have pleased herself. On the other hand there must have been single men, who were not as despised as were women who didn't marry.

Aloud, she said, 'There must always have been men who didn't want to spend their lives curled up with a woman.'

'Or vice-versa,' said Daphne. She was the only one of them who had neither married nor had a child, though Gwyneth and Lydia had not done both.

Evelyn said: 'Well, women are just as bad, some of them,' and then added: 'Bits of the past can change too. You see everything differently as the years go by.'

'That's the benefit of hindsight,' said Lydia. 'What matters is how you felt *then*.'

'I'm not sure if that's really true,' Dorothy said.

'Episodes you thought were nicely packed up and labelled have a habit of bursting out of their parcels asking to be reconsidered?' asked Sonia.

'That's what I mean,' said Evelyn. The tip of her nose was glowing, maybe with the unaccustomed mental exercise.

Sonia was trying to draw her thougths

together. 'How are we to know they won't change again? When they've already changed once — I mean, we've already gone through so many changes? So perhaps the best way to consider them is how you felt at the time, as Evelyn says.'

'Anyway,' said Gwyneth, 'there isn't time to spend your life thinking things over. You have to go on living.'

'There's only one way of pinning things down,' said Sonia.

'How?' asked Evelyn.

'Writing about them. Fixing them for ever.'

'If you keep a diary,' said Lydia, 'you can't bear to read it later!'

'Mm, it's embarrassing to realize what one was once like,' agreed Daphne.

'We have to be prepared to be embarrassed,' said Sonia. 'It would be interesting to read other people's diaries — to know what they think of themselves, never mind what they think of others!'

'What about people with no powers of expression?' asked Daphne. 'They don't write diaries, do they?'

'I don't see why a change of viewpoint or perspective should make anyone feel embarrassed,' offered Dorothy.

'But, Dorothy,' Sonia said, 'if things you'd

158

marked down as Experience — after all, that's what we at our age are supposed to have had! — if *these* things turn out just to have been gigantic 'cons' — or things you were mistaken about — then all the events and feelings you'd seen bathed in a comfortable glow for years might begin to look lurid or even tragic, mightn't they? Wouldn't you then feel — I don't know what exactly — shame? Regret? Anger at your own stupidity?'

'Gracious me!' said Lydia. 'You sound as if you've had a really interesting life.'

'I know what you mean,' Daphne said.

Sonia went on: 'Then that new recognition would work on you and change you — or help you in future. At least it would show you'd learned something.'

'People are always discovering things about themselves,' said Dorothy.

'What if there isn't a next time?' asked Daphne.

'That's right,' said Evelyn. 'We're not given second chances — '

'True. 'Life is not a rehearsal for living',' quoted Sonia. Coffee cups were being refilled. She added, 'I don't think it's really possible to reshape one's life completely.'

'I don't know about that,' said Lydia. She had been listening with a slightly mocking, slightly amused, expression. She said 'I'm a different woman from the one I was thirty years ago.' If I'd been as I am now I'd never have married Maurice, she thought. It was living with him that made me what I am now.

Time came into it all, thought Daphne. It altered everyone a little, even people who never read books or went out into the world, people who could not express themselves. Even if you sat in a room alone for forty years you'd change, change your opinions as well, because you grew older. She said instead: 'The heroines of the novels we've been reading were usually mistaken about themselves, weren't they? Isabel and Emma for example — and Gwendolen in *Daniel Deronda*. You read that last year, didn't you? They changed because of other people, not just because of the things that happened to them.'

'Other people *are* what happened to us!' Lydia said.

'Right!' said Daphne.

'Wouldn't we see the error of our ways without them?' asked Sonia.

'The other people in the books were all good people,' said Dorothy. 'Like Mr Knightley and Daniel and Ralph Touchett.'

'Maybe that's why these characters were

invented — to improve the heroines?' Daphne suggested.

'Is that what other characters are *for*?' asked Sonia. '*We* are other people to everyone else.'

'You mean that you can't be moral on a desert island?' asked Lydia. 'We are meant just to improve each other whilst we're here?'

'Life isn't books,' objected Dorothy. 'It's all fixed for the poor characters. They have to meet whoever their author decides would be good — or bad — for them.'

'But people do it for each other in real life,' said Lydia. 'Even if they're not especially virtuous or villainous.'

'How do we know Mr Knightley was good?' asked Evelyn crossly.

'Good for Emma — probably Jane Austen's idea of a good man,' said Daphne.

'Good people have more effect upon us than bad ones, I think,' Sonia said. Like Gwyneth, she thought. You feel calmer, happier, nicer, when she's been round.

'Bad people reshape people's lives too,' said Lydia.

'Or set them off on the wrong track in the beginning. Like an evil father or husband as in this book for instance,' suggested Dorothy.

She usually denied firmly the existence of evil.

'Emma and Dorothea could at least change,' said Sonia. 'I don't know about Isabel. She *was* good — better than the others. We ought to look for the effect *she* had on the other characters.'

'She doesn't seem to have had one, except to make all the men fall in love with her,' said Daphne. 'She'll never change Osmond.'

I can't change now, I've had my chance, she was thinking. Do the others feel that?

'We don't know whether Emma or Dorothea *went on* improving,' said Lydia. 'I don't think Rosamund did — I feel it's highly unlikely.'

'At least they went on trying,' said Dorothy.

'Yes, but once they had self-knowledge — brought to them, I admit by other people — men in both cases — they became different people, so they could never go back to what they had once been!' said Sonia.

'I think we look for a sort of balance-sheet — someone to draw it up for us anyway — or someone to explain, even someone to absolve us,' said Dorothy.

'Yes!' said Evelyn eagerly.

Sonia said 'Only our inner selves understand our real selves. Maybe our inner selves *are* our real selves — so other people can never really know us?'

'But we show people what we are like only through our words or actions,' said Lydia. 'What good is it having a secret inner self if it never appears and has no reality for others?'

Dorothy said: 'It's *things* happening to people, not just other people, who change them, make them grow up. I mean, women feel differently about their lives now that we've had a twenty-year dose of feminism. Changing conventions change people.'

'Mostly spread through journalism,' objected Sonia. 'Twenty years ago women a bit younger than us were all reading about patriarchy and were told how they'd been bamboozled into doing things for men they could perfectly well do for themselves.'

'But after that, things slowly changed.'

'We knew already what they were banging on about!' Lydia said.

'Women thought about themselves differently afterwards,' said Daphne. 'More of them now do a double job, and are too tired to enjoy either.'

'Yes, it should have been the *men* reading the books!'

'My son Christopher insists on doing half the cooking and sharing the housework with his wife!' said Evelyn. Ron Naylor had never been known to lift a finger in the kitchen.

'A New Man,' murmured Lydia.

'They're both at home though, aren't they, with the business, so it wouldn't be fair for him not to, so long as his wife takes her share in the shop or cutting the flowers or whatever?' suggested Gwyneth quietly.

'We must get back to Henry James,' said Dorothy desperately.

Daphne said 'Pansy was affected by her stepmother but Isabel wasn't going to change Osmond! Emma didn't change Mr Knightley or Gwendolen change Grandcourt, or Dorothea, Casaubon!'

'Yes, it usually seems to be the women who change!' agreed Sonia.

'Mirah was an inspiration for Daniel Deronda,' said Dorothy.

'Isn't it because our books were written in the nineteenth century?'

'By women too, though!'

'I think the heroines have to improve, poor things, whereas the men are lovely or awful to begin with and stay much the same!' said Lydia.

'I expect Emma did keep backsliding,' said Dorothy.

'*We* aren't young but we try to understand

younger people — our children for example — but they don't always want to understand *us*!' said Evelyn.

'Is it just young people who change for the better in books?' asked Lydia.

'It is mostly,' said Daphne. 'The heroines are always young so they're the ones to have to grow up and improve.'

'What about the young heroes then? What about Ladislaw? He was young,' asked Sonia.

'I think she just wanted him as a romantic mate for Dorothea,' replied Daphne.

'Once a woman like Dorothea got him she'd change him all right,' said Sonia. 'I don't think she'd be content just to worship him! She was no longer a young virgin.'

Evelyn burst in unexpectedly: 'I've a lot of sympathy with myself when young. So much was expected of us then.'

'Expecting us to make a 'suitable' marriage?' suggested Lydia.

'I wish Gwyneth would give us her thoughts,' said Dorothy. Gwyneth looked up but remained silent.

'Having children changes people too. Isabel and Dorothea — we never know them as mothers,' said Sonia.

Daphne asked, 'Are babies a relief from thinking too much about yourself?'

'I suppose so. But children make you a hostage to fortune. You can never be truly free again after that.'

'You have to pull yourself away,' said Lydia. 'I know I only had a stepson but I was completely involved with him for ten years.'

'Fathers could do the job just as well,' said Sonia, 'some fathers, anyway — all the things they *don't* write about in these novels are different for men.'

'How else could Nature tempt lazy men to get on with it?' asked Lydia. 'Without some bait they'd never bother with women!'

Nature didn't intend women of our age to be able to sit around talking about ourselves — or about her, thought Daphne but kept the thought to herself.

'It's my mother I'm sorry for — the sexual revolution has been such a shock to her system!' said Sonia.

'I think we should read *Anna Karenina* next year,' said Dorothy.

'*Madame Bovary?*' suggested Lydia.

A ragged discussion, thought Daphne as she put on her coat to leave. But quite interesting. What would Anne have made of it?

She went out with Sonia who was to be given another lift in her car.

166

'Do you feel some sympathy for your younger self?' asked Sonia, putting on the seat belt.

'I see her as a young friend, I think,' replied Daphne, adjusting the mirror in her old car. 'I feel for her but I want to tell her to be careful, not to do silly things. I feel sorry for her as well sometimes.' As I do for Cressy, she thought.

'But did you ever learn anything from novels? By the time I was ready to learn from them I'd in any case changed. I recognized myself — in Gwendolen Harleth, for example — but that's not the same, is it? When we read *Daniel Deronda* the others didn't like it much, but I loved it.'

'The young have to begin everything from the beginning all over again,' said Daphne manoeuvring her gears. 'If only every generation could start out from where their parents left off. It's all so tedious, isn't it? When you've taught for over thirty years you see patterns repeating themselves — and you just know what will happen to certain people. You're usually right.'

Once Daphne had swung her car out of the Naylor drive, Sonia replied: 'I was thinking too, when we were talking about

167

diaries, that there must exist certain things that have never been written down — things unsophisticated people think — people who don't write or communicate well — '

'Some writers have tried. What about Thomas Hardy's Mrs Henchard, or Marty South? The strange thing is that those are the really virtuous characters — yet they're all refracted through a clever person! I'd give anything to know what goes on in Gwyneth's head!'

'I suppose I know her as well as anybody does. She's not like us. Perhaps we just shelter behind words? It's the mystery of personality that attracts us in the novels we read, isn't it? Just as in real life?'

'In some people more than others. I'm trying to understand an eighteenth-century woman poet at present. It's very hard — but would I understand her any better if I'd known her?'

'Was she very different from yourself or is it just the time that's passed since then that makes her more elusive?'

'Both, I suppose.'

'Is it for a book?'

'I hope so. I shan't say anything about it to the others — not until it's finished anyway — '

'Thank you for telling me then!'

8

Women of your own age came nearest to understanding you, thought Daphne as she prepared for bed. She liked Sonia, whom she sensed was a disillusioned romantic and so, like herself, a little cynical. A relief not to have to explain yourself, to have an easy conversation. But she was married, had children, and as she'd said herself, motherhood changed women. The two of them might not have got on so well if they had both lived in Norwood, known each other at school, might even have been academic rivals. Odd, two girls with similar tastes growing up only a mile or two away from each other, going to different schools, different universities only to meet after forty years had passed.

★ ★ ★

She stirred and smiled a little as she dreamed.

There was a plain deal table with three chairs drawn up. A pale brown-haired young woman and two small girls were earnestly reading turn by turn from a large Bible they pushed from one to the other. She heard the ticking of a clock before the woman stood up, pushed back her chair and said, 'Now you can copy the verses you have read in your best hand.' A bottle of ink materialized on the table and two steel-nibbed pens. The only sound then was that of their scribbling away on thin white paper. 'Entreat me not to leave thee,' Daphne read before the dream faded.

The dream lingered longer than usual in her mind. Her conscious thoughts would occasionally seem dream-like too. Engaged in some humdrum task — clearing the leaves from the yard in the front of the house, ironing — she would find her mind full of speculations, images, scraps of dialogue. There were even days when she would actively search for some soothing chore, so there would be a good chance of its giving her interesting thoughts. These flashes of inspiration, or quite long trails of thought, helped colour her ideas when she sat down at her table, but the connecting tissue was not always there, that sense of all the details of another's life. It was all very well 'seeing' inside someone else's head, but that head existed in a vacuum if you were not sure of more mundane things.

She was trying to put herself in Anne's place just as she tried to put herself in Judith's or Cressida's or Sonia's; was happy to think Anne's thoughts for her after immersing herself in Anne's poetry. Only in dreams though did a past background emerge: the table, the Bible, the porridge smeared on the wall . . .

If she were to get on reasonably efficiently with her own life she could not spend all her time thinking about her work. How she'd appreciate a wife: someone to write the shopping list if not do the shopping, someone who would decide what to eat for supper, and when to change the sheets, someone to remember birthdays. It was administering her own day-to-day life that took up time.

★ ★ ★

In the middle of November, remembering she needed the sort of typing paper the village store did not provide, Daphne went into the town. There was still a good bookshop there, as well-stocked as it had been forty years before, so she could browse, once the boring part of her shopping was over. She went on the bus. Parking was such a nuisance. The journey was familiar, one she had taken so many times in her life that she could have driven there blindfold, knowing every bump in the road, every slight incline. The buses belonged to the same company as had operated those of her childhood, and on which she and Mary had gone in the opposite direction to school and back, up the hill first instead of down.

She settled back to look out of the window. The skies were still clear; unusually there had been very little mist or rain in the past week. Had Anne ever sailed across to France? Mary W. had gone over to Paris, had even stayed there during the Terror, but there was no evidence, no mention in any letters or biographies, of Anne herself ever having done so. Daphne shut her eyes, tried to concentrate on the idea of a Channel crossing . . . She recollected where she was when the bus stopped: she'd end up muttering to herself and being mowed down by the traffic.

She did her shopping soberly and was able to go into the book shop before midday. As she pushed open its door she saw Roger Masterson at the back. She didn't think he'd seen her as she now looked fixedly in the opposite direction, wanting a good browse before having to talk to him. She'd go up to him later if he were still there.

172

She scanned the new fiction. Next to that were a few shelves of slim volumes of poetry by local versifiers, published by the many small presses that had mushroomed in the area in the last fifteen years. Most women writers of Anne's time had sold their wares by word of mouth, to subscribers who sometimes numbered hundreds — friends of friends of friends — probably about the same number of people as bought poetry now.

She turned round as she waited at the cash desk and found Masterson just behind her. 'You were smiling to yourself,' he said. 'How are you, Daphne?'

'Fine — glad if I was smiling — my thoughts are sometimes rather gloomy.'

He looked warily at her as they both went out of the shop.

'Nothing important,' she said.

'The world goes to pot daily as my mother used to say,' said Roger. 'Better to ignore it.'

'If you can manage that, perhaps it is,' she replied. 'I'm going to the market — I need some kitchen cups and some old-fashioned potted meat. I can never resist going in there — it was always our treat when Mother had finished her shopping to go into the covered market to spend our Saturday pennies.'

'The place is almost unique,' he said. 'Did you come by car?'

'No.'

'Well, if you want a lift home, I've got the car round the corner — unless you were thinking of shopping elsewhere?' The man seemed destined to offer her lifts in his car.

'Too much of a temptation — other shopping, I mean — I've to get on with writing my book.' Immediately she wished she hadn't said that. But why?

'Of course — you are writing one!' he exclaimed. 'You must tell me more about it.'

She smiled non-committally. What book had he just bought? She might as well accept the lift, and said so. 'Twenty minutes all right?' he asked, telling her where he'd left the car.

'Thanks.'

He went off on some purchase of his own.

She approached the china stall, a riot of shapes and colours. Here you could buy 'seconds', in which only a connoisseur could have found an imperfection, and Daphne was always one for a bargain. She chose some white cups with blue and gold bands and then spent the saving on a pretty cream

174

jug that she was assured was a one-off, having no relatives of teapots or sugar basins. It looked like a copy of a mid-Victorian jug with elaborately curled lip and sides festooned with roses. There wouldn't be anything really old here. Eighteenth-century crockery was always smaller in scale, when tea was a luxury savoured in sips, not drunk in enormous quantities. She thought of Anne's brother Joshua who had painted and sold porcelain, and read an imaginary letter in her head:

Salop. Nov 3rd 1787: Dearest Mother, Anne and Lizzie — I am mightily bored here. We exist in a swamp — the main street is a mud bath and the side streets swollen with the continual rain. Yesterday they showed me the kilns and wheels in the workshop where much of our stuff is made and I tried to appear enthused. But I fear I shall never make a merchant. I shall go on until Christmastide and then shall return to you before Twelfth Night if you can see your way to advancing me the coach fare before then. Or promise a crown when the Rover reaches London about seven of the afternoon of 6th Jny. Money is a great lack to me but more tiresome is the lack of congenial company — if any of these painters upon glaze had a word in their heads not to do with pots and dishes and such like, it would be the more endurable. Give my regards to George and William Dyer and tell them I have started upon sketches of the countryside around here which is pretty when it is not drenched in water. Water-colours are extremely suitable for its delineation. Yr loving son and brother — Joshua.

The young man could settle to nothing but painting pictures, not pots. How disappointed his mother and sisters would have been. However were they to come upon the fare from Broseley to London? Joshua should be helping them, not being a drain upon their finances. It would be his mother who dipped into her savings. Anne would not earn very much at the Dyers and did not even receive her board and lodging there, walking as she did daily to and from their house two miles away . . .

Daphne recalled herself in time to greet Roger again at the entrance to the market and accompany him to his car. On the way back to Heckcliff they chatted about his garden and she told him a bit about her research. After he had left her at the house — fortunately she had nothing very heavy to carry or he'd have been offering to carry it — she went in, lit the fire, Widgery on the rug beside her feet, and forgot Roger to muse once more over Anne's brother and the family financial plight.

Your early twenties were supposed to be the happiest and most carefree years of your life but the more you read of early struggles and remembered your own, the less alluring those years appeared. Joshua was not the only youth to find himself a square peg in a round hole, obliged to work for a living. His father was not a poor man and must have kept the family at least from the worst poverty, but he probably advanced nothing but the cash for bare necessities, the ale house or his bottle of rum being his prime concerns. They would all be dependent upon that, upon their mother's savings and whatever the children could bring in. Anne was said often to have been in low spirits. She did not own a robust temperament, unlike Joshua's acquaintance, Mary Wollstonecraft, who had begged him in that letter she'd read to make more of an effort for his family's sake. Artistic ambitions were all very well for a man, but he must work for his nearest and dearest. The younger daughter, Elizabeth the engraver, couldn't have earned much either. If only some of *her* work could be found — she might not have been as ambitious as her brother so evidently was.

Mary had said she feared Anne's situation was very uncomfortable. 'I wish she could obtain a little more strength of mind.' Evidently fortitude of Mary's sort was not one of Anne's qualities either. Reading between the lines Daphne had wondered whether Anne had been a depressive. Young women always tended to be caught in that trap even if their circumstances were not as gloomy as hers.

Daphne turned up the flames of her fire and considered. If Anne's Platonic lover had proposed marriage, her problems would at that time have been considered over. She remembered her own years of cold-water flats and little money for the small luxuries that perked up existence. Few clothes, many debts. Those would be Anne's problems too, even if the debts were not hers. She was not an independent woman at that time, did not live 'at her own hands' as her friend Mary did. She was in love with a man who loved her only as a friend, yet without that unrequited passion would she have written what she did?

Had she ever been tempted to drink? Laudanum was more likely. Women were

178

not often mentioned as slaves of the bottle, though doubtless some of them were.

'I've no room to talk,' she said aloud to the cat. 'I spent the first half of my life in love with one man after another!' Work had saved her. Had it saved Anne? How delighted she must have been to find a publisher for her verse at the age of twenty-seven! If Anne had had a Charles in her life she might have cheered up, but Anne would never have had an affair with a married man. If there had been an amiable and willing bachelor around who proposed to her she would most likely have married him even if she was not in love with him; that was what women did. Did the Platonic lover — who must surely have been George Dyer, a Cambridge man and friend of brother Joshua — never suspect her feelings for him? She must have been adept at the concealment of feeling necessary for a well-brought-up young woman in those days. She had lived through the most exciting of times: times of a real revolution, not in manners or popular music, but one of blood and terror. Had they talked about it as the tumbrils rolled on over the Channel or had Anne closed her ears to such rumours and sunk back into contemplation of nature and love? There was still so much more research to be done — and much thinking.

Cressida might telephone before she went to bed. Cressy was luckier than Anne, might receive a proposal of marriage. She pulled herself up short. Fancy her thinking this would be a way out of a young woman's problems! But it was still the men who did the proposing — if they believed in marriage at all. Anne had been as attendant upon a man's wishes as Cressy had been upon the whims of that lover of hers. Cressida did not telephone.

Daphne thought again about Roger Masterson. Was he following her around with a purpose?

* * *

She did not dream that night, woke early, before the light, her head full of thoughts of her own youth rather than Anne's. If only Anne, who was a much better writer than she would ever be, had learned to live by herself, had had an independent streak. She fell asleep again.

When the pale beginning of a winter morning slowly lightened the room through a chink in her bedroom curtains she woke again, got out of bed and drew them back. The sun was weak, yet it was there, had returned, as it always did, even if philosophers denied you could even be sure about that.

She pulled on her trousers quickly and went down to feed Widgery and make herself a cup of hot tea to get her going. The paper had already arrived and she cast a quick glance at more headlines, more misery. What sort of God would make it so hard for his intelligent creatures to believe in him? She turned to Saturday's more personal pages: Lonely Hearts.

She began to invent an ad for herself: 'Elderly woman, loves cats, crosswords, roses, opera, obscure eighteenth-century poets, detective stories, no golf, moderate drinker, needs an intellectual companion . . .' The paper was full of such messages. Judith had found the right man without one but she was unlikely to find hers. Men of her own age wanted women of forty, or even younger. The intellectual part was another stumbling block!

She sat down at her typewriter, thinking she would be far more likely to find an ideal intellectual companion in Sonia if *that* was what she wanted.

★ ★ ★

A cold, windy evening, the trees all bare now and Lydia sat snug and warm in her pleasant flat, reluctant to set out for the meeting. She'd enjoyed *Great Expectations*, it was a nice change to have a masculine main character. He had problems, but different ones from Isabel Archer, or poor Hetty Sorell or the Middlemarch women, whose problems were principally to do with men and marriage.

Dickens was easier to enjoy than Henry James in her opinion and probably in most people's. Estella though, would she really have gone off with Pip again at the end? Life did not usually offer you a second chance. She was well aware of that. Perhaps her own expectations had never been great enough? Not like the others, especially Daphne Berridge and Sonia Greenwood, both of whom she imagined had been extremely ambitious.

Lydia counted three and jumped up smartly from her armchair; if you could not do that it showed you were on the way out, according to a health booklet she'd read. She patted her hair in the mirror on the pale cream wall and fetched her make-up bag. She'd never felt able to go out without making her face up, still had her hair well cut every month. Always too, before she left her flat to go out, even if only to shop down the road, she'd check to see her fingernails were clean. The nuns' conditioning had been successful. Clean hands and nails had been on the same level as saying your prayers or telling the rosary. Sonia said it had been much the same at her nunless grammar school: polished boots equated godliness. When you looked round now at the dirty trainers and stained shell-suits, the nuns and teachers had had a point.

She glanced at her engagement pad in its place by the telephone. Next week would be her bridge Tuesday. It kept her mind lively but took less out of her than thinking about characters in fiction who forced her to consider her own life.

She was ready now to go out but looked once again in the mirror, checked that Pause was asleep on his cushion and the door to the kitchen open in case of evening starvation, then locking the outer door carefully behind her she went out to her car which stood in the small carpark behind the block of flats.

★ ★ ★

Pip's sister's bullying ways and her rampages had reminded Sonia Greenwood of her own mother, and his later snobberies had made her wonder if similar ones had been part of her own emancipation. Her mind was stuck again in the grooves of the past. Dorothy always claimed she well remembered their shared youth, but she probably dismissed it from her mind, as you might forget a past miscarriage if you now had the evidence of a fine baby. Somebody had once said that those who did not remember the past were compelled to fulfil it. What did that mean? Gwyneth would occasionally mention the old days, but her memories seemed to be of beloved dogs, or little gardens she had made, and the chilbains and violin lessons at her boarding schools whither she had been pushed off at twelve years old. She'd always returned home unchanged; it would have taken more than the unimaginative regime of St Frideswide's to alter her spartan and stoic nature. Since then Gwyneth had gone her own way on a different path. Evelyn Naylor professed she had no memories of anything that had happened to her before the age of six but it had been Evelyn who had stated 'only the past is safe', and that surely presupposed a reasonably happy infancy, even if she might now deny it? Lydia Robinson often dismissed nostalgia as pointless, a weakness of the over-imaginative; in her opinion it was much better to be grown up.

Sonia was not sure. Lydia said that life was

a struggle but you didn't have to remember it all, better to breathe a sigh of relief that your youth was over and you could now do what you wanted. Lydia always wore a sort of mask, thought Sonia. Did anyone really know her? She looked forward to seeing Daphne again.

★ ★ ★

Dorothy read out the minutes, then looked up and said, 'Oughtn't we to put that we discussed other things than the reading task? I was thinking that we have almost become a debating society!'

'We've always talked about things in general,' said Sonia, 'not always arising from the reading.'

'We're not a university seminar,' said Lydia.

'I didn't mean we shouldn't talk about other things,' said Dorothy. 'Just why not mention that we do?'

'It all arises from the books, doesn't it?' said Gwyneth. 'I mean this Dickens book — it's about growing up and making mistakes, and learning from them, isn't it?'

'You said that was partly what novels were for — criticism of life,' said Evelyn.

185

'Tracts for self-improvement?' asked Lydia ironically.

Evelyn was looking vaguely uneasy. 'I prefer to read for pleasure really,' she said. 'I don't bother my head about ideas.'

'These stories we read contain a sort of running commentary about how to live, what it is to act morally — all that,' Sonia said, and went on: 'All the novels have been about the pitfalls of living, not abstract ideas, but where people went *wrong*. It's only part of the stories, I know, but at least till this century that must have been one reason why they were read.'

'Telling people how to behave!' said Lydia again.

'Wasn't that just the English novel?' asked Dorothy.

'*Madame Bovary* has its cautionary aspect!' said Daphne.

'They are meant to put our own lives in perspective,' suggested Sonia. 'If they make us think, that's good. For example, these 'great expectations' — that's what we all had once, isn't it?'

'Not financial ones,' said Lydia. 'That's what *he* meant, wasn't it?'

'He meant both — and how the idea of them deformed the boy and the man,' suggested Daphne.

'I wish I'd read it when I was younger,' Evelyn said.

'We did it for School Cert,' said Lydia, 'I don't suppose we understood the half of it. Perhaps great novels are only truly understood by older people.'

'We ought to do some close reading,' murmured Dorothy. 'Or we shall end up again just telling each other our own stories.'

'I never used to know what to look for,' Gwyneth said.

'Surely it's the story,' said Dorothy, 'that keeps people hooked? You want to know what happens to the characters — who lives, who dies — all that. There's pure pleasure too of course — '

Sonia looked round Evelyn's sitting-room which did not have many books and had a tousled appearance. It was odd how the tidy-minded Evelyn was not at all tidy in her domestic surroundings. She'd never understand her.

'Gobbling my way through the pleasures of light fiction is a weakness of mine,' said Daphne.

'I still read a lot of detective stories,' admitted Lydia. 'But I think we're getting away from the point about what we read here together. If *we* get our moral rules — rather old-fashioned ones, from some of our authors, it doesn't mean that everybody does. Anyway, most people do read for pleasure — for a good story — a plot — '

'*Great Expectations* has a wonderful plot,' said Sonia.

Gwyneth still looked puzzled. 'If Lydia enjoys her detective stories that's no different from enjoying Dickens, is it?'

'I was always told that 'great literature' was more elevated — enjoyment wasn't the main reason for reading it,' said Lydia.

'We've read scores of books and we've asked ourselves what we got from them — what stayed with us. If they were just lessons on how to live, you might as well say you could learn from Patience Strong or some moral tale for children!' said Dorothy.

'Moral lessons are not the most important thing, but they are there if you look for them,' said Sonia.

'Isabel *was* moral — and look what happened to her. What fault of character did she have?' asked Lydia.

There was silence.

'Questions of morality are powerless to affect you if you don't receive pleasure too,' observed Daphne.

'Hm,' said Evelyn.

'I think life is too short to spend it reading,' said Gwyneth. This made them all feel a little uncomfortable.

'Nobody said you had to spend it reading — it's just that reading was such a big part of the way we were brought up,' said Sonia. 'You're not influenced by rubbish — except in childhood.'

'Why then is any novel better than any other?' asked Evelyn plaintively.

'Some things are just harder than others to enjoy,' offered Lydia. 'I don't enjoy old Henry as much as old Charles.'

'Some people might say we ought to read only what is being written at present,' suggested Daphne, acting devil's advocate. 'It's bound to have more to do with our present problems.'

'Not for that reason!' said Sonia severely. 'The real problems are always the same.'

Dorothy said: 'Well, to get this discussion back on the ground, I think we should remark upon the fact that so far this year we've been reading about the problems of women finding husbands or marrying the wrong ones or mucking up their lives being victims of men.'

'I think we ought to talk about *Great Expectations* and what makes it different — about a man, written by a man, compared with a woman writing about women and a man writing about them,' suggested Sonia.

'Then we must read some women writing about men after that,' said Lydia.

In the end they talked about whether there was a sense of evil in the book and what made it different from *David Copperfield*.

It was almost time for coffee when Lydia said, 'You know, I wonder why there are hardly any *old* people as the main characters in the novels we've been reading — or in any novels really. Except Miss Havisham, I suppose.'

'Some of the minor characters are old perhaps, but all our novels are about growing up — as if the moral choices once made set you forever,' Sonia added.

'As if there were no moral choices to be made once you were over forty,' said Daphne. 'Miss Havisham had made hers long before.'

'How could you have old people in books, if *young* people were to read them for educational purposes?' asked Evelyn.

'Scrooge?' suggested Sonia.

'There are lots of older people in French literature,' said Daphne. 'Old Goriot — it's even in the title. And Cousin Bette. She wasn't young.'

'What about Lear and Falstaff?' asked Lydia. 'They were the novels of the period in a way, weren't they?'

'What could be more about the tragedy of old age than Lear?' asked Gwyneth, and blushed.

'The problems get worse as you grow older — it's just that writers write to be popular and old age is not a very popular subject,' Sonia said after a pause.

'We are not old *yet*,' said Lydia.

They sat on in Evelyn's boring brown room with the creased sofa cushions and the old-fashioned standard lamp and the tiled surround fire where nothing had changed since the house was built sixty years before.

What a picture we could make for one of those Victorian genre painters, thought Daphne — half a dozen women sitting round earnestly debating high-minded subjects, all of us past our prime . . . She saw a ladder was becoming obvious in Sonia's tights.

Sonia roused herself saying: 'I'll think about it and report next time.'

Evelyn rose to make coffee and Dorothy went to help her with the tray.

'I'll list some novels with older characters — we need suggestions for next year too. We planned only until February if you remember,' Sonia went on.

'The next meeting is at your house anyway,' said Lydia. 'So you can root around and find more stories written by women about men!'

'Yes,' said Sonia, consulting her diary. 'The December meeting is at my place — the January one at Gwyneth's. After that we need offers.'

Daphne had not yet offered her home as a meeting place and knew she ought to offer for February.

'*Sense and Sensibility* next,' said Dorothy sipping her coffee. 'There's a moral lesson in *that* book.'

'A bit late for us, surely?' murmured Lydia.

'It's just as much about hope and disappointment as the Dickens,' said Daphne. 'I've just finished re-reading *Persuasion* for the umpteenth time. I always have a Jane Austen on the go.'

★ ★ ★

Lydia Robinson, who had once been Lydia Proudfoot, woke from a dream — and cursed. She usually got to sleep quite quickly but would wake in the early hours, or on better days at about six o'clock, and lie awake, her mind more active than it usually was in the daytime. Sometimes, as this morning, it would be a dream that woke her. Or the dream was evidence of her sleeping become shallower and tipping over the edge into wakefulness. People said that early waking was a sign of depression but she knew she was not depressed — or no more than usual. Sonia had confided that she often woke in the night too and Daphne Berridge had said she dreamed a good deal.

Lydia remembered telling them all that she never thought about the past and here she was just having dreamed of some long-lost day, or no particular day at all, just a memory of the many term-time mornings when she'd walked to the convent. In the dream it had felt like spring, a May day, May, the month of Mary . . .

She would try some yoga breathing. Gwyneth Coultar said it was useful if you could not get to sleep. But she'd probably slept enough. She switched on the lamp and looked at her watch. Nearly six. Oh well then, she might as well have a bath and start the day early. She heard Pause tap at the door. She never allowed him on the bed but he always knew when she was awake and would pad down the hall to her door from the kitchen where his favourite sleeping place was under the table, not on the pretty cushion she'd bought for him but on the vinyl floor. She'd do a bit of breathing anyway, gently and rhythmic, and stretch her toes and fingers.

The dream was still hovering at the back of her mind but would disappear unless she made an effort to keep it there. She'd certainly been in Surrey, walking to school, and there had been a feeling of warmth in the air, flowers in the hedgerow, and something about dressing the altar.

When she had made this short journey to school in reality she had always had a faintly guilty feeling located in her solar plexus, not about anything particular but because that was the way the nuns seemed to want you to feel, drilled as they were in self-abnegation, and wanting you to be like them. Most of the little girls had tried to be good most of the time, but Lydia had always felt guilty. Why? She tried to think. She'd been a pleasure-loving and lazy girl; one nun had called her a sybarite; the nun who taught English and used long words. She'd looked that up in the dictionary at home. Perhaps that had been Sister Clare's intention.

When had she decided to appear hard-working and obedient at school so that everywhere else she could do what she wanted? . . . If I do as they tell me at The Sisters of Mercy, then I can please myself when I'm grown up, and enjoy the rest of my life . . . She had left the convent as soon as her parents allowed, and gone into an office. The nuns had been disappointed, said she had a brain and had just begun to use it. Her best friend Philomena Walsh had stayed at the nunnery and become one of Them in the end. Lydia felt she'd had a lucky escape. If she hadn't decided to behave at school and do what she wanted elsewhere she too might have been caught at sixteen. But Philomena had left the convent twenty years after taking her vows, had received a special dispensation. I wonder what she's doing now, thought Lydia, as she slid out of bed and opened the door to Pause who gave a short squeaky mew and led her to the kitchen for food. Cats always knew exactly what they wanted. If only *she* had known.

When she was well over thirty, after many flings with men who worked in the City, she'd finally taken on Maurice Robinson, a widower with a small son. By then she'd had a good job herself, one reason for not marrying, for she liked her money and her life. She could not remember very well why she had agreed to marry Maurice except that she had thought she might want a child before it was too late. Marrying him had been a sort of task like the ones the nuns used to set them, perhaps a small expiation for having enjoyed herself so well for so long. She hadn't reckoned with Maurice's son Tony. He'd always been too much for her, although everyone knew she'd tried.

Her marriage had been at a registry office, with a blessing afterwards because Maurice wasn't a Catholic. Anyway, for some reason, she had not wanted a 'proper' wedding; the ceremony they did have was only to please her mother. Her father had not been a Catholic and neither had he got on with Maurice, said he only wanted a nanny and housekeeper and Lydia was throwing herself away. He'd been right. She must have been mad. It wouldn't have mattered so much if she'd had a child of her own, but it hadn't happened. It must have been her fault since Maurice had already fathered Tony. Yet she could not help feeling that if she'd married any of those other young men, it *would* have happened. Maurice's work had been transferred north and they had gone there a year or two after the wedding, to Leeds first of all.

Tony had grown into an unprepossessing and sullen youth and then into a man with chips on both shoulders. Fortunately he was not as unpleasant as he had been as a child so maybe her efforts had made *some* difference. If she hadn't looked after him till he was eighteen and intermittently after that, who knew, he might have become a fraudster or something. It wasn't his father's fault. Maurice had not been very imaginative, but he'd tried to do his best by the boy, though he'd given up when Tony was asked to leave his third private school for stealing. Then Maurice had fallen for a young barmaid when he was in his fifties, the classic story, and left Lydia the minute Tony was twenty-one as though a contract had just expired. But Maurice had had a good job, and enough of a guilty conscience to leave her with a small income which she'd immediately supplemented, as soon as Tony had gone for good, with a return to work in a bank.

She'd retired before she need have done, suddenly angry about her life and wondering when it would be her turn to enjoy herself again. Being good had not worked; but she had no desire now to be really bad. All she wanted was a bit of comfort, a nice little place and enough money. She had that, eventually, left to her by her father whose own investments had prospered after many years of stagnation.

It had all worked out well enough, she thought, as she pulled on her pale grey stockings. But reading these novels tugged at her imagination, made her regret leaving school when she had. For a time she'd toyed with the idea of an Open University course, but she'd had enough of commitment to a goal and decided instead to brush up her bridge, acquire a cat, and go on attending the reading circle.

For some time after her release from Maurice and Tony she had also considered finding another husband, but caution overrode her in the end. She might find herself saddled with another Tony, and she was no longer sure whether she wanted what they called a sex life. Sometimes she remembered her young men; one of them was now a grandfather — she'd seen him in Rowell when she'd gone home to sell her father's house, her mother having died long before.

When she thought about her life now it was the convent that kept intruding into her consciousness, even, like this morning, into her dreams. She wished she could go back and meet her younger self, and advise her — but what would she say? There always seemed to have been something missing in her life that she could not put her finger on. Everybody thought she was stable and well-balanced so she supposed she was, but she was cynical, couldn't help that. Now she saw Tony and his wife and young son only at Christmas. She didn't think Tony's marriage would last, though his wife Linda seemed a patient sort of woman.

The only advantage of being older if you hadn't quite forgotten the old days, was that you could certainly advise the young. Really, she was more contented now. Young people only had a few years to remember and regret, had no idea what it was like to be approaching whatever age you admitted to. That was their loss; they'd find out soon enough. She got on all right with the younger tenants of the flats and with some of the younger bridge players in town; she didn't feel old — yet. Was the trouble that as she'd never expected enough from life, she'd survived reasonably intact? It was enough to live in the present, not hope for too much. She'd had her moments before she married, done her duty in that marriage, so she had nothing whatever to reproach herself with. But she needn't have been so self-sacrificial.

All the fault of the nuns; perhaps she'd stored up some good points in that heaven she no longer believed in?

9

As November continued in its usual dreary way towards the more cheerful prospect of December, and Judith put her Christmas 'specials' in the window, Daphne got down to serious writing. She preferred working in winter when there was little else to do in the evenings. For exercise she continued to tramp over to the village shops to chat with Judith Kershaw, and sometimes went further afield.

One morning however there popped through her letter box a stiff white envelope with deckled edges. An invitation from Roger Masterson. Would she care to accompany him to the opera in Leeds?

She'd accept — he intrigued her a little, as well as annoying her. She wouldn't mind a little light flirtation if that was what he had in mind. Nothing heavy.

She telephoned him.

'Shall I drive us there then? It's too far for you to walk this time!' A joke.

'That would be nice — unless you prefer me to drive? I do have a car, you know — not as posh as yours.'

'I'll pick you up on Saturday at one-thirty,' he said firmly. 'It starts at half past two, but with the parking and everything — '

They arranged the details. It was to be *Rigoletto*, one of her favourite operas, to be performed by a northern company. Would Roger Masterson be a suitable companion for mutual indulgence in romantic arias?

★ ★ ★

She'd been surprised when he'd turned to her at the end of the first scene saying: 'The tenor's not bad but Rigoletto sings flat.'

Yet why should she be surprised? Retired architects might be allowed perfect pitch.

'It's such lovely music,' she murmured.

Before, he'd said: 'My wife wasn't keen on Italian opera — we shared most things, but Betty preferred Gilbert and Sullivan.'

'I expect she was a wonderful gardener?' she'd remarked irrelevantly.

'Oh yes, she was — I'm afraid I didn't know what to do garden-wise when she died. I appreciated the results but I never had time for the spadework so to speak.'

'I only have window boxes,' Daphne said encouragingly. Then, without beating about the bush: 'How long ago did she die?'

She had always been prone to a certain directness.

'Almost four years ago. Bertram — our son — had just married. At least she saw him settled. He's an accountant — they live near Chester. They wanted me to move nearer to them but I preferred to stay put.'

Daphne had been encouraged to probe a little further and discovered he had a married daughter in New Zealand, whom he missed.

'We altered the Grange quite a bit years ago, got it just how Betty wanted it. I suppose I stayed because it was home. She'd have wanted me to stay on in Heckcliff. I'm over her death now,' he added.

But you still miss her, she thought.

He had expatiated on Betty's housekeeping and cookery skills. What else did he miss? she wondered. Vaguely she remembered seeing a portrait in oils hanging in the hall of the Grange that time she'd visited in summer and peered in a nosey way through an open window. A fair woman in a fifties'-style, slipper-satin dress. Must have been Betty?

'I mustn't bore you,' he said.

The wicked Duke of Mantua was making his endless farewells. Whilst he serenaded his Gilda she'd been far away with the music, had even forgotten her companion. Such music reminded her of feelings in which she'd once drowned, when nothing had been more important than love. After the duet was finished she woke up and remembered where she was. But the duke's aria after his arrival in his palace plunged her back to the same feelings. Was their reality only a theatrical one? She stole a look at Roger who was studying his programme.

During the interval he said: 'You must tell me more about yourself.' They had made their way to the bar. 'Tell me about your old job.'

'Oh I enjoyed it,' she began, 'but I'd rather have been born creative. I mean, you can be a creative cook or a creative gardener,' — another compliment for Betty. 'All I used to do was interpret and now I gather up details, process them and try to present them in an interesting way for the general reader.'

'You taught English then?' he asked.

'Literature,' she corrected him.

'Was she famous, your poet?' he asked politely after a pause as they sipped their g and t's.

'No, not really — her brother was better known. He was a painter.'

'I must read your book when it's finished.'

'If it ever is,' she said gloomily.

On the way home they talked desultorily. She felt she had not come up to scratch. But it had been pleasant being with a man who was so good-looking, so presentable; she had forgotten what that was like. Pleasant to be driven to the opera, to have tickets and drinks bought for you — though she'd offered him one in the second interval and he'd looked surprised.

'We must do this again soon,' he said as he dropped her at her gate. Ought she to invite him in? She wanted to kick off her shoes, make a cup of tea. There *were* doubtless men who would fit in with her present way of life, who would make themselves at home. Not this one.

'My son's ringing at eight,' he said, absolving her. 'Thank you for a most pleasant afternoon.'

'Thank *you*,' she said. He gave her cheek a small peck and was off.

When he had gone she put on Pavarotti singing the Duke of Mantua.

★ ★ ★

Alan Watson had decided to suggest Paris to Judith as the place for a short New Year's break. She had thanked him for the suggestion, said she'd think it over and finally

told him she'd like to accompany him, but
. . . she had found it difficult to speak, had
blushed, until he'd taken her hand, said he
quite understood. Judith, realizing that single
rooms were harder to find than doubles, and
not wanting to make too pointed a request
— how was she to know exactly what she
might want? — suggested communicating
rooms, if he could find them. He promised
he would look; they were not going with a
travel company, they'd go by themselves and
he would arrange everything.

After this conversation in mid-November
their friendship had suddenly made great
strides. It didn't seem to her now so much a
matter of whether they became more intimate
but how and where.

'There's no need to rush things,' Alan said.
'Take things as they come. Your idea about
the rooms is a good one and we can each
have our own way! *I* shall go abroad with a
woman whose company I love, and *you* will
have a nice holiday with somebody to look
after you and no strings attached.' He was
absolutely direct, and she was grateful. She
believed him when he said: 'I would like to
go to bed with you, Judith, but my idea of
being close to a woman has as much to do
with living together and sharing things. I'm
no longer much of a rake.'

'Were you ever a rake?' she asked him with a glint in her eye.

'No — not really — I fell in love with my wife when I was twenty six and never looked at another woman whilst she was alive. I suppose I'm a bit boring.'

This conversation took place on another of their walks, after which he went back to the flat above the shop and she poured out to him things which she thought she had forgotten about her married life. It seemed to make things easier.

Alan was not a man whose thoughts were principally about his feelings but he had begun to feel quite excited about Judith in a romantic way that surprised him. Women had never been his chief preoccupation because he had been lucky to find Celia after several inconclusive affairs. The few months of his affair with Daphne were different, for he had been immersed in sorrow at that time, which he could forget only through bodily release, and had been grateful to her. His thoughts about her now, when he did think about her, were of a good old friend. Like many people, he could not exactly recall their love-making, or whether there had been anything special about it; he was much more inclined to think of her as a person of whom he had been fond and who had seemed fond of him.

His early memories of his wife were fresher, more real to him now, than those months with Daphne Berridge which had occurred later. He supposed it was something about the pain of that time that had blotted so much of it out.

He thought a lot more about Judith Kershaw than he ever remembered thinking about Daphne Berridge and, after she had told him those things about her husband, found he was aching to help her make up for her marriage which he had found an appalling one. Judith had said, after some of the revelations, 'I've never told anyone about him before — I thought if they knew what it was like being married to him, people would think I was a fool and that I must always have had bad judgement.'

He knew that she had wanted him to think about that, wanted him to realize he did not know everything about her yet. 'You were both very young,' he said. 'I wasn't fit to be married till I was twenty-six, and your husband was only twenty-two and hadn't had a very good example of married life with his own parents, from what you say.'

'It was the physical attraction that threw me over to him,' she said. 'I expect I was as bad as he was. It horrifies me now to think I had those children with a man I had *only that* in common with — I've never been able to talk to them about him. Yet he had some good qualities — at first he made me feel happy. I suppose that was youth too? But if I had accepted what he was like, the children would have had a curious upbringing. Two sex-crazed parents, a mother who put her husband first and overlooked all his carryings-on. I suppose some people survive that sort of family?'

'You got out of it,' he soothed, for he could see she was very upset, had never really come to terms with her past.

'Yes, I felt guilty about that. Did I do the right thing? I know other men have women on the side, and still expect their wives to be faithful to them. Not that there was much time to be anything else.'

'I don't see why you felt guilty,' said Alan. 'You weren't the guilty party — and why should you have accepted being a doormat?'

'Oh, I know women wouldn't put up with a man like Andy now — or they'd see through him earlier. Yet, Alan, you see, he *did* love me, he *did* marry me — I still think it could have worked if we hadn't had the children so quickly.'

He thought over her words after he got home. Was she trying to tell him she'd been a — he struggled to find the right word — a 'sex-pot'?

But his thoughts were not only about Judith's past, for he had other more philosophical concerns and there would always be times when he wanted to be left alone with them. Celia had been sympathetic, and probably glad to have a bit of time to herself too. She'd been a teacher of domestic science when he'd met her, a practical woman who until her illness had whisked him out of her kitchen when he would have been quite pleased to have been useful.

Since Celia's death he'd felt that he was only half a person; there had been nothing to balance his solitudes. Even Daphne had only restored himself to himself after she'd 'repaired' him, hadn't made him feel part of something bigger, that reflected the more general scheme of things. He needed Judith to integrate himself into the world for as long as was left to him. Not that he was sure that there existed any longer a whole world of which he could be an active part, or even a part at all, since recently it had gone mad and all the old certainties been thrown into confusion by changes on the international scene, symbols to him of the transience of everything. Daphne belonged to that now distant time of nuclear disarmament, the Cold War, full employment and muddling through. Of course then he'd been comparatively young, about the age Judith was at present. Daphne and he had both aged and when he saw her or had a chat with her she gave the appearance of having come to terms with that. He'd wondered why she'd come to live in the village after so many years in the city, and had at first ignobly asked himself if she were on his trail. Did she know he was also to retire to the village he'd lived in when he taught at a nearby grammar school? But she had known the place long before he had, might even have been a little annoyed to find him resolved upon living there too. He looked at it that way round and castigated himself for being self-centred. She'd probably forgotten all about him.

He mustn't act selfishly towards Judith. If he wasn't necessary to the younger woman he must bow out of her life. Why should he think he was the one to rescue her? Perhaps *she* felt 'whole' enough, with her shop and her re-discovered painting? But there was still time for her to make a new life for herself, and he felt sure that he could help her to do this, didn't want to change her character in any way. She'd had a bad experience of men, that was all, and if that had taught her caution, she knew that he

210

was fairly cautious himself and was serious about her. He wasn't to rescue her so much as give her a better life. They each needed another person to complement them; each needed intimacy. He didn't come as her saviour, for she could save him too from the narrowness of enforced widowerhood. Their future intimacy had to be thought about, and experiments made. Meanwhile, they needed change. Paris for a few days would give them both a new insight into each other.

Judith was very friendly with Daphne and he wondered if Daphne had ever told her about their affair. Somehow he didn't think she would have done. He thought about his notion of a 'sex-pot'. The word had an old-fashioned ring. Judith wasn't a child of the liberated sixties so much as one whom they had by-passed. Sex was a shortcut anyway, as they both knew, and that might work to both their advantages.

The day after the visit to her flat he sat for a time at his table in the angle of the sunny living room from which he looked out on to the park. The bungalow was built on rising ground, its garden sloping to the wall beyond which he could see paths intersecting in the middle of the open land, but not the war memorial, unless he stood on a chair and craned his neck round. He always took his breakfast at the window and read *The Times*, or the *Independent*, having become irritated with the *Guardian* and chary of the *Telegraph* which he'd always considered a newspaper for the old. He looked forward still to every new day and kept himself busy with a bit of consultancy work — research for a university department on the teaching of mathematics, set up in opposition to the sort of progressive ideas that his college had once favoured.

Well, he said to himself, there are at least a dozen years ahead before I can call myself old. He took exercise daily and though he was on the short side, he wasn't fat, only sturdy. His eyesight was still good; his hands still obeyed him when he had carpentry to do or repairs round the house; his hearing was excellent, and he still had his own teeth, which many men of his age were without, growing up as they had done before the miracles of fluoride in the water. His hair, which was dark, had not gone grey but had a few white hairs in it. One day he might be totally white-headed, not a greybeard.

He enjoyed cooking and driving and listening to his vast collection of compact discs. His pension, along with the fees for his consultancies, was adequate for a reasonable life. His life insurance had matured only that year. He sat on at his breakfast table thinking of these things before washing up. Would Judith want to go on with the shop if she accepted the formal proposal of marriage he intended to make her? How would he get on with her boys?

A short sigh escaped him as he got up and put his dirty dishes on to a tray and went into his modern, compactly fitted kitchen. He wanted to get to know her better, wanted to get closer to her, but did not want to put her off with too much appearance of impetuosity — she'd had enough of that years ago with Kershaw. But he didn't want to appear half-hearted either. He wanted her to take him as he was, if he was worth taking.

Alan did not esteem himself a good conversationalist for he tended to be quiet and unemphatic in manner. She might find him boring? But he was a sound sort of fellow, he thought. He was touched that she'd mentioned he might still have children if he found a young enough partner. That thought had not occurred to him more than once or twice. It was too late. It had been Celia who had been barren, a terrible tragedy for her but one they had rarely spoken about. She'd had tests, and so had he, and after that they'd put it out of their heads — or he had. She'd once said she didn't want to adopt, it was the

213

giving-birth part she said she'd missed. As she was good at her job she'd continued with it and looked after other people's children, teaching in the comprehensive school. No, he wasn't the sort of chap who would want to marry a woman half his age in order to have a son and heir. He would have adopted if Celia had wanted that. As for Judith, he thought, as he wrote out his shopping list, she'd had quite enough of children. He'd be a good stepfather, would not interfere, but would be there in case of difficulty. Whoa there! he said to himself — hold your horses, old man — after a few days in your company she might want less of you, not more. He did not consider that he might want Judith less, because he was sure that more of her presence would only make him keener.

She'd invited him to come round again the following Tuesday because she wanted to finish painting a landscape at the weekend. Tuesday would be the first day of December and he must finalize the holiday arrangements. Her eyes had shone at the mention of Paris. Four weeks to wait, and Christmas to get over first. Would she take the opportunity of inviting him round for Christmas? Three of her sons would be with her. He hoped she might. Or should he offer to cook for them all, invite them all round here? Yes, that would be a wonderful idea! Let the lads see their mother had someone who cared enough for her to cook her a Christmas dinner. The boys wouldn't want to stay too long, he supposed, would have their own pursuits. Judith said that the eldest, Stephen, had been a solemn child. The second boy, Mark, had the reputation of being a good draughtsman. He must have 'caught that from his mother, whom he resembled on photographs she'd shown him. The third boy, Ben, was 'clever', and the youngest, Colin, more practical. He'd seen Colin once or twice on his bike round the village. He tried to put himself in their shoes: never knowing a father, or not for long, being with a mother who was over-worked, and then suddenly finding she'd a man friend.

Would they be jealous or relieved? That was one bridge he wouldn't try to cross until Judith made up her mind. In the meantime he'd invite her and the three eldest over and let her do the explaining if she thought it necessary. He must make it clear she must keep her own bank account, he reflected, as he closed the door carefully behind him. He was scrupulous in that way, always had been — and he wouldn't touch a penny of her own savings which she'd need to help the boys. He'd add to them.

The first day of December arrived and Alan made his way over to the shop at five o'clock. Usually they met on Wednesday, half-day closing, but she'd said they could have a supper together if he'd help her with the accounts. She was still in the shop when he arrived, selling a watering can to an old lady. Curious time to be buying that, he thought. When the woman had left the shop, after taking an age to count the money out from her purse, he went up to the counter. Judith was sitting on a high stool she kept for climbing up to the goods that were too far up for her. He told her she should have a stepladder, that she might fall off the stool, but she laughed and said it kept her young.

'Sure you won't come out with me? We could try that new restaurant up on the Woolsford Road I told you about. You'll be tired after all this.'

'No — honestly, I'd like to have a cosy evening,' she replied. 'You have to see me at my worst — '

He laughed and they locked up the shop, put off the strip lighting, and went up the stairs at the back. He could smell dinner smells as soon as she opened the door of the flat. 'A stew,' she said. 'I did it at lunchtime and put it on low in the oven. Sit down, help yourself to a drink — there's some sherry — I know it's early but I'm always hungry after work.'

She disappeared and he poured himself a Tio Pepe and took the newspaper up from the low table, the *Independent* this time.

He kept up with current affairs, had even written a diary of the events surrounding the pulling down of the Berlin Wall, and was soon immersed in the reports from Bosnia. In politics he regarded himself as middle-of-the-road. So far, he and Judith had not got round to discussing such things, though a few remarks she had made about the present government had alerted him to the fact that her busy life had not prevented her from having opinions on matters other than milk-jugs. He knew she did not go to church, though he had a vague idea that one of her sons had played the organ in the Anglican church in the village. He himself was an agnostic, like most of his acquaintances and friends, but he had found in himself a growing respect for what were called traditional values, which did not mean reactionary ones. Born after the war, Judith would not remember the world as it had been in his boyhood. He remembered talking once with Daphne about that time and he had become angry about what he'd called the new abnegation of conscience. She had seemed to agree, with certain reservations. Even Judith said she sometimes felt a stranger now in the present world of grab and run. Yet you could not ignore the last thirty years of social change. Even here in the village, people led lives beyond the dreams of their grandparents' generation. If there were one place left where folk refused central heating, video recorders, washing-machines and dishwashers it would be up here with its long history of puritanism and thrift, work and stoicism. But it was only the oldest generation who refused them now and he did not go without these things himself. The old ways all belonged to a time, not a place, he thought. Daphne had once said something like that. Would the woman he now heard busying herself with pots and pans and cutlery think he was 'old' for remembering and approving of some of the older ways? Oh well, he wasn't looking for a slim blonde under thirty-five, would find it hard to become intimate with one. Judith could never have been like that; she was old for her age in some ways. It shouldn't be too difficult for them to get together. Intimacy might have its embarrassments at first, he thought, as he used her bathroom, saw her toothbrush neatly hanging up, and registered the tights hanging on the heated rail.

Judith, whipping some defrosted raspberries into a bowl of fool, itself bought from the village 'supermarket' on a quick Saturday sortie, was aware that she would have to do something soon to help him out. The easiest way when she was young had been an uncomplicated sensuality — but look where that had got her. She had forgotten how it felt, but she liked Alan to be close to her and liked the touch of his hand on her arm. It was hard for him to know what to do she supposed.

She went back to tell him to come and eat his supper, unless he wanted another drink. She'd uncorked a bottle of Côtes du Rhône that she thought might go with the tender beef and it was waiting on the table for him to taste. The sherry must have emboldened him, or perhaps the sight of the forlorn little toothbrush, for he put down his glass, went up to her and enfolded her affectionately in a tight hug. She looked surprised but let him keep her like that for a moment before saying: 'You can pour me a drink of wine and tell me if it's all right.' He held her then at arm's length, smiling, and touched a strand of her hair. The last person who had given her such a hug was her youngest, Colin, when he was twelve. She nearly told him but thought better of it.

The beef was delicious. 'I keep thinking I ought to become a vegetarian,' she said. 'But then I taste good meat and my ancestral habits return.'

'The wine is just right,' he said.

'Oh, I'm glad! I do drink wine occasionally and Stephen brings me a bottle now and then.' They hadn't drunk wine very often twenty years ago. It had been more of a treat, and Andy had preferred warm beer. Buying wine for your own consumption might be the beginning of a slippery slope.

'You're a good cook,' he said.

'Not really — years of feeding children makes you lazy.'

'I should have thought lazy was just what it wasn't.'

'Well, you know — it's enough to make regular meals without cooking them for fun as well. Men are usually better cooks because they do it only now and then — not you, I know *you* cook a lot — '

She thought: he's so self-sufficient, I'm sure he can do most things better than I can.

He thought he'd have to convince her, so said: 'I'd have been bored having to turn out two meals a day for five people, you're right.'

He wasn't self-important, not the sort of clubbable man who preferred the company of men.

'Men depend on women,' he said, taking more of the stew from the smart blue casserole.

'Have you made all the arrangements then?' she asked boldly. 'For Paris?'

'Yes — and I've booked in at a little hotel on the Left Bank — near the Luxembourg Gardens.'

'What date do we go?'

'The 30th — in a month.'

'I've only been to Paris twice,' she said. 'Once with school and once to sketch with my cousin Linda who was at the art school with me.'

'Perhaps it will snow and we'll have a white New Year.'

She served the raspberries. She told him about her Christmas arrangements. 'Mark may only come for the day,' she explained. 'He's got a girlfriend in the Midlands who's invited him home.'

'Oh well, if you're only to have him for one day — I thought perhaps it would give you a rest if you all came to *me* for Christmas dinner — but he'll want to have you to himself.'

'No — he's made *his* arrangements — I'll make mine! There'll be four of us, and Colin has promised to telephone from Canada on the afternoon of Christmas Eve.'

She felt, now I've burned my boats. But what a pleasant change not to have to cook the turkey!

'Then you *will* come — oh I am pleased!' He did look pleased.

'If *you* will come over on the Eve for a drink round the tree. There's an old auntie, my mother's sister-in-law, who always comes then — let's give her a surprise!' She felt reckless.

'How long is the French holiday to be?' she asked him when they were drinking their coffee back in the sitting-room.

'Five days. We could go to Notre Dame for the New Year's Eve service? And eat to our heart's content every day.'

Then she felt like saying: I'll have an affair with you, Alan, even perhaps live with you, but I can't commit myself yet to anything else. We'll have to see how we get on. Compatibility throughout the day was more important than nightly passion.

'I haven't had that sort of holiday for

years — holidays are more fun with someone. The boys wanted me to go away by myself last year and stay with a cousin in Devon but I just didn't feel like it.'

'We can go away whenever the shop can be shut,' he said. 'Lots of the old United Kingdom I don't know — Northumberland, the Highlands . . .'

'Oh Alan — you want to spoil me!'

'Yes,' he said. 'I do.'

★ ★ ★

Judith told Daphne about the projected holiday when she saw her in the village the following Saturday. 'My sister and her husband are coming to me,' Daphne said. 'I was going to ask you all to come round but I'm glad Alan Watson's going to do the Christmas cooking for you. You must come over with the boys another time they're with you.'

'How's the book, Daphne?'

'I've just begun it — the first draft anyway, and that's always the best time. I promised to reread *Sense and Sensibility* for the next meeting of the Norwood Reading Circle as well, and I haven't really got the time. You ought to come along to the meetings — they need younger people — all *our* perspectives

223

are similar. Younger women would have different ideas.'

'I don't honestly think I could find the time,' said Judith.

'Never mind — I didn't really think you could. I suppose it's for those of us contemplating life rather than living it,' replied Daphne a little grimly.

'You and your sister and her husband must drop in at my place at Christmas — before the others go off on their walking holiday.'

'I'll see if I can bring them round on Boxing Day then.'

'I wish I had a sister. Christmas was always a bit lonely at home me being an Only. It's strange, my mental picture of Christmas is of the ones when I was a child. Do you find that too?'

'I suppose because someone else did all the work then! The holiday'll be a nice change for me — stop me working all through the holiday.'

'Is your niece Cressida coming to stay with you as well?'

'I'm not sure. She's invited but she may prefer to go to her sister's — Jessica has a little boy.'

Judith was glad that Daphne was to have visitors. Christmas must be an odd time for people who lived by themselves.

10

Daphne looked up from *Sense and Sensibility*. It was hard to imagine Marianne at fifty. Perhaps Colonel Brandon would have died by then. Elinor would be a serenely amused grandmother, whilst her sister would be writing letters, or playing the piano, an adored great-aunt. Somehow she could not imagine Marianne with children even with plenty of servants to help her. But Elinor might have died, worn out from a pregnancy every fifteen months or so? That sort of thing had distressed Jane Austen.

Austen heroines were about twenty when they married, some even younger, though *Persuasion's* Anne had reached the great age of twenty-seven. The novels ended when there was simply nothing else for the heroines to do but get married. They were perfect specimens of romance, with spirited girls for female readers to identify with, dashing young men for them to daydream over, and kindly — if not quite so dashing — thirty-five-ish men for them to consider carefully. And there was always the happy ending.

Did this need for things in real life to end happily owe its existence to novels, or was it the other way round? So-called happy endings in novels were not endings but beginnings. All they told you was that the heroine had got Mr Right, the best man in the circumstances, the one who would be best for her in the eyes of the author and the sensible reader — who was sensible only because the reading of such novels had taught her what to think. Nobody ever asked if the woman was the right one for the hero. The older characters tended to be caricatures. She searched in her mind for marriages of older women but could not for the present recall any. Even Judith would be regarded as old in such novels; as for herself — beyond the pale!

She and Charles had never been able to put the rightness or wrongness of each for the other to the test. I don't think I could have been happy with him for ever, she thought, though he might have been with me. They had both been robbed of the opportunity to find out.

Daphne had always regarded marriage as a burning of the boats. Even in an age of easy and frequent divorce, she still did. In spite of knowing that the end was only a beginning she still saw it as drawing a line under a page: THE END.

As she read she continued to think on and off of marriages, and beginnings, and endings and thought about her fellow readers too: Sonia's gesturing hands and conversation; Evelyn's unhappy temperament; Gwyneth Coultar's amiability and other-worldliness; Lydia's strong sense of herself; Dorothy's goody-goodyness. Judith Kershaw's stoicism, for that matter.

Sonia had said one knew oneself in a way one could never know others, saw a self from the inside out, different from what other people saw. Was there any hope now of someone else discovering one's inner self? It shifted, presented itself differently to different people, unlike a character in a novel 'fixed' for ever by the novelist, described, given certain words to utter and certain actions to perform . . . How would anyone describe *her*, and would their description have any connection with the self she thought she knew?

The novelist and the poet: Jane and Anne. Different as they had been in their domestic and financial circumstances they had both lived in the same England, very different from the present one. Had they both expected to marry, have those children every other year till they were about thirty-nine? Had each recognized her own genius or talent? One had died at Judith's present age, left her novels to survive her for as long as people read; the other had also died a spinster, left one slim volume which only people like herself bothered with. They had both had women friends, the way women still did, for women's closest friendships were usually with other women. Jane's family circle was close-knit, especially when the nieces and nephews came along. Had Anne had any nieces? There was so much she had not yet discovered. Both of them had had one sister, and Jane, with one seriously rich brother amongst others, had not been averse to money, though she satirized those who had wealth and no breeding. Neither woman had direct descendants. Those were what most women would have wanted above all. Grandmothers talked together, enjoyed common memories, as the women in the Norwood circle did, still perhaps rivals as they had been thirty years before over their own children. As they grew old they would discuss change. There must always have been a lot to be said for one's own generation.

Would Anne and Jane have had anything to say to each other? Anne might have felt shy, less socially secure than Jane? Their political and religious opinions would have differed.

. . . I am supposed to be reading *Sense and Sensibility*, she said to herself, not thinking about women and families. She put her spectacles on again and began to reread the novel.

★ ★ ★

Sonia looked round her sitting room in preparation for the December meeting. Her turn had come round once again. However much she cleared up, her house never looked tidy. Too much clutter-books and papers, and plants that never looked as healthy as Lydia's, and pictures and photographs. Never mind. Bob was upstairs working on his computer. Supper had been cleared away, cushions plumped up, and the far from empty room would soon be full of the reading circle. Would Joy and Mrs Reeve come this time? There wouldn't be space if they did.

Only ten more days to Christmas, or what people called the holiday season — the busiest time of the year for those women with families coming home.

Gwyneth's ring at the door was the first, other-worldly soon-to-be-a-grandmother

Gwyneth. Sonia was delighted, for she had not been sure she could come. She hung up the green cloak that looked as if it had once been the uniform of her boarding-school.

'Sorry I haven't finished the book this time — I didn't want to rush it. I brought you some Indian nibbles.'

Sonia took the bag of crisp little twiddley bits and ate one. 'Thanks — I'll brew you some herbal tea if you don't want coffee — you can sip it and go on reading before the others come.'

The others soon arrived — Dorothy, Daphne, Lydia, and finally Evelyn after some fuss about parking.

When the coffee cups were drained and the biscuits crunched and after the minutes of the last meeting had been read they all opened their books. Evelyn said: 'The girls are so young — how can we learn anything from them? They're still full of hope, aren't they?'

'There's always hope,' said Gwyneth. 'You needn't be young to have that!'

Dorothy gathered her thoughts. 'Well, Marianne isn't very happy in her misery, is she?' Dorothy had always sympathized with sensible Elinor Dashwood because when she was as young as Elinor she had not worn her heart on her sleeve either. What had

Marianne really wanted? Was all that passion just the polite early nineteenth-century way of describing what people now called sex? Why did some people need falling in love and exaltation to make them willing to continue to propagate their species? Passion was not of course women's prerogative and lust did just as well for most people. Even in her youth, Dorothy had scorned being 'in love' in Marianne's way but had also disapproved of lust.

Lydia said, 'So long as she can hope for something from Wilberforce she's happy. It's when she knows there is no hope she breaks down.'

'Men are different from women,' said Evelyn pontifically.

'I think we should stick to the book tonight,' said Dorothy.

Sonia thought her sitting room looked quite pleasant now, the flames from the 'Victorian' gas fire behind its brass grating casting a soft glow over Dorothy, nearest the fire in an easy chair, cheeks flushed. Hands on lap, Lydia was sitting straight-backed as usual, legs crossed at the ankle, eyes on nobody. Gwyneth was wearing a mustard wool shift and was as usual looking out of the window whose curtain Sonia had forgotten to draw. Evelyn, away from the

231

fire, a little apart from the others, did not yet need reading-glasses because she was short-sighted. Sonia envied her for this if nothing else. Daphne Berridge was sitting next to her, wearing navy blue cord trousers and a long bright blue velvet tunic matching a rope of blue beads. She had placed her book and file on a nearby table but was holding a pencil between her fingers. Daphne always looked whoever was speaking straight in the eye, never let her attention flag even if they were talking about a matter irrelevant to the novel they were discussing.

'More coffee in a moment — and mince pies,' she said, rousing herself from contemplation of her friends. There would be plenty of mince pies left for Christmas. One thing she always did was to buy them in large quantities from Marks and Sparks. Ralph and Anna would be coming home for Christmas so all she bought were sure to be eaten.

I'm looking forward to their arrival, she thought, her mind not yet completely on *Sense and Sensibility*. Nowadays, events to which she looked forward she often enjoyed in a bitter-sweet sort of way, not to do with the disappointment that can follow too much looking forward, but because she went further into the future and imagined the treats or the visits already in the past. Soon her children's visit would be over and she'd be looking back on it. Bob and herself, she often thought, did not belong any longer to their children's present time. The years passed ever more quickly now, one Christmas sliding into the next.

She made an effort and said: 'I wondered what Marianne would be like when she was middle-aged or old.'

'Yes, so did I,' said Dorothy.

'It's so tempting to speculate, isn't it?' said Daphne. 'We know we should not but we do.'

'The characters go on resonating, don't they?' said Sonia. 'After they both get what they want.'

'Or need to have,' said Dorothy.

'Marianne wants everything, including the wrong man. She gets a much better bargain in the 'old' Colonel,' Lydia put in.

'And Elinor will not allow herself to hope too much,' said Daphne. 'She's not deluded.'

'She's in love, though,' said Sonia. 'Do you think Ferrars was *any* young woman's ideal man? He's not much like Mr Darcy, is he?'

'Well, she does not have to make do with him or settle for him,' said Daphne. 'Elinor and the author know better than the readers or the other characters, don't they? He's just what she needs and therefore, being sensible, she wants him.'

'Why is *she* allowed to be sensible and not her sister?' asked Evelyn. 'It's all weighted to come out right in the end, so does it matter?'

'You mean all poor Marianne went through was unnecessary? A storm in a feminine teacup,' suggested Daphne.

'Well, it does seem a lot of fuss for nothing when she's not going to marry Willoughby.'

'Common sense is not given to all,' said Dorothy.

'Nor 'sensibility',' said Sonia. 'Do you wish you'd been born with more of the first or the second? I wish I'd been more rational and enlightened when I was young, more like Elinor — '

'I don't believe you!' said Daphne. 'I was thinking that Elinor was the sort of woman Charlotte Brontë thought Jane Austen was — and could not abide. But I think Jane Austen herself had been a Marianne.'

'Marianne is only sixteen after all at the beginning — it's a lot to ask of a sixteen year old — to be sensible. It's her sister who's more unusual,' said Dorothy.

'I haven't much sympathy for her,' said Lydia.

'Well, we have more for Elinor because she's so unselfish as well as more sensible,' said Dorothy.

'People *expect* young women to be Mariannes,' said Evelyn. 'You all do.'

'She understood both, I think,' said Sonia.

Lydia polished her smart bifocals with a silky cloth from her brown handbag.

'Romantic girls have always existed,' said Daphne, 'but it doesn't mean that they were always selfish girls or silly girls.'

'But she is very silly, is Marianne,' said Evelyn severely.

'Well, I admit she's very provoking — so totally self-obsessed.'

'Like everybody nowadays,' said Dorothy with a sigh.

'She's taught a lesson,' said Evelyn.

Dorothy took her book and quoted from it: 'At nineteen she finds herself 'submitting to new attachments, entering on new duties, placed in a new home, a wife, the mistress of a family, and the patroness of a village'.'

'Ugh!' said Sonia, 'Poor thing! Was it meant to sound like a punishment?'

'They all had money,' murmured Lydia.

'Yes. Ferrars had two thousand and Elinor one thousand,' said Daphne.

'Pounds. A year. Think what that would be now,' pursued Lydia.

'Marianne could not love by halves,' said Sonia. 'She'd have been the same if she'd been poor.'

'Difficult nevertheless to find a man she could 'esteem strongly' and also have a lively friendship towards,' suggested Daphne, wondering whether Roger Masterson might possibly be one.

'Did none of these women fall in love when they were older?' asked Lydia. Daphne looked at her sharply.

'Not much chance with their 'new duties',' Sonia said.

'She settled for common sense and a good husband — a lot to receive at nineteen,' said Dorothy.

'She's such a snob though, Jane Austen,' said Evelyn. 'Those Steele girls — I know they're meant to be vulgar but it wasn't their fault they were poor.'

'I think the whole book is about how to behave,' said Lydia.

'Marianne reminds me of Maggie Tulliver,' said Sonia. 'But Marianne conforms to society in the end and poor Maggie has to die partly because she can't. I can't help taking sides — I know if the world were full of Mariannes it would probably end in anarchy, but still — '

'It *is* ending in anarchy,' said Evelyn.

'What do you mean?' asked Gwyneth.

'Well, poor Elinor wouldn't get a chance now, would she? Everybody is doing their own thing!'

'Only in the West,' said Daphne.

Sonia said, getting up to see to more coffee; 'I admit I'm more partial now to Elinor than I used to be when I first read the novel years ago. It's so brilliant — almost my favourite of hers, I think. Except perhaps *Emma*.'

'Or *Persuasion*?' suggested Daphne.

'Oh, I prefer *Pride and Prejudice*,' said Evelyn. 'It's much funnier.'

'It's not about happiness, is it, this book?' asked Gwyneth. 'It's about growing up, like *Great Expectations*.'

'Growing up morally,' said Daphne. 'You are right to compare them.'

'Morally being the way the author and her favourite characters saw it,' said Dorothy.

'Could you have a male Marianne?' asked Sonia idly, pausing at the door.

'Willoughby?' asked Lydia. 'No, I suppose as he marries for money in the end he must be on the wrong side — sacrificing love for money.'

'I don't think there are many male

237

Mariannes,' Daphne said.

As she made more coffee in the kitchen Sonia was thinking that the novel didn't deal with experiences beyond the meaning society gave people to make sense of their lives and choices. It was anchored in only one sort of 'reality'. Probably that was why Charlotte Brontë didn't like its author, however much Marianne swooned over trees and Elinor painted them. Was there always something missing from your life if you were a Marianne who had conformed, something not missing from Elinor's life? If romantic love and heady enthusiasms perforce disappeared, anxieties and routines would take over. How would Marianne have managed Christmas? She'd have wanted to make it exciting, no doubt exhausted herself trying to please everybody. For married Mariannes must 'woman's work' always be against the grain?

'What will you be doing for Christmas?' she asked Lydia when she came back to the group in the sitting-room. It was very quiet except for the rustling of pages.

'Tony's invited me for Christmas lunch,' replied Lydia. 'I shall go over to him but not stay too long.' She won't put them up, thought Sonia. That's why she bought a small flat, so she'd not have to.

Dorothy said complacently: 'I'm having

238

the children and all the grandchildren.' We guessed that, thought both Daphne and Sonia.

'Zoë and I are getting together in Berkshire for Christmas at her flat,' said Gwyneth. 'Zoë will do the cooking — it will be nice'. No mention of her daughter's man, the father of the coming baby.

'My daughter in law has offered to do the turkey — for once,' said Evelyn. 'I'm looking forward to that.'

'I'm having my sister and her husband and my niece,' offered Daphne feeling she might as well sound virtuous.

'I am a servantless housewife and superannuated mother,' Sonia murmured to her. 'If you want to come over on Boxing Day you'll be welcome.' She'd already asked Evelyn, feeling she ought to cheer her up. Perhaps she was trying to be too much of a Pollyanna.

'Next meeting at Gwyneth's,' said Dorothy. 'That all right, Gwyn? It's *Vanity Fair* — we'll need two or three meetings for that, I think.'

'It is *very* long?' asked Evelyn plaintively.

'Yes,' said Sonia. 'Very.'

'Perhaps we can persuade Joy to come in the New Year?' Dorothy said.

'And Mrs Reeve,' said Sonia. 'Though

I'm beginning to doubt she'll ever turn up. I haven't seen her for ages but she keeps sending me these little notes.'

On the doorstep, as they left, Evelyn said solemnly 'Happy Christmas, Sonia. Thank you for having us.'

'Happy Christmas!' shouted Sonia, relieved her turn to entertain the group was over for a time.

The night air was frosty and clear. Christmas might not be too bad.

11

Cressida found the company of Jonathan Edwards comfortable. She had just enjoyed another concert with him and had returned home late, looking forward to a hot bath and bed, since next morning she had to get up early. There was some typing to do for a business in South Kensington whose computers had unaccountably gone berserk. She had worked in their offices before and knew the work might be boring but it was undemanding.

Her telephone rang. It was Patrick Simmonds who was to depart on the

Saturday for his working holiday in Japan. She had been dreading seeing him off at the airport but it turned out that he had no intention of her doing so.

'Come round for a drink tomorrow?' he suggested. Tomorrow was Thursday; he'd soon be gone.

'Won't you be busy packing?'

'Oh I don't need to take more than a toothbrush and a change of clothes. I can buy all I need in Tokyo.' He was to make the preliminary arrangements for an exhibition of Japanese nineteenth-century prints and paintings that had been influenced by English poetry.

'How's your Japanese?' she asked.

'Tolerable.' Patrick was clever, had done post-graduate work at the Institute for Oriental and African Studies.

'You will come then?'

She knew it was just for a drink. 'Will there be anyone else coming?'

'Oh, probably, but I'd like to see *you*. What about it, eh?'

Even if it had not been 'just for a drink', she knew their affair was now over. A whole year and a half of her life; it had been dragging its feet for months and since she returned from the north she'd only seen him at the races.

'Thanks — I've a lot of work to do tomorrow in South Ken but I could come over when I've finished it. About seven?'

'Lovely.' Then, with a tinge of compunction — he had a conscience, it seemed — 'Are you all right?'

'Yes — a bit sleepy. I went to a concert.'

He would know it had been with Jonathan Edwards.

'I'll see you tomorrow then. 'Bye.'

She put the 'phone down. If she allowed herself to be miserable she'd never get to sleep. Did she have no choice about the feelings appropriate to his departure from her life? Oh, she'd see him again — one day — but she was angry that he could so quickly change her mood, fill her with longing and sorrow and yearning and hopelessness. He didn't sound at all miserable himself. He had never been in love with her, never missed her. 'Could I *choose* not to miss you?' she asked aloud.

It was all such a waste.

She was certain they'd have been as happy together in the long term as each might have been with anyone else. But she could speak only for herself, and that was not enough.

She went to bed and cried. But there was a tiny grain of relief in her weeping. At that moment, if she could be part of his future

242

life she wouldn't have minded that he would never love her as she loved him. Yet even as she sobbed from misery she knew there was a selfish strand in her love. She wanted to arrange his future for him, wanted to build his own commitment for him. If they had never been lovers she could have released him more easily and he would then have taken his place among that treasure-box of lost opportunities which women like to keep only half locked up.

When she awoke the following morning she did not immediately think of him, which was unusual. Had her hopes finally given up the ghost, allowing her to breathe again in a brighter clearer air?

Instead she was still in the depths of a strange dream about a young strong-faced woman and an amiable looking young man. Why had she been sure the man was American?

The woman had been talking rapidly, standing behind a table by the window of a half-shuttered room. Only when she came out from behind the table did one notice she was slightly pregnant. Cressida felt the pregnancy in the dream as a sensation in her own body, a dragging feeling in the back.

The woman seemed to be explaining something to the man, who just smiled and tipped his chair back as he watched the woman speaking. There was the sound of shouting outside.

But then, unaccountably, the scene changed and there was a view of high mountains from a balcony where the same woman was now seated. Cressida opened her mouth to speak because she was part of this scene, was there, she knew, for some purpose of warning, when a small toddling child appeared under the balcony and she heard the woman say to someone outside the room, 'She's got out again!' Then a door bell sounded and Cressida knew she must answer it herself — and had awoken with the alarm clock sounding in her ears.

She was disappointed; both dreams had been accompanied by a feeling of importance, things to be settled urgently, so that she lay for some minutes after putting the alarm off trying to recall quite what it was exactly. Then she thought, that wasn't the same man I dreamed about when I was at Daphne's. But the dreams had had a similar atmosphere to the one of the man in the garden.

The draggy feeling in her back was still there, not the proof of pregnancy but a sign she was not, unlike the dream woman. She was certain that the half-shuttered room had been in Paris. Who was that woman? She must ask Daphne. Odd, dreaming her aunt's dreams for her, if that was what they were, muddled up with her own preoccupations!

She must telephone Daphne. Her mother had told her at the weekend that she and Cressida's father had decided to take Daphne up on her offer to spend Christmas in Heckcliff. It would be a change, and her parents could go off to Kendal straight after the festival to begin their walking holiday. 'Would you like to come to Daphne's too?' her mother had asked. 'Or has Jessica already asked you?'

Rebelliously, Cressy had asked herself why she should go anywhere for Christmas. It might be nice for once to stay in her own flat and have a few days' hibernating. But she knew that when the time came she'd wish she was elsewhere. Also, she liked the idea of Christmas in Heckcliff, the idea already mooted by Daphne. She'd telephone Daphne this very evening and accept. She had a good deal to sort out about a permanent job for herself, but she could put a decision off until the New Year. For the present the temping would do.

She shrugged on her clothes, made a quick cup of coffee, and was off to the station in no time on her way to the office of *Black Inc.*, her dreams clinging at first in loose

245

shreds around her head but soon dissipated by the walk and the exigencies of twentieth-century commuting. That made you live in the present all right.

★ ★ ★

Cressida had stayed only an hour or two with Patrick, had arrived home at ten, and immediately lain down for five minutes, feeling exhausted. Patrick had said 'goodbye' quite tenderly — but he had made sure his friends were there, his way of indicating that their affair was definitely over, never to be resuscitated. She had not broken down, had managed to appear cool and collected and she hoped that had surprised him.

She got up again, made a quick supper, having declined to eat out with Patrick and his friends, and read through the careers listed in the jobs supplement of her own newspaper. Publishers wanted assistants, and lots of firms wanted marketing staff, but the jobs were all so badly paid. She was dreaming over a job in the publicity department of a charity when her telephone rang. Probably her friend Lucy, with the latest instalment of her love life.

'Hello?' No, it was Jonathan, to say would she like to go to the Curzon cinema with him next Saturday — a new French film — and what about supper afterwards? She accepted, though she knew when the time came she'd want to stay in and brood. He knew she'd be feeling miserable; he was kind.

She listened to a tape whilst washing up and then went to bed at midnight and slept dreamlessly for eight hours.

The next morning, since she had no urgent work that day, she decided to telephone her aunt before telephoning her mother who would keep her on for ages with bits of news and enquiries about her work.

'Hello?' Daphne's voice sounded cheerful.

'Hello, it's Cressy — Mother said they'd decided to accept your invitation. May I too? I'd like to be out of London for Christmas if you're sure it won't be too much work. How's the book going?'

'Oh, Cressy — good — that'll be lovely — and you can all help with the cooking — I was just writing out some of Anne's verse — listen to this — '

She read:

Now winter lights in cheerful fire,
While jests with frolic mirth resound,
And draws the wandering beauty nigher,
'Tis now too cold to rove around . . .

'And it goes on

The Christmas game, the playful dance,
Incline her heart to glee:
Mutual we glow, and kindling love
Draws every wish to me —

'He goes through all the seasons — it's a man speaking — and only in winter does the lady allow herself to be caught — rather nice isn't it?'

'Yes. About Christmas too — '

'I was just thinking about Christmas when you rang. I'm so pleased you'll come — Jessy will have her hands full, your mother says, and I can put up both you and your parents in the two small spare bedrooms — '

'I think I dreamed again about the eighteenth century,' Cressida said, breaking in. 'A woman and a man. It had some connection with what you said about your poet, I think. But it wasn't Anne. She was pregnant, and they were in Paris — and then it changed and there were mountains — I've forgotten some of it, but — '

'That would be Mary Wollstonecraft,' Daphne said briskly. 'She was in Paris with her lover, Imlay — and then she went to Scandinavia two years later and wrote him scores of letters — they were published, you know — '

'How strange,' said Cressida. 'She *was* pregnant though, was she? In Paris?'

'Oh, yes — she had a daughter called Fanny in 1794 in Le Havre. After that she went back to Paris, and then to Norway with the little girl. Later she tried to drown herself from Putney Bridge.'

'She didn't look a suicidal type — she was talking a lot . . . '

'I think I told you a bit about her,' said Daphne. '*I've* been having some more interesting dreams too!'

'Are we mad?' asked Cressida. 'I mean how can we be sure we're dreaming the right century? It's weird — '

'We don't *know*,' answered Daphne. 'But I reflect a good deal on the people I'm researching or writing about — and you probably thought about it afterwards. Have you found that house yet I told you about?'

'No — but I mean to — I've been busy — and then, well, Patrick went off — '

'*I* was thinking about sisters,' said Daphne. 'And Christmas — and Anne's sister was younger than her and quite close — I'm reasonably pleased with what I've written so far — '

'I'm looking forward to reading it. I've

249

been looking for a job — '

'Have you found anything yet?'

'No, but there are distinct possibilities — I've decided not to drop everything to train to be a solicitor!'

'That friend of yours is one, isn't he?'

'You mean Jonathan? Yes — '

'I'm sorry your other man has gone off — but perhaps I shouldn't be — since he seemed only to make you miserable. That other chap — the solicitor — do you like him?'

Daphne was apt to come out with direct questions which Cressida did not resent as much as if they had come from her mother.

'Yes, I do like him as you put it.'

'He wrote to you when you were here, didn't he?'

'Oh, yes — *Patrick* was never one for letter writing. Jonathan says he'll help me to look for that house of Anne's — he's interested.'

Daphne thought, that's the one who loves her. I hope she'll be luckier than Anne with her 'Platonic' love.

'He says I ought to go back to publishing. I suppose I will.'

'Well you've a lot of experience with children's books, Cressy.'

'Yes, I suppose I have. Perhaps I'll be able

to dream up a story of my own!'

'I wouldn't be surprised. Anyway I'm looking forward to Christmas — '

'So'm I.' And she was.

'Must go — I can hear Widgery scratching at the back door,' said Daphne.

'Bye then — see you on Christmas Eve.'

'Bye for now, love.'

* * *

Daphne was making a list of people to whom to send Christmas cards. Each year she made one and then lost it so had to start afresh. She was gathering her forces for sorting out the next part of her book, was still stuck with Anne and her sister Elizabeth and brother Joshua in the 1780s. Joshua and perhaps Elizabeth might have painted small pictures for their friends and family, she thought, as she sorted through some charity cards bought on her last expedition to the village. No Christmas cards in Anne's day, so no way of Eliza harnessing her talents to turn an honest penny.

Daphne still had the worry about which 'Mr Dyer' Anne was unhappily in love with. The son of her employers, or the probable cousin, the critic of the same name? Either could be her 'Platonic' admirer. Anne was

251

still writing about the same man, whoever he was, in a veiled way, when her collection of poems appeared in 1795. But Daphne realized that poets gathered up all their best poems when it came to a book, some of which could have been written long before. Anne might be the kind of woman not to publish such verse until the object of her passion was safely out of reach, or married to someone else. According to all accounts she had certainly been depressed the year before the French Revolution broke out. Mary Wollstonecraft's likely pep talks to her had probably made her feel inadequate. Who would not have felt inadequate in the presence of such a whirlwind as Mary?

Not that Mary herself had fared any better with men. It was in the spring of 1793 that Mary had met her second *grande passion*, Gilbert Imlay, the American. By the August she was pregnant with his child, that first daughter who was to die by her own hand at the age of twenty two. In the October of 1793, whilst the twenty-four-year-old Anne lived her tranquil life in London, Mary was in the Paris of the Terror. The French Queen was guillotined the same month. How had Anne taken that? A traumatic month, that setting for Cressy's dream. Mary had spent Christmas 1793 in Paris with another English woman poet, a feminist like herself, one who lived with a man to whom she was not married. A good thing Imlay had pretended she *was* his legal wife — American nationality had kept her from being imprisoned in the Bastille, as another poetic friend was to be later.

They all seemed so far-fetched, their lives and loves, so far removed from Anne's quiet existence. She felt that Anne would not have fitted into this sort of life. She must have known about it, must have known that some ladies lived with their lovers even if they were driven to suicide attempts.

The high-principled Godwin, a man who could be a friend to a woman with similar interests, one who allowed a woman as much independence as he had himself had eventually married Mary, who had been pregnant with a second daughter, the one who was to cost her her life. Even the headstrong Mary had believed in committing herself in her relationships, had believed there might exist somewhere the ideal marriage partnership. However short her own life, she had produced two children, whereas Anne as far as anybody knew, had no consummated love and no children. Daphne tried to put herself into both Mary's and Anne's shoes but neither seemed to fit.

Christmas in Paris two hundred years ago was still in Daphne's mind as she finished writing her list of Christmas cards. She must tell Judith Kershaw about it all, for Judith would soon be there herself.

* * *

Stephen and Ben Kershaw arrived home together at tea-time on Christmas Eve. Ben could have come earlier but had been reluctant to leave London where he was working in the Senate House library. Mark had arrived unexpectedly the day before, had helped Judith dress the tree and had done the final shopping in the town. He was an extrovert young man and it was not long before Judith had winkled out of him more information about his girlfriend whom he'd first met in the town where he now worked. Judith found herself telling him more about her new friend Mr Watson, whom Mark would remember. 'He's invited me to spend a short holiday with him — in Paris,' she explained. 'For my painting,' she added lamely. 'Oh good,' said Mark registering her embarrassment. 'And he's invited us all to have Christmas dinner with him tomorrow,' she said, her face bent over a carton of Christmas baubles. 'That'll save a lot of work,' he said cheerfully.

'You don't mind then?'

'Why should I mind, Mother — you must make new friends. Can we have a look at your paintings?'

She brought her sketch book to show him after supper that evening. Of all her children he was the one who had inherited her 'eye'.

He told her about his own work in a graphic design studio and she listened carefully.

'Colin's going to ring tomorrow — at least I asked him if he would — as we shall be out on Christmas Day.'

'He sent me a postcard of Central Park — he's got this job in a large department store — did he tell you?'

'So long as he's happy. I worry about him you know — New York and all those muggings — and murders — '

She knew that Mark would tell Stephen about Mr Watson, of whom she had only spoken in a vague way over the 'phone, but had mentioned to Ben in a letter.

At Woolsford station the following afternoon Stephen and Ben were surprised to find they had both been on the same train. They arrived home to find a Christmas Eve tea already laid and Auntie Edith ensconced in the best armchair. Mark joined them for a moment in their bedroom where they dropped their heavy bags. 'Be nice to Mum's friend,' he whispered, 'here any minute — we're to go to him for the dinner tomorrow.'

'Old Watson?' enquired Ben.

'The same — Mum's obviously besotted.'

'Shh!' said Stephen.

'Weird, isn't it, though? He's called Alan by the way.'

'I know he is,' said Ben. 'She told me — in her last letter.'

Ben was the only one who wrote decent letters to his mother and therefore received letters back.

Judith had calculated that Alan would stay two hours or so and would return about six, taking Auntie Edith home in his car on the way. Then she could have a cosy evening with her boys.

They are all determined to please me, she thought when they came back into her sitting room with its Christmas tree and its ancient occupants. It *was* Christmas after all, though that had always been a festival when she had felt guilty that there was no 'Father' Christmas to fill stockings. She knew her sons were fond of her but probably not yet quite old enough to think of their mother as a person in her own right. Mother was Mother and they'd fall in with her arrangements. It would be different when they married, if they ever did. She hoped very much they would find nice girls and settle down. Mark had obviously found one.

Alan Watson arrived just as she was making a cup of tea for the old lady who came every Christmas Eve to her dead sister-in-law's daughter. She sat, dressed in her best, prepared to be entertained. Her husband hadn't had anything to do with the shop but how they'd worried about their poor niece left with those four boys . . . She was a grand girl though!

When Judith brought Alan Watson in she shook his hand with gusto. Christmas was nicer with a few men around. Not that those great boys weren't men by now. They had looked very large last year. She wanted to ask her niece how Colin was finding the States, but kept forgetting.

Mark came in then and shook hands with Alan. 'Do you still play chess?' he asked.

'Certainly,' Alan smiled. Mark had remembered that this was the master who had started a chess club at his school. 'Ben's a whizz at chess,' he said, just as his brother sidled in. Ben was the only one who was short-sighted, and his round spectacles, assumed from necessity, made him look quite fashionable. Ben shook hands too and then Stephen came in bearing the cake which Mark had kindly helped to ice that morning.

'We must have a game soon then,' said Alan to Ben.

Ben, who never liked to waste his time, said, 'Tomorrow? You're on.'

Stephen groaned. 'Last Christmas you played Tom Sutcliffe the whole of the holiday.' He was doing his best to come to terms with the fact that his mother and Mr Watson were obviously rather special friends.

Alan Watson moved over to make a fuss of Auntie Edith and was soon listening to her reminiscences. They all sat down eventually in the glow of the Christmas tree, with the ordinary electric lights out, and tucked into cake and mince pies. Judith was aware that the company was awkwardly assembled and was nervous. Perhaps it had been a mistake to mix the return of her sons with their introduction to Alan? She ought to have waited, let them have first call on her attention? Then she felt, no, I *won't* feel guilty, better get it over . . . The boys began to speak of their work and their friends and as the tea was being poured out for the second time the telephone rang.

'Colin!' exclaimed Judith. 'I wrote and

asked him to ring tonight if he wanted to catch us at home,' she said hurriedly to Auntie Edith. It *was* Colin, ringing from New York. A quadruple conversation, unintelligible to outsiders, was conducted, until Judith finally took the phone. 'We're all missing you — everything OK?'

'Fine — '

'Money holding out?'

'I've found this job in a big store — till mid-January — then I'm thinking of going west — I told you, did I, that Marvyn's here too?' Marvyn was a friend from school.

'He's all right,' said Stephen when she finally put down the 'phone. He patted her arm consolingly knowing that she would have liked them all together. He thought suddenly, it might be our last Christmas here. He was the most conventional of the boys, the most anxious.

They had to tell Edith what Colin was doing, and by the time another plate of mince pies had been demolished it was almost time for the old lady to say, as she did every year, 'Well, must get my beauty sleep.'

'Alan is going to take you home, Auntie, so there's no hurry and no need for a taxi,' said Judith, feeling she wanted a little more time before she had the family to herself. 'What are you doing tomorrow, Aunt

Edith?' asked Mark, knowing that the answer would be 'Going to my other niece,' as it was every year.

Stephen went out for a moment and returned with a bottle. 'You always said no drinks before six,' he said to his mother. 'This is for you — don't waste it on us.'

'Do you mind, Mum, I've a few things to do?' Mark asked.

A 'few things' meant that Mark hadn't yet wrapped up his presents. As she poured a glass of sherry for her aunt and herself, knowing Alan would refuse because he was driving an old lady home — even one drink was more than he allowed himself in the circumstances — Judith thought: they've behaved very well. She knew they would say nothing unless she did and wished for a moment that she'd had a daughter with whom she could be more intimate. Sons were lovely, but apt to withdraw from emotional conversations. Thank goodness though that they were grown up.

Soon after this Alan and Aunt Edith left, and Stephen switched on the television.

★ ★ ★

Daphne and her sister Mary were preparing supper for four. Hugh Miller was enjoying his

260

daughter Cressida's company by the fire in his sister-in-law's snug little house. He was a thin spare man who looked as if a suppressed energy was coiled in him. He never sat still for long. His other daughter, Jessica — 'Jessy and Cressy' they had called them throughout their childhood — resembled him, he always thought. 'Poor Jess — they haven't had a wink of sleep for three weeks, she says,' he said, knocking his pipe out on the hearth.

'You know she always exaggerates, Father,' said Cressida. She felt sleepy. She'd arrived only an hour ago in the cold air, and felt almost too warm now.

'Pity you can't come further north with us on Monday,' he said. 'A walk would do you good.' By a 'walk' her father meant proper fell-walking, for which Cressida was far too lazy, and anyway she had to return to London to find a job.

Hugh went out after supper for a short stroll, leaving the women talking. Whenever Daphne and Mary got together the talk was of the past. He heard it every year, as did his daughter, who wondered whether she and her sister would ever sound quite so nostalgic. Cressida had half-listened, sitting by the fire with a glass of Daphne's Southern Comfort. The sisters were still drinking coffee at the table.

She sprang up to help Daphne with the washing up and the peeling of the vegetables for the next day's Christmas dinner.

'Do you think that as we get further and further away from the time of your Anne that things get more and more different, or do ideas and beliefs come back like the horses on a merry-go-round?' she asked Daphne.

'I suppose the distant past changes according to our own perceptions — but people don't change, Cressy. I'm certain of that,' her aunt replied. Cressida wasn't sure if that was meant to be comforting.

* * *

Christmas Day dawned with a little rain. The weather had changed and now it was relatively mild for the Pennines, unseasonable. Cressida found herself wishing it would come cold again, like the day before, and snow. The sudden change was disconcerting, She helped Daphne further with her 'slaving over the hot stove' and the meal was a success. Jessica telephoned; Hugh went out for another walk before darkness fell, and the women gloated over their presents.

Over at Alan Watson's the four men and Judith sat over the deliciously cooked turkey, pulled crackers and toasted each other and their mother until the young men went out to clear their heads of Chateauneuf du Pape. Judith insisted on washing up, or at least operating Alan's dishwasher. She felt content, would have liked — a little flown with wine and company — to stay with him that night, but had decided beforehand that she would not. She and Ben and Stephen would have Boxing Day together. Mark was getting a lift to Birmingham in a friend's car.

There had been some arguing over politics, in which Alan had joined — and enjoyed himself. He rather missed the young, having spent much of his life teaching them. Ben was to play chess with Alan before they went home and the board was ready on a side table. Judith fingered the silk scarf Mark had given her, designed by himself in swirling colours of green and blue. Ben had given her a new novel and Stephen a large leather-bound diary, and her own presents of clothes had been received politely if not with rapture. She'd presented Alan with one of her landscapes, a pen and wash picture of a local beauty spot, and this Alan was now admiring. Did they look like an old married couple?

'Happy Families,' he said, looking up. 'I think it was that, don't you?' she smiled.

Christmas could have been a strain, and it had not been. He was sentimental. There were bound to be difficulties and she could not say that it was going to be like this always.

'I wish they'd stay on a bit — they always go off just when I've got used to them again,' she complained.

'Did you tell them about our holiday?' he asked.

'Yes — they seemed to think it was a good idea — Mark and Ben anyway. I'm not sure about Stephen, he's always been the one to worry about me.'

'I expect he remembers his father more than the others?'

'Yes — he was the one who did miss him at first. But his grandmother spoiled him — he used to stay a lot with her when I was busy with the little ones.'

'They're nice lads,' said Alan, and meant it.

* * *

Daphne and Mary and Cressida walked the longer way over to Judith's on Boxing Day. Daphne had decided not to accept Sonia's invitation. She'd rather see her alone. She glanced at the Grange as they passed but

264

knew Masterson was staying at his son's.

Stephen Kershaw was introduced, and invited Cressida to join him and his brother for a drink at the Black Horse at seven, an invitation she accepted. She had a pleasant evening talking about the law with Ben, and his job with Stephen. Ben was interested to know she had a friend who was a solicitor. 'Only three more years,' he sighed, 'and then I suppose I'll be one too.' They were a little younger than herself but she found Stephen an attractive young man and Ben intelligent. When they parted Stephen said the two of them must meet in London, but she found herself hoping she need not bother. She was looking forward to seeing Jonathan Edwards again. There was no doubt that those years between the early twenties and the early thirties made a big difference to young men, however pleasant they were at twenty-three.

The third day after Christmas, Mary and Hugh went off to Cumbria for the walking and climbing holiday. Cressy left her aunt the day after and the next day Judith flew to Paris with Alan Watson, her sons all back by then in the south.

Daphne was left looking forward to some solitude in the company of her notebooks. Not for long though. Roger Masterson had telephoned her just before Christmas with an invitation for New Year's Eve. 'A few couples from the old days — thought I'd give a little dinner. You'd be welcome too to see the New Year in.' She had said nothing about this to her sister.

She thought he'd sounded both hesitant and abrupt, unlike his normal controlled self. Was he nervous at introducing her to his friends? Had he for some inexplicable reason fallen for her? Did she want that? She'd appreciated the visit to the opera but had feared he had not enjoyed her company. If he'd been attracted to her in the way she *could* be attracted to him she'd surely have known? He hadn't even flirted with her. Maybe he'd forgotten how.

She ought to see him with his friends, see what he was like with them, though she would really prefer to spend her New Year's Eve with Widgery. But one ought to go out on the last night of the old Year. Was there something wrong with her which made her reluctant? Was it that she feared falling for this man? Or was she deluding herself? She did find him physically attractive — he'd kept himself trim, must always have been good-looking. But he hadn't found a woman of her age attractive, that must be it. Men of his age looked for women of forty — as the ads told you — and occasionally found them. Was he interested in her as a person, a mind? She doubted that too. Fifteen years ago she'd have quickly discovered. Now, it could be embarrassing, though she did not consider herself a woman easily embarrassed. What might he think of one who had never been married or divorced or widowed? She was an oddity, a throw-back . . .

If she took her car she'd not be able to drink more than one glass of wine and she did not honestly feel up to a party without wine. If she walked there he would only offer to drive her home. She decided to use the village taxi service and book a return journey for a quarter to one. That should be long enough, surely?

12

Christmas was in some curious way a safe season, thought Sonia. It must be because of childhood Christmas memories. Not like August, the month in which everything now seemed to happen — old wars, new wars, revolutions, counter-revolutions. Ever since Prague in '67 when the children had been little. Not too young to ignore Bob's depression though. He had been terribly down at the turn events had taken.

There was always plenty to do at this season, one which, redolent of the past, was each year to be lived in the present. She had gone on methodically shopping, wrapping presents, sending off cards and decorating the house, odd thoughts jumping in and out of her head whilst doing these ordinary things. At a time when everyone would be on holiday it made you realize that most people on the tight little, packed little, island were more or less all doing the same things, except for the homeless, the very young, the very poor, and the small number of Scrooges who shunned such festivities.

As far as she could ascertain from television programmes about them, the dispossessed young, living with few of the world's goods in unimaginable squalor on windswept dog-befouled housing estates, their only shops concrete huts selling drink and fags, were, perhaps inevitably, drugged out of their minds. They appeared to spend their time stealing cars, sometimes killing people during their 'joyrides'. A man pulled out the toenails of a sixteen month old baby he was supposed to be looking after. Twelve year olds beat an old man with his own crutches . . . .

Was anger or despair the most natural reaction to all this?

She read an article in the paper criticizing those who 'wanted to go back to three-lane highways and life without penicillin'. Then it was anger that was uppermost. 'Just remember when you are feeling nostalgic that you would not *really* want to go back to such a life,' a young man had said on television. 'Why can't we have the penicillin and do without the motorways?' she shouted at him.

Anna drove everywhere in her van, a world of mobility closed to Sonia unless others consented to chauffeur her. She envied those who took their cars abroad and drove round Europe exploring. Her fear and dislike of driving had made her disabled in this modern world of private transport. She ought to call herself 'differently abled', defective in her dealings with the internal combustion engine as with much else. It was all of a piece with her old failures to skate or swim or ride. As for going ski-ing, you might as well ask her to jump over the moon. She mocked herself: 'What good would *you* be in an older world, digging and planting to grow food, reading by candlelight, getting backache and bronchitis from the cold? You don't have practical skills — gardening and cooking are not things you could ever do well. Gwyneth would manage better than you.'

She tidied up the last of the leaves blown into the garden borders, and felt as virtuous as she did in the summer, planting and nurturing roses, keeping garden pots and urns filled with petunias and nasturtiums, but taking no pleasure in the digging, hoeing, mulching, weeding and spraying needed for more ambitious projects. Bob never bestirred himself horticulturally. At least she didn't buy plants from garden centres already in containers as Evelyn did. Lydia though was a gifted gardener.

* * *

It was true that there had been material progress. Did it matter then if hundreds of thousands of children could not read, or add two and three together, or that their old rhymes and games had been replaced by electric toys their parents could ill afford, and which broke on Boxing Day? She was just an old Puritan writ large, a hard-scabbed warrior from a bygone age who could not accustom herself to the present.

Anna's and Ralph's possible grandchildren, and the descendants of her friends' children, would be in this terrifying new world when

270

she and Dorothy and Daphne and the others were gone. She was afraid of the future, had no faith that evil would ever be eradicated. The world was at the mercy of certain wicked individuals and the misguided attitudes of the soft-hearted towards them. People like her would stand alienated on the margins of the brave new world of technology, speed and conspicuous consumption.

Lydia, who had been brought up on even stronger dogma, would say: 'Why bother? Nothing we do can alter anything.' She was resigned. When these trains of thought went round and round her head in the middle of the night, Sonia knew she was even more pessimistic than Evelyn.

Ralph, with whom she discussed these things, said that the future was by no means hopeless.

'You should have been born a generation earlier,' he said.

The religious festival approached and she decided that Christianity was an invention for trying to deal with evil, not the explanation of it. Jesus was just 'one of us', powerless to prevent evil, indeed a martyr to it himself.

Whenever she felt reasonably contented with her own life she remembered the people who might have been herself or her family and friends bombed to shreds in the Balkans. Tranquil innocent moments, peaceful happiness, had no defence against bombs, only a few of which could destroy beloved places as well as people — a peaceful estuary, an ancient village obliterated, moors and fields pocked and destroyed, Europe itself. Everywhere was open and vulnerable. The violence of the last war had been mostly unreal for northern children. The blackout, the rationing, the shelter drill had been accepted, but hadn't frightened them. Had her parents, Madge and Albert, been frightened? They'd never shown it if they had. 'Of course we shall win,' her father had said. England always won, didn't she? But her parents' generation had been content with little, and now were mostly dead from natural, not unnatural causes.

Bombs and violent men could not kill your past though, so long as you went on existing. But when the old had gone, their skills would go for good, replaced by computer brains.

Some people did not seem obsessed by fragility, went on cruises with complaisant husbands, expecting efficiency, and it seemed that trains and planes and boats still went on appearing as promised.

There was no doubt that action of some kind was the only antidote to all this introspection. A day of sorting and tidying, throwing away junk, cheered her up a little. The world had always been terrible; it was just that you didn't see it like that when you were busy growing up, then building other lives. Now you could hand over what Daphne called the relay bâton to your offspring, who had no time to agonize because they were too busy living. If she had had no children, would she have perhaps have cared less? 'Cheer up Sonia,' she said and went into the kitchen to make supper. Busyness would have to keep her going until after Christmas.

Sonia iced a Christmas cake, fiddling while Rome burned. She thought: Anna has built her defences through collecting the past. She went shopping with her daughter just before Christmas, amazed how people spent money like water, enjoyed acquiring underwear, cushions, lampshades ... *She* bought books and compact discs, those good things brought by technology, mostly to give away as presents because she felt guilty at having too much. A wartime childhood had left its mark.

★ ★ ★

She sat down one afternoon before Christmas to read *Vanity Fair*. Catapulted to the present, would the urbane Thackeray have been able to cope in such a changed world? Would Dickens — who knew all about sordid crime and hopelessness — have made it exciting, sinisterly interesting? Charlotte Brontë would be shocked but not frightened, having a place in her world for evil and pain and misery. All the novelists would have known about riots and scurrilous newspapers and despair, and old people dying from cold in filthy cottages, and carriage accidents rather than car smashes . . .

★ ★ ★

On Christmas Eve, she went to Norwood church with Ralph and Anna who wanted to sample a neighbourhood church service. Last year she had left them to it and they had reported a perfectly awful carry-on in the town with tambourines and people being saved. There was little likelihood of tambourines this year for they were in the parish church, the average age of whose congregation was nearer her own. The vicar was 'High'; the music was lovely and she'd done everything in preparation for the morrow, so she could sit back and enjoy it. Her mother Madge Hartley who had arrived that morning was already safely installed in a spare bedroom, had retired early. Now it was almost midnight.

The church here seemed Laodicean, neither cold nor warm, tolerant, moderate, in spite of the red robes of the clergy and the heavenly choir. The village was full of affluent elderly people possessing cars and dishwashers, spindryers and computers, who had settled here because they liked quiet orderly lives, a sherry in the evening, a bit of gossiping at the post office as long as it was not closed down in some privatization ploy. Most of the descendants of previous villagers were not here — the houses were too dear for them and they'd be lucky to get a council house.

On Christmas Eve Sonia always hoped for some small epiphany, some buried memory of childhood, some whiff of the past. Every December she hoped for a white Christmas but it hardly ever arrived. Years ago at this season it had always seemed very cold, a white world outside, and she and her brother Bill had taken turns to crouch down in front of the coal fire, backs still half-frozen. No central heating then.

'Amen,' she said as the vicar made the sign of the cross. Ralph looked sideways at her. He took great interest in religion.

Were Christians now truly supposed to forgive killers of the old and frail? she was wondering. Who were any of us to 'forgive' anyone else? How hard it must be for those of her parents' generation who were still alive, those who had truly believed in a Christian Hell and truly feared it if they misbehaved. They must feel bitter now when people gave rein to the seven deadly sins without fearing retribution.

'Were you having religious thoughts?' Ralph asked her as they came out into the darkness at about half past midnight.

'Not really,' she answered as Anna took her arm for the walk home.

'Damn!' she said when they arrived home, 'I forgot to take the mince pies out of the freezer.'

'Won't take a minute to heat them up,' said Ralph.

Bob came into the kitchen. 'How was it then, the Establishment?'

'A nice service. Lovely singing.'

'You ought to go more often,' said Ralph.

'Your pillowcases are on your beds,' she said. 'I did them before we went out. I'm going to bed — have to be up to put the turkey in the oven.'

Christmas certainly made you feel needed, if that was what you wanted, and family obligations were bearable if they did not occur too frequently. How luscious Anna looked, she thought, as her daughter stood sipping a mug of coffee. She hoped she would like the silk underwear that was wrapped up in her pillowcase.

On Boxing Day they were to entertain a few neighbours and some of the children's friends as well as Evelyn and her family. Daphne had telephoned to say she could not manage it. Sonia's mother was to stay over until the evening of the twenty-sixth when she would go on a visit to her son Bill. Then, thought Sonia, she'd be able to flop down with a book, banish all thought with a drink — and be relieved it was all over for another year.

* * *

On Christmas Day Sonia cooked the lunch which everyone said they enjoyed, including her mother. Once the washing-up was done and a cold supper laid on trays she went back into the large warm sleepy sitting room as dusk was falling. Madge had dropped off for a snooze, but sensing her daughter was back in the room, immediately opened her eyes and suggested a card game.

'Or Cluedo,' suggested Anna, eating chocolates and reading one of her presents.

'Where's Ralph?'

'He went up to his room for a read — you

know he always does,' said Anna. Hugh was looking through the new videos he'd found in his stocking. 'Sit down, Mummy — you'll be tired — I'll fetch Ralph and we'll play whatever Granny would like,' said Anna. Sonia was sure she'd never been so solicitous to her own mother when she was young.

Ralph came in and said, 'A lovely quiz for you, Ma!'

'Oh, is it a puzzle?' enquired Madge, brightening up. There was nothing she liked so much as puzzles, which she would win, or Scrabble, or crosswords.

'How to tell your character from the Christmas presents you have bought and received,' Ralph read out. 'If you have six or more items the same it says you are fundamentally well-balanced and with friends who understand you.'

'Go on,' said Madge who always gave cheques.

'Well, Mother?' pursued Ralph.

What might be family jokes would be argued about by Madge. It had been tacitly agreed by the four Greenwoods that any argument that might blow up, any minor unpleasantness of family life, would be ignored and later discounted if the presence of this oldest member of the family disrupted hidden boundaries of argument.

Ralph sat down and ate his way through a large bowl of nuts. Anna handed round chocolates.

'In my day,' said Madge, 'a box that size would have lasted us a week!'

Ralph caught his mother's eye and winked. He was inclined to see his grandmother as a character, in a 'when we were lads we lived in boxes' comic turn.

'Mother loves quizzes,' he said to Madge. 'She still wants to know what she is really like, her real self. But the quizzes only tell her what she's already told the setters in her answers.'

'It's not true!' said Sonia. 'I'm just as interested in other people — more than your father is anyway.'

Robert Greenwood was now quietly reading a book given to Anna and did not stir.

'Are you a planner?' Ralph read out from another of the many papers and magazines that littered the floor. 'Was your turkey (a) undercooked (b) over-cooked or (c) did you forget to order it?'

'I thought your turkey was nice, dear,' said Madge.

'What does it say for *slightly* overcooked?' asked Sonia of her son.

'Let's see — yes, you are so keen to make

the party a success that you put your bird in too early and consequently it was rather dry. Try to relax.'

'Better than undercooked,' said Anna. 'What a silly question. What if it was perfect?'

'Quizzes are not for paragons,' said her brother.

'Mother is a planner anyway,' said Anna. 'I'd like to see *you* cook a Christmas dinner.'

This was not quite fair since Ralph, when he was bothered, was a perfectly good cook. But he did not often have to bother.

'Isn't there a general knowledge quiz?' asked Madge plaintively. 'I'd like to listen to the Queen too — we missed her earlier.'

The rest of the evening was spent watching television and a video of *Great Expectations*. Ralph retired once more to his room, whilst Hugh and Anna played chess and Sonia listened to her mother on Christmases past.

* * *

Evelyn hoped she looked reasonably smart in her new dress. Usually she wore grey to match her hair, but she had seen a sale model in the summer of a cherry red two-piece and bought it. She had a good figure, had always been slim. Ron said 'Very nice, dear,' when she asked him if he liked it, but her daughter-in-law said 'Really nice! — put a bit of rouge on your cheeks though, or you will look pale!'

They met Sonia's other Boxing Day guests walking up to the house, which was on a quiet road. 'Oh good, we're not late then,' murmured Evelyn. 'There's Bill and his wife.'

Anna welcomed her friends Victoria, Lucy, and Emma, and took them into the dining-room to consume sparkling wine and crack nuts. 'Thanks for the scent,' she said to Victoria. 'I'm wearing it — gorgeous!' Victoria was known for her expensive presents.

'Can't show you the Edwardian camisole — I'm wearing it!' Victoria answered.

Emma was sampling some of Sonia's books that overflowed in every room. She was a tall, rather forbidding-looking girl, unlike her sister Lucy who had once had a crush on Ralph and still hoped he might notice her. There was no sign of Ralph's present girlfriend Suzanne who was spending Christmas with her parents in Northumberland but who had said she might drop in on her way back to London, so Ralph talked to little Lucy.

'Christmas makes me feel so *old*!' Anna

was saying. ' 'Another year gorn', as Miss Costello used to say.' She and Victoria had once attended the same educational establishment.

She peeked through the dividing doors of the sitting room. Their grandmother was already talking to Mrs Naylor, but she had better go and say hello. Ralph was now talking about his studies to Emma. He was training to be an archivist. Ralph was Grandma's favourite. He was going to have a 'proper' job, unlike his cousin Alex who wrote articles for obscure sci fi journals and existed at present on money earned from acting as a tourist guide.

Sonia entered the kitchen as the others left it. 'Borrow anything you like,' she said to Emma.

'Yes, we still meet to read novels,' Evelyn was saying to Madge. 'Have you read *Vanity Fair*, Mrs Hartley?'

'Oh, ages ago,' said Madge, who could not remember if she ever had. 'Nobody reads Walter Scott now,' she added. 'I used to love him when I was a girl.'

Ronald Naylor came up to be introduced and sat down beside the old lady.

'I believe you are musical?' said Madge, remembering something Sonia had said about the couple.

'I have compact discs of all Johann Sebastian's works. They are enough for me,' Ron replied stiffly.

'Oh — *Bach*,' said Madge, hoping she did not sound too dismissive, but she had never understood what people got from all that churchy stuff.

Evelyn saw that tact was required and led the conversation on to Gilbert and Sullivan. Ronald, who was a man of few words, was quite happy to sit and drink sherry. His son and hers, Christopher, and his wife Valerie were talking animatedly to Bob Greenwood about their last holiday in Czechoslovakia. Thank goodness Chris had improved, thought Evelyn, no longer as silent as his father. Valerie had been good for him. She hoped they'd start a family soon. Her feet were killing her so she sat down on the other side of Mrs Hartley, who reminded her of Sonia, and slipped off her shoes under the chair. They could talk about the old days at home. Old people liked to talk about the past. So do I, thought Evelyn.

* * *

'Was that call from Suzanne?' Anna enquired of her brother who had been hunched over the phone in an upstairs room when they looked for him to go out.

'She's still at her parents' — I'll see her in London next week,' he replied.

The young people, led by Anna, all went out for a healthy walk, leaving the grown ups to deal with Madge and the Naylors and several other neighbours who had also been issued with duty invitations. Bill was to take his mother over to his own home after tea.

The young people ended up in a pub near Eastcliff where they played shove-halfpenny. On their return they found the Naylors and the neighbours departed and Madge in a fur coat ready to accompany Bill home. Anna fingered the fur. 'Yes, I know they don't wear them any more now,' said Madge sharply. 'But it was your grandfather's last present to me!'

'We sell fake furs from the seventies,' said Anna. 'But we're sending the real ones off to Yugoslavia — they're not PC over there, so they will wear them.' Madge looked slightly puzzled.

Sonia was full of compunction now her mother was going. They had still not had that talk about her coming to live with them. Madge lived near Harrogate where she and her husband had retired almost thirty years before. She had her own circle of friends but was getting shaky on her feet. Sonia must go over to see her in the New Year to find out what she really wanted. But she knew what Madge really wanted since she said it quite often. 'Just to die in my sleep — that's what I pray for.' As long as she had the will-power she would stagger on but, ninety-one next summer, even Madge would have to give in one day. Now it was Bill's turn to do his bit.

Bob poured his wife a drink when the taxi had taken them all off. 'A great success,' he exclaimed — which was what he always said.

13

Christmas decorations were still up in the Paris shops but their quarter was quiet and undecorated when Judith and Alan arrived for the midnight mass at St Sulpice on New Year's Eve. They had decided to go to a church nearer their hotel than Notre Dame; the large irregularly twin-towered building was not far from where they were staying in the *sixième arrondisement* and they had walked there after eating in a Vietnamese restaurant on rue Madame. Neither of them would normally have felt obliged to attend a church service on the last night of the old year, but it seemed to them both that to enter properly into the spirit of things abroad one ought to sample the customs of abroad. Neither could conceive of being away by themselves at such a time; neither was an adventurous person who might pack a toothbrush at a moment's notice and fly far away for a change. Paris was not very far.

Most Englishwomen of a certain education would have been in the habit for many years of taking holidays much farther away than the short distance between England and France, but Judith, who had not taken such holidays, found Paris exciting. For so long she'd hoped to have a proper holiday but there had always been more necessary items on which to spend her money. Now there were not so many. She felt dislocated by the flight, the strangeness of it all, and then this dark echoing, incense-laden church, until Alan Watson turned and smiled at her.

He had been abroad more recently than she had, knew Germany better than France, but he felt that being anywhere but Heckcliff gave a spice to their relationship, as if they were marooned together on a desert island. Nobody knew them here, nobody was interested in them as people, apart from being tourists who would spend money in the shops and restaurants. He knew Judith's French was better than his own. She would enjoy remembering it and remembering her first visit to Paris.

At least the Mass wasn't in Latin any more and there were leaflets all over the place in different languages welcoming tourists and asking them to treat the House of God with reverence. The pulpit was mounted by a fat cleric who looked like Mr Pickwick in a long nightdress. He was jolly and spoke of the Eve of St Sylvester as though the saint were a fellow they all knew well.

Judith felt how strange it was now to think that just a week ago she had been spending her Christmas Eve in familiar surroundings amid the familiar rituals whilst the people among whom she now stood had been immersed in their own concerns, their own routines, knowing nothing of her a few hundred miles away. They were at home here as she might have been in the village church as part of a normal week.

Alan was looking solemn she thought when she glanced at him again. He caught her eye, found her hand and squeezed it. He was an affectionate man, and somehow it made her feel on the same level, that they were both strangers in a strange place, dependent upon each other for succour and company. It would be nice to stay here, in this church, for ever; it was warm and pleasant and a little soporific. She stifled a yawn. Travel made you tired.

After the service ended and those who had wished to partake of communion had done so, the cleric announced that the organ would be played for the next hour of the New Year and a collection would be made from those who stayed, the money to be given to those who slept out in the streets of Paris.

'Want to stay on a bit?' he whispered. 'Or are you ready for bed?' She knew he was thinking of nothing but sleep, was probably tired himself after the day's taxis and planes and buses.

'Just a few minutes,' she whispered in reply.

Then the organist, from some dim height far away above them, began to play Bach partitas and the music seemed to cleanse her head of irrelevancies. Bach was Bach wherever he might be found, regular — soothing even — music with which Alan was well acquainted. Those who had stayed along with them were for the most part middle-aged; the young would be living it up in some bar or café, or at a party. But this was a quiet part of Paris.

'One of the best church organs in France,' whispered Alan.

As they came out he took her arm. 'We'll walk in the Luxembourg Gardens tomorrow,' he said. 'Just round the corner, according to the map.'

Judith was suddenly filled with an urge to get to sleep in order to meet the new day as quickly as possible, and refused his suggestion of a nightcap.

Once on the second floor of the narrow recently refurbished hotel he opened her door for her, came into the room and then slid back the connecting door to his own room. 'We both need a good night's sleep,' he said. 'Don't you think?'

She kissed his cheek. 'I'll set my alarm for eight,' she said. 'You'll hear it and then we can have some of those delicious rolls and coffee and get out by nine. We mustn't waste time.'

He laughed. 'Wake me if I oversleep then.' He kissed her goodnight with a smile.

As she brushed her teeth and unpacked her things, hanging her best wool suit up to remove the creases, she heard him moving around too. Once she was in bed she shouted, 'Goodnight, sleep well,' and he replied, 'Goodnight, Judith.'

She lay for some time, images of the journey and the church swirling round her head until she forced herself to breathe slowly and deeply and to think of nothing, to reserve her strength for the morrow.

★ ★ ★

Neither of them fancied a frowsty breakfast among the suitcases and unmade beds and Alan was already up and dressed when she tapped on the door.

'Were you waiting for me? I thought you'd still be asleep,' she exclaimed.

'I woke at seven — had a good sleep in fact. What about you?'

'It took me a bit of time to get to sleep but once I did I slept very well. I'm hungry!'

'Then let's go down — they said breakfast would be served from seven o'clock.'

'We can come back for our outdoor things later — I'm ready.'

They walked down the stairs rather than take the lift. The stair carpet was a dark red and in the alcove of each landing there was a table with dried flowers in a tall vase. Already the smell of coffee was drifting up the small *salle à manger* which was only a room leading off the entrance hall where two large tables, covered with snowy white cloths, were set up with blue and white cups and plates.

'Monsieur, 'dame,' said the young waiter who looked as though he came from India or Ceylon. He pulled out chairs for them at one of the large tables. In the middle of the table stood a large basket of rolls and croissants and in front of each place an assortment of jams and curly butter pats.

'Du café, Monsieur — 'dame?'

'Café au lait, s'il vous plaît,' answered Judith with her best French accent.

'Mais oui!' He swept away. She took a roll and sniffed it. 'Baked this morning — why is it that English hotels never have fresh bread in the morning?'

'Because nobody gets up to stoke the bakery fire,' said Alan.

'I shall dunk it in the coffee,' she said.

'I can see a paper shop,' said Alan, looking out of the window behind him. 'I'm going out to buy a paper whilst we wait.'

She saw when she drew the white net curtain back a little that the street was a narrow one of tall old houses. 'It's like living in Mayfair,' she said. 'All so elegant.'

There were delicate balconies in wrought iron on each second floor and above; few people were about. 'Probably just as expensive,' said Alan, getting up from the table.

'The shopkeepers must come in from the suburbs then,' said Judith. Alan was already off.

She sat wondering what other shops were round the corner. They hadn't had time to look last night before going out to eat, except in the window of an antiquarian bookshop.

By the time Alan returned a few minutes later the coffee had arrived in a large white pot with an equally large white jug of warm milk accompanying it. He sat down and showed her the last copy of *Le Monde* produced before the New Year holiday.

'Something for you to practise your French.'

She poured them each a cup from the twin streams of hot coffee and milk. 'I shall forget my figure for the present,' she said, taking two large pieces of sugar and unwrapping them.

'Delicious — ' Alan got to work on the rolls and, as she had promised, Judith dunked the fresh bread and the pale butter into the steaming coffee.

'I always wanted to do that at home but thought I ought not to set a bad example. I suppose it's very low class?'

'Probably not in France. You know, I

asked the paper-shop lady if she lived above the shop. I think she understood me. She said she came in from Belleville — I suppose that's a suburb?'

'That's what I thought — only the rich live in the centre. Not many even of the rich live in the *centre* of London though, do they? Have a croissant. They're still warm.'

'We shan't need lunch if we eat all this up — yet we're always told the English are the ones with big breakfasts.'

It was all delightful, spotlessly clean, and if not luxurious — for it was only a two star hotel — spacious, and the bread and coffee tasted ambrosial. She wondered, as she got ready a little later to go out, whether it was because she was determined to enjoy herself that she found everything so good. Was that why lovers always went to Paris, because it was the place for happy people?

They took the Métro across the Seine that morning and window-shopped in the Faubourg St Honoré. One pale chiffon dress the colour of moonlight, alone in the window of an expensive clothes shop, took Judith's eye. It was arranged in cunning folds, with a scatter of opals in its lap. 'You'd look nice in that,' Alan said.

'No — twenty years too old for it, Alan!'

They walked to the rue Royale and then

to the arcades near W H Smith's where used to be the English tea shop, and then to the Tuileries and eventually to the river again with its many elegant bridges and silver waters, Notre Dame on its island rearing behind them like a frozen lace waterfall. Then they sat down in a café opposite some bouquinistes on the Quai Voltaire and drank apéritifs.

'It would be nice to belong here,' she sighed. 'There's so much to see. But I feel lazy.'

'May I take a picture?' Alan had whipped out his camera.

'If I can take one of you as well.' He handed the camera over to her and she took him, smiling, in his sturdy Yorkshire overcoat, eyes blue, hair still dark except for the white strand at his forehead.

He was so easy to be with. 'It's nice just walking isn't it? We like doing the same things. But I shall insist on the Musée d'Orsay this afternoon.'

'I'm looking forward to that.'

They were like a long-married couple, she thought, who had passed through their most difficult years and were now equable and easy. Had she expected anything else? She wasn't sure that she wanted anything else but it had to be faced some time. He'd left her alone in her *chambre communnicante* for one night and she wasn't sure what was to happen now. Maybe after a good meal and plenty of wine? . . .

Then he said, 'I suppose I'm rather conventional — I wish I were young again.'

'Why, Alan — I suppose I'm quite conventional too — '

'Except you like your bread dipped in coffee — '

'Well, there is that . . . '

Let's play it by ear, she thought. He reached across the table just as a watery sun came out and for a moment you could imagine it was summer. He took her hand.

'You're nice and warm,' he said. 'What about lunch? There's a good but not expensive restaurant I heard of not far from here.'

'You *have* been doing your homework!'

'No, I asked Philip Halstead, the French expert at my old college.' He grinned a little guiltily, took out a notebook. 'It's all in here.' He read out the name of a restaurant not far away. 'Shall we go there?'

'If we can have a fairly small lunch?'

'I don't suppose they'd mind if we had just one course from the *à la carte*.'

'We could always get a 'self' — that's what

they call self-service over here — I saw it on the way from the airport.'

'If you'd rather.'

'No, of course not. I was teasing. Take me to your recommended restaurant.'

They had agreed to take the same amount of money each and each pay their own bill. Surprisingly, the bill at 'Procope' did not come to an enormous sum, though they both found they were hungrier than they'd imagined.

The vermilion and gold décor and the formality of the table settings, the air of the past, impressed her. 'I'd like to draw some of this — but you can't get the smells into a picture!'

Afterwards they did go to the Musée d'Orsay where Judith was in the seventh heaven seeing at last many of the Impressionists' paintings she'd studied long ago though they hadn't been in fashion even when she was a student. When they returned to the hotel it was growing dark. 'One beautiful day over,' she said and sat on the bed arranging the postcards she'd bought.

Alan sat in the chair at the side of the bed, but then got up and looked out of the window before closing the shutters. Judith got up and joined him there. Suddenly, for no reason, in the midst of all the happiness she truly felt, she sensed a melancholy. Was it that she had never been to Paris when she was young with her husband, or just the weight of the past? There Paris had been, all the time she was being married and having babies and being deserted and working, working, in that northern village which from here seemed as remote as Arabia.

Was it all too perfect? Was she afraid to spoil it all by attempting an intimacy? Yet it was up to her to show Alan Watson she did not object to his sharing her bed that night. He put his arm round her shoulders and they stood silently for a moment with only the light from the small reading lamp.

'I was going to say this after the holiday,' he said. 'But I think I want to say it now.'

'What is it, Alan?' she asked, afraid that he was going to come out with some secret problem, some up until now hidden anxiety.

He turned to her. 'Just that — I know what *I* want. I suppose I'm a bit elderly for romance, or, I don't know — I feel scared sometimes — I do love you Judith — and I was going to say — well, will you marry me?'

'You *are* the conventional one, Alan!'

'You mean we ought to — make love — before we decide anything — before *you* decide?'

'No, not that — just that I'm quite willing to be your lover — you've been very patient with me, and I'm enjoying myself with you just as we are. But I don't know whether I want to marry *anybody* again — and if I say that, I'm frightened of spoiling things — but perhaps you want me only as a wife — '

'Judith! I do want you as a wife — but because you are so attractive — as well as being such a nice person. Somehow I couldn't say it at home. Hell, I'm quite willing to live with you — and why should you marry me — but that's what I'd *like*!'

She suddenly began to cry.

'Darling, why are you crying? I'm a clumsy brute — springing it on you like that.'

'No, no, you're not. You're sweet,' she managed, her voice muffled now against his shoulders. 'It's just nerves, I suppose — all the 'weight of the past', you know — and I don't want to spoil it. I'm out of practice!'

'So am I. So am I,' he comforted.

At last they were close — why had it needed tears?

The tears led to a kiss and the kiss to a lot of laughter before they finally undressed and lay on the bed in his room. 'For you must have your maidenly chamber,' he said, 'when you want to be by yourself.'

Afterwards, he said: 'Well, for two

inexperienced people, that wasn't too bad, was it?' She had been surprised by the passion there had been waiting in his body for her but more surprised that after an initial terror she had found herself slipping into what seemed like a long forgotten strange sort of exercise that unaccountably brought them close.

But she was still uncertain about marriage, needed more time to think. He said he would leave the next proposal to her, wasn't in any hurry now they had begun.

'It wasn't — sex — that was the problem, really,' she murmured. 'It was that I'm not used to being all the time with a grown-up person. I need some solitude — not now, I mean when we get back — just to adjust myself — *re*adjust, I suppose. And marriage terrifies me — my first was such a disaster.'

What was surprising Alan however was the upsurge of love he had felt with Judith. Affection, yes, and tenderness; desire too, though not a young man's imperative need. But a much more steady need to stay with her, be with her, look after her, be her man.

'It's men who are supposed to want only one thing,' he teased her, 'and honestly I'd be quite happy just to be your companion — though this is nicer.'

'Maybe men shouldn't be allowed near women till they are over fifty?' she suggested.

'It would be blackmail, wouldn't it, if I said that I'd be awfully unhappy if you decided against me? Never mind the wedding-ring.'

She thought, how ironic, most women my age would be feeling too flattered at being wanted to have any doubts at all. But Alan was worth more than the resolving of the need for security of a woman about to enter middle age. Then there was the shop . . . However could all that be arranged? She was reluctant to leave her habits, her work.

'We could live together,' he said, as he dressed again. 'Or you could come to the bungalow at weekends. I know it would be a momentous decision for you to give up the shop.'

'You always seem to know what I'm thinking,' she replied.

They went to a big restaurant on the boulevard St. Germain in the evening. Both ate heartily, drank a bottle of Médoc and later, back in Alan's room, fell asleep in each other's arms.

The next day they walked in the Luxembourg Gardens. Judith found it all entrancing.

The holiday was a success. When he

got back home Alan Watson found himself saying to himself over and over again, I don't want her to go — I don't want her to go away now. Please God she won't!

14

Sonia now had to tidy up again after Christmas, a ghost of itself laid to rest in black plastic bags, or in the attic in boxes; still lingering on faintly in bowls of nuts and tangerines. She felt a different kind of depression now, an after-Saturnalia one for the fag-end of the year, and could not concentrate on *Vanity Fair*.

She wondered what Daphne was doing. She had a purpose in life, unlike hers which was to see to the smooth running of a house and home. She suspected that Daphne too had never been able to live for the moment, needed some overarching meaning to sustain her.

Finally Sonia sat down to write some thank you letters.

★ ★ ★

Dorothy decided that Christmas had been a success, in spite of her feeling exhausted from lack of sleep. She'd let Bess and her husband sleep on in the mornings and got up herself to feed little Tom. The other two had been breast-fed for months but for some reason Bess had decided she couldn't pursue that course for more than two months with the new baby.

Her son Sam had stayed over for Christmas too, for one night, clearly making an effort to talk to her about what she might find interesting rather than his own work which was all that really interested him. She'd managed not to mention his present financial plans, property deals being beyond her ken as well as distasteful to her. There would hardly have been time in any case even if he'd stayed longer, for Bess and family had stayed on at her own insistence until the thirtieth. The constant presence of the two older children, allied to the three-month-old Tom's schedule imposed upon them all, had reduced their desire for long *tête-à-têtes*. Thea and Toby had been as good as gold. Noisy and excited of course, but that was natural. Tom was a heavenly baby and she had loved getting up in the morning and being alone with him; he didn't seem to have minded an alien pair of hands holding and changing him.

Her other daughter Ruth, and her partner, had come over just for Christmas Day and that had been nice, though Ruth had kept hinting she ought to put her feet up and that people with three children could not expect to be waited on.

Well, she *was* tired, but it had all been worth it. If Tim could come back to see all his family gathered round her long dining-room table — nine of them if you included the baby, and all except the baby partaking of her well cooked Christmas dinner — the tree she'd decorated glimmering in the background — how happy he would be, I've kept the family faith, she said to him silently. Admittedly, he might not have appreciated the toys liberally strewn in every room or even the wine she had bought, and certainly not Sam's cigars. Only the essence of the family he had left was presented to him by Dorothy in her private communication with him. She still missed him, but with all the evidences of his and her fertility around her, he'd never be forgotten, would be carried on into the future as much as she was. Bess had banished her brother and his cigar to another room, detailing the dangers of passive smoking on her offspring. Tim would have approved of that. Bess was so like her father.

She prepared a mental list of jobs for the morrow when she must organize the house back to its usual tidy cleanliness. She'd bake a few biscuits to send to the children, who had so appreciated them, and ring a neighbour who had declined her offer that he should join in their family Christmas. Then she would continue with *Vanity Fair* and make a few notes with her feet up.

★ ★ ★

Lydia went out for a walk on New Year's Eve. After eating Christmas dinner with her stepson Tony and his wife Linda and son Graham, she'd had them back on Boxing Day afternoon. It hadn't been too bad, though there were occasional silences and a certain strain in the conversation between Tony and his wife — fortunately filled by Graham who was rather whiney. Tony and Linda lived in a small modern house a few miles from Woolsford, too small for them really with all Tony's clutter, and poor Linda had not made much effort to tidy either herself or the living-room. But her cooking had not been totally inedible and Lydia had helped wash up and then read a story to the child. After their own visit to her, which she thought they'd appreciated, especially Linda who liked a change, she'd shut the door, after seeing them off in their Skoda, and breathed a sigh of relief. Bliss to be alone once more in her peaceful flat knowing she'd fulfilled her obligations for another year. They probably thought they were the ones who were obliging, having old step-mum around and dutifully visiting her when they'd probably rather have snored their way through Boxing Day if it hadn't been for young Graham.

In the park Lydia met Evelyn, as usual without Ronald, but with their dog Growler tugging at his leash. They exchanged a few commonplaces about the festive season, Evelyn looking rather rumpled but pink-cheeked. 'I had to give him a run,' she panted. 'Fresh air does good to man and beast after being closeted indoors,' said Lydia.

'We went over to Sonia's on Boxing Day,' said Evelyn. 'I enjoyed seeing her mother. She's wonderful for her age. Have you met her?'

Lydia had only glimpsed Madge Hartley once when she was on an annual visit to Sonia but knew her by repute.

As they stood for a moment in the cold wind she could not forbear to say: 'You ought to get your husband to take the dog out — do him some good. Men tend to be lazy at Christmas, don't they?'

Evelyn laughed. 'It's his turn tomorrow,' she said. Funny, thought Lydia, a couple who were never seen out together, not even on Sunday afternoons with Growler in the local park.

Lydia moved away from Growler's excited muddy paws, saying, 'I'll see you at Gwyneth's then on the 10th?'

'I don't think I shall be able to finish *Vanity Fair* by then,' said Evelyn, and then turned to run after the dog who was chasing a terrified child holding a kite that kept making small attempts to rise but sank back each time as the wind was in the wrong direction.

I really can do without other people now, thought Lydia, as she put her key in the door. Most of the time anyway. And in any case, if I wanted to depend on anyone there's nobody I could depend on.

Pause greeted her, coming into the hall, small tail up, purring. Eventually she allowed him on her lap, when she had eaten a pleasant meal and taken out her book. Like the cat she sighed with content.

* * *

Daphne felt quite blank as the taxi dropped her before the front porch, at the end of the Grange's semi-circular drive. She had worried over what to wear, something she had not done for years, but she didn't want to let Roger down in front of people who had known his wife. Known the competent Betty. Finally, she'd decided on a black dress in a style that had suited her years ago and still fitted though she hadn't worn it since her leaving party at the college. She still had good shoulders and an adequate bust, and the dress, with slightly built up shoulders, flattered them both, and was loose enough around the waist and hips. She wore the only pair of heels she still possessed, so rarely worn they might as well have been new, and a tiny necklace of amethysts with earrings of the same stone. She knew she didn't look fashionable, but she'd pass.

She forgot about herself when she entered the Grange, immediately absorbed in the opulence of the thick carpets, bowls of mimosa and yellow lilies, glittering chandeliers. There was a smell of polish around. He must have a good staff if he'd arrived back from Cheshire only the day before.

'Daphne! So glad you could come! Let me introduce you to Morris and Rhoda Waterman. What will you have to drink?

307

Oh — I forgot — where did you leave your car?'

'I didn't — I came by taxi — I thought I'd want a glass or two on New Year's Eve!'

He looked a little disconcerted, but said: 'Quite right — but I could take you home!'

'No, Roger, I've ordered a taxi back!'

He poured her a glass of champagne and she found herself talking to Rhoda, a stout woman of about her own age with a good complexion and sleek hair of an impossible brown.

Two other couples had just arrived — both very English-looking: a grey-haired man sporting a magenta silk waistcoat, accompanied by a kindly looking white-haired wife in a blue wool dress and specs, and a taller bespectacled man with a much younger wife almost as tall as himself.

Rhoda Waterman was effusive. 'We were all longing to meet you when Roger told us about you!' she began. 'He's such a sweetie isn't he?'

Daphne took a rapid gulp of champagne and Morris Waterman said: 'How do you like Heckcliff then? A bit quiet?'

'I was born here,' she said quickly.

'Really? How interesting — it must have changed a good deal?'

Not so much as I have, she thought of

saying, but said instead 'Less than most places.'

The tall man and his wife were introduced as Nadine and John Ward, the other couple as Adrian and Elizabeth Sanders.

'Roger and I are cousins,' said Elizabeth. She went on: 'I think dinner's ready — Mrs Haigh is making signals.'

They were shepherded into a small dining-room leading off the large bay-windowed sitting-room. Daphne was placed on Roger Masterson's left, Elizabeth on his right. The table sparkled with crystal on white linen, all very tasteful she could not help thinking. He was a practised host.

She saw Rhoda Waterman looking across at her speculatively. They must all think she was girl-friend to this 'sweetie'?

She had decided before arriving to assume a scholarly air, one that had got her through dinners of the college board. She still felt disinclined to say much, but thought she must do her bit to make his party a success. As she had only met six of the guests half an hour ago it was difficult to decide to what level of conversation they would aspire.

She observed them and their host. All appeared to know each other well, though Nadine Ward said little. Talk passed to opera. Here she could hold her own.

She suddenly saw Roger at the head of the table as a 'character' and had an inclination to describe him as 'a silver-haired, well-dressed, charming, polite, well-preserved, widower on the cusp of sixty'. He was obviously a man of substance. Active. Healthy? Why then had he retired? Had he made enough money — or given up his work to look after an ailing Betty? She could vaguely discern what looked like another portrait of her at the far end of the room.

'You haven't met Bertram yet then?' John Ward, her left hand neighbour was asking her as she finished her deliciously sweet portion of melon and sipped cold Chablis. Mrs Haigh was hovering but then disappeared, to reappear wheeling a trolley.

'No,' she replied to John Ward, having remembered the name of Roger's son. (How could a man with a good ear call his son Bertram Masterson? Bertrand would have been better.) 'Only a simple meal,' Roger said to his cousin Elizabeth. 'I took up your suggestion of trout — and then we're to have a cassoulet.'

'And Moira — she's a great girl. We haven't seen her since she went off to Wellington with her husband. But we still see Bertram now and again,' said John Ward.

The talk passed to the Waterman's

burglary, and then the iniquities of the local council. The dinner trundled on ending with a sorbet. Then Stilton and nuts and a dessert wine arrived. She was glad she would not have to drive home.

Coffee was served by Mrs Haigh. The meal had taken so long it was almost eleven by the time they were sitting in a pretty drawing room that showed evidence of feminine taste. Daphne found a downstairs cloakroom and was relieved to discover the taps were not gold-plated.

It was almost midnight when they turned on the television so as not to miss Big Ben chime midnight. They drank to each other as the last notes died away. Daphne saw Roger looking at her and raised her glass to him. When they all sat down again — no Auld Lang Synes here — he came to sit beside her. They exchanged mild conversation about Christmas. He seemed preoccupied. Obviously his friends were watching him hawk-eyed. Soon after, the Wards departed and Daphne's taxi arrived early, its driver grumbling he had three more calls to make. She was glad to breathe in the cold night air.

In the porch Roger took her hand as he said goodbye. She thought he might be going to kiss it but he shook it instead.

She'd have to try to get to know him

better, she supposed. But how? She'd need years to know him well.

Could she fall in love with him? He had nice hands and eyes. Might she assemble the creaking apparatus of desire, call it back? That was one way of getting to know a man. He wasn't much help, she had to admit. Perhaps he wasn't interested in all that?

She'd have him round for a drink.

Did he like cats?

★ ★ ★

On New Year's Eve Sonia and Bob stayed in at home as had been their custom now for years. When they were in their thirties they had sometimes gone over to neighbours who had given self-conscious little parties — once their children were asleep in bed, where they had toasted each other in warm white wine which had given them all a terrible hangover. But that was years ago and it was years since she'd felt the need to be anywhere but home at the end of the old year. This year however Bob opened a bottle of champagne because Ralph had turned up. Anna the workaholic was busy stocktaking. Sonia had gone to bed soon after midnight, still feeling too sober, and annoyed that another year had stolen a march on her. Bob came up soon after

312

her. She fell asleep immediately for once but woke in the night dreaming of two enormous butterflies stuck one on top of the other with the sound of a gentle susurration of wings. In the dream, she said, 'I didn't know butterflies did it like that,' but the sound turned out to be Bob's rhythmic snoring. After about an hour she fell asleep again and was up first on New Year's Day to mutter a self-conscious 'White rabbits', a habit left over from childhood, and to prepare cups of tea for her still sleeping husband and son.

After the warm comforting liquid had sufficiently woken her up she slipped outside to go and buy whatever paper might have appeared on the bank holiday.

★ ★ ★

January 1st was the time to make your New Year resolutions, thought Lydia as she made her face up, but could think of nothing except to try to remember her friend Beryl's birthday this year; to pluck up her courage to ask the freehold owner of the block of flats if she might make a better garden in front; and to finish all the books she was supposed to finish. And not to say she'd finished them if she hadn't quite. That would be enough to be going on with.

Dorothy was on the phone to Bess, discussing the symptoms of chicken-pox which Thea had apparently been incubating all Christmas. She was calming Bess down. 'Even if the baby did get it it's nothing much at that age. Not like whooping-cough or measles.'

'They're inoculated against those — but what a bore, Mum.'

Dorothy agreed it was indeed a bore but promised to have Thea over to stay by herself once the spots disappeared. 'I wouldn't want you catching shingles,' said Bess.

'Is it that way round? I thought grown-ups with shingles could give children chicken-pox but not vice versa?'

'The books disagree,' said Bess but decided to agree with her mother, who was usually right. She rang off, promising to look the matter up. Oh dear, thought Dorothy, Ruth never had chicken-pox, she was the only one who didn't because she was away with my mother at the time. I hope to goodness she doesn't go down with it or she'll blame *me* for having her and Marcus on Christmas Day!

★ ★ ★

314

Evelyn Naylor was giving an extra piano lesson to some child who had missed her last one. The hesitant thumps and tinkles percolated through to Ron who was shaving upstairs. He decided to drop into the office later that day even though no other staff would be there. Give him the chance to catch up a bit on a client's account he'd not been able to finish before being summoned to 'enjoy Christmas'.

★ ★ ★

Gwyneth Coultar, staying on after Christmas for a day or two with her pregnant daughter Zoë, had been up early to meditate and had then gone out in the quiet Berkshire village for a solitary walk. It was there, whilst she was crossing a road, that a car, driven by a youth, suddenly swerved into the road around a hidden corner. Because of her deafness, which was worse than she had ever admitted, Gwyneth did not hear it coming and was knocked down.

Someone on the other side of the road saw the incident and telephoned the police. Gwyneth was taken by ambulance to the Radcliffe Infirmary in Oxford.

Zoë, worried when her mother did not return from her walk after an hour or two, was just going to look for her when the police car arrived, following an address found in an envelope in Gwyneth's pocket, actually an envelope addressed by herself to Zoë the week before which she had forgotten to post.

Zoë was just in time to see Gwyneth before she died without ever having recovered consciousness.

It was apparently a one in a hundred chance of the rupture of a blood vessel in the brain that had followed the knock on her head. The police were out searching for the car. Quite quickly, they came across a stolen vehicle speeding along in the direction of Hungerford and were successful in stopping its further career by the use of roadblocks.

The driver, and the others in the car, all between the ages of fifteen and seventeen, were apprehended.

15

2 January 1993

'But she wasn't walking in the middle of the road, was she?' Lydia asked Dorothy plaintively on the telephone on the morning of January 2nd. She had slept badly in spite of the sleeping pill she'd taken when she'd woken up in the middle of the night.

'Zoë just rang me again — it was a joyrider. No other details,' Dorothy replied. 'The funeral will be on Friday the 8th — in Woolsford. Zoë wanted her — the body — brought back home.'

'Gwyneth was deaf, you know,' said Lydia. 'She mentioned it when we were all talking about growing old — older — '

'I hadn't realized it was as bad as that. But maybe he came out too quickly from a side road for anyone to hear? She'd only just got off the pavement, they think. It was a fairly quiet road off the main one — she must have been about to cross it to return home.' Dorothy forbore to air her suspicion that Gwyneth may have been meditating.

'Perhaps she was miles away — meditating?' suggested Lydia with the same idea. 'How is her daughter bearing up?'

'She sounded quite *compos*. Said: 'Mother wouldn't want me to lose control of myself and hurt the baby.' She sounds a bit too composed if you ask me,' she added. 'But it's true — Gwyneth would have seen herself as of less account than an unborn child.'

'I still can't believe it! It's dreadful,' said Lydia. And Gwyneth was the one of us who

317

wasn't frightened of the modern world and crime and murders she thought. And this *is* murder. 'It's murder, isn't it?' she said to Dorothy. 'Will there be a prosecution now they've caught him? I suppose it was a him?'

'Oh yes, a very young man. Out drinking all New Year's Eve and showing off before he went home.'

'And he didn't even stop? And nobody saw it happen?'

'Yes — a man walking his dog on the verge opposite. He saw it happen and will give evidence. There were four people in the car,' Zoë said. 'No, it didn't stop.'

'Were they drunk?'

'Zoë doesn't know. I should think they were all high on something. I'd better go now, Lydia — I've something baking in the oven. I'll ring you later if there are any further arrangements you ought to know about.'

* * *

Sonia had gone over to Evelyn's and they were sitting in the Naylor drawing room where Evelyn had switched on an electric fire.

'She was the most prepared for death of all

of us,' Sonia was saying. 'But what a way to die — so pointless. And for it to happen to such a good woman.' She thought, it ought to have been me, not Gwyneth.

Evelyn had been crying intermittently ever since Dorothy had telephoned her the previous evening and then again that morning. Yesterday evening Dorothy had also telephoned Sonia with the news. Sonia had thought Daphne ought to know but she was out.

'Is it to be a no flowers thing?' asked Evelyn.

'Zoë didn't say — just that it was to be at the crematorium in Woolsford.'

They were silent, both thinking, then the body will have to come from the hospital in the south.

'I shall send flowers then — they can go to the hospital afterwards — freesias would be nice,' Evelyn said.

'I think we should all share — send heaps of flowers from all of us,' suggested Sonia after a pause.

'Ye-es — I wonder what sort of service they will have?' said Evelyn. Sonia wished they could stop talking about flowers and services. She supposed it was what psychologists called a displacement activity. But what else could they talk about at present, except go over

319

and over Gwyneth's horrible end?

'I am so sad — but especially for Zoë,' she said.

'We ought not to let her in for all the arranging and organizing,' Evelyn replied. 'What if it were you? You wouldn't want Anna to have to do it, especially if she were pregnant — I mean if you hadn't a husband . . . '

'There's no parent or spouse or sister — only Zoë — but I'm sure Gwyneth's religious friends will support her,' said Sonia. Evelyn looked as if this hadn't occurred to her.

Their old friend would never see her grandchild now. That was the hardest aspect to bear, Sonia thought, and might be the hardest for Zoë too, once the first shock of her mother's death had sunk in.

'Zoe will want her mother to have a Christian burial? Gwyneth never actually left the church, did she?' said Evelyn.

'Well, I hope it won't be one of those priests on a rota,' said Sonia, 'muttering over the coffin curtains, though I suppose they do their best. I expect Zoë will have contacted Gwyneth's Buddhist priest, whatever he's called, as well as her yoga friends. They probably knew more about Gwyn than we did.' I only saw part of her life, she thought.

Evelyn said she was glad there would be a religious dimension to the funeral. She did not mention getting some comfort herself from a Christian minister. For Evelyn, thought Sonia, priests were there to comfort the relatives of people who died naturally — she could not imagine them involved in the world of motorways and violent deaths.

'Will you light a candle at St Boniface's?' she asked her.

Evelyn looked at her for a moment as if she might be joking. 'It makes it seem so final,' she said plaintively. Yet it was Evelyn who was the believer. There was nothing more final than death, even if Evelyn believed in an after-life. Evelyn was obviously finding it hard to believe it had really happened. It *was* incredible to be cut off suddenly at a stroke from the world because you wanted to cross a road at the same time as some stupid vicious little idiot who wanted to show off to his friends.

'Motorists who kill are never punished strongly enough,' said Evelyn.

'He was hardly a motorist — the car was stolen. They'd probably been zipping round all night on New Year's Eve. He'll get a stiff sentence, I hope. He's only seventeen and the others in the car were even younger, according to Zoë when she told Dorothy — '

Evelyn blew her nose and said 'I *will* go over to Father Byrne — I suppose because she was a Buddhist I thought it might not be the right thing to do — '

'Go on your own behalf,' said Sonia. Evelyn clearly needed a comfort she could not give her. As for herself she would have to mourn Gwyneth without benefit of clergy.

★ ★ ★

Dorothy and Lydia were on the telephone again. Dorothy felt she had been on it for days, ever since Zoë had rung her with the news and she had immediately telephoned the others. Evelyn had telephoned her again twice since then.

Dorothy sounded angry now. 'I've known her practically all my life,' she said to Lydia. 'She was such a good person. It's so unjust, so unfair. Why her? Nobody really understood her you know, not even Sonia who used to go to art exhibitions with her. I know I didn't really understand her even when she was a little girl. I can't understand it at all — she was never careless even if she was a bit deaf — '

Lydia had already resolved to have her own hearing tested as soon as possible but when she put the telephone down she spent most of the day in a strangely fearful mood before pulling herself together with an effort of will. She saw her own car out of the corner of her eye whenever she looked out of her bathroom window. An instrument of death. She had once had a little cat who had been killed by one of these monsters. It hadn't put her off driving for more than a week but she had never enjoyed her car as much afterwards. We must let Joy Wood know, she thought suddenly. But Dorothy had probably already done that. Dorothy was very competent.

And what would they be doing about flowers?

It was eventually agreed after more calls and discussions that the reading circle would club together and send a large floral tribute.

'Yellow flowers,' said Sonia. 'It was her favourite colour.'

'Daffodils and narcissi and lots of freesias,' said Dorothy.

Sonia undertook to do the ordering and accept contributions later — they would be able to afford heaps. She thought of a coffin under a mountain of blossoms. Dorothy wanted to discuss the wording of the card and added that when she had telephoned Lydia at first Lydia had assumed someone had committed suicide!

'I said, one of us has died, and before I could say she'd been killed, Lydia said 'How did she do it?'.'

'Well it was murder if not suicide,' Sonia replied. She had not imagined Lydia Robinson so pessimistic.

In the end Gwyneth Coultar's coffin was to be covered in white and yellow blooms — white roses and white hyacinths, yellow narcissi and jonquils and freesias with a centre of blue and yellow irises.

The card was to say simply — *To Gwyneth from all her old friends*. Zoë could take that home to keep, to show her that apart from priests and yogis and her one daughter, Gwyneth had not been friendless.

★ ★ ★

The black and white cat was sunning himself under the window of the room which looked out on to the cobbled yard. He purred when Judith Kershaw arrived for coffee and a chat with Daphne the Sunday after her return from Paris. Widgery's mistress had not had much time for him in the last few days. On 2 January Sonia had telephoned her about Gwyneth Coultar. Gwyneth's death seemed unreal until she could talk about it to someone, and she had not said much to Sonia, knowing the two women had once been close.

She had written a short note of thanks to Roger Masterson saying she had enjoyed his party, but had not yet heard from him again. She had returned to her writing and seen nobody.

Judith had never met Gwyneth but was horrified at the news. She looked so happy and healthy herself that talk of fatal accidents seemed in bad taste.

'Will you go to the funeral?' she asked.

'Oh yes.'

'The Johnsons still away?' Judith looked across the yard to the larger house with its shutters that reminded her of Paris except these were green and on the ground floor. In the yard there were several tubs which had held summer geraniums and had not yet been tidied up for spring.

'They've gone skiing,' Daphne replied, bringing a tray of coffee and biscuits in from the kitchen.

The Johnsons were in their late forties, not much older than Judith. Their children had never been much in evidence in the village, having been sent away to school at an early age.

'Must cost a bomb to take all that lot to Savoy,' Judith said, sipping coffee. She wanted to tell Daphne about her own holiday but did not know how to begin and it seemed wrong after the news of an accidental death.

Daphne helped her out with: 'Well, they're not the only ones to take winter holidays! How was Paris?'

'Wonderful.' Judith took up a ginger biscuit but did not begin to nibble it, placed it back on her plate, and stirred her coffee. 'It was nice to come back, though,' she added. 'I didn't think about home for five days, and now I'm back it all seems different.'

She bent down to stroke the cat who did not respond except to twitch a whisker. Daphne said: 'I used to love Paris — but that was years ago. Last time I was there it all seemed less French, you know? The smells were less pungent — everything was more Americanized — except the language, I suppose.'

'There were lots of English words around — but I tried out my French — we didn't manage too badly. The Louvre and the Musée d'Orsay were marvellous.'

Now she had said 'we' Daphne waited for more revelations. Abruptly, Judith said, 'He's asked me to marry him,' and took up the biscuit, but still did not eat it.

'I thought he might,' Daphne murmured.

She did not pursue the remark further to ask her friend what her reply had been, waited patiently to be told.

'I said I wasn't sure — I do like him. Coming back makes it all seem impossible — I feel like running away from him and getting stuck back in my own life, my habits. I mean, it's habits that have kept me going — the shop work and the routine — I think I'm too old to change it all!'

'Oh Judith, what nonsense! You're still young — and habits have a habit of entangling people and making them set in their ways — '

'Yes, I know — but I don't know whether it's just laziness that's making me have cold feet or whether I'm really frightened of change — '

'Probably both — but so long as you like him . . . '

'I think I want to wait — just get to know him better — '

Daphne also waited a moment before she said: 'I'm sure you know him well enough.'

Judith blushed, put down her cup. 'Oh, yes — there was nothing wrong with — all that — though I can tell you it was a shock being close to a man again after all these years. I suppose it was about time, if I wasn't to take the veil once the boys were launched — '

'Then what's holding you back? You like him and I'm sure he *loves* you, you know.'

'I think he does,' Judith replied simply. 'But, you see, I'm frightened of marriage. Life isn't just holidays in Paris — '

'But life isn't just work either at your age,' Daphne said, and poured herself out another cup of coffee, seeing that Judith had hardly touched hers. Judith took up her cup again and frowned.

'No, I know that, but if I did move in with him — whether we got married or not — there'd be all the bother of deciding whether to keep on with the shop or sell it, and I just can't seem to face it all — can't make a decision. I just don't feel ready. And anyway Colin still lives with me — or will when he comes back. He hasn't got a place yet at college and that's a worry — I just don't want to be hurried.'

'Quite right — I'm sure Alan will wait. But in the meantime — '

'Yes, well, in the meantime I've said I'll spend Saturday nights and Sundays with him — this week he's had to go to visit his old uncle in Stourbridge who's ailing. It's nice talking to you. I suppose I need advice. People say 'Do what you want', but I don't *know* what I want. That's the trouble!'

'Well do you want *him* for a start?'

'Yes — I suppose I do — but somehow fitted into everything else — and then, I wonder, am I just seeing him as a person who'll sort me out, be a shoulder to cry on, be *there*? I just can't seem to fall in love like I used to — '

'They tell me,' Daphne said carefully, 'that romantic love isn't exactly the ideal way to begin a lifetime's partnership — '

'Except it wouldn't be a lifetime. We've both had other people — Alan says his own marriage was happy. Am I a coward? Afraid of taking a risk?'

'Life is always a risk — ' said Daphne thinking of Gwyneth. She pulled herself together. 'But honestly, Judith, Alan is the sort of man who is capable of love — I'm sure of that — and also his marriage *was* happy — though I know they were sad not to have had any children.'

'You knew him quite well, didn't you? He likes you.'

Daphne considered. 'Yes — after his wife died we — got to know each other — better — ' She didn't feel it was even now the time to enlighten her friend about her own past affair. 'I think you're just afraid of taking a leap into the dark — but he's not the sort of man who won't wait. I'm sure he would understand. Tell him what you feel.'

'I'm prepared to live with him, even — but not sure whether to get married again,' Judith said after a silence, and then drained her cup, which Daphne promptly refilled.

'Marriage makes things easier — you don't live in a vacuum. Your sons aren't going to tell you you're an immoral woman, but I feel sure they'd like you to remarry. Did they like him?'

'I think so. Mark did and Ben loved playing chess with him — they drew a game each — very long games too! I don't know about Stephen — I think he has an idea I'm his responsibility and he's never got over the actual fact that his father left me. I suppose he thinks I'm vulnerable — '

'I should have said you were rather old for your age, Judith.'

'Well, if I am, that would be a good thing, since Alan is nearly twenty years older than me! I just worry about my own life — you know, apart from the work and the boys — I've got used to living alone now when they're away — I like my own time and I do want to paint more — '

'He's not against that, surely?'

'Oh, no! — most encouraging. But I keep reading all those things feminists say about being taken over — finding you've got the short straw — that men change when they are married!'

'I wouldn't have thought you were the sort of woman to be influenced by journalists, and Alan would be absolutely delighted to have a wife who painted and did her own thing. He'd be very practical round the house too, wouldn't he?'

She knew very well he was, because years ago when she had comforted him he had in return helped her a good deal with her car and the problems of her Leeds flat. She wondered why she was so keen on getting him hitched up to Judith.

She went on: 'It would be too late for *me*' — I mean there comes a time when you know you're going to be alone for the rest of your life — and I love my own company — but then I'm used to it. I decided long ago I wouldn't be a very good wife. But you're *young* — you would have carried on being a good wife, I'm sure. Don't start thinking that what happened was your fault. We often love the wrong person when we're young — and you wouldn't have wanted to miss out on that sort of love, you know. But this will be something quite different — do it bit by bit — see how it goes.'

She was thinking of Charles and how she

would have liked to marry him in spite of everything that was wrong with him and her and them both. But that was thirty-five years ago and she was a different woman now — and it wouldn't have worked. Neither would she really have wanted Alan Watson as a husband. But Judith could be happy with him, she was sure.

'You think I could adapt myself? He's got his own habits too! Always buys a paper — even in Paris — and reads it over breakfast and spends a lot of time thinking about his research!'

'There you are then — he'll give you plenty of time for your own thing, so long as you don't mind doing the same for him.'

'Of course I don't — you don't think he'll change? Want me there all the time — I just couldn't be like that — '

'No — he's got his own ways, as I said. And, just think, you'd be able to sell the shop eventually and paint to your heart's content!'

'I can't believe it — that I'd have time to paint — but then perhaps, if I had more time, I'd find I wasn't any good?'

'Judith, you are very stoical but you've become one of nature's pessimists. You can't know if you don't try!' She felt like a cheer leader, and why was she so sure it would work for them both?

'It's been a help talking,' Judith said when she left. 'I'm going to think it all over. It's all been quite a jolt to my habit-ridden existence!'

When she'd gone Daphne wondered whether she ought not to have sounded so encouraging to Judith? But marriage was right for her and she felt sure Alan had never contemplated less. As men grew older they seemed to get keener about marriage, in diametric opposition to many women who grew less enthusiastic.

She thought too about the silken cords of habit and wondered if *she* could ever manage without them. The news about Gwyneth and her nagging feelings about Roger Masterson hadn't stopped her thinking about her work. Her ideas about Anne and her circle were shifting, strands of research coming together, and she was feeling that little spurt of excitement that meant she might be on the right track. When she thought of Anne's life she felt she'd been right to encourage Judith to accept Alan.

A foray into some old museum catalogues had told her a little more about Anne's brother. She didn't want to write a biography of *him*, or of the whole family, and yet all she turned up was to do with the brother not the sister! Three of the family were gifted with talents she assumed must have come from their mother, Cornish like the mother of the Brontë children. Joshua had sketched in Cornwall as well as in North Wales and Cumbria — mountains had a great attraction for painters of the time. Had Anne ever accompanied him when he painted? A fellow painter was quoted as saying what a hard worker he was, although everything 'kept him from his easel'. Pecuniary worries, she supposed, and the mechanics of living which were even more of a problem then than now.

Judith also had to do with both crockery *and* painting. Joshua — hooray! — had married a French widow when he was forty five! A good augury? If Judith married Alan, how many years of married life could she look forward to, how many years before she became not only his wife but his nurse? She was back again with thoughts of Roger Masterson, thrust them away and returned to her notes.

Joshua, by then a widower, had died in 1847 at the age of eighty. Nobody seemed to know how long Anne had lived.

It would be too much to hope that Joshua might have sketched his sisters, even if he had not confined himself to landscape painting. She'd seen many engravings of his work by now, probably executed by his sister Elizabeth, who had been engaged, like Anne, on tuition. There still remained some memoirs of writers of the time to consult, and further pieces of the mosaic to put together. In an old biography she'd picked up about Mary Hays, the writer of the novel she'd lent to Judith, there had been a mention of her living in old age in Anne's village. Friends because of the long dead Mary Wollstonecraft, the friendship must have had its own momentum, continued long after the more famous woman's death. She had discovered more letters written by this other Mary, had read one that discussed a suggestion she should collaborate with Anne on a novel. Anne was to insert the 'poetical' bits! Nothing had come of this nonsensical idea.

What else might have made Anne and Mary Hays — two very different women — continue as friends, apart from their both having known the famous Mary?

Unrequited love, that was what! It was the theme of Mary's novel, a daring one for a woman, and the same passion had been the driving force behind the gentler Anne's verse.

Daphne began to imagine the two old

ladies meeting in their seventies to chat about the loves of their youth.

There was so much research still to do, but she felt more cheerful now.

When she got up to make herself a cup of tea, Widgery was waiting by his saucer, which meant that he wanted milk. If it were food he would have rubbed against her legs or sat by the door of the refrigerator.

'I'm on the right track,' she said to him. He purred in agreement.

* * *

Not one of the women slept much the night before the funeral, not even Dorothy who usually slept like a log. She got up in the middle of the night and made herself a hot drink, then slept fitfully for an hour or two before the late January dawn.

Bob was away and Sonia knew she would not sleep, so took a carefully hoarded sleeping pill from a bottle she kept for emergencies. It gave you three or four hours but left you feeling muzzy in the morning.

Evelyn lay listening to Ron's snores, wishing she had bought ear-plugs. She was frightened of oversleeping. The funeral was at eleven and she was to drive herself and Dorothy there. Sonia was going by car with

Lydia or Daphne. Would there be any music? As far as she remembered, Gwyneth had never been a great music lover. Did you have to pay extra for music at a funeral? She ought to have offered to play for them. As far as she recalled there was a sort of harmonium in the place but most people had canned music. She decided they'd probably have a record of *Jesu Joy Of Man's Desiring*. It was what people always had who had something chosen for them. Would Gwyneth have preferred temple bells? She wished she knew a bit more about Gwyneth's odd beliefs.

Lydia was up early, examining herself critically in her bathroom mirror, wanting to look her best in company, even at a funeral. When you were with women friends, people your own age, you had to take extra care, for on the look-out for these items in themselves, they would be the first to spot lines and wrinkles and gobbly necks, grey hairs and fallen chins and red-rimmed eyes. There was that friend of Sonia's daughter, Victoria someone, who had announced — Lydia had once dropped in to borrow a book from Sonia and found a kitchenful of young women — that it was silly for older women to bother about their looks as it only showed they had been brought up to put on make-up for men and ought to realize what a relief it should be at their age to stop bothering. A very rude girl. But then Anna, who was a nice girl, had said that she didn't try to look nice for men, it was for herself, and what difference did it make how old you were? In her opinion it was men who should bother a bit more. Goody, said Lydia, delighted with this response, but the Victoria girl hadn't looked as though she cared a fig for anyone else's opinion. Sonia had winked at Lydia.

Afterwards, she knew there was something illogical in her own attitude, but didn't care to investigate it too minutely. You put make-up on for yourself, then for other women, and only coincidentally if you wanted to attract a man. Anyway, she had always made her face up primarily for her own pleasure. She patted on a carefully tinted and moistured foundation on her pale cheeks. Even on the worst days with Maurice he'd never had to complain she'd let herself go.

Lydia blotted her face with a tissue, put her hands under her skirt and tweaked her blouse down under her waistline. Still had a waistline. She drank a cup of coffee, reblotted her lips, applied a little dark green eyeshadow at the corners of her eyes — only a *soupçon* as the French said — and applied a final light dusting of translucent powder on her cheeks and forehead. Then she checked she had turned down the central heating, let in Pause, who had found it too cold outside and, taking her keys and her best brown leather handbag — they were not expected to arrive dressed in black according to Dorothy — was ready to be off. She looked at her watch. Twenty-five past ten. She'd start the car up and bring it round to the front for Sonia.

Lydia shut the door carefully and left behind her empty, clean, light, tasteful flat with its several vases of winter jasmine and its feline occupant, to await her return.

16

When people arrived at their age they had always lost something — innocence, or illusion, or hope. It was worse to lose memories. The middle years of Daphne's life floated at present in some colourless limbo. She was surprised when she found some forgotten old note book or diary or letter, how she would suddenly be projected back into a former way of life. Some things went on being there, like dresses kept because they had never really worn out, and she'd never lost her thirst for knowledge, whatever else she'd lost — optimism perhaps? Lydia and Sonia would agree with her. Dorothy, sitting behind her now in the crematorium chapel, preserved belief in a benevolent universe.

Gwyneth, who had seemed removed from the idea of loss, had lost her life, lost everything. Or gained it — if you believed in the afterlife.

Daphne was sitting next to Sonia and knew that Sonia was trying, but failing, to believe that there, lying in the coffin of shiny pale wood, heaped over with flowers was Gwyneth.

Sonia was in fact thinking that some tough dualism still operated to deny that the body was the same as the person you had known and been fond of. Nowadays, bodies were more important than minds. She tried again to force herself to confront reality, still could not reconcile what lay inside the now closed box with the tall figure of her kind friend. It was beyond tears or wailing and gnashing of teeth. Horror did not show itself in tears but in screams . . .

A shaft of cold January sunlight fell now on them all and on the flowers and it seemed suddenly to Sonia that the yellow and white and blue flowers belonged outside in the world, not inside, all cut and useless.

Gwyneth would have loved them, would probably have wanted to paint them as one of her 'Yellow Studies'. There were narcissi and jonquils amongst her lemons and melons and suns.

A Church of England person was sharing the official side of the funeral with a man who looked Indian, wearing yellow robes. Yellow again. Apparently you could have anybody you chose to officiate and Zoë had asked for them both. She was standing flanked by a young woman friend on the one side and a grey-haired middle-aged man on the other. A tall, dark-haired young woman, she had a quality of restfulness she must have received from her mother. Could the older man possibly be her unknown father? For a moment Sonia allowed herself to hope that he had come to make reparation to his daughter for years of neglect. But no, it could not be. It would be Zoë's trainer of horses and riders.

Behind the young woman on the opposite side of Sonia and Daphne were several other women, all with shiningly kind faces and wearing clothes that looked as though they had been bought at Oxfam. Must be Gwyneth's meditation group. Though she lay alone, Gwyneth was surrounded by women.

Daphne was also trying to concentrate,

to put her thoughts on to a suitable path for a funeral, and was startled when the parson told them they were attending the funeral of Gwyneth Hope Coultar. She had never known Gwyneth's middle name. How appropriate.

Poor Gwyneth, thought Dorothy, so deaf she had not heard that dreadful wagon of destruction that had mown her down like an animal.

The shaft of sunlight disappeared for a moment but then reappeared through a plain side-window. At least it was not raining. The heavens were not weeping for their old friend.

Hope. A tiny shaft of light on the coffin flowers now, all young flowers, Dorothy thought confusedly, not like Gwyneth and her friends.

Evelyn was sniffing into a handkerchief. Was it Gwyneth who had said something about not yet being old? The time they had all been talking about growing older. That awful word, 'elderly'. How old was elderly? Gwyneth was not elderly. Was it the same evening she herself had been talking about crime, the sickening daily reported violence often against the elderly — mixing up having to come to terms with age and having to come to terms with the disintegration of old

England, the place they had always relied upon, trusted?

Growing older had more to do with making sense of life before it was too late thought Sonia. Not too late for Gwyneth; she had made some sense out of her life. Gwyneth had died in that present time in which they all lived for better or worse, a time which would one day fold over them all as they still went on trying to understand. And failing. (She shut her eyes obediently to pray.) Living in the present while the present changed all the time, and was only the tip of the long snake-like coil of the past pushing them all — except Gwyneth now — into the future.

Adapt or die, thought Dorothy, her eyes open. Gwyneth had done both. She'd not been frightened of change. She hoped that she had not had time to be frightened at the end either.

The Buddhist priest, if that was what he was, reading from what sounded like a religious text. No fear of extinction there, and no belief in another place either: 'Your essence was not born and will not die.' He returned to his seat at the front and they were just about to sing a Christian hymn when there was slight disturbance at the back.

Dorothy looked round.

Shuffling into a seat, panting — but she'd

made it, even though she was late! — was Joy Wood! Good old faithful friend, red-faced, wearing a blue hat that had last seen service at her son Peter's christening. If she could not allow herself an evening out she could certainly attend a funeral.

Sonia did not need to look at the words as they sang *A thousand ages in thy sight are like an evening gone* . . . but her eyes were suddenly blurred with tears. She had not yet wept for Gwyneth, only been angry; now *words* made her cry!

Evelyn Naylor looked woebegone. Lydia Robinson, who had also turned round to look at the latecomer thought: that's Joy Wood — I only met her once but I'm sure it's her. How hard these seats are. You couldn't really call them pews. No cushions.

Sonia blinked the tears back. Sentiment easily clouded her eyes but real feelings usually left her tearless. Also, she still felt angry.

' . . . *bears all its sons away,*' sang Dorothy's unselfconscious contralto. At the last funeral Dorothy had attended, of a very old man in Durham, she had been a stand-in for her mother who couldn't possibly go so far in one day. Someone from their family had to go, and Dorothy, greeting the mourners, had been called by her mother's name, Elsie. The

344

mourners were all very old themselves and she supposed she had been the age Elsie had been thirty years earlier when they had been used to seeing her. It had been both amusing and a trifle unnerving to slip a generation. She must look very like Elsie for them to have mistaken her for her mother. There was no family here at this ceremony, except for Zoë and the unborn child.

Gwyneth's parents had died years ago and Gwyneth had been an only child, as her own daughter was. Out of the corner of her eye Dorothy saw Lydia looking straight ahead, lips moving but no sound coming out. Lydia was probably thinking, here is Christianity trying to make palatable what is not. Generations, Dorothy mused on, falling so quickly back the one upon the other; baptisms and weddings and funerals collapsing concertina-like, or seen through the wrong end of the telescope as hundreds of little converging specks. Only thirty years or so of living between one christening and the next, sometimes less . . . Bess had insisted her own babies were christened . . . Only thirty years or so between the death of a parent and that parent's offspring, though now more and more people were living on into their nineties like Mrs Hartley . . .

Lydia looked at Zoë's long dark coat and

thought she could already see, even from the back, that the girl was pregnant. She had looked at pregnant women with such envy once. But Zoë was lucky, the baby would keep her from too many sad thoughts about her mother. She would have something tangible to look forward to because she was young, unlike most of this congregation. It was the looking forward that mattered; funny how it had that additional meaning. That was why youth could be happy in all its misery. 'Are you looking forward to it, Lydia?' her father used to ask her about whatever little treat he might have arranged for her. Those bloody nuns, she thought, they never told you that, how *happy* you could be. But there was always Hope, she supposed, like Gwyneth Coultar's name. Was that what the Reverend Mother would have called a sign? It was Gwyneth herself who had talked about hope. But Gwyneth hadn't been a saint just because she had died.

Perhaps I can't believe, because I don't want to be seen as a supplicant, thought Daphne. The old sin of pride. She and Mary had been well-drilled as children never to break down in public. Still, she couldn't cry. Even at my own funeral, she thought, I mean, even if I was dying, the idea of people mourning me, being sorry for me, myself finally at the ultimate disadvantage, terrifies me and embarrasses me.

Gwyneth used to tease me years ago, thought Sonia. '*Bella figura*,' she'd say when I refused to break down. Gwyneth in those days had cried a lot. She'd been a very emotional person then. One of the very few good people she had known, a really good woman. Calm too, and brave, when she was older. Scarcely ever venturing opinions, or not to her and her friends, though it had been obvious she'd made her mind up on most subjects and shut out what did not concern her: politics, sex, men, the state of society. There had seemed to be nothing and nobody she disliked, and she had never got angry. Maybe she wasn't clever in the way some of the friends were, but she had been happy, whilst professing to believe that happiness in itself was not important. Yet she'd always accepted help if it were proffered.

I can't ask for help from others, even from my children, thought Dorothy. I can't show myself vulnerable. I don't think Sonia can either. Must be something to do with the way we were brought up. Nowadays everybody was always asking for help. They'd even asked Zoë if she needed a 'bereavement counsellor'. Zoë, brought up by Gwyneth to be fairly self-sufficient, had looked puzzled and declined. She was not mourning for herself but for her mother. 'Such a pity, it's such a pity,' she'd said when she'd told Dorothy at first about what had happened on that road. Was it a fault to be proud and independent and self-sufficient as their generation mostly was or pretended to be? It was what you showed to the world that mattered to others.

I would never make an exhibition of myself as Joy Wood is presently doing, thought Lydia. Joy's sobs could be heard in the midst of the record they were playing as they prepared to slide the coffin away. Crying meant you claimed sympathy for yourself, didn't it? Not for Gwyneth, who was beyond sympathy. Or could you just wail for the human condition?

Sonia thought, if anybody had asked me a fortnight ago who'd not be here now, I'd have said Evelyn, who always seems to be depressed. Not Gwyneth, who I thought was invulnerable.

The Christian minister pronounced: 'Ashes to ashes, dust to dust,' and there was time for quiet prayers as the coffin slid away on its journey to the ovens. The sun stayed in when the blue velvet curtains finally closed. To symbolize mystery, Daphne supposed, that slow shutting away, hiding reality.

Was it Hindus who burned their dead in public? wondered Evelyn. I *ought* to think about it, I ought to come to terms with it as they say . . .

Sonia could think only of a poem she'd read about a parent's cremation — a shocking yet wonderful poem about a wedding ring that would not burn. Had Gwyneth worn a ring? She'd never noticed. The Buddhist was now facing them and reading words she had not heard before. She tried to grasp them: 'Life is a bridge, so do not build your house upon it.' Rather like 'Lay not up for yourselves treasures upon earth, where moth and rust doth corrupt', but not quite. 'There is no death,' he went on, 'though every living form must die . . . '

Now it was over, Gwyneth commemorated, suitably or not she wasn't sure. Daphne by her side was staring fixedly ahead.

Dorothy and Lydia and Evelyn sat on together. Lydia kept looking round; Evelyn was still dabbing her eyes with a handkerchief. Dorothy thought, we'll shake hands with the celebrants, and then I must speak to Zoë. The wreaths will be there for inspection too round the side of the building under that sort of arcade.

The parson disappeared, but the Buddhist priest was now sitting next to Zoë, who after a few moments got up flanked by him and her woman friend and walked slowly down the aisle of the chapel. The rest all sat quietly for a moment. A thin shaft of sunlight reappeared through the window. The rest of the mourners got to their feet and moved to the door at the back of the chapel. Joy waited for Dorothy to arrive, took her arm when she did, and they all went out through the porch into the mingled sunshine and wind.

They stood around making stilted conversation, or were silent, according to character, before moving in a phalanx to look at the wreaths and sprays that had arrived, bending stiffly to read the labels, as if they had never seen flowers before.

Zoë reappeared and they all kissed her or shook hands with her and murmured their grief. Evelyn put her arm round her. She looked more affected than Zoë herself. Daphne wondered if she might ask the Buddhist what he had been reading from — all about forgetting the self and putting yourself into the hands of Buddha as far as she had understood it. Very like the 'everlasting arms' in a way. There had not been any incense or temple bells, more of an East-West mixture. But she'd better not ask now. Instead she murmured to Sonia 'I liked the Eastern reading.'

350

'Yes.'

As she looked at the flowers Sonia realized that any desire she might have had to be buried in her past had left her as swiftly as it had slowly come over her since she was fifty. 'Yes,' she said again — 'Every living form must die — but I think I prefer the words of the Old Testament.'

Their solidarity was actually comforting poor Zoë, thought Daphne, for Zoë was now swaying from one to another of them saying: 'Mother had so many friends — you'll help me to remember her.' Dorothy squeezed her hand and even Lydia patted her arm. Joy kissed her unselfconsciously. But it was Sonia to whom she turned eventually, saying, 'The baby jumped this morning.'

'Your mother was so thrilled about your baby,' Dorothy said.

'It hasn't sunk in yet — I mean about Mother. I keep thinking about the baby instead — is that awful?'

'No, it's what she would have wanted,' said Dorothy, adding that Zoë would be welcome to stay with her at any time.

Sonia said a little awkwardly that Anna had promised some baby clothes. 'She's already found some lovely lacy ones — first size — she'll send them on to you.'

There would be no funeral baked meats.

Zoë was returning straight away to Berkshire. The trainer came up then with the Indian and they all admired the flowers once more. Daphne noticed marigolds among them, remembered reading somewhere that they were flowers that meant a lot to Hindus. She would like to have asked what connection they had with the Buddhist priest or the yoga lady. Didn't they belong to a different religion? But possibly Gwyneth had friends in all camps? The rarely glimpsed Joy said then that she would have to go — a neighbour was sitting in with Mother. Lydia offered her a lift but Dorothy bore her away like an endangered species.

The next meeting was to have been at Gwyneth's as they had all remembered, but Dorothy had suggested that as a mark of respect they would all agree to skip that meeting and meet again perhaps in February or even March. As nobody had yet finished *Vanity Fair* this suggestion was welcomed.

All the survivors were soon on their way back home.

Sonia was going back with Daphne. The traffic was building up for lunch-time in clots and mazes and she flinched at what she imagined were near misses as Daphne's car wove in and out of the traffic. But Daphne was driving very carefully. The funeral had affected them all. Fragility they knew about; they were all used by now to sorrow and to a recognition of their own mortality. But it was extinction they had to face.

Life was infinitely precious to both Sonia and Daphne in the car together. Sonia said suddenly: 'Zoë means life, doesn't it?'

'I know — and Gwyneth's being named 'Hope'! You did like the readings?'

'Acceptance of everything? I can't, I'm afraid. If Christianity were true I can't help thinking it would satisfy me better than these Eastern religions . . . Punishing the wicked, for example.'

'Did Gwyneth accept everything then?'

'I don't think she ever left the Church — she was just a religious person, I suppose?'

'Do you still feel angry?'

'Yes, but with whom? — except the youth whose car killed her — but she once said you must show mercy to all living things, so I suppose she would have forgiven him too. It's not for *us* to forgive him though, is it?'

'Certainly not — I agree with you there,' replied Daphne.

'Will Zoë have to see him in court? I hope not.'

'She won't want to, will she? Is she at all like her mother? You knew her better than I did.'

I've known you too only for a few months, she thought, yet I feel I understand you.

'She used to say even when she was at school, you know, that people should live without worry or thinking ahead,' said Sonia.

'Like the lilies of the field?'

'The religions mix quite well in parts, don't they?'

'It was a decent funeral,' said Daphne.

'I was in a church at Christmas,' said Sonia. 'I never thought I'd be back praying so soon!'

17

The Saturday after Gwyneth's funeral, Daphne went to another theatre matinée with Roger Masterson. He made no attempt to get physically closer to her. She was used to his company now, but if *she'd* been a man she'd have expressed feelings more openly. Often he was silent and she did not break into his thoughts but wondered whether he was steeling himself to say something personal to her.

She wished he'd make some decisive move

she could either accept or reject. On the one hand he might have thought it was assuming too much; on the other it might mean he didn't think of her at all as a woman, just a friend to go out with. Yet he'd asked her to his party and his other guests had looked at her in a certain way. Did he envisage a love affair or not?

They both enjoyed the play, a Shaw revival. Shaw had never been a great favourite of Daphne's but he was a lot more interesting than most of the modern plays she saw. They returned by car in the early evening and Roger dropped her at home. Apparently his son made a habit of telephoning him on Saturday evenings, so she need not invite him in. She was glad, for she felt unaccountably tired. It was already dark, but thank goodness the days were now at last growing longer.

The lamp was on in the yard and she saw Widgery sitting on the outside sill of her kitchen window. Funny, she was sure she had left him inside. She hurried to the door and he jumped down. Then she saw that the door was half open and realized in a split second that she must have been burgled. Someone had forced the door open with a jemmy. She went in, switched on all the lights, fearful that whoever had been there was there still and saw immediately that her coffee pot was not on its usual stand in the kitchen. Heart pounding, she ran to her work-room to check that her books and notes had not been taken or destroyed. She was reassured to see that nothing was out of place there. Then she went into the sitting-room. One look told her that her candlesticks had gone — and her silver tray. The cat stood mewing at the kitchen door. If only he could speak. She'd better not touch anything. Did they still take fingerprints or were there so many burglaries now that the police had given up?

She swept into her bedroom and found the drawers emptied on the bed and her jewel case gone, other costume jewellery left in a heap on the bed. No mess apart from this though, thank heaven. She was filled with a burning anger; if the thief had suddenly appeared before her and she had held a gun in her hand she would certainly have shot him. She sat down, tried to calm herself, took her notebooks and wrote down all she could remember that had been taken.

The police first, then a joiner. But there would be no joiner available at this time on a Saturday evening. Daphne had no relish for sleeping in a house whose door would not close, but was no do-it-yourself expert. The door had been locked when she left, and so had her windows which she ascertained had not been opened. She wondered what time they — or he — had come and how long the cat had been outside. Widgery seemed to understand and came up with a sympathetic look on his trim face.

Daphne rang the police, then suddenly decided to telephone Roger. He would help her, might repair the door temporarily?

He sounded surprised at first to hear her voice, but was immediately full of commiserations, said he would look out the correct tools, come round and see what he could do temporarily before Monday.

Daphne waited for the police, her emotions a mixture of fury and annoyance. Just when she was ready to get on with her book there would be all the business of insurance and repairs to see to. She smiled even so then, a small smile, as she waited, almost proud that she had run to the books and papers first, not to her jewel box or her cabinet of small items of silver or her drawer of silver spoons and oddments or even her compact disc player.

She got up and looked round again — the police took their time coming — and discovered further things missing: a silver-backed hairbrush that had been her grandmother's, and a silver inkwell Charles had once given her. She'd been wearing her best jewellery,

357

bequeathed to her by her grandmother, that was one blessing. There was a ring at the bell and she went to answer it. It was Roger, long-faced, bearing a box of tools. Then a screech of brakes, and a police-sergeant and a policewoman leapt out of their car. She'd better make some cups of tea.

It was pleasant having Roger take charge, though he seemed to expect tears rather than fury. He repaired the door for the time being but she insisted once the police had gone away that he went too. She had a headache.

Afterwards she felt guilty; she should have managed by herself; she had 'used' him.

The whole affair pitched her into the present with a vengeance. By the time her initial anger had died down a little she had had a visit from the victim support people. They had seemed to think she was brave in continuing to live alone, had expected she might have a feeling of contamination. Some women, they said, could not abide to think their sanctuary had been violated, went around washing everything, felt soiled, even moved house.

'No, I don't feel soiled, though I expect I would if they'd done some of the disgusting things you hear about burglars doing. I just feel extremely angry,' Daphne said.

'Just be grateful they didn't come whilst you were in the house!' they said lugubriously. She thought this over and decided it wasn't a very sensible remark. She rang the police once more and they assured her that most burglars' last wish was to confront their victims, and that the kind of burglaries found in the area were almost invariably perpetrated in the absence of the owners.

'Get a dog,' they advised. 'Or a burglar alarm. Burglars are opportunists.'

It was horrible to feel she might have been watched. Daphne was not especially fond of dogs, quite apart from Widgery's possible hurt feelings, so decided reluctantly she'd better get an alarm, a thing she'd formerly decided against because it seemed to advertise the fact that you thought you were worth burgling.

All the items they'd stolen were of sentimental value, not enormously valuable in themselves. As time went on she discovered other things that had disappeared, things she had not even remembered she had — a small clock for example that did not go but was encased in silver, given to an old aunt on her twenty first birthday almost eighty years before, and left in a bottom drawer. There was nothing she could do about it and she felt helpless because she could not find the enemy to punish him.

She contacted her insurance office and had permanent repairs made to her front door. It was all very time-consuming. Not only had her burglars stolen some of her property but also banished for ever the village of her childhood. It had really and truly gone, existing now only in her imagination, the way Anne existed, partly her own creation. She must let go of the past. Must she make an even greater effort to belong to the present when the past seemed to be, as Evelyn had once said, the only safe place?

On the telephone her sister Mary had been sympathetic about the burglary but had taken the opportunity to remind Daphne that she lived too much in her own mind. Heckcliff had changed. Sonia on the other hand had been very angry, said everyone knew who the local burglars were. Others might be coming now from further afield who were harder to catch. Not that anything useful was done when they were caught. They ended up eventually in prison only to be paid for during their stay by the taxes of the very people they'd burgled.

Daphne realized that her feelings about the past and her feelings about a recreation of Anne's life were connected. She needed someone to confide in, as she had been

Judith's *confidante*, someone to understand her. She hesitated to telephone Roger again. He might be a tower of strength in practical ways, had said she could always ask for help from him, but . . . She wished she could talk to Sonia. She would be the ideal friend in whom she could confide; all her other women friends lived further away. So far though she and Sonia had mostly talked in the presence of others.

Her work was the best solace, when she finally returned to it after all the upset and disturbance — people ringing to commiserate, burglar alarm salesmen spending a day fitting her house up. What would gentle Anne or either of the fiery Marys have thought about her burglar? Were robberies a commonplace occurrence in their day?

It had been her past that had been violated, bringing her back with an unpleasant jerk to reality. She tried to explain this on the telephone to Cressy who was sympathetic.

'Just the idea,' explained Daphne, 'that I couldn't bear my own grandparents to know — they'd be far more hurt than me. If my grandmother had ever known what had happened to her precious things . . . and that makes it worse to think she'll *never* know — gone beyond recall. That's what makes you realize they're dead, when they can't be hurt any more.'

Cressida thought Daphne had always been sentimental, but it was odd that she seemed to care more for the feelings the dead *might* have had than for the loss of what were after all her own possessions! She spoke of it to Jonathan who was concerned that Cressida's aunt should get in touch with the loss-adjusters as soon as possible. The insurance people had wanted evidence of the value of certain items which had been insured only *en bloc*. 'A pity she didn't photograph the silver,' he said. He was very practical, but Cressida supposed that these were the kinds of matters solicitors would obviously know about.

'She was far more concerned that they hadn't stolen her papers or made a mess of them!' she said.

'We must soon take a look at the house your aunt's poet is supposed to have lived in,' said Jonathan. 'What about next Saturday? I could come over and we could go for a nice walk.'

'That would please her — she says it's one of a row of cottages but there are later ones tacked on to them.'

Cressida had waited in vain for a letter or even a postcard from Patrick. None had arrived. She had not really expected him to write. He was probably enjoying himself with geishas, or whoever the women were provided for Western businessmen. She said as much to Jonathan who was a little shocked. She wasn't sure whether Jonathan's principles rose from high-mindedness or naïvety. He was level-headed and kind though, which made up for a certain lack of those dashing qualities which had seduced her in Patrick Simmonds. She would always yearn for Pat, but she was determined not to succumb again to anyone like him. Whether she encouraged Jonathan was, or should be, a separate matter . . .

The day before the planned walk to Anne's house Cressida received a letter from Daphne asking her to photograph it. She had done so herself at the time of her own visit but something had gone wrong with the camera.

'By the way, Judith returned from Paris looking happy — she still can't make her mind up to marry him — he's asked her. She sent her love to you.'

Cressida felt Daphne approved of Judith's caution, but would be encouraging Judith to react in a positive manner to her elderly swain. In spite of never having settled herself her aunt was always keen to see people settled, though in other ways she was a determinedly independent-minded woman.

Judith would be giving up her independence if she did marry Mr Watson, thought Cressida; she liked her shop; anyone could see that.

Sometimes, when she was exhausted from London and commuting, and work that either took up too much of her time even if it paid well, or paid badly when it allowed her more time to herself, Cressida thought that she would like to throw everything up and go and run a little shop in the country like Judith's and have a peaceful life. The Dales would be nice. She mentioned her daydream to Jonathan as they set off on the Saturday afternoon to try to find Anne's former home. She nearly said that solicitors could easily find work in nicer places than London, but that would be to give him too much encouragement.

'I'd like to keep a village shop and live near a river or a village green with only a few sheep for company . . . '

'You sound like your aunt,' he said. 'But there's no reason why you shouldn't live in such a place, is there?'

She thought, I could marry someone like that son of Judith Kershaw's, the one who wanted to meet me in London — and then we could buy his mother's shop or manage it for her and I could settle into being absolutely ordinary. She did not express these thoughts aloud. Jonathan might think she was quite ordinary enough and it would be ignoble to mention that a young man whom she had in fact no intention of looking up had asked to meet her again. It would either make Jonathan jealous, or make him say, with his usual tolerance: 'Oh, how nice — you must take him up on that.' Jonathan knew perfectly well that she had been in love with Patrick Simmonds, but when she came to think about it he'd never shown much belief in her settling down with him.

All she said was: 'I'm thinking of finding another job — in children's books — I've had enough of temping, I think.'

His face lit up. 'You really must — it would be a shame to throw away all that knowledge and experience.' Last year he had often shared her ribald accounts of some of the manuscripts which came her way written by people who knew no children, or if they had ever known any it had been many years ago. Or by the latest manifestations of hippiedom who wrote about children called 'Cloud' and 'Running Water'.

They were out on the open heath now and it was cold and windy. A few intrepid fathers were out with kites which they were supposed to be showing their children how to fly but which were an excuse for enjoying themselves. The two young people followed a path to the pond and walked past the squat church which was stuck on the corner of the heath like a mid-Victorian toad, and crossed the road in the direction of that part of the 'village' which had been there two hundred years before, leading out of the hollow now cut through by the railway. They crossed another road, walked up a slight rise and then turned in to the right, down a one-way street, at the end of which they followed a narrow road to the right again which turned once more before ending up behind a row of larger houses.

'It was behind there,' she said, consulting her aunt's instructions, 'at an angle made by those three houses on the other side of the road before we get to the bigger ones.' The houses were lower and smaller here, painted white, and a lane led behind them, in a higgledy piggledy way. She stopped in front of the last one, a small cottage, weather-boarded in Kentish fashion. Further on, the lane turned into an open space, a little green, the extreme edge of the old heath.

'There ought to be a blue plaque,' she said. 'Her brother was quite a famous painter.' They stood peering at the house in the grey afternoon.

'Shall I take the photograph?' Jonathan offered.

'Better take one or two just in case.' She handed over the camera, hoping the occupant was not watching them, but the house showed no visible sign of life. Many of these smaller older houses were converted nowadays, having been modernized inside.

'I'd like *you* to be in some of them,' he said. Cressida agreed, and then said: 'I'll take you too — there's a whole roll of film.' She was trying to put herself in Anne's place, convincing herself of the actual truth — that the poet had walked on this very spot in the 1790s, perhaps with her friends the two Marys, about whom Daphne had spoken with such enthusiasm. They had really stood here . . . She frowned with the effort of putting herself there with them, and Jonathan said: 'Now one with you smiling.'

She said: 'It's hard to think back, to really *feel*, that once upon a time these houses were here, recently built, and there were people walking out of them and going to the shops — I suppose there was a shop or two? and taking the coach, all full of their little lives — just as we are, and now nothing left — only the houses, the place — some of the trees perhaps . . .'

'The same sun,' said Jonathan.

'Yes, but you know what I mean — that feeling that everything was there for them just as it is for us now — and what did it matter? They all died in the end — and now there's nothing left.'

'Well there are those poems you told me about . . .'

'Yes — just to leave *something* — to show you were once alive!'

'People's great-great-great-grandchildren are somewhere around,' he answered. 'Somebody's descendants anyway — if not your poet's.'

'Yes, I know — but it doesn't alter the fact that now *those* people are all gone — and then sometimes you feel they are alive still. I think I dreamed about Anne, you know.'

She told him of her dreams as they walked down the hill to the modern suburban village with its busy purposeful shoppers. 'That's what I mean,' she said. 'Here they are all — and us too — thinking we're so important and then we'll be gone too — '

'Not yet,' he said with a smile. 'We've got all our lives to live in the present.'

★ ★ ★

'An unmarried literary critic in his late twenties with a finger in many pies and with a passion for introducing people to each other,'

368

wrote Daphne. 'He knew everybody and sympathized with the female feminist writers.' She looked up. He must have been a nice man. Lamb wrote that essay about him years later. She felt certain now that it had been the critic George Dyer and not his cousin William who had loved Anne Platonically, though she still had no firm proof. She ought to be writing a novel. 'Creative biography,' she thought, with Cressida's photographs in front of her. The poems tell us more about her than the scraps I can reconstruct of her life, peeled of their stage effects to find the raw feeling underneath. Yet if they hadn't been fashioned and formed and given a story and characters to act out their writer's own fantasies, they would have been less good as poems. Fantasies didn't perhaps change very much over time? Southey said Anne was sensitive and full of heart and feelings, that she wanted to retire to the country, longed to leave London, was depressed. It was odd how the same kinds of feelings began to be expressed by different people all at the same time. Was Anne an early Romantic, like Marianne in the novel, full of 'sensibility'?

She looked out at the yard. The rich neighbours, the Johnsons, had returned, and been full of sympathy about her burglary.

Where were her coffee-pot and candlesticks now?

Back to work! But now she was imagining Mary W. telling her little three-year-old daughter Fanny that she was going to marry Godwin. Maybe for all her emancipation Mary did not confide in her own child, left her to a nursemaid so she could get on with her writing. Even 'progressive' people had servants.

* * *

Judith's sons would have to be told soon if Judith decided to marry Alan.

'There must always be a home for the boys,' Judith had said recently, and then gone on to say that she always feared something awful happening to her, to 'punish' her.

'Nothing awful will happen through Alan,' Daphne had assured her friend. 'And if ever anything did, he'd be there to see it through with you.' She was always so firm about advising others to say 'yes' to life. Why couldn't she say 'yes' to it herself and set herself free from the past? Had her burglary been a sign that she must live in the present? Roger had been away on business — although retired he still apparently took on small commissions. Then his son's wife in Cheshire had had a baby. Not his first grandchild — Moira in New Zealand had two daughters, but the first grandson. She had had a picture postcard of Chester from him that morning with 'Regards — R.M.' He was to return soon. She had allowed herself to day-dream a bit about him making love to her, but whenever she did she saw herself as *young*. There was something wrong in that — and she needed a sign that he might feel the same about her.

How nice it would be to be a cat, she thought, as Widgery sidled into the room, tail up. Cats didn't change over the centuries, did not understand about burglars, made quite clear always what they wanted . . .

The snowdrops had been under her window-sill for some time in the cold northern earth and daffodils were already in bud in the Johnsons' garden at the back of their house.

She went back to Southey's letters. At what length they wrote in those days! She must reply to Cressy too. The photographs were very good and she liked the one Jonathan had taken of Cressy in front of the house.

She had spent a day trying to describe Anne's physical presence which appeared to her so easily in dreams but fled when she was awake. All the time she kept seeing parts of her own life flash before her: her early rackety years, her own mistakes. She'd resembled Anne less than she'd been like the two Marys.

* * *

One night in the middle of March she dreamed of a woman standing alone at a casement on a morning of early spring . . .

She was preparing to walk to her work across the heath, the first line of a poem in her head.

Daphne woke out of the dream and wrote it down:

The heath gay-glittered with a shifting light.

After dressing and having breakfast she consulted the small volume of verse and found that it was almost a line of Anne's. But Anne had written:

The plains gay-glittered with ethereal light.

She must have read it and half remembered it. She spent that morning copying out another long poem, a useful way to see the good and bad points of someone's writing.

She would have given a lot to know Anne's state of mind before writing this verse. It didn't matter as far as judging the poem was concerned, but it mattered for her understanding of the woman, and that was, decided Daphne, what interested her most of all. Had Anne said goodbye to life long before she died, abandoned her writing? Nobody seemed to know. Even if the verse had arisen for a large part from unhappy love, it was the poetry that had mattered most to her, just as now it was Anne's life that mattered most to Daphne, in the absence of any poetic inspiration of her own. When you apprehended the solidity of a long life, your own began to fit into the general scheme of things.

Neither would Cressida have a life like Anne's, she decided, not being a writer.

* * *

Cressida, in the interval of working her last week at the temping, was having thoughts which her aunt might have called metaphysical. Thoughts about falling out of love. She had decided that it was more a matter of the imagination than the will, or more likely the imagination aided by the will. Once absence ceased to make the heart grow

373

fonder it was such a relief, even if one also felt a bit guilty towards one's own past self. If the heart recovered it meant only that the imagination had constructed another scenario, aided at first by a little shove from the will that was fed up with suffering. It probably meant too that she was a shallow, superficial person, but it did make existence lighter and brighter. Love could be a fearsome weight. She awoke early one March morning just before dawn and drew her curtains to watch the sky lighten. Then, in a matter of minutes, everything was shiny with new light. That was how she felt, a part of it all, with a new day to look forward to.

18

Dear Cressy — Lovely to hear from you. I'm so glad you're going to try to get back into publishing. I know it's badly paid but it must be more interesting than typing reams of fiddly letters about share certificates. I was amused that you thought I was 'getting at you' about my Anne. You thought I was saying 'Don't be like her', in the sense of missing the boat and leading a solitary life (like me). I didn't mean that. What I was hinting at — and you are quite right to detect a whiff of Your Old Aunt Knows Best, for which I apologize — was that Anne was always (I think, from what I've read of her) longing to retire to the country. I think she wasn't very sociable. I didn't mean to imply that she was left on the shelf. As a matter of fact I think that luck plays a bigger part in all this than people are apt to realize. It's true that Anne was in love with a man who only had Platonic feelings for her, but I think she just didn't meet any men who would have been likely to want to settle down with her. She would know some of her brother's friends — but artists don't usually look to marry young women who scribble. At that time, women 'scribblers' were usually considered by men — and by many women — as either slatternly or licentious or both. Perhaps they still are? So poor Anne, who I'm sure was neither, wouldn't have had much chance when compared with eighteen-year-old girls with modest fortunes from Papa. The man towards whom her affections were aimed missed thereby a woman of delicacy and inner strength. I've become sentimental in my old age and begun to approve of marriage — for the young. I wonder how many of your generation of women are really at the bottom of their hearts looking for a good husband, now they can have children without that item once regarded as essential. How many the same age as Anne when she published — thirty — have just not been able to find a man whom they consider a good enough bet? In my day women almost all wanted marriage — if they were honest. I thought things had changed, but your letter seems to say that they have not. Except for cohabitation replacing love affairs?

Judith continues to agonize. The latest news is that her youngest son, Colin, has decided to come home sooner than expected. He doesn't explain why — she thought he was to continue going round the world until next summer.

Things are looking up here. The grocer now stocks fresh tagliatelle that you can keep frozen, and, being lazy, I'm pleased to find some of the jars of sauce for pasta are quite tasty.

I had another dream about Anne the other night, the first time for weeks. It must have been your letter, combined with the photograph of the cottages, for I'd been imagining how differently they might have looked two hundred years ago, in summer. I had been trying to construct the sort of conversation Anne and her Platonic friend — could have had.

I dreamed of the most beautiful little garden behind high walls. The flowers in the borders were white and there was a white table at which a woman and a man were sitting. I know it was evening. There was a paper on the table which the woman kept glancing at, obviously a poem she'd just finished. All I can recall now of the long conversation which went on, was him saying 'You must polish, polish — it's a pity they called you 'artless'. That can be good, but let it not mean irregular quantities!' She looked most despondent and there was an atmosphere of sadness around, in spite of the pleasantness of the sun which cast low rays on a patch of flowers. She was wearing a white shawl and a white bonnet and a long dress of dark green. I had the impression — no more than that — but woke with it — that the gentleman was about to take orders!

Tell Jonathan that I am to receive what I asked for from the insurers. I found a photo Mother once took of that silver necklace with a valuation from the 1950s and they accepted a figure based on what *the town jeweller said it would now be worth. What a shame — it was something I was going to give you one day!*

Daphne read her letter over and considered. When Charles left her all those years ago, she had been full of self-deception but she remembered a feeling of relief. The trouble with Charles had been not only that they could not get married because he was already married but that they were not right for each other — or at least she was right for him but he wasn't for her. Finally, he'd acted. She'd have made a marriage last if she'd been given the chance.

Had Anne regretted that she hadn't made an effort to meet more people after her lover had made it clear he wasn't in love with her? Had she put as much energy into love as she had into her poetry? Without her unrequited love, would she have written at all?

She wrote a short note to Roger to await his return:

Give me a ring and come round for a drink when you are back — I owe you some hospitality. I'm afraid the burglary distracted me from inviting you. You were very kind and must have thought me rude.

I'm so glad your new grandson arrived safely — D.

Judith Kershaw and Alan Watson were sitting together in the shop one Saturday evening. The shop was closed, but Alan had come round to help her unpack a consignment of crockery packed in straw in tea-chests. The night before, Judith had telephoned him with Colin's news: that he would be home in a week or two. 'I just can't understand it — he was all set for a year in the States — he might even have gone from San Francisco to Japan and then India — though he hadn't made up his mind. Now he says he's coming home!'

'Didn't he give any explanation?'

'Not really.' Now she took out the letter for him to see.

'Here's his letter — it's not very long. Read it.'

She handed over a thin blue airmail wafer and sat on the shop counter whilst he read it. He looked up. 'Do you think he's just missing his home comforts?' she asked.

'No — I think there must be a girl involved — someone who's coming back to England whom he doesn't want to miss!'

'At *his* age?'

'Well, some young men *are* like that — the romantic ones. Perhaps he felt he wasn't earning very much and might just as well find something here. You said he wasn't sure of a place at college?'

'No, his A levels weren't up to much. He works hard at what he likes, but I don't know what he really wants to do.'

Alan was silent for a moment. Then: 'I never taught him but I think I know the type.' Judith waited. Should she be annoyed that he had cast her son as a 'type'? 'At least he's made a decision,' said Alan. 'That's good — and he says here he wants to find a job — that doesn't sound bad, does it?'

'But what sort of job — we're in the middle of a recession!'

'I had a word with your Stephen at Christmas — something he said about Colin? — Yes, he said: 'He's the one most like Grandpa — he likes to be in charge of things but nothing too big or too complicated.' '

'Well — fancy him telling *you* that — I didn't know Steve was so perspicacious.'

'Don't you think that he might be just the person to manage this shop for you?'

Judith was amazed. Colin had always helped her a lot in the shop but she'd thought that was because she gave him more pocket-money when he did. 'But he couldn't take it over!' she exclaimed.

'I wasn't thinking of that quite yet. But

why not let him help you when he returns and then see how he does? Ask him. He's probably the sort of person who doesn't want to bother with further study, just wants to be independent.'

She considered. For a man who had never met her youngest son he sounded convincing. 'Think about it anyway,' said Alan. 'Now let's make some supper before you come back to the bungalow. It's my turn.'

During the meal — sole and mashed potatoes, she thought about it. When they'd finished, Alan, who had been quiet — one thing about him was that he never talked for the sake of it — said: 'I had an idea about expanding the DIY part of your business.'

'Yes?' she said faintly.

'Well — you once said Colin was good with his hands. What if we provided — you provided — a service to people wanting help with that sort of thing? I know a bit about it myself and I could start it off. For love, Judith, not for money!' She laughed.

'Then I could see if that interested Colin?'

They seemed to have mapped out Colin's life for him already.

'What if this girl — or whatever he's coming home for — doesn't live anywhere near here? He'd want to be near her, wouldn't he?'

'He says in his letter he wants to come back to Yorkshire,' Alan reminded her. 'What if he's the sort of young man who wants to save up and have a conventional courtship — I think you said he was that steady type of boy and the only thing that had worried you about him had been his lack of interest in academic work?'

'Yes, that's true, Alan. I think you must be a clairvoyant. We'll put it to him when he comes back.'

'In the meantime, think about my little idea?'

'It sounds wonderful! You've really cheered me up. And if Colin turns out not to be interested, well you could always take over the DIY yourself!'

★ ★ ★

Colin Kershaw came back after Easter. He was a tall quiet young man with a nice smile and a reserved manner. Judith introduced him to Alan, saying: 'This is Mr Watson, Colin.' They shook hands and Colin said: 'Oh, yes. Ben wrote to me,' but said no more then. Later, when Alan had gone home, he sat down with his mother and she waited for anything more he might want to tell her about his return.

'You seemed to like your job in New York,' she began, after they'd finished their supper and he had also demolished three bananas, and poured two large cups of coffee down his throat.

'I *did* like it — but it seemed I was wasting my time — I dunno — I thought I'd rather be home — I met some English people there from around here, and some American students and — ' He stopped, looked at his thumb nail.

'What about them? Did they make you feel you wanted to come back and sort out a course for yourself?'

'No — not really. You won't be cross if I tell you what I thought?'

'Why should I be cross, Colin?'

'Well, I began to think they were mostly pissing around with their lives and I wanted to have a proper job. I thought about being taken on there permanently.'

'You never told me that.'

'No, well it wasn't possible. So I thought, why not get a job back home? I don't think I'd like to live over there for good — everything's such a rush — and when they said there *wasn't* any prospect, I thought I'd come home. I know you wanted us all to go to college — and there's Steve with his accountancy exams and Mark with his graphics and Ben with his law studies — but *I've* never really wanted to go to college.' He paused and cleared his throat. 'I'd like to run a small business. I know it sounds sudden. But I did — suddenly — realize over there — that that was what I wanted to do,' he ended in a rush. So Alan had been right? Colin was looking a little guilty. She had never heard him make such a long speech. When she told him what she'd been thinking of, his face brightened. Colin Kershaw, his mother realized, wanted to carry on the family business! He didn't need a further qualification for that. Later he might take some courses but that was for the future.

She told him too about the idea of a DIY section and that Alan Watson wondered whether that would interest him. Colin said: 'He's sweet on you isn't he? I'm glad.' Then he looked down and blushed and she forbore for the time being to ask him anything about his own love life, or even if it existed. The mention of the students met over in the States might just have included some female ones. But he was so young! Knew his own mind though.

Judith still had a few doubts but only time would tell whether Colin had just been homesick, or was chasing some girl, or was truly keen on learning the trade. She'd always wanted her sons to get out from under and it was ironic that this youngest one should be like his grandfather. It had needed an outsider to see it.

When Alan came over the next day, Colin having gone out on some mysterious errand to the town, she told him he'd been right.

'It'll need a lot of planning. For the moment, strike while the iron's hot and give him a bit of responsibility. I'm sure he's watched you for years and has a good idea of the ordering and the books.'

'Yes, that's the part he might find tedious. He wasn't *bad* at maths, though not as clever as Stephen.'

'It's all calculators now,' Alan said rather gloomily.

'Don't worry — I'll play it softly. I think he's got his own fish to fry,' said Colin's mother. 'There's probably a girl at the bottom of it who'll take his mind off me and you. I think he stayed somewhere in Manchester before coming on home.'

Even so she was anxious that he might not like business when it was a day-by-day grind and not an occasional helping out. Still, he'd worked long hours in New York. He might even have ideas for improving the shop. She felt too old for innovations herself.

I must reply to Daphne, thought Cressida, as she stood waiting to be served in the cheese shop in Jermyn Street. She loved cheese, often bought a tiny sliver of a hitherto unknown variety to tickle her palate. Tomorrow Jonathan was coming to dinner and she'd decided to cook something simple and end with a platter of cheese. Some cheeses were extremely expensive but they saved a lot of time making fiddly desserts or relying on fruit. She was at this moment holding a packet of Bath Olivers and feeling very hungry. During the last year she'd had a time of not feeling hungry at all but since her visit north her appetite had reasserted itself.

The Swaledale was £5.65 a pound! She resolved to ask for four ounces, just to try. Then if it were good she'd take some to her aunt next time she went up north. She'd never seen that cheese on sale up there though it came from a place less than fifty miles from Heckcliff.

Her aunt's letter had cheered her. If Daphne didn't think she was on the shelf, then she wasn't. Daphne was such a one for wanting other people settled but had convinced her she wasn't worrying about *her*. Perhaps though she'd given her up as a bad job?

The problem, she thought as she asked for the Swaledale and half a pound of Lancashire, which she knew was delicious, was that the words 'out of the frying pan' haunted her. She was having cold feet over Jonathan. He hadn't been at all pushy or hinted at anything. It wasn't his fault that she was chary of believing that he had those feelings for her. But when a person wrote letters to you, wanted to see you whenever he had a free afternoon or evening and telephoned you at odd times, what were you meant to think? Did he take her for granted? Was he waiting for her to say something? Nowadays, men found it harder to start things — men like Jonathan anyway, not men like Patrick Simmonds who just went on ahead when it suited them and for as long as it did. Men, like women, came in many varieties.

The other phrase was 'on the rebound'. She'd known Jonathan before she'd met Patrick, and that was the problem. If he'd been a bit quicker with his Platonic or non-Platonic intentions she might never have fallen in love with the other man. And in spite of the slight fear that she was maybe plunging for what was available, she decided, as a man tenderly wrapped up her cheese and gave her a chit to pay at the other end of the shop, that she had better find out Jonathan's true intentions. Over the Swaledale and claret. Or would port and Stilton be better? Never mind. Getting at the truth of a man's intentions through his stomach was so politically incorrect that it couldn't matter really which cheese or which wine she offered him so long as he knew she'd made an effort to please.

★ ★ ★

Daphne put another piece of paper into her old typewriter and considered what manner of Christianity Anne's mother, Elizabeth Batten, might have professed. How did Dissenters bring up their children in the 1760s and 1770s? Her knowledge of such matters was shaky. She must not assume that the household was run on the lines of the Wesleys whose mother had had nineteen children, nor that the *Pilgrim's Progress* was the staple diet. But how 'progressive' might she have been? Progressive enough not to worry about their children's friends when political Radicals made their appearance after the children reached their twenties?

There was no end to this research if you

wanted to be as sure as possible of your facts — or have more evidence for the suppositions you erected over them! She would much rather imagine, and that was not good enough. Her re-creation had to be built on foundations more solid than instincts or dreams. *Had* Anne lived on to be an old lady, perhaps a very old lady? She saw her, tall and erect in bearing, a bit like old Mr Thorpe who was eighty-six and still walked round Heckcliff every day, straight-backed. Women often became hump-backed, or suffered from the rheumatics, even if they lived longer than men. The tyranny of the body again . . . her thoughts kept wandering, a sure sign she'd better pack up for the day. What did it matter whether Anne's mother was an invalid or hale and hearty? Anne had written no verse about old age that she could discover.

The French Revolution must eventually have become only a vague memory for Anne, as the war now was for herself.

She felt more and more strongly that whilst she was recreating Anne, dreaming of her, 'writing' her, she was working out something in herself. It was one way of being positive about life to try to make some sort of sense out of the past; whatever you wrote must come out of your own past experience too, even if you'd forgotten it. You were like a rock made up of different geological strata of which the lower levels had become too deep to excavate. It was only when, quite without your doing anything about it, some secret spring was released from underground, that it brought with it a taste of where it had been.

Roger Masterson might be able to unseal that spring in her if he wanted — but it would have to be soon. She must be told of his feelings and intentions.

★ ★ ★

Judith had come to the conclusion that her own obsessive hard work arose from a fear of feeling redundant. She had thrown so much into the shop in latter years as the boys grew up because she was frightened that when the last one left she'd have no *raison d'être*.

When she pointed this out to Alan, he smiled. 'It isn't as if you'd have nothing to do with yourself, Judith, even if you eventually left the shop to Colin. What about all your plans for painting?'

It was then that she said, 'Oh, but you see I always thought painting was a selfish activity — something I was allowed to do only after a hard day's work.'

'You've got used to overworking,' he said. 'It isn't that the shop makes you feel alive but that it relieves you of guilt. Isn't that true?'

She considered. 'Yes, I suppose I've felt guilty ever since Andrew left.'

'So you took on not only four boys but a shop as well!'

'I suppose that once they went to school — quite apart from desperately needing the money then — I felt it gave me a base — and then I just got used to it.'

'But it wasn't shopkeeping that made you feel *alive*, Judith. It just keep you too busy to think.'

'Yes, you're right. It's my painting that makes me — used to make me — feel alive. I thought it was a luxury.'

'You must do more of it, challenge yourself! Even if you fail — and artists never think they've achieved what they wanted to achieve. Your *raison d'être* has changed now the boys are grown. Women put so much into their children and their only reward is to see them go away to live their own lives.' He looked solemn, had obviously been pondering this speech.

She was thinking: but if I marry you, where will that leave my painting?

He said, divining her thoughts: 'Look at it this way. If you finally do hand over the shop to Colin and take me on, it's a just exchange! I won't take up as much time as the shop did, and all that lovely time left over will be for you to do what you want with!'

She laughed. 'You make yourself sound like a job, Alan. You make things *easier* not harder — '

'So will you believe me when I say that if I thought I'd take anything away from you — time or energy — I wouldn't want to marry you? I believe you have a lot of talent and it will be my task to give you the right atmosphere for your work.' He said this with a flourish. She did believe him: he was one of those rare modern men who combined chivalry and realism. 'Anyway,' he added, 'I've plenty to do myself, wouldn't want you sitting thinking about the spring cleaning.' She laughed. It would be strange though, losing the shop — if that was how it was to be worked out. Her life-line, she thought. It had kept her sane whilst the children were going through adolescence, for without it she'd have had nothing to think about but them. But Alan was right. It had served its purpose. So long as she wasn't a financial drain on him.

Through conversations such as this she began to believe that the future could indeed be rosy. No use hurrying it all up though.

Once she'd said 'yes' to his most important proposal she would speak to Colin. The thought of being finally challenged in her painting did however frighten her a little.

★ ★ ★

Jonathan had enjoyed the Swaledale cheese and the claret. He loved Cressida Miller with the kind of love that went with his steady nature, one that under a veneer of shyness was also a little obstinate. He was modest about his own attractions, if fairly confident of his capabilities as far as work was concerned. Cressy was a lively young woman who never bored him, which so many young women had been apt to do. He'd always thought it was his fault that he found little to say to them. Perhaps though it had not been? Women he had gone out with who were concerned with fashion, being smart, or choosing to present this side of themselves to him, had always disappointed him in the end, even though he'd found them superficially attractive. On the other hand the women he met at work were so ambitious they made him feel stupid. That he accomplished just as much as they did without agonizing had annoyed *them* and made *him* feel a traitor to feminism. Cressy was clever and nice-looking and amusing and just smart enough to look as if she hadn't tried too hard. She was also kind. He had taken over a year to realize that he loved her rather than just being fond of her. It wasn't a great romantic passion — he admitted this to himself. But great romantic passions were often, as he knew Cressy had discovered, a disappointment. He enjoyed doing things with her and she hardly ever talked shop, which was a relief. Aware as he was that she needed a commitment but also didn't want to be obsessed with her love as (he'd observed) she'd been with Patrick Simmonds, he thought that now was the time to stand in his true colours. Even if she turned him down he'd feel better in himself.

Cressy was slightly surprised that she was actually finding Jonathan sexually attractive. She wasn't sure whether he found her so. She'd thought he might be a bit in love with her, or that he thought he was, but his way of going about it was so different from Patrick's that she occasionally wondered whether she'd read the signs wrongly. Also he was a practising Anglican.

When they sat down one evening with their coffee, and she put some Rameau on her cassette player — she was saving up for a CD player — she suddenly realized that she trusted him. If he didn't pounce on her, she told herself, it didn't mean that he was content to go on being just a friend, meant only that he was unsure of her or himself. But she didn't want to say anything unless he did. She'd had enough of romantic declarations on her own part and of ecstatic eroticism on the part of others.

'Have you spent a lot of time being in love with people?' he asked abruptly, drinking his coffee and looking at her over the rim of his cup.

'Do you mean have I often fallen in love? I suppose so. It's been a wasted youth, I fear,' she replied flippantly. 'Have you?'

'A few times — but I've never known people well enough before — '

'You mean you fell in love with them without knowing what they were really like?' she said hurriedly.

'I suppose so.'

'I think that's what falling in love is, isn't it? How can you feel like that when you know someone through and through?'

'It depends on the person. And on yourself. I feel I know *you* quite well by now.'

'But perhaps you don't, and if you did you wouldn't like me,' she said.

'I'm willing to try to discover that,' he said. 'If you'll let me.'

'Well,' Cressy said nervously after a pause. 'I like you — but I'm not in love with you, Jonathan — I mean — '

'Not like you were with Patrick?'

'Well, no — other men too — whom I never knew well enough, I suppose.'

'I'm different from Patrick. People don't fall for me in that way!' he said. She thought he sounded sad, but not self-pitying, quite matter-of-fact.

'Someone might — a different sort of woman from me. I mean someone less selfish.'

'Oh I think we complement each other quite well,' he said and put his hand out and held hers. 'So long as I don't repel you.'

He didn't repel her at all. He was a virtuous man, she realized, when later they extricated themselves from a long embrace.

19

Sonia was trying to lose herself in a yoga session, attending in obscure homage to Gwyneth.

How can my body melt away, as long as my mind's lamp goes on glowing? Did

Gwyneth reach heights — or depths — of meditation? I can't be 'supremely conscious of Being' when I am not supposed to be thinking . . .

For these Oriental sages and their Western acolytes, was mind controlled by body or body by mind, or did they believe they were one and the same when they meditated? They said that all was 'pure consciousness'. But of what? If you opened your eyes you still saw part of your body. Even if you felt you were more than your body — as I knew Gwyneth had been as I stood by her coffin — it was the trapped mind that was doing the thinking. Your fingers or your feet or even your eyes could not know anything; they felt, and the mind received their messages. Eyes were part of both body and mind, the furthest extension of the brain — windows of the soul Father used to call them. A shaft of sunlight comes through the eyes and warms the heart, that part of the limbic system which is also part of the brain. Might as well call it 'self' — or 'soul', I suppose. In blissful dreams one is irradiated with a joy beyond words but it vanishes when you wake up and try and remember. If 'I' exist at all, my body exists. But part of my body is my mind which makes me behave in a certain way.

Come along, body, obey me! Lift your arm, scrunch up your toes. Whose arm? Mine. Not my '*body's*' arm alone . . .

This meditating is no good, it makes me more muddled, not less, and leaves me pondering ancient questions to which I suspect there are no answers. I can't be like Gwyneth. I might feel refreshed and weightless and happy to let my mind think for me rather than to direct it, but I believe too much in words and in that dualistic self which I'm sure is not there when you are dead. My self awareness — the neurotic part of myself? — gets in the way of this pure consciousness, making me take a certain line which I seem incapable of changing or abandoning. I'll go on trying to understand — the exercises at least are good for me, but I can't accept all the philosophy behind them — this 'merging with the universe', when I am perfectly aware even at times of physical or emotional bliss or agony that I am separate, not just a mindless molecule obeying certain laws. I keep my small mind-lamp glowing and fear to lose it even when I am asleep. I don't want to wander as a body or a mind in some ill-defined space imagined by someone else's words . . .

She continued to attend these classes she'd begun after Gwyneth's funeral but gave the

April meeting of the reading circle a miss. Yoga might not be doing her any good but it wasn't doing her any harm. You couldn't live on a plateau of mystical non-being called 'being', when decisions had to be taken day by day.

The fury she felt towards the youth whose driving had killed Gwyneth did not abate. But she had come to a decision that might or might not have to do with that death. You could express your horror through actions or through words. For her, words had always been the most powerful things she knew to alter states of mind. But now she needed to do something. How better to confront present realities than by throwing herself into something quite different? She told Bob that she was thinking of writing something but needed a different sort of life first as a focus for it. He was encouraging. Her husband realized that Gwyneth's death had brought her to a crossroads.

'I'm fed up reading other people's ideas,' she said. 'I need to *do* something and then I shall put down my feelings about it.' Dorothy could take over the reading circle she thought. She'd love to take over the group. Always busy, she was the epitome of those people you ask if you need anything done. Evelyn and Lydia would continue to attend. Daphne might not want to go on with it if she left? It was good that Joy Wood had been able to come to the funeral. Now she'd made the first plunge she might begin to get out in the evenings too, find someone to help with her mother-in-law?

Dorothy tried to dissuade Sonia from leaving the circle, but Sonia could see her heart was not in it.

'The next meeting won't be till May now — don't decide yet.'

Sonia decided to talk to Daphne about it. She wanted to read other things too, catch up on modern novels.

Dorothy informed Evelyn by telephone of Sonia's probable decision but Evelyn wasn't very interested. She'd recently had a big row with Ron, leaving her unexpectedly the victor, and for once she'd not felt guilty. She went out shopping after Dorothy's call, which included a visit to the shop in Heckcliff that sold travel and theatre tickets.

Coming out, she met Lydia who was buying a new type of cat food for Pause. He had indicated that he did not think much of the dried stuff she'd stockpiled before Christmas.

Evelyn looked rejuvenated, thought Lydia. She was wearing quite a decent skirt and a loose-fitting jacket. She'd even been to the

400

hairdresser, if Lydia was any judge.

'You look well, Evelyn,' she said hesitating on the pavement. She'd never found much to say to Evelyn.

'I'm just off to Cornwall for a week's holiday!' Evelyn announced, smiling. 'My daughter-in-law's invited me! They've been asking me for ages and Ron's always said he was too busy so I've said I'll go by myself.'

Bully for you, thought Lydia.

'I've even had to cancel two music lessons,' Evelyn added.

Gracious me, marvelled Lydia to herself, it didn't take much to make Evelyn happy. But she was the same, except she had no grumbling husband to placate about her holidays or plans. But fancy leaving grumpy Ronald by himself at home for once!

'I think Valerie must be pregnant, just have that feeling, you know. So I might be a grandma twice over this year — my son's wife in Australia expects a baby very soon!'

'How exciting,' murmured Lydia, attempting to look thrilled.

'*Isn't* it! But I'll be back from my holiday in time for the next meeting — Dorothy rang and said May. I *still* haven't finished *Vanity Fair*! I'll take it with me on holiday. She said something about Sonia leaving the group but I wasn't concentrating so perhaps

401

I didn't hear aright.'

They parted. How loquacious Evelyn had been. It was high time she became a bit more selfish. Her husband wasn't her fault, and it would be nice for her to have a new friend in her son's wife.

The flat seemed quiet when Lydia returned to it but she gave her normal sigh of relief that unlike Daphne, whose news had spread round both Heckcliff and Norwood, she had not been burgled. It was so peaceful to be home, to put her feet up after her salad lunch and flick through the *Antique Collector*. A vicarious pleasure, but she enjoyed it, and she might go to Sonia's daughter's shop one day and see if she could pick anything up that might blend with her décor. She had always loved shopping for bargains. Meanwhile, tomorrow was her bridge afternoon. Also, the day before, the manager of the flats had responded to her suggestion and said she could have the small patch of ground next to the entrance if she really wanted to do a bit of gardening — plant a shrub or two, spring bulbs, that sort of thing, since nobody else had the time. It was weeks since she'd mentioned it and she had despaired of receiving an answer. She'd always loved gardening, could improve the place no end. Other people might like her to do their window boxes for them too since they were all out at business and couldn't spare the time.

She'd realized at the funeral that she'd been right not to worry about the future. It was enough to be contented in the present and concentrate on what you liked doing. She might even take a leaf out of poor Gwyneth's book and learn to do a bit of yoga, as she knew Sonia was doing. It'd be good for her. She stretched her arms up over her head and breathed in and out. Pause looked startled.

'You and I have survived, Pause,' she said, emptying out some flower water and replenishing the vase with the delicate freesias she'd bought that morning. They reminded her of Gwyneth for a moment but she turned her thoughts away from that kind of contemplation. She'd finish *Vanity Fair* this evening. 'Be thankful, Pause,' she said as she poured him a saucer of single cream. She enjoyed occasionally spoiling him. 'Make the most of it,' she said. 'Enjoy life.' Who knew, she might even book a cruise in the autumn. They had garden tours all over Europe. Some of her bridge friends had been on them and reported favourably.

★ ★ ★

'How's your boy-friend?'

It had been Cressida's friend Charlotte who asked her this one evening in late April, forcing Cressida to perform a rapid double-take. Which man did Charlie think she was at present going out with? Charlotte Lane was not a close friend; they met occasionally for a drink in a wine-bar, having once worked together. She decided to be bold.

'Oh, Pat's fine, I expect. He's in Japan as far as I know,' she said carelessly.

'Pat? I thought you were going out with that solicitor — the tall man I saw you with at a concert — '

'Oh, well, yes, I am.' She paused. 'Getting to know each other better, as a matter of fact.'

Charlotte Lane giggled. 'Is that very hard? He looks nice. Who's Pat anyway?'

Too late she remembered that Charlotte had probably never seen her with Patrick Simmonds, the relationship with whom she had never bruited abroad; only close friends had known about it.

'Oh he was just someone I went out with earlier this year.'

Charlotte must have seen her with Jonathan, with whom she had indeed been going out but only in the old-fashioned sense. Her mother had objected to the phrase: 'Why say 'going out with' when you really mean 'staying in with'?'

'You *are* a dark horse! He looked besotted with you when I saw you — you didn't see me — it was at the Wigmore Hall. I was there with my new boy-friend. He's American and goes to every concert that's going. I've had to make an effort, I can tell you, not knowing my Stockhausen from my stockings.'

For some time Cressida listened whilst Charlotte went into details of her American. Then Charlotte asked her: 'You *are* going out with this solicitor, aren't you? A girl I know used to know him, said he was nice.'

'Yes — yes I am, I suppose. And he *is* nice.'

'You don't look very sure.'

'If you want a further report, Charlie, I'll send you one,' replied Cressida crossly. She wanted to ask who had known Jonathan before but didn't want to appear too interested. People were such gossips. Some men too — not Jon though. You were expected to talk about someone as though he were a commodity on the Stock Exchange when you weren't yet absolutely sure whether you were going to invest in him.

Cressida had been for an interview with a publisher of children's books who knew of her work as assistant to the assistant editor with another publisher of the same kind. They were to let her know by the end of the month whether she'd got the job of assistant editor — it meant less secretarial work and not much money, but she hoped very much that she had. Until she knew, she felt she was drifting, anchored only when Jonathan visited. He'd been a fixture in her life during the past year whenever she'd wanted to go to the theatre or for a walk and had indeed been useful in the Patrick era, had not even seemed to mind that she had used him when she felt miserable. Well, all that would have to change; she couldn't go on being like that. It was all or nothing. Yet she was still haunted by the fear that if Patrick were to return she'd be compelled to see him again and the whole miserable business might start again. She didn't *want* to see him, was frightened of seeing him — frightened of herself, really. She knew she must not, but had no confidence in her resolve. Was she weak-willed? She'd never understood whether 'having willpower' meant having your own way, or fiercely denying yourself something you wanted. Her mother had confused her as a child over this, having given Cressy the impression that a temper and a determination to get her own way were somehow not unadmirable. Anyway, Pat wouldn't want to see her and wasn't due back until July. But in the past he'd often changed his plans, as she well knew, or had had them changed for him, and she was terrified that he might suddenly return and she'd see him by chance and find all her resolve melted away. Then she had to tell herself again that he wouldn't want to see her; the affair was over unless she'd be willing to take him as she found him, go back to being the lover of an uncommitted man.

Jonathan had struck just at the right moment. As long as Pat was away her resolution would hold and she might get over him. The voice of reason that told her she didn't want to see Patrick also made her feel disloyal to her old feelings. But she enjoyed being with Jonathan; not just because his company was undemanding. He was certainly not boring, but it was true she found him soothing.

They had not yet been to bed together; she knew he wanted to. Which was, she supposed, all to the good. He wouldn't hustle her, wanted to get to know her even better, he said. He would certainly not be making love to an exciting stranger. What was that advice agony aunts always gave? That you never made a success of a relationship formed on the rebound from another? But she'd always liked Jonathan and already knew him quite well. If she got the job she wanted with Oaktree Books — which she felt sure she could do well, that would give her even more stability and make her life less hectic. It was only when she was alone and some sad music came on the radio or she listened to a cassette connected with Patrick or with her original feelings for Patrick, that the tears welled up. But she didn't know whether they were tears of sorrow or self-pity or just nostalgia for past feelings. Maybe they were a mixture of all three. Her aunt had once said *à propos* of one of those women whose lives she was digging into, that she was 'a continual victim to the enthusiasm of her feelings'. The woman herself had said so. People hadn't changed much. I don't want to be a victim of my feelings, Cressida said to herself, but was still powerless to prevent those upsurgings of loss, affecting her through music. Daphne had said something too about certain feelings continuing to arise in some people even when they were old. Emotions aroused by a simple song like *Drink to me only with thine eyes* — seemed somehow deeper than the actual feelings Cressida had experienced with Pat when she'd been close to him. She'd always known that he didn't love her, and therefore she must be mourning her own feelings rather than the man himself? Which was sentimental. She must grow up. It really was time for that, even if some people never did. You could not lose something you'd never possessed and she'd never possessed Patrick and doubted anyone ever would. He'd possessed her imagination though, and had not been a complete figment of it. She was torn between this need to rearrange her life, accept new experiences, and an urge to retreat into herself. Time spent alone had not stopped her feeling gloomy. Jonathan made her feel cheerful, which was a good thing. She was sure he thought she must bend to the inevitable. Whether it was as inevitable she should go to Jonathan as it was that she should leave Patrick, she wasn't sure. *He* obviously thought so.

How much easier it would be to live like her aunt's cat, not thinking or planning beyond the day or the hour. She would try to do that, be like that, and see where it led. Being passive would be a nice change.

Was she the right person for Jonathan Edwards, if, as it appeared, he was thinking of a lifetime together? That ought to be thought about quite apart from whether he was right for her. But it was not her problem, was beyond her own control. He was grown up, not a baby, and came to his own decisions.

Whilst getting ready for bed she recalled the chat she'd had earlier in the day with Charlotte, to whom she had mentioned none of her doubts. Now she was suddenly struck by another horrible fear. Did she just want to please Jonathan, not let him down as she'd been let down? But why worry about that? She trusted him, liked being loved, could with a bit of effort see herself as the 'object' of his desires quite apart from her usual sense of herself. That was a healthy sign. She wasn't going to accept Jonathan only as a rescue package.

She loathed being uncertain of her own feelings. Jonathan would just have to wait and see, and she would wait too to discover what she felt like doing when the occasion rose. In the meantime she'd deliberately turn her thoughts to other matters. It was a relief to concentrate on some research for Daphne. What a *coup* it would be to discover an actual piece of china Anne's famous brother had painted two hundred years ago. To this end she began, one Saturday afternoon, to comb all the local antique shops. If Joshua had painted eighteenth-century china, and if that china — or some of it — still existed, he would most likely have brought it home, or encouraged his family, his mother in particular, to buy some of his products. So *if* it still existed and hadn't been smashed long ago, it was likely that it might be in that part of London where they'd lived. If it were signed it would now be expensive, especially if anyone knew that the painter was later to be a founder member of the Society of Watercolourists. She would save up just in case she were incredibly lucky and did find some. It would be a good augury, she thought.

Jonathan's suggestion was that if the man had once worked for a Staffordshire pottery they might ask round museums too.

Cressida wrote a letter and posted it first to Burslem. It gave her a feeling of satisfaction to have done something even if it led nowhere. It was action she needed; to set something in train herself. When she was occupied in thinking about Joshua or his sister she found it quite easy to banish the problems of love from her imagination. Jonathan had asked for a copy of the snap he'd taken of her in front of Anne's house, which she'd given him. She suspected he carried it around in his wallet.

For his part Jonathan Edwards understood instinctively that Cressida Miller was in the process of changing directions in more ways than one. He knew that her previous passion had altered her perspectives on love and on men, but he was sufficiently an optimist to believe that something new always arose from the old, might even improve upon the old. Not all comparisons were odious. Whilst Cressida wanted to go on seeing him there was hope. The time would come when he judged it not too tasteless nor too presumptuous nor too crudely self-seeking of him to expect her to marry him. He was old-fashioned; he didn't mind waiting.

★ ★ ★

In Heckcliff, another old-fashioned young man, one who did not know himself for one, was working hard in his mother's hardware store. Daphne saw Colin Kershaw often when he was in the shop seeing to customers or arranging the new crockery that had arrived from China. China from China, she thought. It was very cheap, and Colin said it would attract people who couldn't afford the English stuff his mother was used to ordering. In early May Daphne went in and bought a new coffee pot from him. She'd never get back her lovely silver one. It was time to acknowledge that.

Daphne was feeling a little depressed, a little deprived. She too had given the March and April meetings a miss. Each time, Sonia had rung to say she was not going and this had decided Daphne too. The evenings were becoming lighter and might have encouraged optimism but there was something about the spring that began every year with the promise of youth and somehow never fulfilled that promise. It was a season for the young, whereas winter was for the old who preferred to sit at home with their curtains drawn. She sometimes felt secretly stern about the advent of Alan, not because she was jealous or envious but because she had reached the age when she had sincerely stopped thinking that a partner was always necessary to happiness. It was ironic that she was the one always telling people to settle down. She was a hypocrite. Then the stupid spring arrived and reiterated quite plainly that there would never be anything but solitude for her in any case. Maybe Judith would find out that painting was less of a compulsion than a new man in her life, a man Daphne did not grudge her. She didn't think that Alan would have yet told Judith anything about her own little long-ago affair. Discretion was the better part of valour — at least until he was sure of his future with her.

Roger Masterson had telephoned to say he would be delighted to come round on the Tuesday week — sorry he had not replied before but he had had to go to Manchester again to settle some old business. She awaited his arrival with a mixture of impatience and trepidation.

Work was the only antidote to feelings of loss and dislocation. It could be done anywhere, did not have to be accomplished in Heckcliff. For the first time she wondered whether she ought to move back to the city.

A magnetic disc had been bought for Widgery and a cat-flap fitted in the kitchen door. Partly this was for Daphne's own convenience so that she need not tramp around at night calling the cat from the bottom of her lawn at the back of the house, a lawn shared with the Johnsons; and partly because since the burglary she had begun to imagine what burglars might have done to her cat. There were so many horrible accounts in the newspapers every day of acts of sadism perpetrated on animals, babies, old people . . . She had also strengthened the locks on her front door. Not that a determined burglar would be stopped by the most secure locks in the kingdom. The cat-flap was a sort of reassurance that at least the cat would be able to come and go. Widgery was not a cat who made friends easily; he'd probably fled out of the house the minute the thieves had entered it and stayed on the high wall of the Snicket or up a tree until they had departed. But the magnetic disc showed she had done her best to allow Widgery freedom and made her feel she'd achieved something for somebody else. It had taken a few days for him to be persuaded to use the flap on his outward journey and he still thought that doors should be opened for him.

She was still feeling a little low and a little guilty too about giving the last meeting of the circle a miss. Sonia would get in touch with her when she felt like it. Her melancholy would lift, was as much a part of her as her passionate interests. She spring-cleaned her study and sitting-room to take her mind off herself. The next day she went to Leeds to look up various matters in the library there. A letter from Cressida, full of enthusiasm, was waiting on the mat when she returned.

We couldn't find any crocks painted by Joshua, but listen to this! Jonathan went on a visit a few days ago to a house in Hertfordshire on a mission concerning an old man's will and was taken on a tour of the house by the owner, Mr Peters, who's ninety and has always collected pictures. In an upstairs bedroom he was shown some old snuff boxes — why he kept them in the bedroom I've no idea — but there were several pictures on the walls, and Jonathan was trying to be polite about them. They were mostly water-colours. It was only because I'd told him about your Joshua's paintings that as they went downstairs, thinking this old chap might be a connoisseur of such things, he asked if he'd ever heard of him. Imagine his surprise when Mr Peters said, 'Oh, I may have one or two of his — I bought them in the twenties.' Jon could hardly contain himself but didn't want Mr Peters to think he thought they might be valuable. He asked to see them. Peters took him into a sort of back kitchen with a Rayburn and an armchair, the walls absolutely covered with more paintings. He pointed to a picture — a drawing — at the top and said, 'That's your man.' But it wasn't a landscape, it was a portrait of three women! There was a girl sitting on one side of a table and on the other side an older woman in profile, wearing a cap. In the centre was a young lady in a musliny-looking dress pouring tea from a small pot. 'I believe that's the painter's family,' said the old man. 'It'll say on the back.' He let

Jon take it down, which he could only do by standing on the kitchen chair and, lo and behold! when he turned it round there was a tiny label at the bottom saying 'Anne pours the tea 1793.' The man said: 'Has he suddenly become valuable?' as though Jon was an expert from Christie's. Jon said it was only that he had a friend who was interested in the painter and had been looking for examples of his painting and could he take a photograph of this one? He got his permission and went back the next day after work — wasn't that sweet of him? He took a flash photo and is having it enlarged. It'll be ready tomorrow and I'll send it on immediately.

Daphne put down the letter. She was actually going to see a painting of Anne? Jonathan might have been misinformed? It seemed too good to be true. She sat down, her earlier lethargy abated, and wrote a quick card to thank Cressy, or rather Jonathan. She wouldn't telephone; somehow the occasion demanded a letter, something old-fashioned, in keeping.

Has old man Peters others by Joshua? Was it signed? Initialled? Very excited. A thousand thanks. Love, Daphne.

417

She took it to the pillar box near the park, for they had the luxury of a last post at half past seven. The days were getting longer. Widgery was waiting by the cat-door when she returned. 'Go in, cat,' she said, pointing to the flap. But he continued to regard her sombrely. Perhaps he thought that he could enter only when she was in the house? Or that she too ought to go through the flap? She sighed, scooped him up and unlocked her door with her free hand. He was purring, must be pleased about something. Each time she returned home she could not repress the tiny fear that she might have been burgled again. Silly.

Widgery jumped down once they were in the kitchen and stood expectantly by his bowl in the corner, tail up. 'I wonder if Anne ever had a cat?' she said aloud to him. Strange that Lydia had one — you'd think she would not be fond of animals . . .

She must tell Judith about Jonathan's finds. She'd be interested, and the photograph would add local colour to what had been so far an excessively literary understanding. Judith might even be able to say if Joshua had been a good artist. Not that it would matter; it was Anne in whom she was interested. She thought of the portraits of his sisters executed by Branwell Brontë where the lack of finish, the flatness of the sisters' faces, brought the atmosphere alive as a better portrait of the subjects might not have done.

Whilst she poured out her own tea, Daphne thought of Anne Cristall pouring out tea for her mother and sister. If they found one of the crocks painted by brother Joshua they'd be incredibly lucky. But it was the poetry that really mattered. Whether the poet had been Mother at the table was only one of those little details one hoarded from the ruins of the past, details which gave life and colour to what was often only a collection of words scrawled or printed on paper that had survived the years. Poetry also arose from the contemplation of the everyday, and painters, too, often took the everyday as their subject when they were not painting wild landscapes.

She reread Cressy's letter. The child sounded pleased with her boy-friend. He must be a nice young man to bother so with his girl-friend's aunt's concerns, must be keen about her or else he wouldn't make the effort. She dismissed the idea that he might be insinuating himself by such means into her niece's life. Nasty people didn't bother with helping others.

* * *

419

Colin Kershaw was proving himself exceptionally capable and not only in his mother's eyes, though it might be expected she would want to find him so.

'I don't know why you're surprised, love,' said Alan after they had shut up shop on the Saturday after Daphne had received the letter from Cressida. Judith felt a little guilty about Colin when she spent Saturday night over at Alan's, but Colin said he didn't mind. He liked to go to bed late, and get up late on the Sunday, and Judith suspected he spent a lot of time on the telephone to a mysterious girl-friend. She left him enough food in the freezer to heat up for himself until she arrived back on the Sunday evening. Colin said he was perfectly capable of cooking and could always fetch some fish and chips at any time.

'The fish-and-chip-shop isn't open on a Sunday,' said his mother.

That evening Daphne Berridge was to come over. Judith knew that Alan was eager for her to see them as a settled couple. Daphne was not the sort to linger on and on when bedtime came, or ask embarrassing questions.

Judith had not painted much since returning from France but had done a good deal of sketching around the narrow valleys they called cloughs to the west and north of Heckcliff. Alan had taken her by car whenever she wanted to go and they had then walked by streams and fields and woods. Judith remembered the places from her childhood. For years she had been too busy to visit them. Occasionally during the children's early years she had taken them on walks but at that time sketching had certainly not been possible, the boys usually managing to fall in the beck or into a cow-pat, scrape a knee, stay up a tree, or fight with a brother.

'I wish I could find some porcelain painted by that artist brother of the poet Daphne's researching,' said Judith to her lover as she set out coffee-cups and a cake in Alan's immaculate kitchen. Daphne had phoned, full of Cressy's friend's discovery.

'Have you looked in all the antique shops?' enquired Alan, busy measuring coffee into his special filter which he swore was the only way to make coffee taste as good as it smelled.

'I've looked in most places but they don't have eighteenth-century stuff round here usually. They might in Harrogate, in places where tourists go. There *might* be some unworldly old ladies living round here who prefer nineteenth-century ornaments, who think the older things are too plain. They *might* 'lose' them in boxes in their attics.

Daphne was to bring along with her that evening the photograph of the drawing found in Mr Peters' house.

'I must look for a little booklet on teapots I once bought — or someone gave me,' Judith went on. 'I've a feeling that apart from the Chelsea ware the Staffordshire stuff wasn't painted awfully well until the end of the eighteenth-century — not like the French porcelain.'

'Did the French drink much tea then?' asked Alan.

'As much as anyone did — but our teapots were usually plain white earthenware — apart from the Chelsea pottery, or the Wedgwood later.'

'I once saw a very pretty little cream-coloured teapot in a Leeds museum,' said Alan. 'Quite plain.'

'I didn't know *you* were interested in teapots,' said Judith.

'No — it was Celia who was interested in such things — I went along with her on trips to museums.'

'Oh, darling I'm sorry — I should have thought — '

'Judith — what's the matter?' She looked distressed.

'I'm always putting my foot in it,' she muttered.

'Look, I'm happy to talk about her — I don't mind — I like you to know that sort of thing we did together — '

'Really?'

'Of course — and Celia *did* like that sort of thing. She wasn't artistic like you but she had good taste and she was interested in everything about domestic life in the past. Many's the time I've tramped around museums with Celia looking at flat-irons and old ovens.' Judith was able to smile.

Daphne arrived at a quarter past eight and they all sat in the room that overlooked the park. The sun was about to set over the high hill in the west, tingeing the sky dark pink and purple.

'So peaceful here,' murmured Daphne.

'Isn't it peaceful where you are?' asked Judith in surprise.

'No — I mean it's always peaceful in other people's houses because you can just sit down and relax and not think about the washing-up or the jobs you've lined up — or burglaries.'

'And drink a perfect cup of coffee,' added Alan handing over a small white fluted cup.

'Oh how pretty!' she exclaimed.

'Show us the photo, Daphne,' said Judith, knowing her friend was dying to do so.

Daphne drew out an envelope from her capacious handbag which she carried everywhere with her and slid out a colour photograph, quite a large one. 'He had it enlarged for me, did Jonathan,' she said. 'What do you think?'

Judith took a look. It was a reproduction of a drawing in a Victorian-looking frame. The young woman in the centre of the picture was facing the artist, looking straight at him, whereas the other two women were seen in profile.

'The one in the middle holding the teapot is Anne,' said Daphne.

'She'll drop that teapot or pour the tea over the table-cloth if she's not looking at what she's doing,' said Alan.

'I expect her brother wanted her to pose. There'd be no tea in the pot,' said Judith.

'There must be some reason for drawing her holding a teapot.'

'It *must* be because *he* painted the design on the pot! You can just make out some flowers — or trees.'

'This is probably a sketch for a later painting,' said Judith. 'Something he was going to work up — probably did, and then someone didn't throw this away and it was sold in a job lot when he died. Still, he must have been well enough known afterwards for the old man's family to have bought it.'

Alan was looking at the young woman. 'She has a look of you, Daphne,' he said.

'Me?' She was astonished.

'Well, I mean when you were younger — '

Daphne put on her spectacles and took back the photograph.

'The *line* is good,' murmured Judith. 'He's a competent draughtsman.'

'You can just see his initials,' said Daphne. 'Jonathan — Cressy's friend — said they were quite clear — 'J C'.'

'It would be nice to find that teapot or one like it,' suggested Alan.

'Cressy's been looking everywhere but if any exist as old as that they'd be in a museum.'

'Yes — Alan was just saying — '

'I think it will prove impossible — but it's a nice thought,' said Daphne. 'I'm so excited over the drawing though. Do you think this Mr Peters might sell it to me?'

'Hasn't Cressy's friend asked?'

'No, he didn't want to put the old man off. He was there only officially as his solicitor. You can hardly start to bargain with a client for his possessions.'

'*I* shall go on looking for you,' said Judith. 'You never know.'

425

20

Judith had searched high and low for any piece of crockery or porcelain painted by Anne's brother Joshua. On her half-days and, more often now, on a Saturday afternoon when she could leave the shop to Colin, she'd scoured local antique shops and attended any house sale that came to her notice. With Alan she'd gone further afield to York, to Harrogate, to Ripon and over into Lancashire but nothing had come to light. If anything of Joshua's still existed it must be either in London or in some Staffordshire warehouse or museum in spite of Cressida's drawing a blank in both places.

'He was quite famous later,' said Daphne, 'but his sister was just as well-known earlier on. Joshua came into his own when the new century dawned. I expect, because he was a man, people took him more seriously — but Anne's poetry was highly regarded.'

She had already told her friend about the glass and china shop he had managed in Aldgate and how when its owners, who had been very fond of Joshua, died they had offered him the shop in their will, and he had refused it. 'You can imagine what his family thought about that!' Daphne had added.

'I wonder if Colin has artistic talents we've never suspected,' said Judith laughing. 'At least he wouldn't refuse my shop.'

'Maybe he has,' said Daphne. 'Artistic talents, I mean.'

'What did Joshua do then, after all that?'

'Went to Shropshire, to a china factory — but spent all his time sketching. He asked if he could be their traveller, and I believe for a time he was, but eventually he left.'

'He seems to have been a leaver.'

'Well he knew he was an artist — of course Anne knew she was a poet, but she couldn't up and leave her governessing and travel around with a notebook, could she?'

'I suppose not.'

'He worked as a clerk for a time and then started to paint china himself.'

'When would that be?'

'The very early 1790s — that's just when he painted the picture we saw. None of his early jobs lasted long. In November 1792 — according to my reading he'd be about 26 — he became a student of engraving in the Royal Academy school. He helped to found the Society of Painters in Watercolours about twelve years later — and twelve years after *that* he became its President.'

'I suppose it's like nowadays. Young people are about twenty-five by the time they're qualified to do anything. Stephen's twenty three and only just beginning to earn enough to have a decent life — he didn't go to university though. Mark's better launched. I suppose your Joshua might have been a student of graphic design if he'd lived in our century. Do you think he was too pure to make money commercially?'

Daphne looked pensive. 'I keep thinking — these people were in their early thirties at the turn of the eighteenth century, almost the same age as Cressy and her friends and your boys are now. Then in the *next* century everything in Britain changed so much even though there wasn't a revolution. Will the twenty-first century change everything again?'

'We're still only in the nineties,' said Alan who had been half listening to all this. 'Maybe there will be an *English* Revolution?'

'Telescoping people's lives in the past cuts one down to size, I feel,' replied Daphne.

* * *

Judith was recalling this conversation in the market-place of a small town in the Dales.

She wandered among the stalls and booths, Alan having left her there whilst he went to see an old colleague who had retired close by and whom he had absolved Judith from meeting. Now she felt herself transported back to a market two hundred years before. There had been one then on these very cobble-stones, probably selling what they were still selling — seconds from some china factory. But she knew she would not find anything as old as that here. The bookstall was piled high with paperback bestsellers and the jewellery looked vaguely eastern in provenance. Spring flowers covered every available inch of the next stall and their scent wafted in the sun. Unfurled daffodils were stacked in boxes. She imagined them growing by some Wordsworthian field. They were late, but it was pleasant to find them, their tardiness a proof that they at least were not imported, were late northern blooms. She bought a few bunches to take home and then wandered over the square to see if there were any second-hand bookshops or antique shops. A sign at the corner of a street leading off the market looked promising: TREASURE HOUSE. But it might be full of modern artefacts, mass-produced 'in the style of — '

It was not. The window had an old

sewing-basket and several candlesticks, a trunk covered with a vaguely William Morris-looking bedspread, and a bookcase. On the bookcase reposed a teapot.

She caught her breath, it was exactly the shape of the one in Daphne's photograph of Joshua's picture. It could not be the same one, for it was not decorated, but it looked authentically late eighteenth century. She went into the shop. The teapot would cost the earth, but she could ask, and then tell Daphne about it. If she told Alan he'd insist upon giving it to herself as a present, for he was very generous. A middle-aged man came forward from the back of the shop. Scruffy tweeds and a mournful face. His manner however was rather abrupt.

'I'd like to look at the teapot you have on the chest in the window,' she began. He looked wary, probably sizing her up as a potential customer.

'You realize it's genuine?' he answered. Probably he didn't want to spoil his display, she thought. She knew the feeling.

'Yes — I thought it was — about 1790?' she hazarded.

He looked gratified.

'It would cost you two hundred pounds,' he said snappily, waiting for her surprise at such an outlandish figure. Yet if it were genuine it wasn't outlandish.

'I'm looking on behalf of a friend,' she said quickly.

He went slowly to the window and after much shuffling brought it out. Plain-looking, of creamy-coloured earthenware with a delicate twisty handle, and a short spout, it had an open daisy as a knob.

'Leeds ware?' she hazarded, at which the man's stern face relaxed. 'It's quite big,' she said. 'The earlier ones were much smaller, weren't they?'

'The Japanese ones are still small,' he replied.

She thought, if I could afford it I'd *give* it to Daphne. But I will tell her about it. 'It doesn't need ornamentation,' she said. 'Though I like some of the designs on the earlier ones.' The man seemed to think she'd proved her credentials, put the pot carefully down on the counter of the shop, an old high desk, but held on to the handle. 'Still, it's dear,' she went on. 'I'll tell my friend. Give me your card will you? I suppose such things are bought chiefly by American tourists?'

'Oh, we get some Americans,' he said. 'But they're always on their way to somewhere else.' He handed over his card and stood contemplating his teapot. Judith was thinking, I'd rather enjoy painting designs on crocks — perhaps I should forget about landscapes and go commercial!'

Unexpectedly he said 'You might get something not quite so perfect — but cheaper — at auction.'

'Thank you, anyway,' she said. 'It's lovely.' She took his card, leaving him still contemplating the pot. She'd like to look at his shelves of books but then there wouldn't be time to do a bit of sketching before Alan met her outside the George at the prearranged time.

She returned to the market place and took out her sketch-book from her shoulder-bag and stood by each stall in turn to see if there was anything worth recording. It was the market as a whole which would be a good subject, but for that she'd need to stand at a corner where she could see the pattern of the stalls and the cobble-stones, the spire of the church beyond, the spring sun slanting down on awnings that looked incongruous, belonging to a hotter, sunnier climate. Finally she found a vantage-point on the opposite side of the road where she could lean against a lamppost, and executed a few rapid line-sketches. Then she found she was drawing the teapot and decorating it with daffodils. She'd do a rapid sketch of the flower stall before going to meet Alan.

She recrossed the road and made a few notes about the colours of the spring flowers on the stall where she'd bought her flowers.

'I found a teapot Daphne would like,' she said to Alan when he came up to the entrance of the George having left his car in the small car-park. 'The same period as the one on her photograph. Plain — very beautiful.'

Perhaps he'd say, hadn't she had enough of teapots at home in the shop? but he didn't, asked only: 'Did you get any sketching done as well?'

She showed him her sketch-book when they were sitting in the car for a while before going out for lunch to a place he'd found in the guidebook, apparently starred, quite famous.

The daffodils were on the back seat. 'You like Daphne, don't you?'

'Of course I do. She's the most interesting person in Heckcliff — apart from you of course!' she replied laughing.

Over the meal he seemed a little preoccupied, told her little about his friend except to say that retirement didn't suit him and that he was trying to find work with a charity. 'It's a big growth area — all the charities are run like businesses now.'

In the car on the way home, Alan driving

433

since he'd had no wine with his lunch, though she'd offered to drive back, he said: 'Daphne helped me let go of my past, you know.'

She waited. There was obviously more to come. He stared straight ahead, was concentrating on the road though it was empty and would become busy only when they joined the main road that led to Leeds. 'I wanted to tell you but didn't know how,' he went on. 'It was just after Celia died — sixteen years ago. We had an affair.'

'Oh!' said Judith, surprised.

'We weren't in love — at least I don't think she was and I know I wasn't. But she was very kind to me and I'm still grateful. We don't talk about it.'

'Did you ever think of asking her to marry you?'

'No, I did not. I knew she wouldn't, you see. And I had no wish to remarry at that time.'

'But she might have liked to be asked.'

'I don't think so. She guarded her independence even then. It's only this last year — getting to know you — that I've felt I would like to marry again, but she *was* very good to me.'

'Poor Daphne!'

'No, not really — she's got enough in her

head to keep her going!'

'When *we* get married,' said Judith carefully, 'we ought to give her that teapot. From us both. As a sort of non-wedding present. Yes, let's both give it to her? She'll know why.'

'I wish I could stop the car,' he said. 'You've just said you'll marry me!'

'No, you go on driving,' said Judith. 'I'm glad you told me about you and her.'

'You don't mind then?'

'How could I mind, Alan?'

'Well, some women might.'

'You mean I ought to mind that Daphne wasn't asked?'

'No, of course not. I'm very fond of old Daphne but it would never have worked. When shall we get wed?'

'I'll let you know,' said Judith laughing, knowing he must now feel sure of her to have told her his secret about her friend. 'As soon as I've sorted out the boys — '

'September?'

'Whatever date we decide,' she said, 'we'll do it secretly. I don't want anyone to see me burning my boats. It must be a *fait accompli*.'

He laughed now and felt for her hand. 'You ring up that shop on Monday,' he said, 'and we'll both buy the teapot for

435

her and give it her when we're officially one flesh.'

★ ★ ★

Daphne was arranging the daffodils bought by her friend on her return from the Dales. 'They're just like daffodils from anywhere, I suppose,' Judith had said. 'But I like to think of them growing wild far away.'

Daphne knew nothing about the teapot, for Judith had decided Alan's idea was a good one and they would send for it. She felt it looming over her future as a sort of symbol of Alan's turning to her, sealing off his old friendship with Daphne for good.

She had worked hard all day and was glad to sit down when Judith had gone. The flowers reminded her of her first attempt to grow a flower from a bulb and her ignominious failure. Standard 2 had been the class she was in and she had watered her own bulb too often so that when everyone else's had blossomed hers had not. When Miss Mason had taken them out of the cupboard her own had not even had a green shoot. Miss Mason had explained about overwatering, but Daphne had felt ashamed. The other children laughed. Something Daphne Berridge could not do! She must tell Sonia about that. She was to come round next week.

She went over to her steel filing-cabinet where she had placed old photographs and mementoes in neat folders when she first came back to Heckcliff. She hadn't had time to look at them for a year or two. There must be a picture somewhere of Standard 2?

She found instead an old newspaper-cutting of her class in the war years, two years after the daffodil fiasco, a group photograph which for some reason her mother had kept. How staid and neat and tidy they all looked: mothers with round spectacles and wearing calf-length skirts, and hats, or, if unhatted, with neat perms, and all of them holding knitting-needles. Knitting scarves for the troops it must have been. Some local war effort. The children stood in front of their mothers, the small girls also knitting. Knee-length stockings for both the boys and the girls — obviously home-knitted too — and strapped shoes. She and Mary were at the front, their hair tied back with clips and ribbons.

She laughed out loud, remembering her own failure to finish any knitted article. A failure pretty well all round. She wondered whether women had done much knitting in Anne's time. They must have done — all those *tricoteuses* in France . . .

She made herself a cup of coffee in her second-best pot, bought from Judith's shop, and sat in the growing dusk thinking about Anne and her blighted love. She had been a sensitive, introverted woman, probably a great writer of letters. It was a pity none, as far as she knew, had survived. Anne must have longed for stability and continuity and for financial equilibrium. No pensions in those days, but stability and continuity were at any time found only in the self. Mary W. had had no business to say she ought to 'summon up more strength of mind and fortitude'!

Roger Masterson would be coming round in two days' time. She still dreaded this a little, had the feeling he'd been putting it off for some reason. Perhaps he could not make up his mind about her?

She looked at the picture again before shutting her eyes for sleep. The teapot Anne was holding in the picture stood for the continuity of things — human, domestic, used.

★ ★ ★

The next day Sonia telephoned her.

'I'd ask you to come over for a cup of coffee but I know you're busy. All I wanted to say was that I've decided to give up the reading circle for good.'

Daphne expressed surprise but was not in fact surprised. Sonia attended principally out of loyalty and might have more urgent things to do with herself.

'Well, you'll carry on reading anyway, won't you?' she said.

'Oh, yes — but it's my daughter — she asked me not long ago if I'd like to go in with her. You know she has a little business selling survivals from the past? Clothes and toys and books and things. Well, I thought it was about time I did something different with my life. I might as well give it a go and see if I can be of any use to her.'

'I think it's a wonderful idea, Sonia!'

'I've been feeling restless for ages. I seem to be wasting my life. Housekeeping doesn't suit me — Parkinson's Law, you know. I began to feel I was being taken for granted. I thought it would be easier once the children had gone and there'd be less to do but it's a big house and the work's never ending. I'm not good at it either so I'm going to get somebody else to clean and wash and garden. I can go on doing my share of the shopping and cooking . . .'

Daphne interrupted the flow, saying: 'You'll find you care less about the house if you can get out of it.'

'Yes, and I might one day bring in a bit of money — who knows! At least to pay for the help — though Bob's quite willing to fork out a bit at first and says he will do more shopping and cooking in preparation for his retirement!'

He could hardly be short, Daphne thought, since he was still working at the university, had chosen to go on there till he was sixty-five. Sonia hadn't gone back to work before because she had become disillusioned with teaching in secondary schools. Daphne did not blame her.

'Even if *he* thinks of it as therapy,' Sonia went on, 'I might even find I'm good at it — I can be quite organized over work you know, even if housework defeats me.'

It was about time that her new friend took on a new challenge, Daphne agreed.

'It'll keep me young anyway,' said Sonia. 'Anna can do all the travelling and I can keep the shop in Woolsford and do the accounts and try to have some bright ideas. I'd been helping her with the catalogue before.'

Daphne wanted to ask why she had decided so suddenly but Sonia told her.

'It was Gwyneth's dying that made me reconsider my life — to realize I was stuck in a rut. That's why I decided to give up the meetings as well and I suppose I might want a rest in the evenings. Do you think I'm too old to change? Shall I resent not having so much free time?'

'Parkinson's Law needn't operate if you don't want it to,' replied Daphne. 'I expect your free time was taken up with jobs around the house and garden?'

'It surely was,' said Sonia fervently. 'But I think people our age ought to work at something, don't you? I mean, if I were talented I'd write a novel, but as it is — well I might still try to write — and I'd have more to write about, wouldn't I?'

'I'd go mad if I didn't have my own work,' confessed Daphne. 'I don't miss *my* old career — I resented never having enough time to myself. I'm happier now than I've ever been.'

'Our generation put so much into either work or home — sometimes both. If I hadn't married I'd have wanted a job like yours. I suppose if I were young now I'd have to do both — home and career? It isn't that I didn't want to look after my own children but, you know, once you've started on that you're left with all the rest of the mechanics of living for ever and ever! Anyway, I wanted you to be the first to know.'

'I shan't go on with the meetings either,'

Daphne said. 'I'm so busy writing and researching. I've enjoyed coming across new faces — they're all such nice people — but at present I'm so involved in my book that I can't do it or the novel reading justice. I think *my* book might turn into a novel, you see!'

'Let's meet soon for a proper talk,' suggested Sonia.

'What about a week on Wednesday — you come here,' said Daphne. 'I never entertained the circle but I'd like to entertain you.'

★ ★ ★

Daphne had washed and polished some glasses and arranged them on a tray covered with a lacy cloth, on which she also placed a bowl of crisps, a bowl of olives, a bottle of whisky, a soda-siphon and a bottle of Tio Pepe. She was nervous. The best thing he could do would be either to kiss her, or make it clear there was to be nothing between them but friendship; then she would know where she stood. She had held off and held off expressing any of her own embryonic feelings of romance or desire and it really was time for him to sort himself out. He had obviously put it off so many times because he had to tell her they must be 'just friends'.

When he arrived she took his driving coat and settled him at a seat by the window near the table and the tray.

'I'm so sorry it's been so long — what with a contract I had to finish coming at the same time as the arrival of my grandson.' He looked around at his surroundings with interest, seemed cheerful.

'That's a nice landscape you've got there,' staring at a small picture of Wharfedale painted by Judith.

She poured him his choice of whisky and soda and they discussed Judith for a moment, whose shop he knew. She found herself talking then about his new grandson and the names to be bestowed upon him — Benedict Roger. She was damned if she was going to make it easy for him. She began to tell him of her latest discoveries about Anne's family.

His eyes looked a darker brown today and she noticed he was wearing a tie she'd never seen before though she supposed he must have hundreds. A tie of pale turquoise and yellow.

Now he was looking at her piercingly, straight in the eye.

Was he going to hold her hand? Did he want to kiss her?

She sat down opposite him.

443

No, it seemed he was about to make a speech, for he cleared his throat.

'I think we know each other well enough, Daphne? People our age can't wait for ever for things to — develop — so I'm going to take the bull by the horns. What do you feel about our going off for a little holiday together? Somewhere warm, I thought — '

She was astounded. Was this a proposition, or just an invitation to a companionable voyage? She waited.

He went on heavily: 'You see — ever since Betty died — I've wanted to marry again. I'm no good alone. We get on well, don't we? You're very easy to be with, Daphne — and we're both old enough to know our own minds — '

She looked searchingly at him. What could she say? I find you attractive, but that's not what concerns you, is it? If she could not have a man falling in love with her, would she rather have a sexual proposition? What did he mean by a little holiday?

'Marriage is different,' she found herself saying, quite briskly.

'Yes — yes — *I've* been married so I know that! A very happy marriage — but we're not getting any younger you and I. I'm sixty-two — content in my own way. But I'm lonely — I confess that.' He lowered his

444

voice. 'I'm not looking for — er — passion, Daphne.' He sat back and appeared to expect applause.

She was pale with shock. How did he envisage this union?

It was clearly a speech he had prepared. He went on: 'I can offer you a lovely place — holidays abroad — I know you're a bit of a stay-at-home — but it would be different, travelling as a couple. I've enjoyed our jaunts to the opera and the theatre.'

She was tongue-tied.

'You could have the garden the way you wanted — have plenty of help there. We could make a go of it, couldn't we?'

'Roger,' she began, took up her own drink then put it down again. 'Like you, I've enjoyed our 'jaunts' — and you've been very kind. You're an attractive man — '

He looked startled.

'But you must see I couldn't decide about — marriage — on the spur of the moment!' (I could if you desired me, she thought.)

'We could see how it worked to begin with if we had a little holiday together. You could move into the Grange as soon as we were wed!' He sounded excited now.

'I need time to think. I'm honoured at your suggestion — but what do you want *me* to give *you*, Roger? I'm not a — wifely sort of woman.'

'Don't say that!'

'It's true! I need time and space to myself.'

She meant: if you were in love with me, if we were in love with each other, or if you showed you were even *attracted* to me . . . if you wanted me in a more primitive way . . . if you took me in your arms and said you needed love — or sex — I wouldn't need to mention time I need alone!

Silly.

'Couldn't we just go on being friends?' she went on aloud.

'We *are* friends and I believe in friendship — shared tastes — between man and wife — but it would be so much more convenient for us both if we were married, Daphne!'

We had a sort of friendship anyway, she thought. Trips to the theatre, to the opera, an *amitié amoureuse* would have been compatible with all that. But this man — over whom I have occasionally felt I *might* have expended such passion as is left in me is just not my type! I'm old enough to know that. Why can't I say any of this?

'My work,' she said. 'That's my reality now.'

He thinks it's just a hobby.

'You'd end up disappointed in me,' she added weakly, shifting the blame to herself. She suddenly had the thought that Roger Masterson ought to meet Lydia — she'd be just right for him! He looked at her blankly and there was a tiny pucker on his forehead.

'All I ask is that you think it over, Daphne. I know Betty would have wanted me to remarry. And my friends like you — '

'What about your son and daughter?'

'They'd be delighted! They're always saying the Grange is too big for me to manage alone.'

That was it then — he wanted to replace Mrs Haigh with a wife, who wouldn't cook half so well.

'Have another drink, Roger. I — promise I'll think it over.'

She thought: he obviously expected me to be coy — or overcome with gratitude. Even to herself though she sounded uncaring, dismissive. She went up to him, poured him another drink, took his hand in hers. His was dry, inert. But he had not finished trying to persuade her.

'I know your work means a lot to you, Daphne, but what I'm offering you is the real world!'

That made her bridle. How did *he* know what was real?

447

'Good grief, Daphne — I'd like to make your life easier, not harder!'

I know you would, she thought. By having me take care of that enormous house — and cook and garden and live as Betty lived but with no family of my own as compensation for the toil! She touched his arm. 'What about — love?' she asked.

'Well, I am fond of you,' he answered hesitantly.

There was a long pause.

'I promise I'll write to you. Let's be friends meanwhile,' she offered. He got to his feet then, looked disappointed.

When finally he'd gone, giving her a peck on the cheek, she poured herself another stiff drink. *Too big for me to manage alone.* The phrase sounded the death knell of his hopes if he had only known.

★ ★ ★

She declined his proposal in a short letter a day or two later. '*You need a woman more like your wife.*' She wanted to say a good housekeeper. *It's too late for me to be like that. But it's not too late for you to find one. It's not your fault, it's mine* (the usual kind of half-truth women produce, she thought) *— I've lived too long alone and I'm happy*

*as I am. But you have been very kind and
I don't want to lose you as a friend . . .*

This was not strictly true. They had
little in common. She could never speak
unselfconsciously to him about teapots or
Anne Crystall.

Why could she not just say 'I wanted you
to want me?'

21

MINUTES OF THE MEETING OF THE NORWOOD LITERARY CIRCLE HELD ON 19 MAY 1993 AT DOROTHY GREY'S.

PRESENT; D Grey (Chairwoman); E
Naylor (Secretary); L Robinson, J Wood,
N Reeves, P Sparks, C Taylor, V Smith,
H Maudesley.

The chairwoman welcomed new members
and an old member, Joy Wood, who had
been unable to attend during the past
year. Gwyneth Coultar's daughter Zoë
had written to the circle again in reply
to a letter sent from the meeting in April.
She thanked them for their continuing
support.

Dorothy Grey then read out letters from Sonia Greenwood and Daphne Berridge.

Sonia had decided that after so many years' attendance at the circle she thought it was time she now left it for others to carry on. She was going to help her daughter with her business which would leave her little time for reading. She wished the circle great success in the future and hoped that new members would derive as much pleasure and satisfaction as she had herself from the regular meetings. After all members had expressed their great regret over Sonia's decision, a vote of thanks in her absence was moved by the chairwoman and seconded by L Robinson. This would be conveyed to Sonia.

Daphne Berridge was now busy writing a book and would no longer have time to attend the meetings as well as to read the novels with the attention they deserved. The meeting received this resignation also with regret but wished Daphne well with her book which they hoped one day to read.

The chairwoman then said how pleased she was that Mrs Wood had found it possible to attend now that her mother-in-law had been placed in a nursing home. Mrs N Reeves then apologized for her protracted absence from the circle during the last two years. Having retired at Christmas from her work as library coordinator for local schools she now hoped to attend regularly.

It was proposed by E Naylor that an effort should be made to recruit younger members. All promised to bear this in mind.

There then ensued a lively and prolonged discussion of *Vanity Fair* and the character of Becky Sharp. The meeting broke up at half past ten, members having agreed to read *The Old Wives' Tale* before the next meeting which was fixed for Wednesday May 19th, Wednesday being an evening most members would find easier to attend than Monday.

Signed: E Naylor (Secretary.)

On the very evening that the members of the Circle were attending their May meeting, Bob Greenwood drove his wife over to Daphne's.

'I feel so guilty telling Dorothy I'm too busy now to attend, and then coming over to you!' said Sonia as she came into the low-ceilinged sitting room.

'Same here! But never mind — I'd much rather talk to you.'

Daphne pointed to a comfortable chair, brought up a decanter of whisky and then sat down opposite her friend.

'I know you are *really* busy, unlike me. I shall be next week when I start properly in Woolsford at the shop. I don't count housekeeping.'

'I have to stop work sometimes, you know! The book's not going too badly.'

'May I read it when it's done?'

'Yes — but that might not be for some time yet.'

'I always wanted to write,' said Sonia. 'I know that's what a lot of people say, and if they were serious they'd have written — but I *did* write — unfortunately not well enough to publish.'

'I expect you couldn't put it first?' suggested Daphne sympathetically. 'Neither could I when I was so busy teaching. It's only now I'm retired that I can.'

'I think I was trying to write the wrong sort of thing. Over the last year I suddenly realized that I was much better at reporting conversations and describing real people than making things up — there'll be plenty to write about in future — you see all sorts in the shop — not that I'll have much time, but still — '

'I think you'll be my ideal reader,' said

Daphne. 'I often wonder what I'd have done if I'd had children and been forced to put them first. I wouldn't have had the energy to write whilst they were in the cradle as some women do. I'd have wanted to stay at home too whilst they were small, I know I would. Not for too long but, you know, to get them started in life — it's the first five years that count, they always say.'

'Yes, I often think that what's good for children is diametrically opposed to what's best for women,' said Sonia, savouring her whisky. 'But it's a bit too late now to wish I'd carried on with a full time career.'

'You can start two new ones, then.'

'It would seem,' said Sonia, 'that if I am not to go bonkers, getting out of the house is now a priority. I really hate housework and housekeeping — I'm very bad at it, you see. It takes such a lot of energy to do it badly!'

'Well, obviously you need a change — '

'Yes, and I'm lucky to have a daughter willing to give me a job rather than a grandchild. But I do envy you spending your days writing. Not that I feel I'd be capable of disciplining myself now to putting it first.'

'I think if I'd been like you and had had to run a home for other people I'd have gone mad,' said Daphne, wanting now to tell her about Roger's proposal.

'I think I've been a little mad for years — reading kept me going. But I never had the intention to go on at the Circle for so long — the others will get on quite well without me — I apologize for dragging you in too.'

'If you'd been a man,' said Daphne, 'you'd have been able to do a job properly *and* have children — not many men write, though, as well as having full time demanding jobs — it's a punishing schedule.'

'Except there's usually a wife tending to him,' said Sonia, grimacing. 'When I got really tired — when the children were small, my fantasies were of having heaps of servants — gardeners and laundry maids and cleaners and professional shoppers and a nanny and a Cordon Bleu cook, so I could just — you know — *be* instead of *doing* things all the time! Now here I am wanting to *do* because I don't know any longer how to *be*. Gwyneth knew how to. She lived in the present, you know — she enjoyed just living. I've never been able to do that for more than a short time.'

There was a silence whilst they both thought about Gwyneth Coultar. Then, 'It's just your temperament,' said Daphne. 'I'm the same. And I wish I had had a child — though I wouldn't confess that to anyone but you. My fantasy was to have a grown-up daughter return to me at eighteen after being brought up by a faithful servant, and then to find I had a real soul-mate. But I've noticed that people's children are rarely soul-mates and it would be unfair to want them to be.'

'I know,' Sonia sighed. 'You have to detach yourself from your children. Anna goes her own way — she'll keep me up to the mark though. Young women are encouraged now to put their own interests first. At the end of each day I sit thinking about what I'll have to do the next day — I want all the housework done at once and when it's done all I can think about is that it will all have to be done again the next day. Anna says, leave it — it won't hurt to let it slide for a bit. But I suppose it was my early training that made me impatient — everything had to be done 'properly' and I couldn't do it 'properly' even if I'd all the time in the world. I don't regret having children, though,' she added after a pause, as Daphne refilled their glasses. 'I don't suppose I could have been any different.'

'I realized not long ago that I see my writing in the same light as I might see a child,' said Daphne. 'I find it hard to detach myself from it — especially from the woman I'm writing about at the moment.'

She took Sonia into her work room and showed her all the notes she had made about Anne and her brother and sister.

'I wish I could write a *novel*,' she said. 'Most of my facts would be true though.'

'Some biographers invent just as much as novelists,' said Sonia. 'It's more honest to call it fiction.'

'Just recently a man wanted me to marry him,' said Daphne carefully. 'I couldn't accept. If he'd been a passionate man, had cared about finding the real me under all the years. But he wasn't — isn't. He's kind and competent — but what he really needs is a housekeeper-cum-cook-cum-gardener-cum-travelling-companion all rolled into one, like the wife you were just talking about! Like his first wife. He could afford them all and they'd do the job better than I could even if I wanted to. I received the impression that things like having a partner to go on holidays with were more important than sex. Never mind love. Which he never mentioned, though I gave him the chance. I know women our age are often said to be less interested in 'all that', but you'd think he'd at least have tried to find out!'

'So you said No.'

'I wrote to him and explained why I couldn't accept — more politely than I've expressed it to you. I would like — would appreciate — a close man friend — a man who was less interested in surface things. As for sex — love — well, I only wanted him to acknowledge its existence even if it were to be a Platonic marriage. He could have called it up in me but it was not in him — '

'An academic would suit you — like my husband — '

'I suppose that would be more my line,' replied Daphne, remembering Alan. 'If I'd wanted a husband. But how can you make a man understand that, even if you are our age, you'd like to be valued as a mysterious sentient being, a person who might even change — and change him too? Roger would never be able to — or want to — change. Perhaps I couldn't change either and it would have been too late even if I'd met the right man.'

Sonia was looking at her with a very serious expression.

'You know I think it's easier to rely for most things on women friends even if Mr

Platonic Love bowls you over!' Daphne added.

'Roger Masterson? Up at the Grange?' Sonia asked after a pause.

'Yes.'

'He had a nice wife — absolutely devoted to him. I believe her family had money — some business or other.'

'Betty.'

'Yes — she had cancer — died a few years ago. A good woman. Did a lot of charity work.'

'Not like me at all. Roger needs a widow,' said Daphne. 'Someone used to a husband!'

'I certainly can't see you with him. A different sort of man perhaps, yes. One who lives more simply — not that academics live all that simply nowadays even if they are always grumbling how poor they are. But a man of our age who'd never married — he'd be even less adaptable than a woman! Men are very habit-ridden.'

'That's partly what I was afraid of. I wouldn't want to become a habit. Yet, you know, we went to the opera — he's musical — and when I was listening to the love arias from *Rigoletto* it made me realize I *could* feel again like that — it was only waiting to be called out. But not with Roger — '

'No Duke of Mantua!'

'I was quite prepared to flirt with him, you know. I'd have enjoyed that — but he didn't know how!'

'You are just not bourgeois enough,' said Sonia. 'You'd have to look elsewhere for a man like that!'

'I wouldn't want a toy boy either! It's unsettled me, all this. I was perfectly happy — and now I feel so guilty about the poor chap. He thinks I don't live in the real world.'

'The guilt will pass off,' said Sonia.

They took their drinks into the study and Daphne showed Sonia the picture of Anne and the teapot.

After that they talked of Cressida and Anna and Judith Kershaw whom Sonia had once taught a hundred years ago — a 'dark horse' she called her.

By the time Bob Greenwood called for his non-driving wife, both women felt their new friendship was firmly based. They would share some of their preoccupations with each other in future.

'Will you advise me if I do manage to write some Village Vignettes?' Sonia asked as she left.

'They might be libellous,' replied Daphne.

'Then *I* shall call them fiction!'

22

Once she started her new job in earnest Cressida's search for Joshua's porcelain or pottery went into abeyance. She was kept late, had energy in the first week or two only to eat, wash and crawl to bed. Things improved once she got the measure of the work, to begin with mainly a clearing-up after an incompetent assistant and keeping up with current correspondence. Jonathan understood she would be busy and advised her to unwind alone at week-ends. By the beginning of June she was feeling less tired and welcomed his suggestion that he should come over and cook her a nice supper on Saturdays. He pointed out that her kitchen was better equipped than his own and her flat was nearer to his father's house if they drove over to see him on Sundays. He too had been busy. She was not surprised that he was such a dutiful son, though most young men of thirty-two were not usually so solicitous of a parent. His father was a widower and his sister lived in Scotland, so a visit once every fortnight or so was perhaps not too much to ask. Fortunately Jonathan was well organized and seemed to have plenty of energy for both work and family and social life. His father was a shy man, considerably older than her own father who certainly did not appear to expect such filial devotion though he appreciated it when it arrived.

Was the Saturday idea Jon's way of saying he wanted to stay with her on Saturday night?

When she thought of this time last year and her ups and downs with Patrick and the uncertainties about her summer holiday she was cheered when Jon asked her if she would like to go away with him when she had accumulated enough leave. They pored over Greece and Turkey and decided provisionally to go to Cyprus in late autumn. The past receded, the present beckoned, and she began to feel released from those unsettled feelings that had been part and parcel of her for so long. On the first Sunday of their new arrangement, when they returned from visiting Mr Edwards, Jonathan took her back home. She had been surprised that he had not taken for granted that they should make love the night before. Now he said: 'We could go to Cyprus for a honeymoon, I suppose?'

She was too taken aback to do anything but catch her breath and stare at him in a bewildered way. She hadn't expected this quite so soon. She felt a little aggrieved, even asked herself: is he presuming too much? — and was then immediately ashamed. Wasn't it what she wanted above all?

Jonathan Edwards smiled and said, 'I thought I'd be original and ask you that before I made love to you.'

She was amused that *this* was the reason for the proposal, and said so.

'You know what I mean, Cressy.'

'Show me,' she said, 'and then I'll answer your question.'

'That's not fair!'

'It was you who put it that way.'

But she knew that it would be all right.

It was. Jonathan might be a New Man, whatever that meant, but his instincts were fairly ancient.

★ ★ ★

'Of course if you'd prefer for us just to have a bitter-sweet affair, it could be arranged,' he murmured afterwards.

He'd made her feel drowsy, contented; she'd been his equal in desire and her own passion had surprised her. Even later, she

462

said, 'I have to ask you too — otherwise it's not 'fair' — you might have found me disappointing.'

'I felt I knew you so well already Cressy,' he said. 'It was only that I had to offer you a way out, you see — ' He did not say, but she knew he was thinking of Patrick and that he knew she knew that.

They were lying entwined together, a little light from the early summer evening entering the room through a chink in the blinds.

'What time is it?'

'Don't ask — I'll have to leave you and I don't want to.'

She realized that she didn't want him to go and that the sooner there were no more partings the better.

She said: 'Are you still going to ask me to marry you, Jon?'

'Certainly, the sooner the better I think.'

'I always thought you were rather conventional,' she said. 'But you're not, are you?'

'We could live together at first if you wanted,' he replied. 'But it would be much nicer to be married — so you see I *am* rather conventional.'

'Well then, I agree,' she said.

After this they made love again and it was eleven o'clock before he left. An hour later he telephoned her. 'Get to bed and go to sleep, lovely Cressida.'

'If you promise *you* will. Will you think of me? I shall think of you.'

'If my thoughts stray to the line of duty,' he said, 'I shall allow you to think about tomorrow's work too.'

They arranged to meet on the Tuesday at his flat in Bloomsbury. He wanted to put an announcement in the paper and to buy her a ring. She felt extremely happy but wanted to nurse her future to herself for a little while before telling her mother and father and sister — and Daphne. Her mother was not the sort of woman who dreamed of white weddings but she would be pleased that her daughter had decided to marry. It could be done fairly quickly, before the summer ended, if they could find somewhere to live that was not too far from both their places of work. Jonathan was willing to commute from the suburbs to begin with, he said, and there were flats and even small houses near Cressida's present basement flat where they could begin. Larger Bloomsbury flats were too expensive. Once a flat was found it would not matter when the ceremony took place. A big wedding would be a problem. She had so many friends. A small one, and a party later in a new house would be best.

Once she knew her future was as secure as anything is secure in an uncertain world, Cressida felt her past sliding away from her like a boat receding as she stood on a firm shore. Or perhaps she was the one sailing away from a country she once knew but would never visit again. She described this conceit to Jonathan and he said, 'We shan't be always moving away. I'd rather think of us as anchored for a time and sometimes setting out to sea together.' He was sweet, said the sort of sentimental things Patrick Simmonds would never say to anyone. She knew that she would remember Patrick later. Aspects of herself which had belonged to a particular time of her life might surface again in the future. But she had no wish whatever to have left any part of herself with Patrick. Her experience had altered her and the changed Cressida was the Cressida whom Jonathan loved.

Over the next few weeks, both busy at work, they planned and announced and flat-hunted and enjoyed themselves, both happy, a little astonished that life could be so simple. Cressida felt she now knew how to make the most of what she now had. She wasn't sure if love was the word to describe what she felt for this man, or if that mattered. She trusted him and that was the main thing. And she was determined that his trust in her would never be misplaced. Also, he loved her.

Dear Cressy
I am very happy for you and looking forward very much indeed to meeting your intended (love that word!) I gather Jon's mother is dead and that the father is in his seventies? Do both come North for a weekend whenever you want, before or after the wedding. Thanks for inviting me. Once you've fixed the date I'll look forward to coming to London. (I hadn't imagined you'd want to get wed in Berks with marquees and orange blossom.) Mary says you are spending this weekend with them and that your father has put off a walk on the Ridgeway to welcome a future son-in-law. Tell me what you'd like for a present. Something practical? In haste.
Your loving aunt, Daphne.
PS: Still working on Anne. I have been telling Sonia (Greenwood) all about it. I think we are going to be firm friends — she is going to work with her daughter, having decided not to waste the rest of her life on running a house. We've both decided to leave the readers' circle to others.

Dear Daphne

We think we've found a small house that costs not much more to buy than a flat so long as we both go on bringing in a decent salary. It's not far from your Anne's old place! We're not making a wedding present list, just telling people, so, as you ask, I think giant bath towels yellow or dark blue or tablecloths same colour. I leave them to your taste. Father got on very well with Jon — who is easy to get on with but shrewd enough to notice things you might not think he would. Father even remembered to call him by the right name. I was dreading his saying the name of my first boy-friend years ago who was the only one Father really met before — William — but he didn't, and took Jon off to the pub for a drink, doing his best to act normal. I'd told Jon our family were all mad but he didn't seem to think they were, just a 'bit unworldly' is what he said. All details later as soon as we know them ourselves. Glad you have been enjoying Mrs Greenwood's company — I think you are right to stop going to those meetings — you have enough to do.

Love Cressy

It was a hot July and Judith Kershaw was quite glad of the cool of the shop during the day. She'd begun to paint again, could now call herself a 'Sunday painter', but Alan said it did not adequately describe her. She was sticking to water-colours at present which were much more a test of painterly skill than oils in her opinion, even if people thought they were for amateurs. Gradually, as she was able to give herself several hours at the easel now set up in Alan's spare bedroom, she found the very act of painting was giving her a sort of peace and that a current of thought accompanied it without her volition. Alan would leave her alone to get on with it and would have a meal ready when she stopped, and sometimes Colin would come over and eat with them, before going back with her to the flat above the shop in time for Monday morning and its opening. But this was becoming more and more of a nuisance and she knew she must soon get her family together and explain she was soon to move over permanently to Mr Watson's. Colin's nineteenth birthday passed without anything being arranged. It was quite difficult to assemble all four of her boys together.

Her thoughts told her she had had too much 'life' too young but that she now had years in front of her to make sense of it and release herself from the past. It was not to be expected that the sons would all be delighted that she had found a new man — Mark and Ben might be, but Stephen might not be too pleased. She wrote to them telling them about her painting and her plans to give the management of the shop to Colin and pay him a wage, whilst investing the profits — such as they were — as she had always done, to be given eventually to them all in equal shares. 'My painting gives me peace,' she wrote, for she could not bring herself to go into details of the sort of peace Alan's presence in her life also gave her.

To Daphne she said only 'I can understand your Anne's poetry better when I'm painting — painters and poets are doing the same thing really — making new worlds out of the one they know.' She spoke more to Daphne now on this sort of subject than on more personal matters, in order to avoid talking about Alan. She felt a little embarrassed about his past and that she knew something about her friend that Daphne would not realize she knew. But she underestimated Daphne.

One evening that summer Daphne had come across Alan at the library and had walked part of the way back home with him. Then she told him she was glad he'd found the right woman. Alan had for once alluded to their past, saying 'I don't regret anything and I hope you don't.' They'd kissed each other on the cheek when she'd left him to walk on further and she'd known that the subject had been discussed with Judith. She wanted to let Judith know that she knew Alan had spoken to her about their old affair, but to do it indirectly, casually. Then they would all feel more at ease. She was fond of Judith, felt even a little maternal towards her — which was odd, considering Judith was the mother figure. Judith must be led to feel her old friends would not desert her when she took up to a new life. Daphne greatly admired how she had brought up her family and civilized her sons. If all the world were like Judith there would be far fewer social problems around, boys who had never been 'gentled' and socialized. Above all, Daphne hoped Judith had stopped feeling that irrational guilt about which she'd so often spoken to her. Guilt was one thing she could dispose of — including any misplaced guilt about taking Daphne's long ago place in Alan Watson's bed.

She had so far received no reply from Roger Masterson, which worried her a little. He obviously didn't want her friendship if he couldn't have her as his second wife!

She had just discovered in the course of further research that Joshua Cristall's death in 1847 at the age of eighty had followed on his being knocked down by a cab. Her sources also claimed that he had been older than his sister. She had also discovered the precise date of their parents' marriage; her supposition had been correct: the young, well-brought up daughter of a Cornish merchant had been seduced by a twenty-years-older Scottish mariner who was also a widower. There had been less than eight months between the wedding and Joshua's birth.

She had not yet found the date of Anne's death. She'd been sure in her own mind that Anne had lived to be very old, but now she was not so sure. Where had she lived? Her friend Mary H had died in Camberwell in 1845. Had she gone there when her friend Anne had died? Mary's last known address was that of a girls' school in Greenwich. Daphne was willing to believe that Anne too had eked out her life teaching in that school until she was too old to do so. There had been no pensions, except for certain charitable almshouses, and no Society for Distressed Governesses until much later.

If her supposition had been wrong and

Anne had died earlier she would have to rethink everything. She had preferred to follow her own theory until it was proved wrong, had finished her study of the verse half-hoping she might never know the correct date, but confessing she wanted Anne to have lived to a great age. She had the conviction that if Anne lived to be a very old lady, then so would she. This was sheer superstition, she knew. It would not matter if Anne had died at any time up to the age of sixty, now that she was herself that age. She was stupid to identify herself with the object of her study, even to the length of life, but it could not be helped.

'Let Anne survive her brother and live on to her eighties,' she said often to herself. Sonia would sympathize with her, but her sister and even Cressy might tease her for it. Nobody she had consulted so far had bothered to note that date of death, whereas she had found Joshua's death recorded so far in two places. If the censuses of 1841 and 1851 drew a blank she'd have to investigate other parish registers for burials. They'd have been passed to some local history library, necessitating a search during her next visit to London. She could combine that with Cressy's wedding. If it were not for Widgery she'd stay on there longer, perhaps look after their house for the newly-married couple whilst they were away.

I've loved men who are now dead, she thought, suddenly depressed. Am I trying to get under the skin of a long dead woman to give meaning to my own life? Should I have waited before answering Roger Masterson? Alan Watson too had loved someone who was now dead . . . Judith's husband was dead. A widow would soon marry a widower.

Poor old Joshua knocked down by a cab! He might perhaps have been deaf like Gwyneth? Or gone blind? Since he was a painter, she hoped it had been the former. Whilst waiting for an answer from the local history libraries, and to take her thoughts off death, she weeded her garden, tidied it, and gathered roses to put in pretty vases that had fortunately escaped the attention of her burglar.

Judith's and Cressy's lives would move out of her ken: she was under no illusions about that. Both of them had been close to her and she'd played a little part in their lives, but she hoped they had both now found happiness. Anne's and Joshua's lives would have the pattern she imposed upon them. Whether what she created was the truth about those once flourishing human beings was another matter. As the members of the Literary Circle had so often asked, how did you discover the 'truth' even about people whom you knew well? About yourself? She and Sonia would doubtless discuss that again one day.

What was still the most difficult task for her was envisaging the ordinary day-to-day life of these people in the past. Human reactions could be imagined and you could understand something about a writer from her poems, but still could not know all those other details which they would have taken for granted. Had they had to draw water from a well in their garden? Had coats and top clothes ever been cleaned?

How far did the practical side of living affect people? She asked Judith.

'I expect you know as much about that as I do,' Judith said as she sat one evening at Daphne's with a portfolio of her new water-colours on her knee, which her friend had asked to see.

'Even I remember existing in a much simpler world,' she went on. 'No refrigerator when I was a little girl, and no washing-machine, except an ancient gas-boiler Mother used. No central heating — cold bedrooms, dresses made by Mrs Bowlby unless you went for a treat into Woolsford and bought something ready made.'

'Oh those party-dresses,' said Daphne

reminiscently. 'We had Mrs Bowlby too — I suppose there was more variety when you didn't buy off the peg?'

'We didn't have much pocket-money either.' Now Judith had begun she was enjoying remembering her own childhood in the fifties. 'I think we were much more polite, don't you? Had to behave, or our elders and betters would come down heavily on us.'

'My own childhood — if not yours — was much nearer to one in the eighteenth century than the childhood of your sons!' Daphne said.

'I suppose you made your own amusements? My mother said they used to sing round the piano, go on long walks. Your family still do that!'

'Yes — there was a lot more walking then,' said Daphne. 'So we were thinner. Also, because we didn't eat so much sweet stuff — crisps and cokes . . . '

'Think how tiny-waisted the Brontë girls were,' Judith said. 'Even the tall one, Emily.'

'I think most people were thin. We're all too fat. Have another biscuit.' They laughed.

Daphne took the portfolio and looked at the sequence of local landscapes Judith had begun.

'That's Moon Woods,' she exclaimed in delight. 'And the old church!' They were small pictures, the colours delicate but bright, and evidence of a decided talent. 'I wish I could paint as you do — sometimes I think words are no good. Oh!' she exclaimed as the final picture was seen to be a small portrait of Alan Watson reading a book. Judith had caught his absorption and the way he would put his head on one side as if half listening for something.

'It's very good of Alan,' she said, with a quick look at Judith. Judith had put this painting there for a purpose she was sure.

'I'm very pleased about you and him,' she went on. 'Alan told you about us? — years ago — it seems like a hundred to me.'

'Yes, he told me. Isn't it odd?' said Judith. 'I feel you probably knew him better in a way than I do.'

'Being the same age?'

'Yes — there'll always be a bit of a gulf between Alan and me because of that — but I suppose I may catch up with him one day!'

'Cressy has decided to get married in September,' said Daphne turning the subject slightly but not really fishing for any information about Judith's own nuptials.

'Will it be a big wedding?'

'No — just the close family and a best friend on each side I think.'

'I must send her a present,' said Judith.

'She's asked *me* for towels and tablecloths. But, you know, she'd love one of your water colours!'

Judith looked doubtful. Although she had enough self-confidence now to know that some of her work had been a success even in her own estimation, she was never sure whether others might want examples of it.

'She once said to me she wished you'd paint Sholey Hall,' Daphne went on. It was not quite true; it was she herself who wanted a picture of that place. Leading Judith in that direction might result in more than one painting.

'I've often thought about painting the Hall,' said Judith. 'But I could never rid myself of the idea that an architectural drawing would convey its quality better. You'd need such a sense of atmosphere to make a successful picture.'

'Like a John Piper — colour-wash and ink?' suggested Daphne, whose taste in painting was irredeemably romantic, from the time when she was young and such painters were fashionable.

'A pity the sun doesn't *actually* set over it!' she added, and laughed.

She must one day ask for Judith's help in evaluating Joshua's water colours; she must judge the painting as well as the poetry against the backgrounds of other works of the period.

Judith went home thoughtful; a whole series of paintings of local halls might be a commercial proposition.

When she had gone Daphne went back to her books, suddenly sure that she could never now present her book as a straight biography. It was a little dismaying. The 1790s, when everything was in tumult and continued to be so, in spite of what people thought about Queen Victoria, had caught her imagination. The modern world had begun with the French Revolution, but she wasn't an historian . . .

She sat down to look through her notes and her mind kept straying to the beginnings of the feminism that had been taken up with some success in the last half of the nineteenth century and had provided the impetus for her own notions of independence. The notions hadn't been at all fashionable when she was young. To achieve perfect equity you'd have to have women who didn't give the name 'love' to their sexual longings or believe that 'love' was what was also uppermost in the minds of men. It seemed clear that Cressy's

Jonathan was capable of that emotion — and now she was older she didn't equate the two — much good that had done her with Roger!

She took her thoughts back again to the aspirations of Anne and her siblings: to publish a book of verse, to paint landscapes which others might buy, or to be paid for engraving them. They were not impossible things to want, yet they had had a hard struggle.

Anne and Joshua and the little sister Elizabeth . . . they sometimes seemed to represent herself and Judith and Cressy. How she would love a talk with Anne. She was herself in possession of knowledge about the world in the years between their lives which Anne could never have guessed or imagined. Whether Anne would have much to say to her, was more problematic.

She returned from wool-gathering. Even such a modest study as her own, however successful it might turn out to be, had made her shift her imaginative focus just a little whilst she had tried to recreate the past in her mind. But it was still a fiction in which the chief characters were her own invention. If only she could dream a really useful dream in which Anne, recalled from the past, read her own book and gave her frank opinion. She must return to the harder, more analytical study of the words Anne had used — their variety and order. That was probably a better way of empathizing with a long-dead woman and understanding another's mind. Art was something perfect left over from a chaotic past. What more could one hope for?

★ ★ ★

Judith had bought some water-colours, feeling a little guilty at the expense. The morning after her purchase was a Sunday and she and Alan had been determined not to waste the day, were to walk up to Sholey for Judith to sketch the Hall in its garden of monkey-puzzle trees. On the way they were greeted from across the road by a Mrs Hudson who had apparently just returned from Canada with her husband. Judith had been at the same school but in a lower form and was surprised at her appearing for she had thought all the Hudsons were settled down in Ontario. They had sold up eighteen months before and she had almost envied their apparent freedom to pull up their roots and depart.

Mrs Hudson obviously wanted to stop for a chat, and this made Judith feel restive. Alan however, once reintroduced, though he didn't remember teaching her offspring, listened to a long story of her inability to settle, homesickness and 'a recession over there too', with every appearance of interest.

'We've had to be rehoused by the council,' said Mavis Hudson. 'Only me and Jim — the kids decided to stay on. But we decided this old place meant a lot to us.'

She even had a slight Canadian accent, Judith noted. After only eighteen months? It must be harder to lose your northern accent in London than in Toronto. Her own boys still had it.

'My grandchildren will be Canadians,' said Mavis Hudson. 'It's a place for the young. Too cold for us — Dad and I just didn't fit in!'

When they had finally waved farewell to her, Judith said 'Fancy coming back to Heckcliff to live far away from your children. I suppose it's because they are married — the children, I mean?'

'You wouldn't want to go far away from Stephen and the others, would you?' Alan asked her.

'No — I wouldn't — not so far away. I suppose I'm still a bit too maternal, Alan. I did think once of emigrating — all of us together — when the boys were little but it would have meant pulling us out by our roots.'

'It's natural,' he said. 'I'd feel the same. I'm a natural conservative. The Empire would never have been built by me!'

She took his arm. Mavis Hudson was known for her garrulity. Now it would spread all over the estate, to anyone who might know her, that she was seen out with that Mr Watson one Sunday morning and they didn't look as though they were going to church.

When they arrived at the high wall of the Hall in its lonely lane and Alan had helped her to sit atop it, she concentrated on looking very carefully at the handsome unoccupied house with its daisied lawn and unweeded path.

Alan lit a pipe and was content then to go off and explore the neglected gardens, before Judith rejoined him to look round the back. She made a few quick sketches of the front of the house and found herself thinking again of Daphne's suggestion. Pen and wash would do very well here. The skies were a pale summer blue at this time of the morning and there were a few swifts flying around. As she turned her head to sketch the side wall that must have been built in the same century as the house, though it had been repaired since, she thought how much she loved this village with its vivid Pennine green fields and black walls. The Hall was a little incongruous here, for all the other halls were still standing in their original seventeenth-century stone. As her fingers flew the charcoal over the pages of her sketch book she remembered walking here the previous autumn with Alan.

How much of what she would paint when she returned home would be what she had actually seen and how much what seemed to create itself once the paint-brush was in her hand? There was less of the serendipitous with water colours; even so she wasn't the kind of artist who relied only on an exact as possible representation. The paint had a will of its own, of which a trained hand and eye were only the servants. It wasn't the other way round; there was always the actual paint to consider. Often when painting in oils she'd thought that she'd let the paint dictate to her too much, for she wasn't an abstract painter and had often been surprised at what had appeared on the canvas.

When she joined Alan in the neglected garden she said something of this to him. The nice thing about Alan was that he actually liked talking about such things and always gave her his full attention. Yet he'd never interrupt her at her work, just as she would leave him to his, which needed concentration more than imagination.

'You mean the painting paints itself?' he said. 'You'd better not tell Daphne that — she wouldn't agree that words do the same.'

'Oh, I don't know, Alan, she once said that the pen ran away with her thoughts and it wasn't till she reread what she'd written that she realized what she'd been thinking!'

'Still that isn't the same as working with a brush that makes a concrete statement each time you put it on the paper. You can't 'see' words — they have to *mean* something. Did you hear from Ben?' he asked her.

'I forgot to tell you in all the excitement of my purchases yesterday! — he and Stephen could come up mid-September. Mark's buying a car so he could bring them. I just have to tell Colin, that's all.'

'We only need three weeks for a licence,' he said and caught her up in his arms. 'Or only a few *days* for a special one!'

'Then we won't tell anyone else, just the boys, and get it done with,' she said gaily.

'Then come home — no honeymoon?' he asked, straightening the curls on her forehead.

'Let's take a honeymoon later — in the cold weather. When everything's organized and some new things bought for Colin in the flat and I know he's OK.'

He released her, smiling. 'Did Daphne say something to you the other day?' he asked as they walked out of the drive and back to the lane.

'She knows I know — I'm glad you spoke to her.'

'What did she say?'

'That I was the right person for you.'

'Let her be the first to know we're actually married. Then the teapot can be accompanied by a little message,' said Alan. They both laughed and ran down the road like children.

23

August meant work for Daphne, and for Sonia and for Cressy and Judith, a busy time. Daphne was starting a new draft; the younger people were busy moving furniture and possessions, and Sonia was scouring FOR SALE adverts in newspapers and attending house clearances. You never knew what might be on offer. Only well into September would Judith and Cressy relax their efforts. Daphne knew she would be occupied still at her desk.

But Cressida had also found time to do something for her aunt, and by the end of the month something arrived from her.

Daphne sat excitedly, having read Cressy's letter. With the letter had come a thick sheaf of photocopies.

The girl had gone to explore an old tucked-away art gallery one Saturday morning and returned the following week to reap a harvest. It concerned matters which Daphne had not yet followed up, and which now effectively altered her perspective on the family, if not on Anne. Too much was written here about Joshua for her to assimilate all at once but it seemed clear that there would be no pots found painted by him. What there *had* been at his death were *over six hundred* drawings and paintings sold at auction!

'We thought there might be more information about Joshua in these proceedings of old painting societies and 19th century art magazines that you hadn't yet got round to finding. Nothing much about your Anne here, except that the date of her death *is* mentioned in one of these articles I've found for you. A lot more about the family . . . '

She had immediately turned to this. One of the children, a brother, had been a bad lot, variously described as idle and dissipated. Well she'd known a bit about that before.

He'd ended his days in 1848 in the Union Workhouse.

She read on: *Later that same year Anne too died, only a mile or two away from the home of her youth* . . .

★ ★ ★

1848! Daphne was overcome with joy. Anne had been eighty when she died. She *had* been younger than Joshua, if only by a year. She read and reread this page many times, her imagination running over the facts, encouraging more and more speculation.

Their mother had died in 1801, that she already knew, but it had been at Christmas, and the father, then aged eighty, had died two months later at the same age at which his two eldest children had died. In his will he had called his elder daughter 'Nancy', the girl who only seven years before had produced her 'Poetical Sketches'. Had Nancy along with her elder brother known that old pensioner, a 'decayed Turkey merchant', who had just turned up in Cressida's sheaf of papers and who had read aloud to Joshua from Dryden's translation of Virgil and fired the little boy with a love for the classics?

Like her brother, said the writer, Anne had had 'natural talent, quick perception and great perseverance' as well as 'refinement of feeling'. Joshua had, he said, been particularly attached to this sister. Elizabeth, who had learned engraving from him, had died two years after Anne, three after Joshua, for whom it appeared she had at one time kept house. All but the youngest boy were dead by 1851. There were several mentions of the small competence that had belonged to the mother and with which she had helped her favourite child Joshua when he was young and struggling. The father had left half his money equally divided between his daughters. They must have survived with that and their salaries as governesses. It appeared now that Elizabeth had died in the same area at a grammar school. Perhaps Anne had taught there too?

Anne's book had come out in 1795, but by then Joshua and Elizabeth were not living at home. Was she left with the parents and wastrel brother? The youngest brother was called Joseph, and he was later to carry on his father's business, Joseph might even have living descendants? The 'Miss Cristall' mentioned who was 'loved Platonically' must be Anne since that was always the appellation of the eldest daughter of a family. The story must have come through Elizabeth after her sister's death.

488

It was both frustrating and rewarding to know all this. Cressida had enclosed several examples of Joshua's work which Daphne was surprised to discover consisted not only of landscapes but of classical figures, and peasants and country people of his own time.

The very last item, which she read again before looking up and discovering that two hours had passed whilst she had been engrossed, was the statement that one of the many pictures left by Anne's brother was of *The transformation of Daphne into a Laurel, according to the Metamorphoses of Ovid*. This gave her an authentic shiver down the spine as well as surprising her.

She felt now completely convinced that she must write the whole story as a novel. She rose in a dream and made herself a cup of tea, munching a biscuit as she did so.

'I'm going to rewrite it,' she said to Widgery. 'All of it. I shall make Anne and Elizabeth the heroines of my novel, and Joshua can appear only as a very minor character.' That evening she sat down to make a completely new beginning.

★ ★ ★

Whilst Daphne was embarking upon her novel and Sonia was taking many taxis to sales and auctions, Judith and Cressida each moved house. Alan had offered Colin a room in his bungalow but had been secretly relieved when Colin had expressed a preference to stay over the shop.

'There'll be room for the others too when they come north,' Colin had said to Alan. 'I've always wanted to do a place up — and I'm only a five-minute walk from Mum — that's if she'll let me stay here by myself.'

Judith was relieved, but could not help wondering if Colin felt in any way aggrieved. *He* wasn't the one leaving home; it was she who was doing that! When they'd all talked it over, Alan making concrete proposals for helping her son with a DIY department and with repainting the flat, she relaxed. There was room at the bungalow for all her possessions. Both she and Alan had thrown out a good deal of junk and their marriage was now fixed for 18th September, a Saturday. Her boys were to arrive the previous night and would sleep over at the flat which had begun to look cleaner and brighter after Alan and Colin's ministrations. Colin had painted his own room a dark blue and had bought a new duvet and cover for his divan, with curtains to match. Judith would stay for her last night as a widow at the flat, in the little bedroom she'd used for the last eighteen years. She did not feel sentimental about it since Colin was so patently pleased to have a place of his own.

When the others arrived they were frankly envious. 'I can see Colin as a businessman,' said Ben.

'Oh, Colin's working very hard,' said Judith. 'And the flat goes with the shop. If any more of you want to come and be entrepreneurs, you can!'

'No thanks, Mum,' said Mark. Stephen had been less ebullient but, alone in the kitchen with her for a moment, had said, 'I'm glad, Mummy' — unlike the others he'd kept the childish name — 'Now I shan't have to worry about you.'

The flat was to be kept in her name for the present. If a wife materialized for young Colin one day there'd be a home waiting which she would let them buy from her. She'd explained the financial considerations to them all and that they would all receive any profits made by the shop, with Colin getting as well a living wage. He seemed willing to accept this for the time being. She'd sell up only if one day he wanted a bigger store, or tired of his work.

★ ★ ★

Cressy and Jon had exchanged contracts on a small modern house, about a mile away from Cressy's old flat. Their wedding was to be the same day as Judith's, though not even Daphne knew when Judith's was to be. She intended to combine her presence as wedding guest in London with a few days' further research in the British Library and elsewhere. No need now to check parish registers! She would visit St Catherine's House to check the date of Anne's death, within the period of public registration. Widgery was to be fed by the Johnsons whilst she was away and they had been given the key to her house and had the mystery of the cat flap explained.

It was a bright September morning when she awoke in a small hotel near Cressy's flat, the lease of which did not expire for another two weeks. Cressy's parents were sleeping there. Cressy herself was already in her new home but Jonathan had decided he would not stay there until he was married, would stay in his Bloomsbury flatlet. 'Most proper,' Hugh had said with a laugh. The marriage was to be in a nearby church. This was Jonathan's wish. Cressy would have been quite content with a registry office, however depressing, but did not mind one way or the other.

It wasn't the large parish church but a

small church at the edge of the heath and she had attended it the Sunday before, feeling a fraud. All she wanted was to survive the ceremony and be off to Italy. They had eventually decided against Cyprus. The rest of the arrangements could wait, including the furnishing of the house. They had bought it from a couple with a baby and a toddler and it needed a good deal of paint-work. But it was now theirs, and they were lucky.

Daphne got up, dressed in her finery which she had last worn at the wedding in Leeds of the daughter of a friend, and ate a hearty breakfast. Through the window of the hotel dining-room she could see a view not dissimilar from the one Anne had known.

The night before she had entertained her sister and brother-in-law to a drink at her hotel. Cressy wanted an early night so had joined them only for half an hour, after which Daphne and Mary had chatted. Not about the wedding so much as about life in general, a habit which both weddings and funerals, though not christenings, always seemed to encourage. Hugh as was his wont had gone out for a brisk walk across the heath and the women had therefore felt that lessening of the restraint which even Mary said she still felt when talking to her sister or women friends in her husband's presence, and which most of her married friends said they felt too.

'Cressy is at last joining the real world,' said her mother.

The same words as Roger Masterson had used.

'Really, Molly, you don't need to be married to do that!'

'No — I didn't mean that. I meant she'd made a choice and will stick to it. She'll probably enjoy her work better for having a husband.'

'Provided she's not overworked. Women nowadays have to do too much,' said Daphne.

You have never had to fit in the needs of a husband and children into your life, thought Mary, but said: 'Tell me about the book. How's it going?'

'Cressy and Jonathan found me some more old magazines and proceedings of painting societies which had some priceless information about the woman I was writing about. I've changed my tack because of that — I'm going to write a *novel* about her now.'

'A novel. Really? But how will you fit in all you've written about the verse you told me about?'

'I'm not sure yet but I shall use it

as a sort of background to my heroine's unrequited love.'

Her sister looked doubtful, but Daphne went on: 'Many of the poems were about that. The trouble was I didn't know for sure who the man was. I'd realized already that, as I didn't know for sure, the book was skewed. Then Cressy came up with all this further stuff. There was a mention of Anne being loved, platonically, by 'a critic'. I'd already come to that conclusion myself and so I could now write a biography but I don't want to any more. I want to write a novel!'

'How long will it take, do you think?'

'I just have a few more facts to check and then I shall let my imagination rip. I felt constrained before, couldn't really do what I wanted. But I haven't wasted my time.'

'I wish you luck. I'm glad Cressy helped.'

'Yes — in more ways than one. It was thinking about that man she used to be in love with — '

'Patrick? You knew about him?'

'Oh, she told me an edited version. I could see quite clearly last year that Jonathan was the marrying sort when he kept writing to her when she was staying with me.'

'I thought you didn't like the 'marrying sort' of man?'

'Just because I didn't find that sort of man

495

myself when I was young — and probably didn't deserve one — doesn't mean I don't think women are happier with someone like Jonathan. But some of them have to suffer first.'

'Or never find him,' said her sister, draining her whisky and soda.

'Or never find him. It's partly luck. I knew a man once when I was about forty-five who was a bit like Jonathan, but it didn't turn into marriage and I'm glad it didn't. Now he's about to wed that nice woman at the hardware store I told you about.'

'But would you have married him if he'd asked you?'

'I don't think so — I'm glad I didn't, because I know myself better now and I really do enjoy living alone. I wasn't miserable about him — don't get me wrong — it was too late for children, even then.'

'Are you nostalgic about that other man you lived with years ago?'

'Charles? A bit. Sometimes. I suppose past misery has become a subject for nostalgia. I shall use that idea in my story. Anne makes use of the unhappiness of her unrequited love in her poems. Not that she went on writing a great deal as she grew older — or perhaps she did and we don't know. At least, it was never published, except occasionally in the

Gentlemen's Magazine.'

'I shudder to think what would have happened to Cressy if she'd stayed with Patrick,' said Mary. 'Have another drink?'

'No, I must get my beauty sleep. I agree with you. But perhaps we are maligning him. He at least knew he wouldn't be good for her in the long run.'

'He made her grow up,' said Cressy's mother. 'Not being able to have what she *wanted* she realized she *needed* something quite different.'

On this the sisters parted, Daphne having decided to say nothing to her sister about Roger Masterson. She might one day.

Hugh came back into the foyer from his walk. 'The heath is prettier at night,' he said. 'See you in the morning.'

★ ★ ★

Daphne stood now amongst the congregation. Only three or four pews were filled. Invitations had been restricted to the close family and friends of the bride and the groom. The parson looked as if he had long ago retired and had been recalled for an emergency. Cressida was only one minute late when she entered on Hugh's arm, wearing a rose-pink silk dress and carrying a

497

bunch of late roses. The bridegroom, waiting at the front in a neat grey suit with a similar rose in his button-hole, looked more nervous than she did.

It was good to hear the words Jonathan had insisted upon having from the old Book of Common Prayer and she heartily agreed with its stern admonition that marriage was not a matter to be taken in hand 'inadvisedly, lightly or wantonly', but 'reverently, discreetly, advisedly, soberly'.

That the procreation of children had first mention she found refreshingly realistic. As for the 'remedy against sin', that might still be necessary for *some* people — whatever you thought of the sin involved. The third injunction — that marriage was ordained for the 'mutual society, help and comfort that one ought to have of the other', was the best watchword for the future. Roger Masterson ought to have spoken more of all that — except it was a shame she did not really need constant help and comfort . . . Both Cressy and Jonathan looked as though they would provide both for each other. The 'Jane Eyre' clause having been intoned, and no obstruction found, the two made their vows in quiet but clear tones, and Hugh gave away the daughter who had in fact lived away from home for eight years, eleven if you counted university.

'Let no man put asunder,' the old parson ended firmly, with a fierce look at the small congregation. Then Cressida Georgina and Jonathan William were pronounced man and wife, and Edwards Senior was seen to wipe a tear from his eye. The couple were then blessed and the God of Abraham prayed that they should be fruitful.

After a short sermon, which Daphne gathered was about the temptations of the modern world — she supposed the parson knew more about that than she did, being the priest for a part of the parish which abounded in social problems — the ceremony ended with an organ fugue. Daphne was thinking of Anne, who if she had ever married could have done so in this very same church, the very same words resounding in her head. That was a comfort to a literary person.

Cressida had not objected to this ancient form of service except to say she would not be happy about promising to 'obey' her husband, words which, it turned out, Jonathan certainly did not require to be intoned.

The secular feasting that always followed such a ceremony Daphne had always considered a bit of a come-down, even if you couldn't live on seventeenth century

Prayer Book heights for ever. Photographs were taken before they all adjourned to an hotel on the edge of the heath; the cutting of the wedding cake and the consumption of a good deal of champagne followed, and at four o'clock, the couple departed in a taxi for Heathrow.

Mary and Hugh and their elder daughter Jessy, complete with husband and small son went off shortly afterwards, squeezed into one large car in the direction of the M4 and home.

Daphne went back to her room in her own modest hotel, put her feet up and pored over her notes. In the evening she went for a walk to see the little house on the row where her — now fictional — family had lived. She would return home on Wednesday after two days' further research in London.

* * *

Daphne settled back in Heckcliff to work.

On the following Saturday afternoon there was a knock on her door. On the threshold stood Alan Watson and Judith Kershaw.

'Can we come in? We knew you'd be busy — but we have something for you, Daphne.'

Widgery took the opportunity to sneak out

into the courtyard and Daphne gestured her friends in, apologizing for the untidy state of the sitting-room.

'This is for you,' said Alan solemnly and handed over a small parcel.

'We wanted to give you something — to commemorate — well, we got wed last Saturday,' said Judith. 'It's from Mr and Mrs Watson!'

'Congratulations,' Daphne managed, and sat down to unwrap the parcel. 'Oh how beautiful!'

'It wasn't decorated by your Joshua, I'm afraid,' said Alan. 'But Judith couldn't resist it. It's authentic late eighteenth-century Leeds ware.'

Daphne put the small plain lovely object on her table. 'How very kind of you — just the sort they really used — wherever did you find it?'

They explained and then Judith said, 'We thought when we got married we'd rather give our friends a present than ask *them* for one — it seemed a better idea.'

'Then we shall baptize it straight away,' said their hostess.

'No. Let me. Sit down and I'll make you your first cup of eighteenth-century tea,' Judith said, taking the pot and moving to the kitchen.

'I'm so pleased — and how kind of you to want to give *me* a present,' Daphne said. It set a seal on the past.

She knew they had all been thinking that.

When Judith came back with the teapot on a tray and some of Daphne's cups and saucers, she said, 'Tell us about the wedding in London then. Ours was on a conveyor belt — but quite satisfactory.'

Daphne wondered if, on the previous Saturday Judith had thought of her first marriage, but that was something she would never know. She did her best to describe her niece's wedding, dwelling on the words of the old service. 'Not that Cressy really needed them, I suppose, but they were very impressive.'

'Our boys were splendid!' said Judith. 'We're waiting for the proofs of the photographs they took. Colin's got the flat beautifully arranged. The others were quite sad to leave it.' Daphne noticed the 'our'. *At last* Judith's sons would have a father.

'You will be our first guest,' said Alan.

'Alan is to practise his culinary skills and give dinner parties. I am banned from the kitchen till further notice.'

'I found out a lot more about Joshua,' said Daphne to Judith when they were leaving. 'I'll show you when I come to your house — you'll be able to tell me what you think of his paintings. Meanwhile I'm writing a novel — not about him but about his sisters. I'll give you a copy as a present when it's finished.'

'She'll always find something to do,' said Alan when he and his wife were walking back down the Snicket. The first leaves had just fallen in a small scattering on the cobblestones.

'I always thought she would write a novel,' replied his wife. 'Daphne has too much imagination to confine herself to biography.'

'Back to your easel tomorrow,' said Alan fondly. 'Do you think she liked the teapot?'

'You saw her face. She was touched. She's such a nice woman — I'm *sure* she was pleased.'

24

Roger Masterson never replied to Daphne's letter.

She was sure he would have written to her if for some reason it had never reached him and he was still awaiting an answer. But the post was perfectly efficient . . .

Then she heard from Sonia that the Grange was to be sold. Its owner was moving to Cheshire to be near his son!

Not even to acknowledge her letter was unlike the man she thought she knew, but she put it down to hurt pride. She had done her best to write in a friendly, but sensible and truthful manner, thanked him for his company, hoped they would always be friends, even over-stressed her own inability to change her life. But it could not have been friendship that he had initially envisaged when he invited her out and paid so much attention to her! Nor love. Nor an affair . . . Had he been shocked that she had mentioned love?

Well, it was too late now to regret that; she had been right to expect a mention of things other than gardens and houses and travel. She had not written again or telephoned him. It had nagged at her that she might come across him locally and would feel embarrassed on his own account if not her own. That he was leaving filled her with ignoble relief.

She was able to forget him in the autumn when she sat at her table every weekday from nine o'clock to six o'clock writing the story of Anne and Elizabeth, allowing herself half an hour's break for lunch and sometimes a short walk in the afternoon if it were fine. All her previous year's work was coming in useful, yet as she went along she found she was altering details from those 'real' lives; the story was to be the inner truth about the sisters as she understood it.

At half past four there was sometimes a knock at the kitchen door. By this time she had usually begun to make herself a pot of tea in the famous teapot and she would open it to the young daughter of a woman who lived across the Snicket and with whom she had got into conversation at the library.

Beatrice Alderson was twelve and a voracious reader. Daphne wondered whether the child had some way of knowing when she would be welcome. It was not every day that she was. On the days when Daphne did not want to tear herself away from her work Beatrice never came, and when she did never stayed for longer than half an hour. The girl's mother, Joyce Alderson, was a teacher of music at the new grammar school in the next village which, having survived for over three hundred years, was now taking girls, and as a result of reorganization, had become 'Independent'. Beatrice was, unfortunately for her mother, not at all musical but made up for this by her marks in English and History. She was an old-fashioned child and

Daphne enjoyed their conversations, aware that she could not resist instructing. Her previous career had made her a little tired of twenty-year-olds, but a twelve-year-old was a joy, especially when her conversation was so amusing.

'You are just eighteen years younger than Cressida,' she said to her one October teatime. Just as she herself was about seventeen years older than Judith Watson, and Judith older than Cressy by not much less, so this child continued the pattern. A half-generation or a two generation difference between people seemed to work the best. Children went on growing up, with them one might carry on a sensible conversation, perhaps especially if the child were almost of an age to be your granddaughter. Daphne remembered having the sort of easy flowing talk with her own grandmother that she had never managed with her mother. She felt no responsibility for Beatrice except the general one the elderly have towards the young.

Beatrice had heard a lot about Cressida, having admired the photographs of the London wedding which were at present on Daphne's kitchen mantelpiece. Joyce Alderson never got home before six, as she gave two music lessons after school, and was grateful that her daughter should not return every afternoon to a dark and empty house.

'When *I* am thirty,' said the girl, 'I shall either be in the Royal Shakespeare Company or the mother of twins.' Daphne knew that she spoke only half-jokingly, that these were her daydreams, but Bea was a determined person and if she didn't become an actress — which Daphne privately thought unlikely for she had too many ideas of her own — she might very well become a writer.

'Twins are very tiring,' offered Daphne. 'And not so common either unless you have them already in your family.'

'Or have gone in for fertility treatment,' said Beatrice composedly.

'Or if you are a cat — but then — you have quins or quads or even more.'

'I wonder why — do you know why?'

'You'd better ask your biology teacher,' answered Daphne. 'Elephants only have babies in ones, I think.'

Beatrice enjoyed Daphne's chocolate biscuits. Thank goodness she seemed to have no tendency towards the anorexia of so many high achieving girls, but her mother was a sensible woman with a hearty appetite who did not mind being slightly overweight.

'My homework is to write about an old building,' said Beatrice. 'I thought I'd do the Hall at Sholey. I have to imagine what it must have been like to live there, but I don't know much about the seventeenth and eighteenth centuries.'

'Then you will make it up,' said Daphne firmly. 'And one day when my book is finished you can read it and find out.'

Beatrice was a ready recipient of scraps of information. It was times like these when Daphne felt her own work was worth doing. The youngest generation must become interested in the past if civilization were not to come to a rapid end. Beatrice would soon be grown up, but the seeds sown before puberty were the important ones. Her parents were divorced and the father took his daughter out once a month. Beatrice had talked a lot about that to her and asked her for suggestions as to where she could go with him, since he never had any ideas of his own. Daphne had probably heard things about Mr Alderson which Beatrice did not even tell her mother. She did not seek these confidences but accepted them when they came. Beatrice never overstayed her welcome but skipped off at five o'clock so that Daphne might have another hour's work before seeing to her supper.

Judith had not visited since the day of the Teapot and Daphne did not expect her to come over so often now.

She would reread her sister's last letter over supper. The young newly-weds were very busy painting and decorating their new house. Cressy was enjoying all that. Her sister Jessy was pregnant again — a surprise. Mary said she'd got used to the idea, though this second baby would certainly be her last.

She had had a postcard from Florence from Jon and Cressida but did not expect that her niece would continue as good a correspondent as she had been in the previous years. She had quite enough to do without writing letters to an aunt, and had already done so much to help her.

So much had happened to them all in the year since Cressy had visited her last autumn. Most of what had happened to herself might appear negative: being burgled, a botched proposal, almost a year spent writing a book only to realize she'd done it all wrong. But she'd found a kindred spirit in Sonia Greenwood, who had already been over a few times and promised that she would look for eighteenth- and early nineteenth-century fashion prints to help the fledgling novelist's feel for Anne's and Elizabeth's time. Sonia was much enjoying her forays into the world of old objects.

Daphne had not dreamed of Anne for

some time: she was using her imagination, and so her unconscious was occupied during her daytime life. There'd be one more dream before she'd done, she felt sure about that. There were already more faint stirrings in her mind about the London of the early nineteenth century when the second generation of Romantics was sharpening its swords. Charles Lamb, the friend of Anne's George Dyer, had been only seven years younger than Anne, and his life and the lives of his friends in middle-age would lend themselves to fiction . . .

She tried to decide whether Anne would have been happy if her Platonic lover had moved out of the realms of the Ideal and actually married her. Anne might be essentially a man's woman, unlike herself? Might very well have declined into a wife if she'd ever found requited love?

Sonia thought she would. Most women did, she said. Daphne privately thought that Sonia was what she might have become herself if she had married.

'I often wonder what I'd have been like if I hadn't married,' said Sonia. It was not marriage but children, she said, that changed your outlook.

★ ★ ★

Daphne had been a few times to Kershaws for some electric light bulbs, and had observed Colin Kershaw, who resembled his mother in facial features and had the same curly black hair. He knew her; his mother must have spoken to him of her, for the first time she met him he said, 'Can I sell you another teapot?' and laughed.

'No, I am using my present,' she replied. 'I don't believe in putting nice things away on high shelves or behind glass cabinets. How are you getting on?'

'Fine — Mum pops in now and then. They're going to St Petersburg to see the paintings next February.'

'At the Hermitage — lucky them! I hear your step-father has been giving everybody Do It Yourself lessons. I ought to come and listen.'

'Saturday mornings at eleven, Miss Berridge,' said Colin, ringing up the till.

Did she wish it was herself going with Roger to St Petersburg? she wondered as she left the shop that time. No. But she mustn't become a complete stay at home. She must take more exercise, make a start perhaps by accompanying Sonia to her yoga classes. Writing meant you never moved from your desk unless you were forced by lack of light in your bulbs or nothing in the fridge.

She didn't somehow think she'd be queuing up to hear Alan's words of wisdom on home repairs or decoration. She often passed the Watson bungalow on a walk but did not linger.

Widgery was always waiting for his fish when she returned and always gave the same imperious mew when he saw her full shopping basket.

'We are both selfish,' she said to the cat.

Sitting at her table she often thought, Anne is dead and gone, but I have enough life left in me to recreate her. Even if the life going on around me often seems at one or two removes from my own. Life might be for living, but it was also there to write about. And in a novel you could change the past, make it over!

The postman came one day with a letter from Cressy telling her that Jonathan was to give voluntary help to various conservation groups. She was pleased, bethought herself to send off a small cheque to Greenpeace. Charities were the growth industry nowadays. She'd support them in the hope that she never became an object of charity herself. Sonia understood that too.

* * *

Marriage was already giving Cressida a new perspective on life. This surprised the recent bride, but she realized that novelty accounted for part of her new feelings. Shopping was boring, but more fun when you could share it; entertaining friends was just as much work, but nice when there were two of you to do it. On the other hand she felt more responsible if she forgot to pay the milkman or shirked washing the kitchen floor and this made her feel guilty that she was not living up to her feminist convictions. Jonathan took his share of everything, and this was an improvement upon so many men she knew, the husbands or partners of friends, who expected their women to shop in the lunch hour and have a meal waiting magically for their arrival back home even when they also had full-time jobs. Her mother had always done these things, if she remembered rightly, and it must be some osmotic transference which was responsible for any slight feelings of guilt. It was sensible to share out the jobs. Jon for example, liked digging the garden and took more of an interest in car engines than she did, so she supposed it was not too much of a surrender to the womanly stereotypes if she let him get on with it. He was as good a cook as she was but not as tidy a one. Neither of them was an assiduous cleaner but Cressida found that each was grateful if the other spent an hour or two tidying up. Indoor plants as opposed to outdoor ones were mysteriously her own province since Jon professed little interest in them. Although the washing could be done by either with the new washing machine, a present from Mr Edwards, the ironing always fell to her, except for Jonathan's shirts, which he sent to the laundry. She found ironing soothing and allowed her thoughts to wander, as they did when she shone up the small items of silver they'd acquired as wedding presents. By the time of their first party before Christmas that year they had settled into an easy demarcation of the chores in which such a large part of living together seemed to consist. They both had to bring work home now and again but she approved of his extra work with groups who were in dire need of solicitors who were sufficiently sympathetic to the 'earth' not to charge for it. Jonathan at present drew a larger salary than she did but they shared the correct proportion of expenses. Life was good.

She had a surprise postcard from Patrick Simmonds, forwarded from her old address. He was now in Toronto. She'd debated whether to ask him to their party and was relieved she didn't have to make the decision.

In the week before Christmas they gave their party, a great success. The next day, feeling in need of fresh air, they took a Sunday walk to an ancient monument in the district, a sort of folly on a hill overlooking the whole of London.

'The guide book says it used to be a girls' school,' she said. 'I wonder if Daphne knows about that?'

'We must photograph the view from here,' he said. St Paul's was dwarfed by tower blocks and city skyscrapers, Canary Wharf's silver light was flashing regularly like a lighthouse.

'We can save up for a camcorder too,' said Cressida.

They walked arm in arm back home across the heath in the dusk. I hope things will always be as easy as this. We've never argued yet about anything important. I suppose we shall one day. But we agree about most things, she was thinking.

★ ★ ★

Judith put the finishing touches to her portfolio of water-colours of the halls of the district. There were ten in all, the majority belonging to Heckcliff and Norwood though she had allowed herself to count in two or

515

three a few miles away.

Alan admired her technique. Each picture had a sky to suit its own character: dark and lowering for an early nineteenth-century mansion; pale cream, with gold from a hidden sun, for a low-built hall on a hill, a sky of mackerel-shredded clouds and soft dove grey for Sholey Hall.

'You must show them to Daphne,' he said. 'We haven't seen her for ages. I was thinking, we ought to have a little luncheon party when we come back from Russia — what do you think? As we didn't have a wedding breakfast . . . '

'So long as you arrange the menu,' she replied. 'You know, I think I ought to do another of Sholey at sunrise as companion to this one. One or two of the others seem rather unfinished to me.'

He knew better than to argue. She knew he'd always give her his honest opinion in the end when she had agonized a little more.

* * *

By March of 1994 Judith had much more to add to her portfolio, for she took her sketch book to St Petersburg and drew the Winter Palace and the Neva, returning with many new drawings, but unsure how best to

516

make use of them. She'd enjoyed the change, seeing grand unfamiliar buildings, but really and truly she preferred to draw old familiar places. It wouldn't stop her enjoying future holidays abroad with her husband, when she could recharge her batteries.

They gave the luncheon party on their return. Mary was staying with Daphne at the time so they both attended. Afterwards, Mary remarked to her sister that Alan, nice as he was, would not have suited a woman who kept the hours Daphne kept at her desk, longer ones even than those spent by Alan's new wife at her easel.

Whilst Mary was staying with her, Daphne had the dream which turned out to be her last of Anne. She was about to start on the last chapter of her story, had up till then written at a great pace. This last part was not an easy one to write. She wanted Anne to continue to write her verse in old age, but as there were no examples of any poems written by the real Anne after the ones which had appeared in the *Gentleman's Magazine* of 1806, Daphne felt she must try to provide a few pastiches herself. This was proving exceptionally difficult. What would Anne write about when love had left her life?

It had been Beatrice who had given her an idea the day before. The child had come over one late afternoon. Both sisters were in the kitchen chatting. Mary was to cook a complicated supper that evening, for Sonia and Bob Greenwood were to come over.

Beatrice had just had her thirteenth birthday and her father had taken her at her own request the previous Saturday to the opera in Leeds. She rhapsodized over *La Traviata*, an opera which her mother had dismissed as nineteenth century romantic nonsense.

'She says it has some good tunes but they are hackneyed,' said Beatrice. 'They were so sad though, the best ones. Does opera make you cry?' she asked Daphne.

'Sometimes,' Daphne conceded.

Afterwards, Mary said, 'It's hard to remember that there's always a first time, old things excite new people as time goes on.'

'I think it's better to encourage enthusiasm rather than a critical sense.'

'I agree — no point having a critical sense if you don't care one way or the other. But how can you *make* people enthusiastic?' asked Mary.

'Beatrice is already,' said Daphne.

'Nowadays enthusiasm is all — which makes me suspicious,' replied her sister.

'Little Beatrice is lucky — you have to be swept off your feet first. Her mother forgets she took years to refine her own taste.'

'I suppose your heroine — from what you've told me — had to learn a craft? Enthusiasm wasn't enough?'

'As a matter of fact the critics said her verse was too free and that she didn't always know the rules! But she had an instinctive genius, according to the kindest of them.'

'More ammunition for you then!'

'I wouldn't stop Beatrice at her age expressing herself, pouring out her feelings. Eventually I expect I'd want her to learn how to express them better, if she was going to be any good. We don't always wheel in our critical apparatus when we read, or look at paintings, or listen to music though.'

'You spent your life teaching, telling people how to read — '

'In the end it depends on the student — how much they need from you — or how much criticism they can take, I suppose.'

The sisters went on walks together just as Daphne had done with Cressida. On one of those walks they met Judith and her husband who were sitting on a wall looking over to hills in the distance which Judith was drawing. Alan looked younger, thought Daphne. You could guess from his attitude that he was happy and that he adored his new wife. Judith too had put on a little weight and it suited her.

* * *

That was the night Daphne dreamed of looking from an upstairs room over a large garden, with walls which resembled ramparts, and the view of a river in the distance. Then she found herself transported to the garden itself, where she was sitting on a bench that curved into the high wall by a gravel path. Beyond the path was a lawn with a sundial and towards her two ladies were walking. They looked to be in their late fifties or early sixties. In the dream she assumed a welcoming smile, preparing her lips to utter a 'good day', but it seemed they did not see her.

She knew as she sat there that she was dreaming and that the taller of the two ladies was Anne, an Anne very different from the Anne she had first encountered, but one whose hair was still dark and whose eyes were still bright though she walked stiffly and was thinner. The other lady was dressed in a higgledy-piggledy sort of way with a slightly dirty ruffle at her neck and an over-bodice that was too tight for her, but her hair was white; she was older than her friend. When Daphne looked beyond them she saw a line of little girls come out of a large arched doorway and start to wind their way in a crocodile in the direction of a gateway at the end of the courtyard which had been hidden from her view until she craned her neck round and looked out at one side of her garden seat. Then she saw one child break away from the line and come running up to the two women. 'Mrs Browne wants to see you, Miss Hays,' she said quite clearly and then turned tail.

'You see she cannot leave me alone. The woman is mad,' said the older of the two women.

'Listen to her and make a pretence of following her counsel,' said Anne. 'If the worst comes to the worst you can always go and stay with your brother in Camberwell.'

'It is not the same for you, Nancy!' said Mary Hays. 'You come only to give your lessons in grammar and rhetoric, whilst I depend on my salary, as you know. I ought to have been given as meek and gentle a character as yours. I suppose I shall have to go and eat humble pie once more.'

'Promise me you will come on Tuesday to Lizzie's — Mr Dyer will be there and one or two of my brother's old friends. We shall cheer you up.'

Mary kissed her friend on the cheek and then pulled her cloak around her rather ample figure and walked towards the school. Anne stayed for a moment and then turned towards Daphne as she sat quietly on the smooth seat watching her.

'Be thankful,' she said — and Daphne knew she was addressing her — 'that you live in a century which, if more barbarous even than mine, at least allows some women their dignity.'

Daphne thought the woman was going to touch her, but she seemed to look right through her as she added in a low voice, 'Keep faith with me and with all of us. My grave is in the old churchyard down the hill — leave a few flowers for me there.'

The light faded and the strange house and garden grew dark, though Daphne could hear the voices of children in the gloom. The moon rose over London and she awoke with the same moon streaming through her curtains far away in the north.

Epilogue

Judith and Alan Watson continued to live contentedly together. Judith exhibited her Yorkshire Halls all around the county, and they were so well-received that she was eventually commissioned to paint a series of landscapes for the Council for the Preservation of Rural England. Here she came into contact with Jonathan Edwards who was representing various conservation groups in enquiries into the building — or rather not building — of a new motorway. Judith finished a second series of illustrations of other nearby halls and made a book of them.

Colin's brother Mark married in the same year that his mother published this book. Colin continued at the shop, now renamed C KERSHAW, and became officially engaged to the American student, Diane, whom he had met in New York and who was attending a college in England on a special course for Americans who wished to 'understand Europe'. Stephen and Ben Kershaw both stayed in London working hard, frequently going north to visit their mother and stepfather.

* * *

Jonathan was very happy in his work though it took him away a good deal. A son, Thomas, was born to the couple two years after their marriage. Cressida combined her maternal duties with work for a publisher, reading children's books. She was hoping to go back to full time work eventually, though they wanted another child in two or three years.

* * *

The Reading Circle enjoyed *Cranford* and *Esther Waters*, but Dorothy Grey then suggested that the group might extend their reading to biographies, an idea to which Sonia had always objected. The members agreed that the lives of writers were often easier to absorb than their works, and were enthusiastic.

* * *

Dorothy's grandchildren came over to Norwood on ever more frequent visits — frequently, but separately, so that she could concentrate upon the special nature of each. Dorothy continued with her other activities and remained chairwoman and convenor of the Reading Circle. She saw little of Sonia, who was busy with *Tit for Tat*, her new name for Anna's venture, one which Dorothy felt was an unfortunate choice. Occasionally, Sonia's old friends would visit its new premises in Woolsford where modest profits were being made, even though the recession was not completely over. Anna sold several of Judith Watson's water-colours there, for Judith had no objection to finding herself amongst older survivals.

* * *

Dorothy had begun to see quite a lot of Evelyn Naylor who always reported that Sonia was 'thick' with Daphne Berridge. Evelyn was a changed woman. Having once faced up to her husband, intimating that if he did not take a little more interest in his marriage she could always move to Cornwall where there was plenty of room for her, she realized she had the whip hand. Ronald was too amazed to be angry, and so dreaded the thought of his own retirement that he thought it politic to make an effort and began to attend concerts with his wife. To please him Evelyn scoured the papers for concerts of organ music. He then said plaintively that he supposed Chris and his wife might one day invite him too as well as his wife for a holiday in Cornwall? Eventually they spent a fortnight together at their son's. Ronald welcomed his new grandson quite warmly. Their other son Jim remained in Australia with his wife and baby daughter, where another child was soon on the way.

★ ★ ★

Lydia Robinson continued as member of the circle, enjoying a mild battle or two with Dorothy. She continued also to relish her Bridge afternoons, and received permission to extend the garden by the forecourt of the block of flats. On a holiday arranged to show tourists round the Gardens of Tuscany, she too met an admiring widower and saw him several times on her return to England. When he asked her to marry him Lydia found she did not want to marry again. She was amused to discover that after her own refusal he went on another similar holiday and met another widow who did.

Dorothy had spoken to her son Sam about

the difficulties Lydia's stepson Tony was having finding permanent employment and Sam found him work on one of the building sites he directed. To everyone's surprise Tony found he enjoyed the work and was in demand for his electrical knowledge. His wife Linda kept her fingers crossed.

★ ★ ★

Zoë Coultar's baby, a girl, was named Hope. Zoë gave up her intensive riding, but married the baby's father after his divorce and opened a riding school.

★ ★ ★

Having given up attendance at the circle, and being busy with the cataloguing of her daughter's 'objects', along with the further development of a mail order facility, Sonia had still found enough energy to begin a diary, which included vignettes of friends, neighbours and customers, scarcely fictionalized characters whom she enjoyed describing. One day she hoped to tidy it up to see if it could be published, for it seemed to have turned into a modern version of the *Life of a Provincial Lady*. Daphne encouraged this project.

Sonia's mother, Madge Hartley, as game as ever, was regularly visited by her family, in a residential home in Harrogate. She had firmly refused to live either at her son Bill's home or at Sonia's. She was delighted when her grandson Ralph qualified as an archivist.

Madge hoped that one day soon would see the marriage of her granddaughter Anna to a Suitable Man — but for the time being she was Living in the Present.

★ ★ ★

Daphne Berridge finished and eventually published her novel, *A Water-Coloured Life*, based on Anne Cristall and her family and friends. Its jacket reproduced a painting — found by Anna Greenwood in the attic of a recently deceased old lady — of women gathered round a well. It was one of the six hundred by Joshua auctioned off after his death in 1848.

★ ★ ★

Daphne is now reading up the lives and background of several women writers involved with the Romantic Movement and is planning a new novel with great enthusiasm. Anne will be part of it too since she lived through forty

528

eight years of the new century. Daphne has visited her grave in that old churchyard, but has never dreamed of her again.

Just as Anne had her writing and her friends old and new, I have mine, thinks Daphne. As Anne grew older — and old — she continued to write, and knew all the new Romantics in their youth.

Sonia and I both live in a Present that includes the Past. Sonia remains nostalgic for the just departed, and I continue to imagine a more distant past.

In my next novel I shall see life through the eyes of Anne, as an old woman in a changing world, and through the eyes of other women who gathered round with their friends to discuss Love and Nature and Art — and sometimes wrote themselves.

... We may lose our old loves through death or dissolution and may imagine we have lost our old selves, but the bedrock of the self does not change whatever is heaped upon it by the years.

Such thoughts could have been Anne's too, and from them Daphne composed her stories. Of what you truly possess, she knows, you cannot be robbed, and of her imagination no one can dispossess her.

Other titles in the
Ulverscroft Large Print Series:

THE GREENWAY
Jane Adams

When Cassie and her twelve-year-old cousin Suzie had taken a short cut through an ancient Norfolk pathway, Suzie had simply vanished . . . Twenty years on, Cassie is still tormented by nightmares. She returns to Norfolk, determined to solve the mystery.

FORTY YEARS
ON THE WILD FRONTIER
Carl Breihan & W. Montgomery

Noted Western historian Carl Breihan has culled from the handwritten diaries of John Montgomery, grandfather of co-author Wayne Montgomery, new facts about Wyatt Earp, Doc Holliday, Bat Masterson and other famous and infamous men and women who gained notoriety when the Western Frontier was opened up.

TAKE NOW, PAY LATER
Joanna Dessau

This fiction based on fact is the love-turning-to-hate story of Robert Carr, Earl of Somerset, and his wife, Frances.

McLEAN AT THE GOLDEN OWL
George Goodchild

Inspector McLean has resigned from Scotland Yard's CID and has opened an office in Wimpole Street. With the help of his able assistant, Tiny, he solves many crimes, including those of kidnapping, murder and poisoning.

KATE WEATHERBY
Anne Goring

Derbyshire, 1849: The Hunter family are the arrogant, powerful masters of Clough Grange. Their feuds are sparked by a generation of guilt, despair and ill-fortune. But their passions are awakened by the arrival of nineteen-year-old Kate Weatherby.

A VENETIAN RECKONING
Donna Leon

When the body of a prominent international lawyer is found in the carriage of an intercity train, Commissario Guido Brunetti begins to dig deeper into the secret lives of the once great and good.

A TASTE FOR DEATH
Peter O'Donnell

Modesty Blaise and Willie Garvin take on impossible odds in the shape of Simon Delicata, the man with a taste for death, and Swordmaster, Wenczel, in a terrifying duel. Finally, in the Sahara desert, the intrepid pair must summon every killing skill to survive.

SEVEN DAYS FROM MIDNIGHT
Rona Randall

In the Comet Theatre, London, seven people have good reason for wanting beautiful Maxine Culver out of the way. Each one has reason to fear her blackmail. But whose shadow is it that lurks in the wings, waiting to silence her once and for all?

QUEEN OF THE ELEPHANTS
Mark Shand

Mark Shand knows about the ways of elephants, but he is no match for the tiny Parbati Barua, the daughter of India's greatest expert on the Asian elephant, the late Prince of Gauripur, who taught her everything. Shand sought out Parbati to take part in a film about the plight of the wild herds today in north-east India.

THE DARKENING LEAF
Caroline Stickland

On storm-tossed Chesil Bank in 1847, the young lovers, Philobeth and Frederick, prevent wreckers mutilating the apparent corpse of a young woman. Discovering she is still alive, Frederick takes her to his grandmother's home. But the rescue is to have violent and far-reaching effects . . .

A WOMAN'S TOUCH
Emma Stirling

When Fenn went to stay on her uncle's farm in Africa, the lovely Helena Starr seemed to resent her — especially when Dr Jason Kemp agreed to Fenn helping in his bush hospital. Though it seemed Jason saw Fenn as little more than a child, her feelings for him were those of a woman.

A DEAD GIVEAWAY
Various Authors

This book offers the perfect opportunity to sample the skills of five of the finest writers of crime fiction — Clare Curzon, Gillian Linscott, Peter Lovesey, Dorothy Simpson and Margaret Yorke.

DOUBLE INDEMNITY
— MURDER FOR INSURANCE
Jad Adams

This is a collection of true cases of murderers who insured their victims then killed them — or attempted to. Each tense, compelling account tells a story of cold-blooded plotting and elaborate deception.

THE PEARLS OF COROMANDEL
By Keron Bhattacharya

John Sugden, an ambitious young Oxford graduate, joins the Indian Civil Service in the early 1920s and goes to uphold the British Raj. But he falls in love with a young Hindu girl and finds his loyalties tragically divided.

WHITE HARVEST
Louis Charbonneau

Kathy McNeely, a marine biologist, sets out for Alaska to carry out important research. But when she stumbles upon an illegal ivory poaching operation that is threatening the world's walrus population, she soon realises that she will have to survive more than the harsh elements . . .